The Discovery

P. J. Bailey

This is a work of fiction. Names, characters, places, and incidents are products of the author's imagination or are used fictitiously and are not to be construed as real. Any resemblance to actual events, locations, organizations, or persons, living or dead, is entirely coincidental.

World Castle Publishing, LLC
Pensacola, Florida

Paperback ISBN: 9781953271327
eBook ISBN: 9781953271334
First Edition World Castle Publishing, LLC, November 16, 2020
http://www.worldcastlepublishing.com

Cover: Karen Fuller
Editor: Maxine Bringenberg

Chapter 1

The jarring ring of my office phone startled me out of the research I was wrapped up in. I was completely impervious to the goings-on of my office, but the obnoxious chimes that were set by my assistant, Katherine, because she was tired of answering my calls when I was immune to sound, were nearly impossible to ignore.

"Eve Monroe," I answered as steadily as I could, letting my heart steady out.

"Love." I knew with that one pet name and southern accent, it was my former professor Shawn. He was one of the most influential people in my twenty-six years. His work had taken him to London over three years ago, and I had always wondered how his cowboy hat, boots, and snug jeans fared overseas.

"Shawn! It's great to hear from you. The last time we spoke was two months ago. How's London?" There was envy behind that question. I had always felt bound to England and was drawn to the history, almost as if some unnatural force wanted my feet tethered to the land of the monarchs, but I never had a chance to visit.

"London is fantastic. Actually, that is why I am calling. I could really use your help out here. I am drowning in the archive, and I have to teach on top of that. I need your help."

I mentally went through my checklist of all my projects and when a good time to take a vacation would be. "I would love to visit and help, but right now, I am in the middle of research at the museum. A new grant came in for my work. Would you still need help in the next month or so?" I was hoping he would say yes.

"Eve, you're misunderstanding me. I want you out here for more than a visit; I want you to leave Colorado. I have already arranged a contract with the university, and they have accepted my proposal."

I stopped all my bodily movements; the pen I was using as a drumming instrument slipped out of my fingers. "Are you joking, Shawn?"

A snort reverberated in my ear. "Trust me, Eve. I would not joke about this. You know your history, and you're smart and efficient. I need an archivist, and I want it to be you. I have to be honest, though—the pay isn't like what you are making now. But the uni has arranged board for your service, so that might help a little with the cost. Regardless, this is what you have always wanted, and the chance is up for you to take it."

I almost forgot how to breathe. This was what I had always wanted. There was no possible way I could say no. "Yes, absolutely!" I screamed into the phone, not even giving it a second thought. "When do you want me there?"

"I already booked you a flight. It leaves Denver late tomorrow night. I will email you the details. I'm thrilled to have you working for me again."

The phone clicked on the other end. He had hung up on me before I could interrogate him any further or pose objections. I tried to call him back, but his phone went straight to voicemail.

Staring blankly at my computer, I held the phone away from my ear. How was I supposed to get everything in order in a day and a half? I didn't even know if my passport was expired or not. I thought back to how many years ago I had gotten it for a family vacation to Mexico with my mom and sister—the trip ended up getting cancelled because I couldn't get out of work. It had to have been seven years ago, so with any luck, I still had three more years before I had to get it renewed. I would also have to quit my job that I really liked. The work I was doing on the Ute Indians for Colorado was interesting but ultimately was not what I wanted my focus to be.

The phone started to make the dial tone noise, forcing me to take action. I pulled myself away from the desk. I was making the right decision and knew what I had to do next.

Making my way to my supervisor's office, my palms pooled with sweat as my head poked through the cracked door. The shiny, bald head of my boss, Mr. Sharp, was the first thing I saw. I knocked lightly on the door to get his attention.

"Miss Monroe," he said, waving at me to come in. "I was about to call you in. Take a seat, please." I sat in the uncomfortable, square wooden chair that was strategically positioned on the other side of his desk. Wiping my hands on my trousers, I clenched the chipped arms of the chair. "It has been a pleasure working with you, Eve." He straightened out a stack of papers.

"What?" I exclaimed, lifting myself up in the chair.

He gestured his palm down for me to sit again. "I received a call from Shawn Austin. I don't know if you knew this, but Shawn and I used to be in some of the same classes at the University of Florida. I was a few years ahead of him, but we were still good acquaintances, anyway." He rolled his head, getting back on track. "Shawn explained to me the offer he has made you and the importance and urgency with which he needs you. I'm familiar with your background. I couldn't imagine you passing up this opportunity. Am I right?" I nodded, having nothing to say. "That's what I thought. Since you are in the middle of the grant, here is what I am proposing. Take your research with you, and put in a few hours a week of work. Katherine can do the majority here, and we will keep you on the payroll for your hours until the grant is up."

"Wow, Mr. Sharp. I don't really know what to say," I responded. "This is more generous than what I was expecting."

"Eve, you have done great work here, and to be honest, if this had come from anyone other than Shawn, my propositions wouldn't be so generous."

"Thank you, sir," I said as I stood, giving him an awkward curtsy. "I will continue to produce solid work for you."

"I have no doubts," Mr. Sharp replied. He typed something on his computer. "Get your things ready for Katherine, and then you can leave. I'm sure you have arrangements to make, and if you don't mind sending in Katherine, she'll be thrilled to hear about her promotion."

"Thank you again."

Scrambling out of the room, I knew I needed to move quickly.

~*~

My eyes were blinded by the harsh light coming in from the small sliver of the airplane window. Tears formed on both ends from the sudden change to daylight. Being en route for ten hours, which felt more like ten days, didn't help any of my senses. I could hear the man five rows back ever so silently wheezing through his nose as he slept. There was enough consistency to it that it was starting to drive me mad. I sucked in a massive sigh to try to relax, but instead, all I got was a big whiff of week-old peanuts and stale airplane coffee. I was going to be sick.

"Flight attendants, please prepare for landing," cracked the pilot over the static loudspeaker.

I was almost there; about forty-five more minutes. I wasn't normally this moody of a traveler. I loved to fly, and that smell of peanuts and coffee usually got my blood boiling with adventure, but I was stressed and exhausted. Everything had happened so fast. When I left work, I had called my mom. She was equally excited and saddened about the news. She had also called me ten times since the first call, crying each time. I managed to get most of my belongings in three large suitcases, paying absurd prices to check them, which probably cost the amount of my seat. I tossed the rest of my household items in boxes for storage. My apartment was now vacant, but my landlord assured me it would be rented by the end of the month, and I wouldn't need to pay for the next month. I racked my brain, trying to make a list of everything I had forgotten to do, but I was falling short. I guessed that my life back in Denver wasn't as complex as had I thought.

Anxiety filled me, and a need to see my new home called to me. To appease some of the unease, I wanted to lift up the window curtain and peek through the tiny window at the city that held all my dreams. I didn't, though, because those windows always made me airsick, even if the plane wasn't moving, and I didn't want to spend my first minutes in London in the Heathrow bathroom throwing up my breakfast of coffee and pretzels.

The plane rattled as we descended onto the runway. The pilot's voice crackled over the intercom again. "Hey folks, we will be taxing for a few minutes, so please keep your seatbelts fastened until the seatbelt indicator light goes off. The weather here in London is sixty-five and rainy. The time is 8:45 a.m." The weather was slightly cooler than I had anticipated for late July. Luckily most of my wardrobe was acclimated to Colorado's constantly shifting weather.

A buzz went through the aircraft, indicating that we were now safe to move about the cabin. I slowly stood up, knowing my legs would be a little wobbly and stiff from sitting for so long. As I stood, I stretched out my arms until my fingertips hit the ceiling of the plane. I could hear each vertebra in my back pop back into place. I grabbed my small carry-on bag that held all of my travelling essentials from under my seat. I didn't bother turning on my cell phone; I knew it wouldn't work internationally. I would have to find a different cell provider. That would be on my checklist of things to do this week.

Sucking on a gummy worm, I watched all the people waiting in line to get off the plane. That was something I never comprehended. Why did passengers scurry around the aisles, and then after finding a spot in the long line that literally didn't move, they had to dodge for their lives as people tossed their luggage from the overhead bins?

I felt safer standing by my seat and out of the way of the missile-like luggage and enjoying my candy. After thirty minutes of waiting for the cabin to clear, I eventually sauntered off the gateway. Heathrow wasn't much different from the Denver airport, except for the British accent on the loudspeaker announcing people that were being paged. I knew it was kind of mundane, but that little bit of London got my heart pumping. It took me a while to get through customs and find my way to baggage claim. My bags were the only three remaining on the turnstile.

Heading towards the arrival gates, I had no idea what to expect. In Shawn's email, he said there would be a car waiting for me. I didn't know if that meant a car service if Shawn was going to pick me up himself or have one of his teacher aides do it. Shawn was notorious for having other people run personal errands for him.

I didn't have to wait long to find out about the whole car debacle. A very tall and gorgeous man was holding a sign that read, "Eve Monroe." The man was definitely not part of a car service unless the English had drivers that were male models. He had to be over six and a half feet tall, and I could tell that his body was in impeccable shape by how well he fit into a pair of slacks and how his chest bulged out of his collared shirt. He had a tan that suggested he was from the Mediterranean area. His dark hair complemented his skin, but his bright, piercing turquoise eyes were such a contrast to the rest of his features that it was stunning.

This was a good way to welcome me to England.

I gave him a toothy smile to let him know I was the person he was waiting for and then stumbled over the wheels of my bag. Being awkward around people was normal for me, but when I encountered someone as beautiful as this man, it became painful. I approached him, sticking out my hand to introduce myself, but was abruptly cut off.

"You're late. What took so long?" came a deep voice layered with a British and Italian accent.

Caught off guard by his coarse words, I stuttered my excuse as to why I was a few minutes past my arrival time. "I...I...I got a little lost trying to find the baggage claim."

"Hurry up. I have places to be, and this is not one of them." He stepped around me, not even offering to help with my bags.

I followed him through the exit doors to a black Jaguar parked at the curb. Of course, someone that attractive would be a complete jerk. I had to load my luggage in the car, but only one suitcase would fit in the trunk, forcing me to shuffle around two of his personal bags so mine would fit in the back seat. One of the bags appeared to be a gym bag, and when I moved it to the floor mats, a scent of sea salt and smoky pine wafted from it. He revved the engine to let me know he was in a hurry. I deliberately took my time walking around to the passenger door and fiddling with the contents of my backpack before I crept up, opened the door, and got in the passenger seat.

"About time," he huffed, his conjoined accents slurring his words.

"It was nice of you to help me with my luggage," I mocked. "I am Eve, obviously."

He responded with the sound of his tires peeling away from the cement of the arrival gates and sped onto the airport's exit ramp.

We didn't make it far before hitting traffic. I kept my attention ahead, focused on the standstill we were in. The silence was gnawing at me. There was no talking on either end. I was annoyed with him, and he couldn't be bothered by my presence. The radio was off, and the sound of the rain on the car completely muted any noise from the world outside. This was going to be worse than my flight.

"I would have been better off walking," I mumbled to myself, not exactly keeping my voice low.

One side of his mouth twitched up. "I heard that."

"So," I said, crossing my arms and squinting out, trying to see some type of scenery. But the rain was distorting any kind of view I could be enjoying. "I'd rather be drenched in this downpour than be stuck in here with you." I had half a mind to unlock my door and dive out, but I didn't know where I was going.

He let out a deep laugh, which thundered through the tension in the car. "I'm Malcolm."

"Malcolm, I wish I could say it was nice to meet you, but honestly, it really hasn't been." My fingers absently tugged up on the door lock. It would be so easy right now.

Malcolm pushed a button on his steering wheel, and my door locked automatically. "Do I need to set the child locks?" He looked at me in a way that could only be described as a disapproving fatherly glare. The traffic let up, and we slowly rolled forward. "So, how do you know Shawn?" he addressed me with his eyes on the road.

Without anything to see out the window and the general lack

of boredom, I let my stubbornness dissipate and answered. "I have known Shawn since my third year of college. He had just become an associate professor and took an interest in me after a few of his lower level students came to me for help with their papers. I was almost obsessive-compulsive about organizing, and I had a knack for pulling information out of sources and putting it into the right places. Shawn heard my name through word of mouth, and it didn't take long for him to find and mentor me. Shawn was pretty young when he took me under his wing. He is only about ten years older than me." I stated this for no particular reason. I was sure that Malcolm already knew how old Shawn was. "So, we made fast friends after I got used to him subjugating me to do his personal errands, which I am assuming is how you landed this daunting task."

"Sort of...Shawn does have a way of talking people into doing things." His comment came out snide. I wondered if that was intentional. "But I'm not a teacher's aide. I'm a researcher working on my second graduate degree. I work with Shawn on several different projects, and I'm not much older than you. Two years, to be exact."

I put his age in my mental notepad but wasn't sure why I would do that. Malcolm was pretentious and impudent, and I couldn't picture myself even being a colleague with him.

The conversation deteriorated after that, and I began to make patterns from the raindrops on the windshield. There were a few times when I flinched because I had not adjusted to the passenger being on the opposite side of the car. Every time we passed a bigger vehicle, especially in the roundabouts, I would suck in a sharp gasp and ram my foot down on the pretend brake pedal. In my peripheral vision, I could see Malcolm chuckling, which made me think he was intentionally getting closer to cars so he could see my over-dramatic reactions.

When he finally parked in a spot on the street, my hands were trembling from nerves and excitement. I felt like I was on the edge of my seat, ready to race out into the unknown. I had no idea where I was living, what kind of work I would be doing, or how I was going to make it from one meal to the next. My stomach grumbled with the thought of food. I hadn't had anything to eat besides pretzels since early this morning on the plane, and now the sensation of hunger hit me. I was about to have a panic attack. I wasn't sure how, where, or when I was going to get to eat. I knew it was kind of a minute and stupid realization, but it was the only thing I could focus on. What was I thinking, leaving everything behind and coming overseas without a plan or knowledge of what I was doing? Shawn had assured me that he took care of everything, leaving me with little detail, and I trusted that. But I hadn't seen Shawn in over two years. He could have changed into a completely different person in that time.

I was going to be sick. I could feel my blood leave my veins. Closing my eyes, I tried to refocus, but it wasn't working. A strong hand ran the length of my lower thigh and squeezed at my knee. I had almost forgotten that Malcolm was still in the car and watching my very personal and private breakdown.

"Are you okay?" He squeezed once more.

Blood began to burst through my veins again, and I was brought back to reality. I suddenly became very aware of how close Malcolm was leaning into me, and his hand felt like a heavyweight that was permanently seared to the spot right above my knee.

I twitched my leg aside and lunged for the handle of the door. "I am fine, just a little hungry." I was out of the car and into the wet, sticky, London air.

Chapter 2

I wished I had a chance to take in the sights of the university, but the rain was cascading down. By the time we got my luggage out of the trunk and raced through the campus's main corridor, we were drenched. There was about an inch of water in my shoes, and they were slowly draining out into pools on the wood floor of a dark hallway, causing a squeak every time I took a step.

I felt like I had taken a step back in time. The long hallway was ominous, almost as if I was being escorted through catacombs filled with dark shadows and no light to guide me through to the end.

Malcolm stopped when we neared the end of the hallway and opened a door that I didn't see a handle to. I followed his lead inside to an immaculate room. The rich chocolate wood from the hallway flowed into the room, but the large window that was now casting dark stormy light somehow eased the eeriness. Several large book-covered oak desks were scattered throughout the room, all appearing to be as old as London itself. Past the desks were floor-to-ceiling shelves that held similar books.

Just beneath the large window stood the most enormous desk I had ever seen. Stacks and stacks of books bordered the perimeter. In the center was an ancient computer with files piled on top. Evidently, the only use for the computer was as a filing cabinet. This must have been Shawn's desk. He really hated using technology, and he was not very adept.

Rounding the corner, Shawn came into view with an open book in his palm and his face buried in it.

"Good to see you haven't lost your ability to read and walk

at the same time in your old age," I said.

Shawn was tall and lean, with muscles that curved around his arms like chains. His light brown ever-present five o'clock shadow matched his light brown hair, which was always an inch too long and mussed like he had just finished riding a motorcycle. He had an easy personality and a natural flirtatiousness that everyone loved.

Startled by my voice, he quickly tore his attention away from the book, almost dropping it. "Hello, love." His tone was weary from the surprise, but he stretched out his arms wide, ready for me to receive him. I dashed forward, letting him gather me up. I sucked in his citrus cologne, and something familiar washed over me, immediately bringing me to ease. He embraced me with a grunt. "I'm glad you are here. It's been way too long."

"I wouldn't miss this opportunity." I beamed up at him. "Thank you."

He gently situated me back on the ground and uncoiled from the hug. "You haven't changed one bit. You're such a goddess."

I rolled my eyes. Shawn was always very complimentary, and it drove me crazy. Sure, some days, I saw my reflection in the mirror and thought I was pretty. My silver eyes went well with my long, wild, curly hair, streaked with auburn, copper, orange, and bright red. It was all natural and sometimes looked like a red color spectrum had thrown up all over it, but I never had the heart to dye it one solid color. I was average in height and had curves that most women would hate, but I loved. I was pale because I was always cold in Colorado, even in the middle of summer. But I was no goddess. There were many times when I thought I was a monster or something out of the old horror classics, and my hair was an unruly mop that had a life of its own. Most of the time, I kept it up and out of my face unless it was behaving.

"Glad to see you aren't wearing a cowboy hat anymore."

He placed his lips on my forehead and said with a throaty laugh, "I knew you hated that hat. So how was your trip? Sorry I couldn't pick you up. I got in over my head here." He gestured to all the books scattered over the tables. "I hope Mal was a good tour guide."

"Oh yeah, he was a real joy to be with."

Malcolm stood passively in the background, but his full attention was on us.

Shawn choked. "I missed your wit, but don't mind him. He is agitated because he had to miss his lectures today."

I whacked him in the arm. "Shawn, I can't believe you made him miss class. I could have taken a taxi. I am sure you can get notes from someone," I said hopefully to Malcolm.

"I could, but I don't attend the class. I give the lectures."

I ran my fingers through my hair, but they didn't get very far before they found a knot and came up damp with the moisture from the rain. "Thanks for picking me up, I guess."

"It was a pleasure."

Malcolm's luminous eyes burrowed into mine from across the room. The way he said it led me to believe he really thought it was. We stood there in silence for a few moments, staring. Something jolted around in my stomach, and I couldn't determine if it was good or bad.

"This is uncomfortable, watching you two stare at each other. Let me show you where you will be staying." Shawn took me by the elbow and steered me to the door, and Malcolm vanished into the abyss of the bookshelves.

The rain was still not letting up. All I could see was the dark red cobblestones with brilliant green specs of grass rising up through the cracks. I was starting to wonder if I was ever going to see the campus, or London for that matter. The constant rain was dampening my hope of exploring.

We crossed the threshold of an apartment building with large glass sliding doors. As I stepped inside, the bright fluorescent light that flooded the already stark white lobby was a big contrast from the deep brown hallway that led to the archive. My eyes burned. The lobby was empty except for one person, a security officer behind a white vinyl-covered counter. Shawn ambled over to the man behind the counter and began to chat. I stayed put and took in my surroundings. I suddenly flashed back to when I was eighteen and had moved into the dorms in college for the first time. The layout was eerily the same.

On the left side of me sat two chairs and a modern couch that was navy and boxy. On my right side was an old beat up foosball table, and I was sure that if I inspected it closer, there would be some missing players that were no longer bound to their metal rod. At least I wasn't going to be a freshman again, stuck in a dorm room with somebody who never washed her sheets, and having to share a bathroom with twenty other girls from the hall. I bet the post-graduate housing I was moving into was similar to some of the Denver lofts I had lived in. I was already expecting it to be small, with a tiny bedroom, bathroom, living room, and kitchen, but I would take small any day of the week over a dorm room and crappy cafeteria food.

Shawn found his way back to me, jangling a pair of keys in front of my face. "You ready to see the place you will be staying until your contract is up with the uni?"

"About that—you never did say how long this would take."

"It would take most people over a year to do the work, but I know you will have it done in six months or so." Six months was no time at all; he must've read the disappointment in my face. "That's why I have a list of projects for you to do. So I have you contracted for two years."

My spirits perked up. I would have two years here, if not more. My mind ran through everything I would be able to see and explore. If I saved enough money, I could travel to different countries. I currently had a small stockpile of money that would last me about a year's worth of expenses. I knew the university was paying me a small amount for my work, and with the part time work for the museum and my housing being covered, I would be traveling in no time.

I followed Shawn in a daze, my mind listing off all the places I wanted to see. We climbed one small set of stairs; I counted eight of them. He came to a sudden stop, and I nearly ran my face into his shoulder. "Here we are, room 102," he said, drawing out the numbers in his southern accent. "Before we go in, I want you to know that I took the liberty of buying you a few essentials, like towels, sheets, cleaning supplies, and a few other things."

"Shawn, you didn't have to do that but thank you. How

much do I owe you for all of it?"

"Not a thing, sweetheart. It is a thank you for helping me out, and don't ask me again because the answer will still be the same." He closed off any further discussion about me paying him back.

I gave him a thank you pat on his shoulder.

Shawn opened the hefty orange door. "Welcome home." He gestured me in with a swoop of his arm.

My eyes combed the room, and I was filled with sudden terror. The room was about the size of my bedroom in Denver. There was a small twin bed in the corner of one wall, diagonal from a small window. To the left of the bed in the other corner was a distressed computer desk. A few feet from the desk was a tiny kitchenette, home to a sink, a hot plate, and a black miniature refrigerator with a small white microwave on top of it. On the wall by the entrance was a tan leather loveseat with a green throw on top of it. Both were new. Next to the couch was a thin hallway that I assumed was where my closet was.

"Um, Shawn…is this a dorm room?" I almost hyperventilated.

"Well, love, this is one of the housings for the undergraduates. You are acting as an advisor."

"What?!" I glowered at him. "I am what?"

"Listen, Eve, this was one of the stipulations the university had for you coming here. Besides, being an advisor here is much different than it is back in the States. Yes, the rooms are similar in size to dorms, but the students aren't all first year. It is less babysitting and more like being a landlord. If there are any problems, you have to report them. There is another advisor here to help you too. It's not as bad as I know you are thinking."

"I thought when you said they were paying for board that it would be post-graduate housing. I have got to be the oldest person in this building."

"Not the oldest, exactly," he shrugged. "Think of it as a second job. You are in this room for two years, so make the best of it."

"I, uhhh…."

Before I could muster a thought, Shawn was out the door.

His bailing out on confrontational situations was beginning to irritate me. I had forgotten he did that.

I was stagnant for nearly thirty minutes. My mind was filled with thoughts of crazy college drunken nights, drama-filled hallways of crying girls, and shower shoes for the communal shower.

The thought of a bathroom made me take a step. I really hoped I had my own. I walked the short distance to the hallway. There were two doors, one to my left and one to my right. I went to the right first. I held my breath as I gripped the brass handle and released it when I saw that I had a bathroom. It was on the smaller side, but it was my own. The smell of bleach burned my nose hairs. The pedestal sink stood next to the toilet, which was directly across from a rather large stand-in shower. It could easily fit three people, if not more.

I moved on to the door across the hall, and with a little twist of the door handle, it flew open. My heart nearly stopped from amazement. It was every woman's dream come true. The closet was more than double the size of my bathroom, and I could almost fit my bed in there. Shawn had undersold it when he told me he had bought me a few things. Besides the leather couch that I was pretty sure was brand new, there was a mini-fridge, a microwave, and an elaborate deep purple and dark green bedding set on my small twin bed. The closet was stocked with all kinds of goodies. There were several bath towels that matched the colors of my bedding, which happened to be my two favorite colors. I knew that was not a coincidence on Shawn's part. There were paper towels and toilet paper, and next to a year's worth of cleaning supplies. In the corner of the closet were two pairs of rain boots. I was impressed by Shawn's taste in shoes. One pair was dark green with pink polka dots, and the other pair was mock, black motorcycle boots.

When I went back into the main part of the room, I investigated a little bit more. He had bought storage drawers for under the bed and organizers for the desk. He must have spent a few thousand dollars getting all this. I was glad he insisted that I didn't pay him back because I wouldn't have spent so much money on the basics.

I chose to stop brooding and get myself settled in. This was my home, and I had to deal with it for the next two years. I made quick work of the room and closet. I didn't have many clothes, only two suitcases full, and one of those was pretty much full of shoes. I hung everything on the hangers that Shawn had supplied and thought that later I would have to do a little bit of a shopping spree to fill the rest of the closet. I unpacked the suitcase that held my work files from Colorado and pictures of my family, organized my desk with all the office supplies, and hung up all the pictures around my room. I didn't know if I should be sad that it only took me a few short hours to set up my old life or happy to know I could quickly adjust to a new place.

The time difference was catching up to me, throttling me into exhaustion, but I didn't want to sleep just yet. I needed a shower to get rid of the dank rain that was leaving a residue over my skin. I was about to strip off my clothes when a heavy conk came from the door. I wasn't sure what visitors I would be having. It could have been the security officer from the lobby, but I also remembered Shawn saying there was another advisor here.

Cautiously I opened the door. Malcolm was propped up against the frame, and he was more muscular and handsome than I remembered from only a few hours ago.

"Can I help you? Or did you come by to make fun of my new living situation?"

"No." He lunged into my room without being welcomed in. "I thought you would like to meet the other advisor for the building."

"Sure." I stretched my neck around his mass of muscles to get a glimpse at my new visitor.

Malcolm's laughter echoed off the bare walls of my room. "It's me, Eve."

"What? How did you get suckered into this job? With your position as a researcher and a professor, apparently, I thought you would be living in some swanky loft, with your fancy car." I pointed toward the small window, where his Jaguar was parked somewhere outside.

"I have no choice but to teach, but I am not a professor. You see, I was coerced into teaching, foregoing that 'swanky' loft, whatever that means." His accent almost sounded southern when he repeated swanky. "My father is the dean. They pay for my living expenses and other arrangements I have made, and in exchange, I do some teaching and miscellaneous work for the uni. I get little pay for working with Shawn, but as you can tell by my car, I am not really in need of money."

"So now I have to work with you in every aspect of my life?"

"I am not that awful." He took a step closer to me, a little more at ease and softer than before. "I know we got off to a bad start, but I can be nice."

"I don't believe you can be." Twisting away, thinking he was too close for comfort, my body wanted him closer, but my mind was yelling at me. How, in such a short amount of time, could he affect me so much?

"You're right, but on the rare occasion, I am nice. The living situation isn't ideal for me either, but there are many things I enjoy about the uni. Also, my sisters will be living here, across the hall from you, and one of them is a bit unpredictable. I'll be able to keep a better eye on her."

"Sisters, as in more than one?"

"Yes, they are twins, though completely opposite. I am protective of them both. I was counting on you to help me out with them."

"You are already demanding favors from me?" He was delusional if he thought I would do anything for him. "I barely know you, and honestly, you are rude."

"I know we haven't been acquainted for very long, but we will be spending a lot of time together for the next few years." I was expecting him to finish his sentence, but it hung there, his vivid blue eyes blazing back at me, waiting for an answer.

I rolled mine in response. "Fine...whatever."

He smirked, the corner of his lips slanting up, creating impeccable height to his cheeks. It made me want to strip my clothes off, but I quickly vetoed the idea.

"The new term begins in over a month. Most of the students

are away for the break, but the building will be full a few days before classes. For now, you should get some rest and a shower. You kind of smell like an airplane." He turned to walk out the door. "Oh, and Shawn is going to pick you up for dinner tonight."

Ready to wash the long travel day and Malcolm's words away, I hooked a new plush towel on the rack and ran the shower. Shawn had replaced the showerhead with a brand new rainfall one. I stepped in with so much excitement; it was almost unbearable. The hot water pounded on my tense muscles, loosening them and making me weak and tired. Once I forced my arm to turn off the water, I moved at a glacial pace to my bed, and as soon as my wet hair hit the pillow, I was out.

Chapter 3

I woke up startled and perplexed. It took me a few moments to recognize my new surroundings and to realize that someone was banging on my door. I stumbled out of bed, twisting my hair into a bun, knowing that it was unmanageable because I had slept on it wet.

"What do you want?" I crudely requested when I saw Malcolm's face.

"Whoa, calm down. I brought you dinner." He lifted up a brown paper bag that he was holding.

"I thought Shawn was taking me out to dinner." My voice clawed at the surface of my throat. I was still groggy and cranky from my nap.

A playful smile spread across his face. "He would've, but after a quick lunch at the pub, he met an appealing—well, depending on your taste—woman and decided to get to know her a little better."

"I should be upset, but I am not really." I gestured Malcolm into my room, but he stood at the door.

"Actually, there is a social lounge that has tables and a tellie, and I have a pretty big movie collection."

"A movie sounds nice." At least this way, I didn't have to worry about making myself presentable for public viewing.

"I will go get one. I'll be back quickly."

I pulled on a pair of stretchy black yoga pants and a T-shirt and waited for him outside my door. I hadn't had time to explore the halls, so I wasn't sure which room was his and which way he would be coming from. I saw him on my left out of the corner of my eye, coming out of a door that wasn't more than fifty feet away from my own.

He closed the gap between us in a few wide strides with his long legs. His black hair swept across his forehead and his plump lips grinned when he saw me.

He was more approachable than our first encounter, and I couldn't help but smile when he looked at me the way he was doing.

"Listen, I appreciate the dinner, but you could have stayed out with Shawn."

"Not really interested in that. Shawn's choice in women is different than mine."

"You don't strike me as a guy that has a particular type of women. Not that I know you at all." I didn't know him, but if he always carried the same attitude he had with me earlier, a decent woman wouldn't want to stick around.

"You're right. I don't really have a type. What about you?"

I followed him into a room around the corner from the main lobby, and I bounced onto a stiff orange couch facing an obscenely large television. "Nonexistent." It was only fair that I answered him. I was the one that had brought it up in the first place.

Malcolm went up to the television and inserted a DVD into the player. He joined me on the couch with several remotes in hand, fiddling with a few of the buttons, and the movie came to life. "I figured your first meal in England should consist of English food, and since fish and chips don't travel well sometimes, I went with meat pies." He retrieved two white containers. "I hope that's okay?" He smoothed his palm over his jaw.

My gaze descended to his neck, where muscles strained under his defined jawline. I wanted to run my finger over it and stroke every plane. I drug my eyes up to his mouth, hypnotized by the way his lips moved as he spoke. His tongue lightly ricocheted across full lips. I wanted to know what those lips felt like, and I knew I was insane for it. I barely knew Malcolm, and what I did know wasn't pleasant, but perhaps I wasn't giving him enough of a chance. He was nice to me and brought me dinner when he didn't have to. He stopped talking, lowering his eyes to mine, the mineral hue storming into ash.

I had to say something, anything, before I humiliated myself any further. "I like pie!"

My cheeks burned. I couldn't believe I said that, and what was worse was that I basically yelled it. Picking my food container up off the table, I tore open the white tabs. I was too embarrassed to see his reaction. I stabbed the crust of the pie with my fork and watched the steam rise through the four tiny holes. When the steam evaporated, I smashed my fork on the golden top, taking a bite. I inhaled a piece of the crust and choked as it got stuck in my throat.

"How do you like teaching?" I said, trying to play it off that I couldn't chew my food properly.

He picked up his food and followed my lead by smushing the top crust. "I enjoy teaching on the subjects that I am passionate about, but it's difficult to process that I am influencing young minds. I don't consider myself a great role model, and, if you haven't noticed, I am not very social. But the students expect me to be, so I am forced to be friendly."

"I don't know how you can do that. I could never stand in front of a hundred students." Adjusting myself to face him, I crossed my feet under my knees.

He got out a water bottle from the food bag, twisted off the cap, and handed it to me. "I wouldn't have thought that of you. From what I've heard from Shawn, you seem outspoken."

"I would call it awkwardly outspoken. I have a tendency to let whatever I am thinking slip out, but in groups of people, I clam up."

The conversation flowed easily. We went back and forth, asking questions and answering truthfully. The movie had never started—it had stayed on pause at previews from the beginning of dinner. Malcolm got up from the couch and threw away our dinner containers, then ran his hand over his jaw. I was beginning to think it was a nervous thing, but for some reason, whenever he did it, my stomach dipped.

"My mates are up the street at a pub. Did you want to go out and get a drink?"

"Yes, I could use a drink. Let me go change really quick. Give me five minutes." I dashed out of the room, but his long legs caught up to my pace.

"I lived with two sisters. I know that five minutes actually means twenty. So why don't you come to my door when you are ready?" He lunged into his room before I could make a snide remark.

I rushed around trying to prove a point that when I said five minutes, I meant five minutes. I hobbled around on my toes, trying to stuff my hips in a pair of skinny jeans and a black, deep V, long sleeved shirt that I tucked into my pants and secured in place with a belt. I swiped on some mascara and lip gloss, but then I hesitated on my shoes. I saw through the small rectangular window that it had stopped raining outside. I wasn't sure if it would rain again or if I would need my new boots and a jacket. I checked my phone for the weather forecast out of habit but realized it was off and that I had no service. Padding over to my desk, I lifted up the lid of my laptop. It took several minutes for my laptop to boot up, connect to the university's Internet, and search for the weather. I was at eight minutes. I cursed as I waited for the mouse to finish spinning its wheel. I really wanted to prove a point that I could get ready in five minutes. After discovering there was no forecast of rain for the rest of the night, I opted for ankle boots and no jacket. I stuffed my keys and cash in my pocket—I wasn't much for purses—and was out the door.

Malcolm was waiting for me outside his door, leaning against the wall, stabbing angrily at his phone. "How long have you been waiting here?" I asked. He had changed into a white shirt and jeans. I never knew that such a simple outfit could be so alluring.

He folded his arms across his broad chest and replied, "Only a minute or two."

"I thought you said that when women need five minutes, they actually mean twenty."

He nodded, yes. "You don't appear to be the type of woman that needs that much time to get ready."

"Thanks, maybe…actually, I don't know. Was that a compliment?"

"I don't know, was it?" He launched himself off the wall and winked at me before beginning down the stairwell.

I stalled in the hallway. What was that supposed to mean? Was I that unkempt? I contemplated circling right around and marching back to my room, but the idea of beer nudged me to follow him.

There wasn't conversation as we walked the two blocks to the pub. The streets were busier than I expected. I didn't know why because I was fully aware that London had a population of over eight million. I had a picture in my head of sixteenth century London, with small boats on the Thames and people strolling around in corsets, cloaks, and robes. I knew how foolish that was, but since most of my studies revolved around that century, my perception had become skewed.

I wasn't focused on much more than the tall buildings and envisioning them as thatched roof houses when I felt an arm loop around my waist, my feet lifted off the ground, and my back slammed into something concrete. A black taxi zoomed past me as my heart nearly vaulted out of my chest.

Hot air danced along my cheek and traveled up to my ear. "Careful, traffic is on the opposite side here. You have to look the other way."

Malcolm's bicep contracted, flattening me closer to him. I could feel every solid ridge of his chest. He exhaled, his stomach bumping into my back, forcing me to stiffen in response. I cocked my head to the side. His lips grazed the bottom of my ear.

"Thanks for saving my life," I said sweetly.

"You're welcome, doll." The way he rolled his R was tantalizing. He moved his thumb that was clutched onto my waist in circles. Excitement and irritation prickled my skin.

"You can let go of me now," I urged. When his hold didn't loosen, I pried his fingers off me and gave them a little twist.

"Why so aggressive?" he said, shaking out his large hand.

"You can't go around grabbing people."

"I grabbed you to save your life. Next time I will let you take care of yourself."

"Thank you!" I angled my chin up and shoved the corner of

my shirt back into my pants. We crossed the street, and he kept a good distance between us, but as we approached a courtyard, people were huddled into small groups on every inch of the large cobblestoned slab. A noisy hum of conversation filled the area.

"Is there a festival going on or something?" I asked.

Malcolm was puzzled by my question.

"All these people…." I gestured with my hand.

He chuckled. "In London, we like to drink outside."

There were two pubs across from each other, with men in business suits and women with black shift dresses and black tights, clearly enjoying some beers and socialization after work.

"Is this how it always is?"

Malcolm searched the crowd for his friends. "Most of the time, even when the weather isn't great, people still prefer to drink outside."

He signaled to a man he recognized. I followed his eye line and uncertainty yanked deep in my stomach. He began walking, and once again, I was speculating if I should run back to my room and hide away until the morning.

"You coming?" he hollered back at me, waiting for me to catch up with him. I put on a brave face and set one foot in front of the other, and walked straight towards three men with Malcolm by my side.

Malcolm gave them a nod. "This is Eve. Eve this is Wesley, Logan, and Owen."

I had that blundering moment where I didn't know whether to do the same and nod or shake hands. Going around the small party, I softly repeated my name to everyone.

"Hi Eve, I'm Wesley." Wesley was the shortest of all the men. He was on the heavier side, but not by much. His thick jaw, well cut bronze hair, and charming face made up for the fact. A silver band glinted from the bar lights off his ring finger. "When did you get into town?"

"About nine hours ago," I answered, letting Wesley take a long scan of my face. He didn't look anywhere else on my body, though.

"Well, welcome," said the man standing next to Wesley. I

guessed that he was Logan. He had a smile that could draw in a crowd. "We all feel like we know you already."

That was astonishing because I had no idea who these people were or who would be talking about me. Before I could find out, Malcolm came up with two pints in his hands—I hadn't even noticed he had left. He passed one over to me. The dark, foamy liquid sloshed in the glass.

"Thanks. How'd you know what I liked, and how much do I owe you?"

"I remembered earlier that you said you prefer dark beer, and you don't owe me anything. It's my treat tonight, to make up for my behavior earlier." Between dinner and now the drinks, I had no choice but to forgive his earlier actions.

"I don't think tonight will be enough, but thank you." My lips tipped up at the corners; I couldn't hide my forgiveness very well, and he mimicked me, knowing his actions were a thing of the past. Conversation seized the group. I took a large sip of the bitter beer, realizing that our interactions were the center of their attentions. "So," I said, swallowing down the foam rim. "I am interested to know how you guys knew who I was."

"Shawn joins us on occasion, and your name pops into the conversation quite a bit," explained the tallest man of the group, which by elimination had to be Owen. He had lanky limbs and milky blue eyes that reminded me of a wolf. His accent suggested he was from the Scandinavian area.

"That's odd," I mumbled into my drink. Shawn and I were close—for the most part, we talked once a month over the phone—but he hadn't been a major character in my life for over two years.

"Honestly, I thought you had a relationship at one point by the way he speaks of you," Malcolm explained.

I barked out a single laugh. "Absolutely not. He is not my type." The idea of Shawn and I together was almost comical.

"Is that your natural hair color?" blared Logan, blinking rapidly at my mane like he was gaping at the sun.

"Yes," I answered timidly. I had to make sure my hair hadn't run loose from the bun it was tethered to. From what I could feel, it was still mostly secured to the top of my head.

"It's pretty. That shade of red isn't something you see every day," Logan complimented with that smile again, and I swear I saw a girl in the group next to us fan herself.

"Thanks." I twirled a finger around the end of an escaped strand, uncomfortable with the attention.

"Don't you like redheads, Mal?" Wes snickered.

I pivoted my head up to Malcolm as his eyes shifted darkly onto Wesley. "I like your husband. He is the only red haired person I know, and when have you ever seen me date a redhead?" Malcolm tapped two fingers on his glass.

"When have we ever seen you date anyone?" Owen jabbed Malcolm in the shoulder.

Malcolm held a cold expression. I couldn't decipher whether that was true or if they were giving him a hard time.

"How do you all know each other?" I asked, trying to investigate their bond further.

"We have all been friends since we were eleven," Wesley answered. The way they badgered each other made sense now. It was the same way my sister and I behaved.

With each change in topic, I had a new beer in my hand. I found out that Logan was a year younger than me and was Wesley's cousin. The only family resemblance I could see was that they were both attractive. Owen was in finance. I stopped listening when he launched into details. I did catch that Malcolm had some type of accounts with Owen. Logan was a commercial investor, and Wesley was an engineer. They were all very successful for being so young. I felt I was successful too, but not monetarily like them.

The beers had slowed, and I was beginning to feel the effects of the four I had consumed. The sky was now onyx; little sparks of yellow burning lights poked through the clouds and city sky. It was nothing compared to the night sky of Colorado, where you could see the stars for miles, but there was something very satisfying about where I was viewing the stars from tonight.

Malcolm gently elbowed my side. "I think I'm going to call it a night. It's been a long day, and we both have an early start tomorrow."

I was tired too. It felt like I had been awake for days, and I was sure the dark rings under my eyes were proof of that.

"We are going to leave," Malcolm announced.

"I have to say, Eve, it truly was a pleasure, and I think we can all agree that we expect you to have drinks with us again, and soon," Wesley said, taking my pint and stacking it on top of his.

"It was nice meeting everyone too. I will be taking you up on that drink," I said, shaking all their hands and stopping at Wesley.

"Promise me." He held firmly onto my wrist.

"She promises, Wes." Malcolm wiggled Wes's fingers free from my arm.

"Sorry, my friends are so intrusive," he apologized once we got some distance from them.

"They are really great, Malcolm." I yawned into the back of my palm.

"Good. Now, if you're not too tired, I would really like to show you something." Malcolm was barely audible over the constant traffic.

"I think I can manage," I replied, really hoping I could. My eyes were low, and I was dragging my feet.

We roamed for about thirty minutes, taking dark and dirty alleyways. The direction was leading us toward the Thames River. "Are you taking me into an alley so you can kill me and dispose of me in the river?"

His body vibrated from holding in laughter. "Not yet. I thought you might like this spot. When I first moved to London, I came here a lot. Still do. For some reason, this place helps me to think."

I was moved by the gesture and thoughtfulness, but was he still trying to make up for earlier, or did he really think that I would enjoy it? Malcolm side-stepped out from in front of me, and what was before me took my breath away.

The dark waters of the Thames laid a path to the Tower Bridge, which was floating above the water. Large spotlights bounced off the old towers, underlined with cobalt light. The suspensions were wired with white glowing lights. The structure glistened off the water, making the whole scene seem right out of a dream. It was as if the city stood still. All of the chaos had ceased, and for a moment, it was just me.

A well of pure joy hit me. Tears brimmed at my eyelids, making me breathless.

"Are you okay, Eve?" I found Malcolm's voice somewhere around my distant thoughts.

Forcing the tears down my throat, I cleared my voice before it was obvious I was crying. "Yes. For as long as I can remember, I've wanted to be here," I explained. "The feeling has always been resting deep in my bones. I know how bizarre that sounds, but standing here right now, I know this is where I belong. I have never felt so much at peace than in this very moment."

"I completely understand."

His azure eyes glowed in the night. They were almost as breathtaking as the stunningly lit bridge. I didn't back away when he took a step closer, my eyes never leaving his.

Small drops of water fell, cooling my boiling cheeks. A rumble of thunder cracked in the skies, opening up pounding rain. Malcolm took my hand, and we ran towards a busy intersection. I found shelter under an awning, and his muscular arm rose up as he called for a cab. It only took a moment for one to arrive. He held the door open for me, taking the brunt of the rain. He sat beside me instead of across. I felt every fiber of his shoulder when it would sweep against me with each jolt of the cabby's jerky driving. By the time we made it to the university, my skin felt like it had been seared by his touch.

"Do you remember how to get to Shawn's office?" he asked when the cab came to a stop at the apartments.

I squeaked once as confirmation. He stayed in the taxi when I stepped out. "Are you coming?" I asked, holding the door open for him, getting wet.

"I have to make a stop first. Work is at eight tomorrow."

I was curious as to where he had to go but wasn't comfortable enough with him to ask. "Thanks for the day, Malcolm."

His full lips curved into a smile. Taking control of the door, he closed it for me.

Away from Malcolm, I let sleep plague my muscles, slowly lurching down the hall and up the few steps that felt like they took an extra thirty minutes to climb. I slid the key into the lock, tossed my wet clothes in the shower, and that's the last thing I remember.

Chapter 4

I could barely keep my eyes open when my alarm went off. I was on the verge of ripping it from the wall and throwing it across the room. After one hard smash on the small end table, the beeping slowly decreased in sound. I was positive I had broken it. Once I flopped onto the floor, I hunted for any type of coffee but came up short and had to settle for water instead. My normal morning routine was thrown off. I was lost on what to do first. I sat on my bed for fifteen minutes in a blank glaze. The screen of my laptop flicked on as if it knew what my next move should be.

"Mom!" I said out loud to the room. I had forgotten to let her know I arrived safely. Knowing her, she had most likely already called Shawn. I typed out a quick email telling her that I had made it and that I would contact her with my new phone once I got a new plan. I took an extra-long shower in the world's best shower, tousled my hair dry and twisted it into a low messy bun, and was out the door with plenty of time to make it to the archive.

I only took two wrong turns and made it to work with a few minutes to spare. Shawn wouldn't have cared if I was late, but it was my first day, and I wanted to be punctual. Shawn and Malcolm were sitting in the chairs beside the large desk, drinking what I assumed was coffee. I zeroed in on the cups, envious, and plotting on how I was going to steal the caffeinated nectar. Malcolm slid his cup behind him. He knew what I was going after, not wanting to give his up.

"Morning, Eve!" Shawn sprang up from his chair, pleased to see me. "I hope you slept well, and I am sorry for cancelling on you last night."

Words. It was only words that I could manage to gather as Shawn continued. I had one focus, and it had a name. My mouth nearly watered, thinking about it. "Where can I get coffee?" I shouted.

Shawn cackled. "I didn't forget your obsession, love." He plucked a white cup from somewhere on the desk. "If I remembered correctly, you prefer mochas."

I squealed with excitement. "Thanks, Shawn, and I forgive you now."

"I thought that's all it would take. And for your information, there is a coffee shop on campus and one across the street. I would suggest going to the one across the street. It's not as busy."

The way the liquid burned my throat was a welcome feeling. "So, what's the plan for today?" Taking another drink, I thought if I didn't slow down, it would be gone in seconds.

"We actually have faculty meetings all day, so you are on your own. But your job is to organize everything and then come up with a system to record and track what we have."

The room was twice the size of the file room at the museum in Colorado, and not a single item was in place. There wasn't going to be enough coffee in the world for me to be able to organize all of it by myself.

Malcolm clenched his hand on my shoulder, squeezing on the stiff muscle. "It's best to start by region, then century and topic."

"Thanks for the advice," I said, wriggling out of his hold. But I wasn't bothered by the contact, like yesterday.

"Once it is all organized, we will begin the process of digitizing everything," added Shawn.

Taking my coffee with me, I stumbled around to the bookshelves. The rows went on and on. As I went further and further in, several of the overhead lights were burnt out, creating the illusion of a never ending room with each shelf housing hundreds of books.

Finally, I stopped at the last shelf, panting dramatically at the mess. The life of an archivist was daunting. Beginning with the shelf that was labeled ancient history, I was quick to realize that the labels didn't hold true. I was finding books all the way up to the Vietnam War. Several hours in, I was proud of the dent I had made. Stacks were piled high into their respective regions.

I was nearly done with one case. I had one more row left, and unfortunately, it was the top row, which was out of my reach. As I put a foot on the metal shelf and hoisted myself up, the bookcase creaked under my weight but held sturdy, so I began my climb. I carefully removed a book at a time, trying not to damage their old bindings. My fingers that were supporting my weight were aching, but there was one book left, wedged in the back. I reached for it, but it wouldn't budge. Climbing up higher, my fingers burned. I gave the book one hard yank, and it broke free, but my fingers gave out, and I fell back. I braced myself to hit the piles of books below me, but instead, arms cushioned my fall. I clutched the book to my heart as I looked up to see who had prevented me from having weeks' worth of back spasms.

"That's twice now that I have saved your life." Malcolm's accent flowed off his lips.

"I would hardly call this saving my life."

I heaved myself forward. He dropped my weight, but the motion made me stumble on my feet, my knees crashing into the pile of books anyway, which was going to leave a bruise.

"You are very stubborn, aren't you?" He cocked his head to the side, throwing his hands on his hips.

"I like to call it strong-willed." I recreated my pile of Eastern European books, still clutching onto the one that had caused all this trouble.

"That's a good word for it." He helped me with the scattered books, but instead of putting them back in my piles, he read over the covers with a look of interest on his face. He shrugged, keeping three books for himself. "I think we are done for the day. Want to get something to eat?"

"Done for the day? What time is it?" I searched around the walls for a clock.

"Just after fifteen."

"It's three?!" I didn't mean to shout it out. It was supposed to be a mental excitement that I figured out the time without having to subtract twelve first. "I mean, the day went by fast, and ending at three is kind of early."

"We don't do the typical nine to five here, and when there is a chance to get done early, we take it. Plus, when all the students come back, the job becomes twenty-four hours."

"Then, food sounds good since I didn't eat lunch." I wanted to go back to the room and check some emails and change first. "But can we meet back up in a few hours?"

"Yes, but we are going in the same direction." I had almost forgotten we were neighbors.

"Let's go then. Do you know where I can get an international phone plan?" I asked, thinking I was going to get a lecture if my mom didn't hear my voice soon.

"Yes, we can do that before we eat." He held the door open for me.

~*~

Not till I was in my room did I realize I still had the old book in my hands. The binding was torn and frayed at the ends. There were no words on the tarnished and tattered cover, only a symbol, and it was one I had never seen before. A line with curved ends rested between two half circles that pointed at the ends and flared out. As I carefully opened the large text, the smell that came from the ancient pages almost made me weak in the knees. The smell of old books brought back so many memories of me falling in love with reading, and reading was what ultimately made me want to be a historian and archivist. I smiled as the pages that were barely held together by the binding crunched with each turn. The writing was in a language I wasn't familiar with, and the symbol on the cover appeared throughout.

I went to the Internet for help with the translation, researching all the ancient languages I could think of, but nothing was matching up. I was frustrated in myself that my vast knowledge of languages had gotten me nowhere. Maybe Malcolm would know. I opted to suck up my intellectual pride and went knocking on his door.

He was quick to answer, standing halfway in his clean room. His shirt was off, and his pants were hanging low on his waist.

I slowly climbed my eyes up from the indents at his hips and found flawlessly formed abs, expertly divided in six sections. His chest was shielded with muscles, creating his broad frame that ran down his perfectly sculpted arms. I was in a trance and was completely aware that I was marveling at him in a way that would possibly get me arrested.

"It has not been a few hours." He didn't even attempt to cover his body, almost like he knew how immaculate he was.

"I...I.... I need your help with something." I felt like a fool. It was not like I hadn't seen a half-naked man before, just never one this beautiful.

"Sure thing. Let me throw on a shirt first unless you would like to continue to check me out."

My mouth suddenly became dry. I was at a loss for words and utterly embarrassed. "Okay. Yes, yes, a shirt." Why couldn't I form full sentences?

He faded away into his closet, which was good because I couldn't articulate anything else. Our rooms were nearly identical in size, but his desk acted as a stand to a very large television, and there was a couch in the same place as mine. Bookshelves ran along the wall near his bed. They were filled with all types of genres: history, fiction, nonfiction, comic books, and even a romance book or four. His bed was covered with a black comforter, and the pillows were stuffed in black satin. The major difference between our rooms was that his bed could comfortably fit his large frame and another smaller person.

"You ready?" He came up from behind, startling me. A black T-shirt stretched over his muscles.

"How did you get a bigger bed than me?"

"Dean's son," he said, wiggling his thumbs.

"That would do it." He followed me to my room, and I directed him to take a seat at my desk chair. "I can't figure out what this language is. I was hoping you would know."

He skimmed through the text with delicate fingers. "I am actually not sure. Where did you find this? What is it?"

"In the archive room, as I was organizing, and I am not sure. That's why I was hoping to translate it."

"I have yet to see something this old in the archive, but in all fairness, there could be books older than the creation of civilizations, and we would have no idea." He adjusted the laptop to him. "Did you try Runic, Etruscan, or Canaanite?"

"I have, but the lettering doesn't match up."

"Some of these characters are familiar. This word *potestatem* is Latin for power, and this...," he pointed to a word in another paragraph, "is God in Greek. I think there is a mix of languages here. As far as I can tell, this book is written in ten different languages. There are more languages that I don't know and several hieroglyphics. Whoever wrote this, which seems like multiple people by the style of the writing, really wanted to keep its contents indecipherable."

Every time he turned the pages, I held in a gulp of air for fear that they would tear.

"Then why even write it?" I closed the book on him and stole it back, not being able to handle the sound of the pages anymore.

He swiveled in the chair with amusement from my actions, "I don't know. Maybe it was something worth writing, but it's presumably something worth hiding, which leads me to believe it could be valuable, or maybe even dangerous. Your theories are as good as mine."

I scrunched up my nose, wrinkling my forehead and creating deep creases, trying to hypothesize what it could all mean.

"I can help you translate this if you want. I am actually pretty interested myself now, and if we can translate this, it could be huge for us. You could have potentially stumbled onto something big."

My heart beat rapidly, trying to escape out of my rib cage. This was a historian's dream. A discovery like this could bring in grants, job opportunities, book deals, and our names made well known throughout the community. "I think working together would be beneficial, but can we agree to keep this between us until we have some substance? This includes Shawn. He has a way of taking the lead and not giving it back." I didn't say I wanted to keep the credit of the discovery to a limited amount of people, knowing how selfish that sounded. "I think with the knowledge the two of us have, we don't need any additional help."

"I think it would be best." He stuck out his hand for me to solidify our verbal contract with a shake. I didn't know Malcolm very well, but I had a strong sense that I could trust him unconditionally. Our immediate connection was undeniable, and I couldn't ignore that.

I cupped his hand, and a jolt went up my arm. "We have a deal then, and we should pick up a few things, like a lockbox and some gloves."

"Let's go then. We have a lot to do today." He rose from the desk, looming over me. There was excitement behind his callous disposition.

I didn't want to leave the manuscript behind, but I knew it was best to keep it here. Removing my suitcase from under my bed, I packed away the book, using my luggage lock as added security. I shoved the bag back under my bed and dragged Malcolm out the door behind me.

"I can walk without you pulling me."

I let go of his wrist. "Sorry. I am really excited." I tried to refrain from skipping. "You should lead anyway since you know where we are going."

Once we stepped out of the lofts, the blaring sound of horns startled me. It was so much louder than inside the apartments. A large tour group cut in between us, taking photos of the architecture and oddly wearing binoculars around their necks.

"Does London ever slow down?" The newer structures glistened with the flare of the sun from the hundreds of windows. I wondered if the people in the windows could hear all the noise below.

"No." He looked the opposite way, as I did, before crossing the street to the mobile phone store. "It's crazy, but it has been my favorite city to live in. You know how you were explaining last night that you were connected here? I feel the same way, and I have lived in a lot of places." He held the door open for me, and we took a place behind a line of people waiting to be serviced.

"Where have you lived?"

"I was born in Italy and lived there until I was ten when we moved to England. When I went off to uni, I studied in Germany, Turkey, and Japan. For my Ph.D. I also lived in Scotland, but I have travelled almost everywhere except for America."

That was a lot of places. I couldn't imagine living in that many countries. "I have only lived in Colorado, and this was my first time flying over an ocean." It wasn't for lack of wanting to. My education had been my focus since I was eighteen, and so had student loans.

"Why not? You seem eager to."

"Money mostly. Education is expensive, and I also have a problem with not being able to pull myself away from work."

"Shawn mentioned something about you working more than most people should."

"I guess that's what happens when you love what you do. I really can't get enough history."

He was about to say something, but the line had dwindled down, and I was face to face with the cashier. Malcolm left me to go fiddle with the display phones while I took care of business.

~*~

Malcolm was patiently waiting for me outside for the half hour it took me at the phone store. Plucking the phone out of my hand when I was back outside, his thumbs flew quickly over the screen. "Now you have my number if you ever need it." He slipped it back in my palm.

I tried not to read too much into it. We were coworkers, after all, and now we were working together on my new discovery. I opened up his name and typed out, *hello*, sending it over to him. His phone chimed. "There's mine if you ever need it."

He smiled at my message. By the way his lips awkwardly went rigid, I could tell it was an unfamiliar gesture for him, but over the past two days, I had seen him smile more at me than anyone else. "Are you hungry?"

I bowed with a yes when I realized he was waiting on a response.

"Fantastic, because I am too."

He took off up the street. It was difficult to keep pace with his long legs, but lucky for me, he stopped after a few shops at a red brick building. I followed him inside. The smell of melted cheese and freshly baked dough wafted in the air. Malcolm found a table in the back away from the rowdy conversations. A pretty young blonde waitress came swaying up to the table.

"Mr. Archer!" she announced cheerfully.

"Alissa," he responded politely. "Hope your summer is going well. Are you ready for the new term?"

"I'd be more ready if you gave me all your exam answers." She tossed her hair over her shoulders, her voice an octave higher.

He let out that deep, sexy laugh that had quickly become one of my favorite sounds. Apparently, that sound wasn't strictly reserved for me. Alissa brought her pen up to her mouth, biting on the cap.

"You already know the answer to that. How many of my classes are you taking this year?"

"Two, but I know they will be my hardest courses."

"If you need help, I'm sure that Ms. Monroe could point you in the right direction. She is our new archivist."

I responded with a finger wave. "Nice to meet you, and Mr. Archer is right." It was odd calling him that; it was so formal.

She gave me a stiff smile. I wasn't as interesting as he was, apparently. "Are you having the usual?"

"I don't know. What do you like, Eve?"

"I'm good with anything. Order what you normally do." Alissa nodded with my instructions and left without writing down the order. "Do all your students flirt with you?" The question came across more possessively than I intended.

Malcolm tipped his chin downward, meeting me at eye level. "Honestly, yes. A majority of them do. I don't flirt back if you were thinking that. But I can't help what other people do."

I made little balls with the wrapper of my straw for my water. I didn't know how to respond to him. He was right.

Malcolm reclined in his chair with his arms crossed, watching me in silent amusement. The small paper balls grew into a fortress with the lack of conversation. Alissa came back, dropping a pizza in the middle of the table, but didn't offer any more assistance. I had a feeling my presence was preventing any further pursuit of him.

I placed a slice on my plate, picking off the mushrooms. "So, is your mother the one from Italy?" I quizzed, trying to pick the conversation back up.

"She is. How'd you guess?" He took the mushrooms off my plate and piled them onto his pizza.

"Your father is the dean. I assume he is the one from England. I'm thinking your parents divorced when you were young and that your mom stayed in Italy because you still haven't dropped your accent."

"Most people don't hear the Italian unless there is a particular word I am saying. Now that you have guessed a little about me, can I know something about you?"

"I'm an open book." My feet bounced underneath the table in anticipation of his question.

"You and Shawn really never dated?"

"Really? Of all the questions, you want to know that one?" My feet stopped bouncing. I peeled off a pepperoni, popping it in my mouth.

"I want to know a lot of things about you." He propped his elbows on the table, ready to listen to everything I had to say. "But I think I should get this one out of the way first. It's none of my business, really. I'm only being intrusive to feed my curiosity." His hand ran down his jaw.

Fascinated that he wanted to start with that and why his friends had thought the same, I decided to answer him. "No. Although he is handsome, I am not and was never attracted to him. I'm not sure why." I shrugged. "Maybe because he was my boss or had a different girlfriend every month, but he was just someone I wasn't interested in."

"I don't think he feels the same way about you. We all think he believes you are the one that got away."

I'd never thought about Shawn feeling that way. We lacked the chemistry that made a romantic relationship. "Monogamy isn't in his vocabulary, especially with me."

"It's only my observation." Wiping his hands on a napkin, he said, "We should get the rest of the supplies and get to work on the manuscript."

"I thought you had more questions." I reached for another piece of pizza, not ready to leave yet.

He did have more questions. Once I told him to continue, they were nonstop for the rest of the day. By the time we got back to the room, I felt like he knew me better than anyone else had before.

We stayed up until the early morning, trying to piece together the languages. Malcolm called it a night around three in the morning, but my determination was greater. I stayed up another two hours and made some leeway on the first page, which was the easiest because it was primarily written in Latin. Once he helped me brush up on the language, I was able to translate full sentences.

The greatest power of all time was created by the first known god and his children. The relic was forged in blood and bone. Whoever wields it holds the power of the gods themselves.

I could no longer focus on the words—all the letters scrambled together. Tucking myself into bed, I attempted to sleep, but two hours before I had to wake up, I knew it wouldn't happen. I kept on trying to piece together what it all meant. Could there really be a relic out there that held that power? If it were true, it could potentially change the world as we knew it. What was the relic, even? All I could picture was the Holy Grail. Had many people found it, and if so, how did they use it? History was littered with war and power struggles. Which of those events were because of some mystical item? There were so many unanswered questions, but it was going to take some time to translate the whole manuscript. I would have to stay up to all hours in the morning every day.

Rolling out of bed, I went straight to the bathroom. My hair had gone on strike. There was no way I could stay up every night doing this. Someone would end up sending me to a psychiatrist by my looks alone. I splashed cold water on my face in hopes that would reduce the puffiness in my face. I parted my unmanageable hair, braided it into two sections, and ran out the door with only a minute to spare before I was late. I wasn't paying attention to my surroundings because I collided face first into Malcolm's stomach.

"We have to stop meeting like this. Every time I see you, you have a part of your body pressed against me," he teased, but in a way that made me think he didn't mind it. I lightly slapped his chest. My hand recoiled off the rock-like surface. "I like your hair like that," he said suggestively. "Also, I figured you stayed up all night after I left and thought some coffee would help. I added two extra shots to get you through the day."

A smile spread across my face. I knew how ridiculous my expression was, but I didn't care. The gesture was so thoughtful. "Thank you, and you're right. I stayed up all night. It was worth it, though. I got some of the first page translated."

Digging in my backpack, I found the notepad I had scrolled on. He read it while we walked to the archive.

"What does it mean? Do you really think there could be such a powerful entity out there? Or what if this was some elaborate tale that made its way secretly through the centuries? What if there is a society we don't know about, like the Knights Templar or the Black Hand?" A sudden spring hit his step. He was steaming with all the potential.

"There is only one way to answer that." I took my coffee from his hand before he dropped it and devastated me greatly. "A copious amount of research."

"Why do I get the feeling that is going to be your favorite part?" He tucked my notepad under his arm.

Shawn found us in the courtyard. He was coming from a parking lot, but I knew he didn't drive to work. I never thought to ask him where he lived or to see his place. He flagged us down and jogged over, ending our discussion of mythical relics.

"Long night?" I asked when I saw the sleepiness in his eyes.

"Early morning," he yawned, "and late night. Sorry I couldn't go to dinner with you two yesterday. New faculty was hired for this term, and I had to show them around. I should really introduce you to the rest of the history department—Malcolm isn't the only one."

"That's not necessary. I will meet them eventually." The idea of forced socialization sounded dreadful.

"Eve, I know you hate talking in groups, but it is a done deal. You should give yourself more credit. People are drawn to you." Shawn threw his arm around my neck. Normally I would find the gesture friendly, but after what Malcolm had said last night, I second guessed the act. "So how was your first day yesterday? Make any progress?"

I let him keep his arm around me. If I acted uncomfortable, that was exactly how things would be. Shawn and I had never had an uncomfortable moment in our relationship, and that's how I wanted to keep it. "It was fine. Time went by quickly. I got one bookcase cleared, so only fifty more to go. How did it become such a mess in the first place?"

"It was like that before I came here. The whole room was filled to the ceiling about five years ago through donations. I've tried to organize it, but every time I get free time, something else comes up. Some students work on it for extra credit, but they always get lost in all the text and don't know how to properly archive it all. I had one student that hid behind the shelves and slept for three months too."

Malcolm veered in a different direction from the archive. "I have to work on my lesson plans."

I inclined my head toward him. An energy that was low in my gut wanted me to follow him, but I waved at him instead.

"He has taken to you quickly." Shawn brought me in closer to his side. "He's typically very guarded."

"I think we get along. It's not easy to tell with him." Scooching my hand around his back to his side, I knew it wasn't the most professional. But Shawn and I were more like family; at least I hoped we still were.

"He is definitely the silent type." I wanted to disagree with him. Malcolm was nothing but talkative—after the first few hours, that is. "Despite his father, he is smart and a diligent worker. I couldn't ask for a better assistant. Well, besides you, of course."

"We haven't worked together in two years. My talents could have slipped."

"I highly doubt that. They probably got better with age, like you. But even if they hadn't, I am really happy you are here. I've missed you.

"I've missed you too. I have never felt more at home than I do now." My phone buzzed loudly in the courtyard, making me skip a step. I had gotten used to the lull in activity. My mom's number flashed across the screen. "I better get this. It's my mom, and she hasn't heard my voice in days. I'll meet you inside."

"Tell her hi for me."

Shawn saluted me and left me to my mother's unbelievable ability to tell a story with no point.

Chapter 5

Over the past four weeks, I had made headway in the archive. I wasn't as far along as I wanted to be, mostly because Malcolm and I worked closely every day doing Shawn's bidding that had nothing to do with my work. I had spent almost every hour of my days with Malcolm, except for the few hours a week when he went off to do his own work and when we slept. At night we put our focus on the ancient manuscript. I had figured out that the further we went into the pages, the more complicated it became to decipher the text. The language switched to something completely unknown to both of us, and it took nearly four nights pursuing what the language was.

Malcolm entered my room right as I clicked "send" on my email to Katherine with my latest research. "I got it!" He was clutching his laptop in one hand and the manuscript in the other. "It's North Picene, and unlucky for us, there are no cheat codes online for it. It's a foreign language to everyone."

"Guess we will have to figure it out on our own, then." I typed in the language in the search engine of my computer, but nothing that was helpful came up. Only information on where the language came from.

He raised an eyebrow. "Only you would try to translate a language that can't be translated. You know that you have been so buried with the archive, the book, and your work in Colorado that you haven't had an opportunity to even see all the historic sights of London."

"I know." I exhaled into my palm, depressed by that fact. "And with everyone moving in this weekend, I will hide away and become a shut-in until next summer."

"I hope not. I've become accustomed to seeing you all day long." He bowed over my chair, reading my recent search. His scent caught my nose. It reminded me of spending a day at the beach; it was so tantalizing. "Dig out a big camera and your walking shoes, and put your hair in those bloody cute braids. I am taking you sightseeing tomorrow. We are going to be tourists for the day!" He stood up, full of excitement, and bounced around gracefully, having total control over his large body. "I need to prepare. I'll pick you up at eight." He left the room with an accidental door slam just as quickly as he had come in.

I wondered what he had to prepare. I assumed we would be seeing the major highlights. No matter what we were doing, I was excited. London was filled with history, and I had yet to experience it. I brushed my teeth and showered quickly, eager to get to bed so tomorrow would get here sooner.

~*~

Malcolm rapped on my door exactly at eight. I already had it cracked open, ready for him to enter. I finished knotting the laces of my shoes and slung a backpack over my shoulders. "Ready!" I called out to him.

He glided into the room, wearing a red shirt. The color bounced off his naturally tanned skin, creating a glowing light that illuminated him. Dark hair hung low in his eyes. His hair had grown since I first met him. I knew he hadn't had much time to cut it, but I didn't mind the new style at all.

"Where is the big camera around your neck? I am disappointed, but those braids really do something to me." He clenched a braid in each hand and tugged, sending heat all the way to my toes. I gnawed on my lower lip. "We should go. Don't want to be late. I have made a very packed schedule."

"So, what's first?" I crammed my phone and wallet into my bag. "Is anything even open this early?"

"Nothing historical, but we are getting a traditional English breakfast first, blood pudding and all."

We took the path along the Thames that I had taken many times before. The river was brown and murky, but there was something peaceful about the gentle ripples in the water and the muted streets of the city on an early Saturday morning. Fog had settled over the river, creating a haze and making every building slightly out of focus. I stopped in the middle of the bridge and snapped a few pictures. I also took a few pictures of myself and a candid one of Malcolm. "Getting into tourist mode," I told him.

"I like it, but you're not full tourist until we take a picture of both of us." He gathered in beside me, stretching out with his long limbs holding my phone. He clicked the button about ten times and then moved in closer, resting his temple on mine. He took more pictures, but I wasn't focused on the lens. I was too concerned with his proximity to me. "Much better. Now we can call ourselves tourists. Be prepared for more of those." He checked out the pictures he'd taken. "I am sending this one over to myself." Flashing the screen at me, I saw his turquoise eyes staring straight ahead at the camera. He was gorgeous, no doubt about it, but I looked crazy. I was gazing at Malcolm in a way that a couple would look at each other. How could he like that photo? I must have come across as insane to him. But it didn't seem to bother him because he pushed forward, walking and taking pictures of me and the scenery with his phone.

The streets began to pick up with traffic and people once we made it to a pub. It was dark when we went inside, the walls covered in antique wallpaper and old paintings. We chose a booth at the front window because I wanted to people watch. Malcolm went up to the bar to order two English breakfasts and coffee.

I inspected the people outside. It was hard to tell who were tourists and who weren't. Most everyone had a bag on them and were on their phones. No matter how hard I tried, I was still disappointed that I wasn't in the sixteenth century London I had always imagined.

"See anything interesting?" Malcolm asked, taking a seat across from me.

"Not outside," I grinned. "So, what is on the agenda for the day?"

"I can't tell you that. It's all going to be a surprise, but I'm sure you can guess what some of the major highlights are."

The waiter came by to give us our drinks, but his fingers fumbled with the coffee mug, and the heated liquid splashed on the table and dripped on my jeans.

"I'm so sorry," yelped the waiter, mopping up the mess with napkins.

"No problem at all." I smiled up at him, trying to make him feel better. The mug tipped in his fingers again. This time the coffee spilled to the floor. He cursed out loud and scurried away, taking my coffee with him.

"But my coffee," I mumbled, dabbing my napkin in my water and cleaning up the spots on my pants.

"Take my coffee. I can wait." Malcolm slid the cup my way and cleaned up the rest of the table with the remainder of the napkins.

It was like he had handed over a priceless piece of art. I circled my fingers over the hot ceramic. "When I think you can't get any better."

"I am only better with you."

"Why is that?" When he didn't answer me, I continued. "I have talked to several people, and they all say the same thing about you. They all say you are one dimensional with your emotions and that you keep to yourself. But you don't have that problem with me?"

"I don't really know why. From the beginning, it's been easier with you. In some ways, we are very similar. We both love history; you can talk about it for hours, and you get really passionate about it. You throw your hands up in the air and get flustered and excited and go off on tangents. You're smart, and even though you get anxious a lot, I'm relaxed around you. I don't have to pry out a conversation, and you listen to every word I say. It's impossible to keep to myself and be one-sided around you."

"You make me sound pretty amazing." But everything he listed off about me was exactly how I felt about him.

"That's because you are. You have no idea of your effect on people, do you?"

"What do you mean?" I said, driving my eyebrows together.

"The waiter." He pointed in his direction. "He spilled the coffee because he was paying attention to you and not where the table was."

"Why?" I snarled at him in my response.

A portly rumble came out of him. He hung his head low between his shoulders as if he were giving up on me. "You're beautiful, Eve." His voice held steady, giving truth to his confession.

The waiter returned with more coffee and two giant plates of food. His hands were steady this time, but he didn't look up at us either. Malcolm forked my pile of mushrooms onto his plate, knowing my dislike.

"Wow, that's a lot of food." My plate was piled high with meats, tomatoes, and potato cakes. I dug into the mound, doing my best to eat everything except the baked beans.

"I can't believe you ate the blood pudding but skipped the baked beans. What kind of American are you?" His plate was completely empty. Where did all that food go on his body?

"Baked beans are awful! They sound like they should be savory and salty, but when you bite into them, they are sweet and mushy. It mystifies my taste buds." My stomach made weird sounds trying to process all the different foods.

"Baked beans aside, what did you think?" He twirled a spoon around in his coffee.

"It was good. However, I don't think I will be hungry for lunch, and I couldn't eat it every day."

"I guarantee that you will be hungry for lunch. We have a lot of walking to do, and the English can't even eat this every day." Malcolm got up from the table, came around to my side, and pulled out the chair for me.

"How much was my half?"

"Nothing, and don't say anything. You know I don't mind paying for you."

"I know you don't, but I do, so I am paying for both of us today." I narrowed my eyes on him, sticking out my chin.

"It's kind of hard to say no to that face." He placed his thumb tenderly on my chin and pushed it back down to level.

I eased off in my small victory, but I knew we would be having this conversation again. "So, where are we going next?"

"The lady doth protest too much."

"Shakespeare's Globe Theatre," I quipped with a cocky kick to my step.

"Smart, like I was saying."

Chapter 6

The thatched roof of the theatre stood out amongst the modern buildings surrounding it. Even though it was a replica, I could turn my mind back in time and picture myself standing in the center of the floor. Bodies crushed against each other, bad smells coming from every direction, ale sloshing at my feet, but loving every minute of the performance.

We were sitting in a tour group listening to the presentation. The woman leading the group was very energetic, but her facts on some of the Shakespearean history was off. I wanted so badly to correct her, but I didn't know how rude that would be. Malcolm was the first one to raise his hand. She seemed eager to call on him, and like with every woman, her voice got higher and filled with interest.

He politely corrected her last mistake, and her face fell flat. He glanced at me to seek my approval as to whether he had done the right thing. I gave him a discouraging head shake, raised my hand, and called out another mistake she had made earlier. By the end of the presentation, she had stopped calling on us and stormed out once she called it quits on the tour.

"I almost felt bad for her," I snickered as we trekked over to the Eye.

"I don't. If you're going to be a historical tour guide, then you should know the history."

I swayed my head in agreement. "That's why I said almost."

"At least this time, I had someone else to agree with me. Everyone learned a long time ago not to do this kind of thing with me because I will shamelessly correct people. Apparently, it's embarrassing for all parties."

"I am personally happy I am not the only nerd anymore. Granted, you're the sexiest nerd that I know...." I forced my tongue to stop, jamming it to the roof of my mouth. Had I really told him he was sexy?

"It astounds other people too." He winked at me.

I jabbed him in the shoulder. He lunged to the side, creating a wide void between us. He laughed robustly, turning several heads. I loved seeing this carefree side of him.

After the Eye and the thousand plus pictures we both took, we headed over to Parliament Square and Westminster Abbey. Malcolm was incredibly patient with me when I studied every tomb in the Abbey. We had been there for several hours, and I was finally nearing the end.

"Hell," he cursed out from behind me. He was squatted, his hair combed out of his eyes, studying a tomb intensely.

"What?" I placed my hand on his shoulder to balance myself as I got in the same position as him.

"I think I see the symbol, but I can't be sure." He pointed through the elegantly carved wood gate to a large tomb. A woman lying down with arms crossed was mounted on top of the tomb. Her gown was adorned with rich royal colors of navy, burgundy, and green. Roses created of stone detailed the tomb. At the furthest edge of the casket was a symbol. The way the half circles curved up at the ends was very similar to our symbol, but it was hard to tell from this distance.

"I think I might be able to get a picture." He pulled his phone out of his back pocket, hiding it behind his large hand since photos were prohibited in this area. "Block me, so the security guard doesn't see me."

I shifted to his other side, swinging my backpack to my front and pretending to search through it, trying to take up as much mass as possible to cover his large, very noticeable presence.

"Done." He stood up, his chest skimming my back. Static ran in the small space between us. "I'll enhance this on a computer," he breathed into my ear. I wondered if he knew what his proximity did to my body. The more we spent time together, the more I noticed it. "How are you doing?" He wasn't going to move away.

I turned to face him. His eyes were sultry, nearly blinding with desire. "Tired, but it is all so worth it. I am having such a great time, but I'm hungry," I whispered; all the air had left my lungs.

"Me too." His finger slipped down my shoulder to my wrist, leaving a trail of fire. "I mean," he cleared his throat, "I've got a place in mind."

We hiked the trip to Chinatown, where red lanterns lined the streets, stopping at a restaurant to eat lunch, and for the second time that day, I had way too much food. Malcolm was going to have to roll me out of the restaurant.

My stomach churned loudly, and I sobbed with discomfort.

"Don't worry, doll, we will be walking it off." He patted his stomach, but it wasn't protruding like mine was. "The British Museum will be the second to last stop. I figured we would both want to be there for a while since we both love museums. We'll have to do another tourist day in order to see the rest of the major sights. I was thinking that while we are at the museum, we should explore the antiquities for anything that might have to do with the relic."

"I was thinking the same thing." We hadn't made much headway in the last few weeks, and every night the puzzle of the relic gnawed at me. I knew we were on the verge of something big, but without proof of its existence, we would never get anywhere. The fact that some sign of it showed up randomly today was remarkable.

When we entered the museum's doors, Malcolm was immediately approached by a very slender and attractive woman. The navy pinstriped pencil skirt that reached her knees showed off toned, tanned legs. Her pink button-up blouse was nearly bursting at her bust. Long chestnut blonde hair was gathered into billowing waves at her shoulders. Her arms looped around Malcolm's neck. He embraced her with a large smile, and a ping of jealousy zinged straight to my heart. What a senseless notion that I should have that feeling when she hugged him. It's not like he was mine, I reminded myself.

"Eve." He let go of her. "This is Rose. She has been a close friend since I was twelve and is married to Owen."

On her ring finger, there was a giant amber diamond the size of my knuckle. "Owen is a lucky man." I closed my mouth; sometimes, I wished I could zipper it shut.

Rose grabbed Malcolm's elbow, clearly comfortable with touching him. "I like her already."

I stuck my hand out to introduce myself. "Eve."

She put her slender, delicate fingers in mine. "Nice to meet you, but I feel like I already know you." She swooped in, locking her arms around me. "Malcolm has nothing but good things to say about you."

I glanced over to him. He was looking all around the lobby except at me. "Rose is the volunteer coordinator here, and she wanted to say hello."

Rose agreed, releasing her hold. "And to meet the only woman, Mal has ever talked about."

"That's enough for introductions. We should get to it before the museum closes." He tugged on the strap of my backpack.

"Calm down, Mal. I won't embarrass you anymore," she teased, "I thought I might be able to get you both a sneak peek of our new exhibit about the Vikings."

"No luck?" Malcolm asked.

"I was actually able to pull some strings, mostly because Eve has a reputation with the lead historian. He wanted me to tell you that you needed to catch up with lunch and talk about the influences of 'Greek gods in today's culture,'" she said, using air quotes with her fingers.

It had been years since I had that conversation, that late night debate with Dante over gin and tonic, lasting for hours. "You can tell that pompous ass that I am right!" I said in seriousness.

"I think he would try to get me fired if I said that back to him."

By her reaction, I could tell she didn't like him. Knowing Dante, his blunt and aggressive attitude was probably off putting.

"Dante was an old professor and mentor of mine, similar to how Shawn and I are," I explained to Malcolm and Rose. "But

I haven't heard from him in years." I was thrilled to learn that he was living here again. There was no single word to describe Dante. He was one of a kind, with his long grey beard and white hair. I was almost positive he was a relative of Merlin.

"He is interesting," she said warily.

"He is harmless, I promise you. You can give him my number."

Rose laughed. "Malcolm, can you text me Eve's number? I will be sure to pass it along to Dante."

Malcolm went rigid with his arms crossed, puffing out his chest. "I don't know."

"Malcolm!" Rose slung up her hands. I had a feeling she did that a lot with him.

He was unaffected by her irritation. "You sure you can trust him?" He leaned into me, acting protective.

"I can. Hopefully, he remembers how to use a phone. After all, he is about seventy years old," I told Rose, but she already knew his age. The knowledge was for Malcolm's benefit.

Malcolm loosened his statuesque stance and exhaled. The motion was not lost on myself or Rose.

"Anyway, why don't you two look around for a few hours? Let me know when you're done, and I will take you to the exhibit, and don't forget to send me that number."

"Sounds great." Malcolm gave Rose a pat to the head. She flicked him in the arm and tossed her hair with the turn of her back. Her heels clicked off the tile floors as she sauntered away.

"I like her, and you wouldn't get it, but it's nice having a woman around."

"I don't really, but as long as you two get along, that is all that matters. It's important to me." We stepped into a large circular area. "So, what do you want to see first?"

I thought about asking him why it was so important, but he didn't give me enough time before he walked up to the kiosk and retrieved a map.

"Let's start upstairs and work our way down. But first…." He left my side again and made his way over to a coffee cart, ordering me a mocha and himself an espresso.

"It's like you read my mind," I said, taking the freshly made drink from his hand. I stood up as tall as I could on my toes and softly kissed him on his cheek. His skin was sweltering under my lips. That was the first time I had gotten that close to him, and I almost regretted it. I wanted to leave my lips there longer; the pull of his sweet-tasting skin was nearly devouring. He breathed out a word, but I couldn't make sense of it. Finally, I backed away, licking my lips in the process, reveling in the tiny sample I had of him. He went up the stairs slowly, in a distant haze, but his sea colored eyes never left me.

I was truly inspired by the extensive artifacts of the museum. We examined every inch of every piece of work. I felt like I could spend a week there and still not see everything. I found some very interesting pieces, but nothing that held that symbol we both so desperately wanted to know more about. After we finished the last floor, I got to see the famous Rosetta Stone. Well, sort of got to see it. Even with the building coming to a close, the room where it was held was packed full of people. Cameras were out, and everyone was throwing elbows. I got a glimpse, and with Malcolm being the tallest in the room, he was able to take some pictures for me.

"When work slows for Rose, I will get her to let us stay after hours so you can see it. That usually happens after the holidays."

I scrolled through my pictures of the stone. "This will do for now. Your height comes in handy." I made a straight line to the gift store to buy useless items that I didn't need. Malcolm had realized by the second place we visited that I was a gift shop junky. I demanded to stop in every single one and buy one thing.

I was rummaging over the books when Malcolm's heavy hand landed on the base of my spine. "I think it funny that you are an archivist and see books every day, and yet I find you in front of the book section."

I turned to him with an amused smile, "This coming from the guy that has a book collection in his room that includes a handful of romance novels."

"What can I say? I like to read anything and everything."

I swooned. Malcolm was a living character out of a romance

book, and it was kind of surreal that I was sharing air with him and calling him a friend.

"Find anything interesting?"

I flashed the cover of the book I was holding in his face.

He held a lopsided grin. "Ancient Languages. That could be valuable."

"Most of these we already know, but I figured any kind of source would be good," I explained over my shoulder as I waited in line at the cashier.

Rose materialized from around the corner, and Malcolm went to chat with her. While waiting, I saw an array of pins with various images on them. I picked out one with a book on it to give to Malcolm as a thank you and a memory for the day. I maneuvered the book in my bag, which was getting full from all the other trinkets accumulated throughout the day, and palmed the pin.

"Hey." I touched Malcolm on the shoulder, pulling him away from his conversation with Rose. "I got this for you as a thank you." I opened up my balled up fist to show him what I had bought.

He beamed. "It's a book, that's fitting! Thank you!' He swung his backpack around and pinned it to the front. "This will always remind me of you." He swept his fingers over the image. His eyes held some question that I didn't know the answer to but really wanted to find out. Their normal azure brewed into a stormy grey.

"Wow." Rose's voice surged over our trance. "I think I should go take a cold shower." Malcolm nervously played with the zipper of his bag. "The museum will be closing in an hour, and I know you want to see this exhibit."

We followed Rose's swaying hips up the long circular staircase. She swiped her ID badge on a keypad on the second floor. "I can't stay with you guys. I am in meetings for the rest of the day. Don't touch anything, and if you run into any problems, call me." She winked at me as she let herself back out the door.

The overhead lights flickered on in the room, showing off glass cases that ran the entire length of the space that were ready for public viewing. Malcolm and I went separate ways to observe what was in the cases. Weapons and helmets were the majority of what was on display. A sword was hung up on the wall. According to the plaque that was below it, the sword was thought to belong to Freydis Eriksdottir, the daughter of Erik the Red and a Viking warrior princess. It explained that the intricate design of the hilt was what led archeologists to believe it was her sword.

Glancing up at the hilt, I saw that there were three outer circles, and encased in them appeared to be what was the symbol we had discovered. I almost ripped the sword off the wall to exam it more closely. The symbol was barely etched into the rusted-out sword, but it was definitely there.

"Oh my god," I puffed out, barely above a whisper.

"What?" Malcolm buzzed in my ear, standing right behind me. I hadn't noticed that he had crept up.

"Freydis's sword." I pointed to it. Malcolm scanned it, his eyes brighter than mine. He reached for it, about to lift it from its display. I yanked him back by the elbow, keeping his arm dangling in midair. "Don't! What if that is the relic? We don't know what it would do."

"Only one way to find out." His free hand released the sword from clips before I could object again. He delicately held it between his hands, examining every inch and waiting for something, anything, to happen.

"Do you feel anything?"

"Nothing." He sounded disheartened with the inactivity. "It could just be a drawing, and maybe Freydis knew about the symbol. She was considered to be a fierce and volatile warrior, and if the manuscript is correct about giving the possessor great strength, this would make sense. We know that this," pointing to the hilt, "is cross-cultural, with all the ancient languages from all over the world. This is big, Eve. I know we can't be the only ones to discover this, but maybe we will be the first ones to unmask it."

The sound of a cracking door made both of us jump. Despite Malcolm's normally controlled movements, he stumbled, causing him to fumble the sword, but he caught it before it crashed to the ground, causing a number of damages. He swiftly attached the sword back on the hanging clips in one movement.

"Everything okay in here?" called out Rose's pretty accent.

"Yes." Malcolm whipped around, clearing his throat. He put an unnecessarily large amount of distance between us.

"All right." Rose eyed us suspiciously.

"We better get going," he stated to the room. He had turned white, his chest inflating heavily with each pant.

"That's a good idea. I don't want to miss the next item you have on your list." I rapidly leaped to the door.

"Mal planned the whole day out?" she challenged. "That's unexpected."

"What can I say. He's full of surprises." Taking him by the hand, I rushed us out of the room. "It was great to meet you, Rose."

"You too, Eve. I'm sure I will see you soon," she called out to me as we rushed out the door.

Malcolm mumbled what sounded like a goodbye to her when we hit the stairs, a little too late for her to hear anything. His usual calm demeanor was erratic. He clutched the back of his neck, forcing the bottom of his shirt to rise up an inch and giving me a sneak peek of his amazing body.

"I can't believe I almost destroyed a thousand-year-old artifact."

"Yeah, that was a close one. Come on, I will buy you a beer."

The air was cooler outside, with the afternoon giving way to the evening. He followed me down the street to the first pub I could find. I sat him at a table and left him to contemplate almost destroying a rare piece of history and possibly getting his good friend fired, as I ordered us some beers.

I put the lightly colored lager in front of him, and he took a long drink. "Better?" I sloped forward with my elbows on the table.

"Much. Thank you." He gathered my hand and cradled his over it as a gesture of gratitude. Color came back to his high cheeks, "Your friend Dante is the one that put that exhibit together. Do you think he would know anything about the symbol?"

I cast my gaze down on his hands as if they had caught fire. "I can talk with him about it." There was a good chance that Dante had seen the symbol before. He was well versed in most areas of history.

"Can I go with you if you meet with him?" He chained his middle finger with mine absentmindedly.

"If you want to. But just to forewarn you, he is eccentric."

"I have been warned and will be prepared. There is one more thing to show you, and we need to be there shortly." Our fingers unlinked, dashing away my cravings for him.

My glass was still full of beer. Shrugging my shoulders, I drank it in one breath. I got up from the stool and tripped on my feet. "I swear I am not drunk, only clumsy."

"I had figured out a while ago that you weren't coordinated, but I better be cautious anyway."

He placed his arm around my back, clutched a hand on my waist. He slanted to my side, connecting us at his hip. The evening air held a bitter chill, causing a shiver to run all over my skin. Malcolm moved forward, the tips of his toes touching mine. I stood there with my arms dangling to the side. I tried to shift my eyes away from his magnificent face, but it was impossible. I wanted to get lost in the way his lips curved up so slightly at the ends when he found me amusing and how the muscle running down the side of his neck tensed when he didn't quite know what to say to me, but I could tell by his eyes that he wanted to say so much.

A gust of wind blew past us, forcing his black hair to fall forward, skimming over his eyebrows. "It's getting cold. We should get going." His voice was thick and lazy, the Italian more recognizable.

I rocked my head yes and took a step back. My head was cloudy from his proximity as I followed him to our unknown location. Most of the tourist spots were closed, and I was getting hungry again.

I was busy thinking about food when my face bounced off Malcolm's back. He had stopped walking, and I hadn't noticed.

"Sorry," I mumbled.

"It's all right." His hands tossed in his hair. "Listen, I didn't mean to upset you back there. It's that—"

Having no idea what he was talking about or why I would be upset, I interrupted. "I was thinking about food and not paying attention to where I was going."

"Oh." His arms fell to his side, almost looking disappointed. "We are going to eat soon, I promise."

Gazing ahead to see where we were, I found myself standing right next to the Tower of London. The structure jutted out in the middle of the street. Stark green grass surrounded the property, rolling down the hill that used to be a moat. As the grass began to incline again, a wall of stone acted as a divider to the main complex. Situated right on the edge of the Thames, I could imagine how it would be threatening to intruders. "I don't think we can get in." We approached the main entrance, but the gates were closed.

"Not exactly." He rubbed my shoulder.

From a cobblestone street that led around to a back gate, I saw Wesley's thick frame heading toward us.

"Thanks for coming!" he exclaimed from the road. He must've read my confusion. "For dinner. Did Mal not tell you?"

"No, MAL didn't tell me anything we were doing today."

"Intriguing." Wesley scratched his chin like he was deep in thought.

"Don't hurt yourself thinking so hard." Malcolm punched Wesley in the shoulder as he glided past him.

Watching Malcolm retreat through an open door, I asked, "I am stumped. Do you live here?"

"We do. My husband, James, is one of the horticulturists for the grounds. Most people that live here are the families of the Yeoman Warders, but we managed to negotiate an apartment."

"That is...incredible! I can't believe you get to live in a place with so much history. It must be amazing to walk the same steps as so many people from throughout time."

He stopped and whirled around to face me, his long pause unknowing.

"What? Is everything all right?"

"That is something Mal would say. In fact, I believe those were his exact words when we first moved in."

We were historians, after all. "We kind of live for this stuff. That's most likely why we became friends so fast."

"You see, the thing is," he crammed his hands in his pants pockets, "Mal doesn't make new friends. Sure, he has us, but we have been friends for so long we no longer count."

"What about Shawn and other people at the university?"

"Shawn forced himself on the group, but it took over a year for us to meet him, and even then, Shawn had to invite himself. As for his colleagues, they are only acquaintances. We haven't met a single one by Mal's doing. Don't get me wrong, he has other friends. Granted, he isn't as close to them as he is to us. But we all met you the first day, and he hasn't stopped talking about you since. I am guessing he hasn't spent one day without you, has he?"

"No," I answered timidly.

"Mal doesn't plan surprise days. He doesn't talk about the women he meets, friends or otherwise. He has never introduced a woman to us, not even me, and I'm his best mate."

"Oh." I wasn't sure what he wanted me to say. "Sorry, but we are friends. I don't know why he acts differently around me. We are very similar, and we both have a passion for history," I said, repeating Malcolm's words from earlier. "That's all. I mean, he was as eager to go sightseeing today as I was. I think he was happy to have someone really appreciate what he loves." I didn't really know why I was explaining myself or felt like I had to come up with an excuse for us to be friends, but it felt like he needed some justification.

"Whatever you say, but you don't need to be sorry. We like having you here and want to see you around for a long time."

"Thanks." I wasn't sure if that was worth a thanks, but I went with it anyway.

"Come on now, let's get out of the cold. James is excited to meet you. He has been preparing all day for your arrival."

The small foyer of their apartment was modern for the age of the facility. Light wood floors covered the space. The living room spread into an open kitchen, making the small room appear larger than it was. New appliances and furniture added to the modern touch. A man with beautiful, wavy red hair that coiled at the ears stood tall in the kitchen with a wine glass in his hand. He was wearing a white button-down collared shirt. The sleeves were rolled at the elbows, exposing strong forearms. The shirt was stretched over his chest, suggesting he had a defined body. The black slacks he was wearing were formed to his hips. I suddenly felt underdressed and self-conscious of my braids and T-shirt.

"That is your husband?" I was stunned by the beauty of the man.

"Yes." Wesley drew in air, similarly awed by him.

"Holy crap! Did you marry the Prince of England?"

Wesley's lips twitched up. "Yeah. Yeah, I did." I couldn't help but laugh at the way he admired his accomplishment.

"What are you badgering about?" Malcolm asked with curiosity.

"We are admiring my gorgeous husband," explained Wesley. I rattled with agreement. Why were all of Malcolm's friends so attractive?

James squealed a high pitch sound. "Malcolm, she is wonderful and gorgeous. That red hair is beautiful, kind of like how mine is." He swooped his hair to the side so dramatically I thought he would pull a muscle in his neck.

I, on the other hand, danced on my toes, not comfortable with the compliments. "Thanks for having us over, and it's nice to meet you, James."

James shook his head fervently, removed a wine glass from an overhead cabinet, and filled it to the brim with dark crimson liquid. Then he tipped the large glass towards me as a gesture to see if I wanted some.

"Yes!" I answered a little too vigorously, hoping that wine would help alleviate my awkwardness.

"Dinner is almost ready. I have a few items left to prepare, and after we eat, we can go on a tour of the grounds."

"Really?!" I tried to contain my excitement, but it wasn't

happening. I was getting a private, no lines-to-wait-in or view-obstructed-by-the-crowds, tour. "Can I help you finish up?" I offered.

"Yes, and this way I can get to know you better." He handed me a knife and a carton of mushrooms to chop. Wes and Malcolm went to the couch to talk about a rugby match that was on in the living room. "I know Malcolm said you don't like mushrooms, but go ahead and do the whole container. It's Malcolm's favorite, and he will eat your portion." I saluted him with the knife as confirmation, "Have you always lived in Colorado?"

It was a little off putting that these people knew about me before even meeting me, but I chalked it up to Malcolm or Wes, telling him where I was from.

"Always. Went to college there, and up until a month ago, the only time I left was to visit the surrounding states. What about you. Where are you from?"

James went to the stove. The space was small, and he had to cram in next to me, thumping me in the side as he mashed the potatoes.

"I'm from London. Never lived anywhere else either. Wes and I went to uni here. We met during our first year and have been together since then."

"So, you were interested in him right away?" I made sure that each mushroom was sliced evenly.

James took the knife out of my hand and diced up one of my neat slices, creating jagged edges. He handed it back over to me with a mischievous grin. "I did. I remember the first day he walked into class. He was adorable and so nervous, but the moment we made eye contact, it was as if sirens went off. He sat next to me, and throughout class, I caught him catching little glances. I have to admit I was doing the same. After class, I followed him to his next class. Even though it wasn't mine, I sat through the whole lecture anyway. Afterwards, he introduced himself, and from there, it was history." A pan for the mushrooms came down on the cutting board. "You know, he was nervous for me to meet Malcolm at first."

"Why is that?" I asked, tossing slices in the pan one at a time.

"Malcolm is so closed off and kind of aggressive about it. We got along fine, but it took several years for him to open up to me. If he hadn't been Wes's best friend, I wouldn't have put so much effort into it, but now I can say it was worth every effort." He took the pan back from me, throwing in a stick of butter. "So tell me, Eve, when did you know you liked Malcolm?"

"Oh, I...I don't like him, not in the way you are thinking." I blamed the hot kitchen for the sudden change in my temperature.

"Come on." He pointed his spatula at me. "I have only seen you interact with him once for a half second, and I know those sirens go off for you too."

I finished off my wine with a large gulp, adding more to the glass. "Regardless of what I feel, it doesn't matter."

He deserted the spatula and took my hands. "It matters a lot, Eve."

He was going to say more, but Wes came into the kitchen, taking a bottle of wine out of the refrigerator. "Is dinner almost ready?"

"Yes, dear." James kissed the top of his head.

On the door of the refrigerator was a collage of printed-out pictures, many that appeared to be recent, over the past few years. Malcolm hadn't changed a bit. He was strong and muscular, with the same haircut. In the center of all the photos was one from when they were all younger. It was easy to tell who each of them was. Rose was maybe the most different. Her hair was lighter, and she was wearing an oversized baggy shirt, looking more like one of the boys. Even as a young boy, Malcolm was striking. He was darker in the picture and taller than everyone but Owen. His hair was longer and wavy, covering his eyes, but the blue still pierced through his hair. He had the cold expression that he still wore daily. The rest of the group was smiling, but he was the only one scowling at the camera. On his right hand, there was a red cast that went all the way up to his elbow. I couldn't help but get the impression he was sad.

"We were thirteen in that picture." Wes sipped his wine close to my ear. "Malcolm always had that same face, even to this day, but I have noticed that lately, a smile comes across when he is lost in thought. There is one thing that has changed in his life over the past month."

"I can set the table!" I shouted to James. Malcolm turned to me from the couch to see what was going on, but I desperately wanted to get away from what Wes was talking about.

"Thanks, Eve, but we are eating outside. The table is bigger."

James handed me a plate and piled it with food. Malcolm was the last to get his plate, emptying out the remainder of food onto his. I followed them outside but wasn't prepared for the chilly night air. I hugged myself, trying to warm up, but my teeth wouldn't stop chattering. Malcolm took a seat next to me, his body acting as a barrier from the breeze coming from his direction. But the moment he put his plate on the table, he got right back up and went inside.

When he came back, there was a sweatshirt hanging from his arm. "I was prepared. I brought an extra one for you."

"Thanks, Malcolm. You really did think of everything today." I stood up from my chair and drew the sweatshirt over my head, loosening my braids in the process. Pieces of hair fell forward into my eye. Sitting back down beside him, I was instantly warm. Malcolm's arm shot out, his fingers landing on a strand of my hair that had fallen. He gently tucked it behind my ear. His hand lingered, and he etched his thumb along the ridge of my jaw.

"Much better." His deep voice cleared the soundless air.

Eyeballing my lettuce, I counted how many leaves I had left. Wesley mouthed something in order to get the table talking again, but I was still focused on that lettuce. When I peeked up through my lashes, James's stare was glittering.

"Did you enjoy your day of sightseeing?" Wes asked both of us.

"I did. Eve was great company and didn't complain once that I made her walk around the whole city. She also taught me a few new facts that I didn't know." He nudged me in the arm with his elbow. My piece of steak fell off my fork.

"Malcolm didn't teach me anything new," I joked. "Well, besides the fact that he likes to take a lot of pictures."

Wes coughed on his wine and spit the remainder that was

in his mouth out in a napkin, forcing an icy glare from Malcolm. "I've got to see these pictures, and I don't think Malcolm has ever taken a picture of us willingly."

Wes quickly snapped up Malcolm's phone and went through his pictures. Malcolm didn't seem to mind that he violated his privacy without really asking. He was concentrating hard as we ate our food. I wasn't able to finish all of mine. I had consumed way too much food today. Malcolm traded plates with me and finished off the rest of my portion. I watched him as he devoured my food. I couldn't believe he looked the way he did with how much he could eat. It was worth being envious over.

"You ready to go explore?" Wesley leaned across the table to get my attention. He had water in his eyes, and I wasn't sure why. Did I miss something important while my attention was on Malcolm's eating habits?

"I am so ready!" I vaulted out of my seat, letting Wes's random spring of emotions fall to the side.

"Why don't you two go up to the top of the wall and wait for us there while we clean up? The view is amazing." James gathered my plate in his hand.

"You sure? I don't mind helping with the cleanup," I offered.

"I insist," he urged, casually shifting his eyes to Wes and hoping that I would pick up his hint that he wanted to talk with him. "It won't take us very long."

I took Malcolm and began to walk away.

"Wait," Wes demanded. "Take these." He handed us plastic glasses filled with wine. "Better to take plastic than glass."

Malcolm took the cups from him, and I followed him to the top of the wall. Small slits in the stone ran the length of the wall where arrows used to be shot through. We reached a spot where the Tower Bridge was most prominent, and the city lights across the Thames sparkled in the dark. That overwhelming sense of belonging hit me again.

"You're getting that feeling again, aren't you?" Malcolm spoke softly in my ear.

"How can you not?"

"I don't know because I feel the same way."

He slid his arm around my back, and I rested my head right below his shoulder, soaking it all in. I don't know how long we stood there like that. I spent a long time enjoying the thought that life had come to a halt, long enough for me to memorize how many lights bounced off the water and to watch the remainder of the night dwellers on the cobblestone walkways. Their chatter bounced off the walls, solidifying to me that I needed to appreciate more moments like this.

Someone's throat cleared from the distance. Malcolm's arm released from my shoulder, but I kept my head on him. Wesley and James stood hand and hand, each holding a cup of their own. "As much as I don't want to interrupt this moment between you two, we are ready. Since we are here for you, Eve, what do you want to see first?"

"How about the white tower?" I knew exactly where I wanted to go.

"The white tower it is!" Wesley sang out. I think the three bottles of wine that he had consumed on his own was affecting the volume of his voice.

"I should drink your wine." Malcolm reached out, thinking the same thing.

"Nonsense." Wes yanked his cup close to his body, standing behind James for protection, although I wasn't sure who would protect who. James was taller only by a little and had more muscle, but Wes was bigger.

There was something haunting about touring the tower at night. It was as though I could feel the spirits of all those who had died there. I was in a historian's dream. I stopped at every plaque and read everything, taking my time, examining every piece of history, buzzing around everywhere. All three of them were keeping up with me without protest. Many times they would probe me about an event, date, or person, and I would answer in a long detailed response. I think Malcolm was even impressed by my extensive knowledge.

"She is smarter than you," I heard Wesley tell Malcolm as we were making our way over to the St. Thomas tower. Since they had been drinking, they were talking louder than they realized.

They were probably also hoping I was daydreaming, much like James, who was traipsing around us in circles.

"I know," replied Malcolm. "I am honestly not used to someone being able to keep up with me." He didn't sound intimidated by it, which was something I wasn't used to.

"Thanks, ass."

"I mean professionally." Malcolm quickly caught his mistake.

"I know you are smarter than me, but thanks for trying not to be a complete ass like normal," Wes mocked.

"Honestly, I like it." Malcolm paused for several seconds. "I like her more than I should," he confessed to his friend.

"I'm not sure what that is supposed to mean."

"It means that I can't allow myself to feel this way. I don't want her involved in my messed up life. She deserves more than that."

"I can understand how you would feel that way. You know, I do. But a woman like that doesn't come around very often, especially for you. You act differently around her, better, and I think she would understand what you had to and do go through."

"I do know how I am around her, but I still can't subject her to everything. Which is why I think we would be better off as friends. We could also potentially have a long career together, and I don't want to ruin that either."

A horrible emotion sat low and massive in my body and tore into me. It felt like I was on a plane and that the dip from the turbulence had caused me to be nauseous.

"You're wrong," Wes spoke bluntly. "You deserve something good, Mal, and she is it."

What could be that bad or messed up in his life that caused him to stay away from any type of relationship? I climbed up steps to the tower, seeing that Wesley had his hand cupped on Malcolm's shoulder.

I was so focused on them I hadn't noticed that I missed another step before hitting the landing, and I tripped on the large stone, flying forward with my limbs straight out into the doorway of the tower. My face planted on the cold stony floor, cracking my nose on impact. Dark red liquid poured from me and cascaded down my chin. I pinched my nose closed as I sat up and rested my head against the wall.

"Eve!" Malcolm sprinted up, crouching next to me with his hands on my face, attempting to examine me through the coat of blood.

"I am fine. Just hit my face. Don't think I broke my nose, though." My ego was bruised too, but I didn't say that.

"Damn it," Malcolm cursed, more upset than me. I was used to injuring myself at least once a week. He called to Wesley and James to go back to the apartment and get some towels. "Keep on pinching it until it stops. I will get you cleaned up soon. You know, you are the smartest person I know, but you are also the clumsiest. I should carry around a first aid kit when we go out."

"Funny," I garbled, trying to let my embarrassment deflate.

I zeroed in on the stonework on the archway across the room, studying it closely, so I didn't have to endure the crack of amusement on Malcolm's face. The light from outside was hitting the stone just right, defining the dirt and crevices that had been built in over the years. Where the mortar hit the stone were shallow cuts that resembled the symbol that held one of the half circles. From a distance, I couldn't tell if it had the other markers.

"Malcolm." I stood up but swayed. The blood loss and face dive had weakened me, and I had to use his arm as a stabilizer.

He wasn't seeing what I was seeing. The circles weren't visible without the small amount of light. Dirt had filled in around them, seemingly causing them to be passed over thousands of times. "Do you have keys or something sharp on you?" I held one hand over my nose and the other one out in the air.

He pulled out a small knife from his front pocket and flipped open the blade. "I always carry a knife with me." I took it out of his hand and carved the dirt away. My suspicion was right. It was the symbol. "Oh my god. I can't believe you saw that."

"The light caught part of it. Do you think there is something behind the stone?" I started digging away at the mortar, trying to pry the small stone away from the larger pieces.

"Eve, you can't destroy historical property."

He reached for my hand, but I moved it away before he got

to it. I was thinking back to the exact conversation we had earlier about Freydis's sword.

"Malcolm, don't you find it odd that there is one small stone near the larger ones? There has to be something behind there. I can put it back. No one will ever notice." I really hoped that was true. I could be put in jail and charged a large fine for destroying property.

My hand rattled as I carved a small indent around the grout, trying to make the least amount of damage possible. It didn't help that it was difficult to see, with my other hand in the middle of my face holding my nose.

"Here, let me do it. Concentrate on your nose, and when James and Wes come back, distract them."

"Okay, but be careful."

He pursed his lips at me like I didn't need to tell him that.

I stood in the entranceway, on patrol. My nose was trickling now, but my hands were covered in blood. I heard drunken chatter from below. Peeping over the edge, I saw that they were almost to the stairs.

"Hurry up, they are coming," I buzzed to Malcolm.

"Almost there." He kept his hand steady on the knife, careful not to make any unnecessary marks. "Tell them I got a call from my father—it will give me time."

Not sure what that meant, I did it anyway without asking. "Malcolm is talking to his father. He needs a few minutes." I hoped I sounded convincing enough.

"That's going to ruin the night." Wes banded his arms around my waist, helping me off the last step. Apparently, my prior missteps warranted me needing a guide.

"Let's get you cleaned up." James wiped my face with a wet cloth, and I washed off my hands with another one. "Sorry if it is a little cold."

Wes handed me an ice pack for under my eyes. Hopefully, it would help, but I knew my face was going to hurt in the morning.

"I'd better make sure he is okay," Wes said, heading for the first step.

"I am sure he is fine." I stood up too quickly, getting vertigo.

My vision crossed, but I rushed to block the stairwell anyway. "I mean, it sounded pretty personal."

"I know. That's what I am concerned about. You don't get it." Uneasiness had jaded his soft features.

I was beginning to feel bad for lying. "Then explain it to me."

"It's not for me to tell you, Eve. All I can say is that his father is not a good man, so if you don't mind...."

He used two fingers to push my shoulder to the side and stepped around me. My pulse quickened. If Malcolm was caught tearing apart the tower, his friends would be angry, and we would both have a lot of explaining to do.

Luckily, Malcolm's silhouette came into view, and he headed down the stairs. "I am fine, Wes. Just discussing work. Thanks for dinner, but I should get Eve home. She hit her face pretty good."

"It's getting late anyway," James added, securing Wes to his side and drawing shapes on his stomach.

"Thank you so much for tonight. I am so happy to meet you, James, and to spend more time with you, Wesley."

They walked us to the exit. Wes was still anxious about Malcolm's pretend call, and I was on pins and needles wanting to know if he had found anything if the vandalism was worth it.

The seconds ticked by slowly. We made it one block, and I burst out, "I am dying to know if you found anything."

He paused for a long time. It was torturous. He finally handed over a small tube from his back pocket. Tarnished leather was stretched taut into a cylinder. The edges were burnt off into crisp ends, and the only weight was from the material.

"This kind of container was used for passing messages in order to keep the paper safe from damage. Since it is still sealed, I'm assuming a note of some kind is in there and that whoever it was supposed to reach never received it."

I sighed. As much as I wanted to rip it open, I knew better. It had been sealed for who knows how long. "We need to take precautions and open it in an airtight chamber."

"I bet Rose can set it up for us to use the one at the museum. I will call her tomorrow."

"I'm not a patient woman." Surveying the tube, I saw that

the seam down the center was cross-stitched with black thread. It would be too easy to pop the thread and find out what clues lie beneath it. "You better keep it." I handed it back to him. It was like handing over a child. "Was there much damage to the wall? And I didn't even think about cameras until now."

His long fingers engulfed the casing as he took it from my hand. A sudden feeling of yearning crept over me from the departure. "Only the major rooms with artifacts and jewels and the outer walls have cameras, but there is nothing along the walkways or in the stone towers. I was able to place the stone back with minimal damage. If someone examined it closely, it would appear to be normal wear and tear. What we did was highly illegal, so we need to keep this our secret. Not that you need a reminder; it's something I need to say out loud, though."

The secrets we held were getting easier and easier to keep with each new criminal act we were committing. "I'm sure I can keep this one too."

"We are in this together. If you get caught, so do I." He knocked his hip into my stomach, asking, "How is your face doing, by the way? I hope you didn't mess it up too badly."

"Why? Afraid to have to see my ugly face all day?"

He seized me by the shoulders and drove us under a street lamp. His fingers tickled right under my left eye. "You can't do anything to this face to make it ugly. It will always be beautiful." His finger held still on my skin. The way the dark shadows hit his cheeks highlighted his eyes, making his confession believable.

I did nothing and said nothing. I was cemented to his words.

"Most people say thank you or piss off." He backed away from the street lamp. Even in the dark, he stood out.

"Malcolm, can you tell me about your dad?" I had to jog to catch up to his long stride.

Anger blazed across his face. "Why would you ask that?"

"I have pieced a few things together. Mainly what you said about being on the phone with him and that Wesley told me he wasn't a nice person. Also, you only call him your father, not your dad, which implies you don't have a good relationship with him."

"I don't want to ruin our good day by talking about him."

"I won't force it, but you can tell me anything. I want you to know that I am here to listen to and support you when you're more comfortable with me."

"I am comfortable with you now, more than I expected, but Andrew Archer is someone I never want to discuss." He ended the conversation of his father with an almost demanding force. I wasn't bothered by it. I knew it wouldn't be a pleasant topic.

We lazily strolled back to the university, letting the breeze that rolled off the Thames tickle the hairs on the back of my neck. Even with my exhausted muscles, sore feet, and throbbing nose, it had been the best day I'd had in a really long time. The pressures of my work had dissolved the moment Malcolm stepped through my door that morning. I was finally able to see and explore all of the places and artifacts I'd spent years researching and reading about. "Thank you for the day, by the way. I don't think I said it yet, but it was absolutely fantastic."

"You're welcome. I had a great time too, plus...." He waved the leather tube in front of me, causing me to cackle with excitement.

Chapter 7

My left eye had a dark purple ring under it, and there was a dull ache on that side of my face. I was lucky I hadn't broken my nose. The sunglasses I was wearing protected it from the sun on my way to the archive. There was no one else in the room when I got there, which was a rarity. The large piles of books had diminished to almost nothing. I had about two weeks left of organizing, and then I would transfer them to digital copies. I had to pat myself on the back for being excellent at my job.

I took my time drinking my coffee and nursing the unexpected hangover while one-handedly organizing the books back onto the shelves.

Shawn eventually showed up thirty minutes late. "Sorry, I am late. I slept in," he called out to me.

"You're the boss. You can show up whenever," I hollered from behind a pile of books. It was almost like playing a game of Marco Polo.

"That's what I like to hear," he called out again. "I have zero accountability. Where's Mal?"

I got up from behind my books and emerged into the aisle, about to say that I didn't know, but Malcolm entered with the creak of the door. Both of them had unkempt hair with slouching shoulders, and sleep was heavy in their eyes.

"Whoa!" The three of us yelled at the same time.

"What happened to you two?" I knew Malcolm and I had some drinks last night, but it wasn't that damaging.

"We went out late last night. Shawn came around one in the morning and forced me to go out." Malcolm wasn't too happy about it.

I was stunned by that because we had gotten back after midnight.

"I only got back to my flat about two hours ago. It's almost too easy to pick up women when Malcolm's around. You should have seen what we picked up last night."

"Oh." I paused, scowling at Malcolm.

He started for me but then thought twice about it. It hadn't bothered me that Shawn was telling me this. I was used to it from him. But the envy I felt that Malcolm was with another woman pierced me worse than expected. I forced that feeling deep down and mentally stomped on it.

"What happened to your face?" Shawn pointed to my eye.

"I stumbled and fell. Nothing exciting." Shawn was well versed in my utter lack of ability to put one foot in front of the other.

"Does it hurt?" Malcolm stepped forward.

I stepped back. "I'm fine." I spun my back to him, marching down the aisle to my corner of books, where I felt the safest.

I was silently pouting for half the day. No matter how much I tried, that awful taste I had for Malcolm came back and burned my throat. I kept my distance from both of them. I was short on my answers and sour with comments. I put my headphones in halfway through the morning so they would get the hint to not talk to me. I was very content in my space, lost in an Ottoman Empire book I was reading until Malcolm tugged out one of my headphones.

"What?" I demanded harshly.

He flinched. Words were at the tip of his tongue, but he hesitated. I brought the music back up to my ear.

"We are going for lunch. I really want to you come!" he nearly shouted, trying to get my attention off the music.

"No, I am not hungry." That was a lie. My stomach was eating itself alive as we spoke, and I had been hungry for the last four hours. I put my headphones back in, hoping he would get the hint to go away, but he pulled them out again.

"Can we talk?"

"About what?" I grunted, grating my teeth together.

His hand went to his jaw, trying to rub away the tension. Why did I find that so attractive? "About me going out with Shawn last night."

"I really don't think there is anything to talk about. I am not your mother or girlfriend. You can do what you like with whom you like." I knew the words coming out of my mouth were true and that he didn't deserve my behavior, but I was upset, and no matter how hard I tried, I didn't truly believe what I was telling him. I blamed it on those damn sirens that James talked about whenever Malcolm was near.

"Eve I…."

I put my headphones back in and turned up the volume, ending the conversation before I cried.

He left me alone like I wanted, and neither of them came back for me. Shawn knew me well enough to know that when I was in a mood like this to leave me to my thoughts. I was nestled up in the back of the room, reading a book about the imperial harem, when my eyes felt weighty, and the books looked like really good pillows. I rested my head on them to take a small nap.

Books descending on top of me scared me out of my sleep. The lights were bright in the archive room, but a black shadow cascaded from the aisle. Books crashed to the floor on the other side of the shelf. The vibration caused one to bounce off my foot. A man cursed. More books went flying, and the shelf rattled like it was getting hit by an earthquake. I was trapped in the corner like a caged mouse. The more the man rattled the shelf, the more I could be exposed, or he would eventually come into my row and find me back there. I had to get out.

The shadow moved a few feet closer to the aisle. I didn't know if this man was violent, but I did know he was enraged. What if he attacked me for being in the room? Through a slit between the books, I saw that his back was facing me. This was my chance to sneak out. I softly moved to my toes, holding my breath. I could hear my rapid heartbeat and hoped that he couldn't hear it too. I picked up the thickest hardcover I could find and raised it up, ready to swing if I needed to.

Taking one tiny step at a time, I found myself in the aisle. If my timing was off, he would see me, and I didn't want to think of what he would do to me if I was caught. My plan was to sprint down the aisle as soon as I stepped into it, but I halted. Books covered every inch of the wood floor. Pages were ripped out and scattered everywhere. All of my work was destroyed, but I couldn't think about that. I had to concentrate on making as little noise as possible while stepping over them, trying not to damage them more than they already were.

I made it to the other side of the shelf. The man was still turned away, a black ski mask over his head. Black pants and a long sleeved black shirt made him look like a robber, but what could he possibly be stealing here? All this stuff was free to use for students and faculty.

I kept my focus on him, watching for any movement in my direction, but not watching my feet was a mistake. I stumbled over a book, making enough noise to grab his attention. The man rotated around, almost in slow motion. He was motionless at the sight of me, obviously surprised that someone was there so late. The shock wore off in a second, and he lunged for me, but I was ready for him and swung the book at his head with all my force. He did a full spin and crashed to the floor.

I ran as fast as I could, abandoning the book and hurdling over the ones on the floor. I ran down the long wooden corridor, my footsteps echoing in the hall. I kept my head up, sprinting through the courtyard, flying through the apartment doors and taking three steps at a time up to the floor, stopping at Malcolm's door. I hammered with both fists for several seconds, glancing behind me to see if I was followed. I was relieved to find that I hadn't been. The lock clicked, and the door flew open. I leapt inside, slammed the door behind me, and twisted the lock.

"Eve, what is going on?" His accent was lazy and sleep induced.

I arched against the door, throwing my head back, trying to catch my breath and calm my nerves.

"Eve?" His fear grew heavier on his voice when I didn't reply. "Damn it, Eve!" He placed both of his hands on my face, his thumbs at my temples, and his forceful fingers brushed circles on the back of my neck, helping me to calm down. "Please tell me what is going on!"

I took a deep pause, steadying my composure. "I had fallen asleep in the archive, and I was woken up by a man throwing around books."

Malcolm exhaled sharply. "Did he hurt you?" He made a quick check of my body.

"He was searching for something. All the books were tossed from the shelves, and half of them were destroyed. Anyway, I tried to sneak out. He saw me and went for me, but I hit him with a book, and he fell to the ground. Then I came straight here."

"You're okay, though? He didn't touch you, right?" He needed me to say the words; seeing me wasn't enough.

"I am not hurt. Just kind of shaken up and frightened."

He dropped his hands from my neck and weaved me between his arms. It was only when my face was scrunched against his chest that I realized he wasn't wearing a shirt. His skin was smooth like silk and cool against my hot cheek. My hands found their way around to his lower back and splayed out over his muscles. We held each other for a few minutes.

"I am sorry." He spoke to the top of my head.

"It's okay. I'm all right."

"I know you are. I meant I am sorry for last night with Shawn. I didn't do anything with that woman." He held on tighter, almost as if he was afraid to let me go.

I took another large breath of relief the moment he said it. "You don't need to apologize. It really is none of my business what you do." His earlier indiscretions were now a distant memory.

"I needed you to know."

"Thanks." My shoulders slumped, needing to put some distance between us, "What should I do about the man?"

"I will call Shawn and security. Take a moment to gather yourself." He took a bottle of water out of a cabinet. "It might be a long night."

I chased down my fear with the water. The clock on his

table read that it was almost two in the morning. I balled up on his small couch, trying to unwind, but it didn't last long after Malcolm came back into the room.

"All right, we need to go back to the archive. Security and Shawn are going to meet us there. I can call back and tell them you will speak with them tomorrow if you want to rest up, though."

"No, let's get this over with."

He lifted me off the couch and let me attach myself to his side during the walk. The early morning sky wasn't helping my anxiety. The clouds covered any stars and the moon. It was eerily dark, and every noise or pop of a car made me turn my head or twitch. Malcolm didn't give me a hard time for it and held onto me when I got skittish.

"I'm sorry I woke you up and got you involved. I know you needed sleep."

"Don't ever be sorry, doll. I am here for you, always. And I don't care about sleep as long as you are safe."

The sense of safety was tangible standing next to him, and it had nothing to do with how tall or strong he was. I knew I could trust him, and that was more comforting than anything.

I halted at the long corridor that led to the archive.

"I am right here."

He held my hand as we approached the room. The door was set ajar. I hoped the intruder was gone or wasn't dead. I didn't think I hit him hard enough to kill him, but it could only take one lucky swing. I tightened my grip on Malcolm's hand when I saw a man dressed in black in the middle of the room.

"It's all right. It's the security guard." He dislodged his hand from my grasp but leaned in to reassure me that he was with me.

The security guard faced us. The first thing I saw was his large round belly and thick chunky cheeks. "Oiy, Malcolm." He was also Irish. "What a mess. Is this the woman who was in here?"

"Yes, sir. I'm Eve." I stuck my hand out. He mimicked me, his chubby fingers encasing my hand. It was like holding uncooked sausages.

"Frank." He removed his security cap, showing off an

extremely shiny, hairless head. "Sorry to meet you this way, Eve. Can you tell me what happened tonight?"

I cleared off some books that were tossed on the brown chairs. "I had fallen asleep in the back corner and was woken up by books falling on me. That's when I heard someone else in here. He was throwing books around and getting angry that he couldn't find what he wanted. Anyway, I was trapped in the corner, but when I could see that his back was toward me, I made an escape. I didn't expect books to be all over the aisle, and I tripped on them, causing him to hear me. He tried to grab for me, but I hit him in the head with a book, and he fell to the floor. After that, I ran back to the apartments and got Malcolm."

"Can you give me a description of the attacker?" Frank requested.

"No. He was wearing a mask, and when I hit him, I didn't even think about taking it off before I ran. Should I have done that?" I was rethinking my actions now.

"No, you did the right thing," Malcolm assured me.

"Oh, god, my books!" Shawn scrambled angrily into the room, taking in the disaster.

I leapt up from my seat, startled by his entrance. "I'm sorry, Shawn. I shouldn't have fallen asleep in here. This is my fault."

He shot towards me, collapsing his arms around my shoulders and squeezing. "Are you all right?"

Air was closed off in my lungs. I opened my mouth to say something, but nothing came out except for a squeak.

"Sorry." He let go, holding me away from him to make sure there weren't any visible injuries. "Tell me what happened." I relived the events of the night again for him. "I am glad you got out of here safely, and it sounds as if the intruder took a beating from you."

"I guess." I should have figured out who the masked man was and ended the investigation before it even started. "I will make sure to clean up what I can as quickly as possible."

"This isn't your fault, Eve. I have slept in this room so many times I have lost count, and most of these doors stay unlocked anyway, especially when classes begin. They are open for students to come and go as they please. I think this would have happened regardless."

That made me feel a little better, but I still held onto some guilt.

"I think I should report this to your father," Frank told Malcolm.

Malcolm cursed out a string of words in a language I couldn't place. It wasn't English or Italian. He ran his hands through his hair.

"I will do it," Shawn offered. "I am the head of this department. It is my responsibility." The way his lips folded into a grim line said otherwise. "If it comes from anyone else, especially you, it will be worse. I have no problem taking care of this as long as you get Eve back to her room and make sure she gets some rest."

"I can do that," Malcolm agreed quickly. "Thank you, Shawn."

"But what about the mess? I should stay and clean up." I began stacking books, but I felt defeated. I knew this was going to take weeks, not just a few hours.

"The books will still be here in the morning." Shawn stopped me. "I will call both of you and tell you when to come in. Eve, please try and get some sleep. You have been through a lot tonight."

"I am not tired, though." I wasn't lying. I didn't think I could sleep even if I tried right now. My adrenaline was through the roof.

Frustrated, Shawn mouthed to Malcolm for help. Malcolm took me by the forearm and tugged me to him. "Can we please go, Eve? I know you don't want to sleep—you would rather be helpful here. But my father will show up as soon as Shawn places the call, and trust me when I say that you don't want to be here for that." He begged with pleading eyes.

"Fine." Not able to resist him, we left Frank and Shawn standing in the middle of the trashed room.

"Why don't we watch a movie in my room and try to rest?" Malcolm offered.

A movie wouldn't help me sleep, but the company might

help calm my nerves. "I want to change first."

I went to my room to change into a thin tank top and silk sleeping shorts and yanked my comforter off my bed, making it into a cloak. I staggered over to Malcolm's room. The door was open, but he wasn't visible. I made myself comfortable in a cocoon of my blanket on the couch. The door to the bathroom opened, and a hint of what smelled like the ocean wafted into the air. My body reacted to the smell in a way I wasn't used to.

He chuckled at me, all swaddled up. "Comfortable?"

"Very, but can I get a pillow?"

He tossed one off the bed. It flew in the air and hit me square in the face. "You didn't play many sports, did you?"

"Is my hand/eye coordination really that noticeably bad?"

"Considering that every day I have seen you trip, slip, drop, and fumble, I am going to say yes." I flung the pillow back at him, but it missed his face and crashed into a lamp on one of his bookcases. Luckily it didn't break, just bounced off the carpet. "Need I say more?" He picked the lamp back up and strutted over to me, gently folding the pillow behind my head. "What kind of movie do you want to watch?"

"Horror."

He browsed through his collection and slipped a movie into the player. "You know that after most people get attacked, they would want to watch a comedy or something lighthearted."

"Not me. Whenever something bad happens to me, I like to watch a horror movie because it makes me feel stronger. If the main character can make it through two hours of a machete-carrying psychopath, I can make it through whatever it is I am going through."

"You are interesting," he reveled.

"I hope you mean that in a good way." I fluttered my lashes and crossed my eyes, making me look deranged.

His laugh was powerful, sending ripples through my legs. He went over to the light and switched it off. Taking a large step to me, he bent over. His mouth was an inch from mine. Our noses lightly touched.

"It's a very good thing."

I watched his magnificently formed lips move as he talked. It was like silk waving in the wind. My tongue ran the length of my bottom lip. I was anticipating his touch. The glow from the television ignited his face, and his eyes flashed deeply with desire. My willpower was going to cave. I was about to make a move if he didn't, but then he adjusted and touched his lips to my forehead.

"Let me know if you need anything, and try to get some rest."

Chapter 8

A masked man wielding a butcher knife was chasing me down the hallway to my room. I tried to run as fast as I could, but no matter how hard I tried, my legs moved in slow motion. The fear was creeping up the brick walls, almost suffocating me. A sharp pain pierced my shoulder blade. The man had caught up to me and jammed his knife into my back. Falling forward, bracing the fall with my hands, I yelled out. My weight was too much for my back to bear. My hands crumpled, and I rolled onto my side as I saw the knife rise in the air. The blade came plunging into my stomach. I screamed at the top of my lungs, convulsing and shuddering with the large open wound.

"EVE! EVE!" My screaming stopped, and my eyes flew open. Malcolm was shaking me, his face a ghostly white. "Eve, you're having a bad dream. Wake up!"

I escaped from his grasp and hurdled into the air, landing on my feet. I lifted up my shirt to inspect my stomach—nothing. There was nothing there. I wasn't stabbed; it was only a dream, but it felt so real. My heart rate slowed, but Malcolm was vicious like he was about ready to attack someone.

"Perhaps I shouldn't have watched a horror movie before bed, after all." A nervous giggle bubbled up from my throat.

"You think?!" Malcolm rubbed his jaw. "I went out to get you some breakfast, and when I came back, you were screaming at the top of your lungs. I ran in here, thinking someone was attacking you. You nearly gave me a heart attack."

"Sorry." I was still choking on the fear from my dream.

"No need to be sorry." He closed the space between us. "I am happy you aren't being tortured." His fingers danced along the exposed skin of my stomach; I had forgotten to roll my shirt back down. He slowly traced his hands up my sides to the edge of my shirt and pulled on it, covering me up again. "Shawn called. He wants us back in an hour."

I had almost forgotten about the archive. "How did your father handle the news?"

He rubbed his jaw. "Shawn said he was displeased, which is the nicest way to describe his temper. We have to inventory the cost of damage for insurance, but since most of it was donated, I don't think there is much to claim."

"Do you think the intruder wanted our book?" The thought had crossed my mind several times in the night.

"I don't know, Eve. We hadn't told anyone else about it, so if he was after the book, then he knew it was there already. He could've been looking for something entirely different, but that would be too coincidental."

"Have you had a chance to talk to Rose about using the oxidation machine?" The strap of my tank top had slipped off my shoulder. I shimmied it back up with my finger.

He watched me like I was some type of prey. "No." He removed my comforter from the couch and draped it around my back. "But, I will try again today, and I might stop by James and Wes's to see if anyone noticed the damage to the tower wall."

I wanted to go with him, but I had a lot of work to do, and I knew Shawn wouldn't let me leave early until everything was back in place, especially since the students were arriving at the end of the week.

~*~

The condition of the books was devastating. Most of them were primary sources and as old as the university. No repair work could be done to them. All that could be done was to piece them back together as best as possible. It almost brought me to tears to witness such a disregard for history.

The week had come to an end. I spent almost every possible hour, puzzling everything back to normal. I had taken a break from the archive tonight. My mind was so consumed with history that I needed a break before I actually saw the knights of the crusades. Shawn had given me the next day off to preserve my sanity.

Malcolm's phone had been buzzing on his bed for the last half hour, and it was driving me crazy. I was about to smash it into pieces when he came through the door with a pizza box.

"You left your phone, and someone really wants to talk to you. I haven't been able to focus on the manuscript because of it."

"You could have answered it."

"And say what exactly? What if it was your dad or your ex-girlfriend?" I smacked my pencil off my notebook.

"You could have said something like 'This is Malcolm's incredibly attractive assistant,'" he badgered me. "And I don't have ex-girlfriends."

I tossed a pencil at his head, but it landed by his feet. "Your assistant, hilarious." He would only be so lucky if I were his assistant. Then he wouldn't have a pile of ever changing lesson plans surrounding the base of his TV.

He placed the pizza on a small table, and I lunged for it, snagging a few slices.

"See, it was my sister. She probably wants to talk for the hundredth time about moving in this weekend. I will call her back in the morning."

"Wait. Did you say you don't have any ex-girlfriends?" the thought now processing through my mind.

"I did. You already know I'm not good with relationships." He tossed the pencil back. It landed directly on my paper.

I was envious of his aim. "I know, but I thought there would've been a woman mixed in there a few times."

"Doll, there have been, but they don't stay around for a long time." He winked at me.

"Oh." I knew what he meant by that: long enough to share a bed, and that's it. I wasn't one to judge what he did. I didn't have much experience in relationships either, but I hated that I was envious of all those women. I was eventually going to have work past all those feelings if I wanted to continue to be friends with him.

"Rose called. She scheduled us for the machine at ten tomorrow." He sat next to me. I ignited with heat; it was a sensation I was beginning to get used to. "Get anything out of the manuscript yet?"

"Pieces, but I think only a few people are actually able to wield the power of the symbol. I can't tell what it really does, though. Do you really believe this could be real?" Had there actually been something that held the power of the gods out there from the beginning of time? I didn't even know if I believed in this, but I did know that the idea of magic had existed throughout history. From Salem and witches to Merlin, to the Greeks and Arabian folklore magic, there was a common theme, and it would be unwise to totally discredit the idea.

"I wish I had a yes or no answer, but I am sure we have the same view. There is too much literature throughout history to have a blind eye."

I inhaled deeply and slowly began letting out the balmy air in my lungs. This was too much to process right now, and I was tired from the busy week. I put down the plate of food and rested my head against the back of the couch.

"I should get to bed. We have a few long days ahead of us."

"Don't remind me." He took my remaining pizza from the plate and put it on his. "Want me to walk you to your door?"

I smiled at the silly gesture. There were houses larger than the space between our rooms. "I can manage. Plus, this isn't a date."

I stood in front of my bathroom mirror two hours later. The thoughts of magic and gods were keeping me up. I splashed warm water on my face, but that had the opposite effect and woke me up more. I really needed a distraction from my thoughts. Before I knew what I was doing, my legs moved me to Malcolm's room, and my hand knocked on the door. I hoped it wasn't too late, and he was up.

The door slowly opened. He stood lazily with squinting eyes and tousled hair. Even when he was half asleep, he was remarkable. "Everything okay, Eve?" he asked when I didn't say anything.

"I can't sleep. I have visions of dragons and warlocks in my head. I need a distraction."

His shoulders perked up. He scratched at the hair right below his belly button. "You want to use me for my tellie, don't you?"

"You know me so well." I sheepishly grinned at him.

He snarled, "Not well enough." He let me in and went straight back to the bed, hiding under the covers. I locked up and went for the couch. "What are you doing?"

"Going to watch from the couch. Where is the remote and a blanket?"

"You won't get anything until you get into bed with me." He waved the remote at me. It was so small in his large palm.

"But I…I'm fine with the couch."

"I know you are fine with it, Eve. But the bed is more comfortable, and there is plenty of room for both of us."

I stepped away from the couch to the bed and back to the couch again. I was getting irate with myself, also kind of cold. I was an adult, living on my own in a foreign city, and I could choose whether I wanted to share a bed with my friend, who was a man—a very attractive man and one that I had feelings for, but nevertheless a friend.

"I don't bite…well, unless you want me to. I will even sleep all the way on the other side of the bed." He drafted a line with his finger. "I won't cross the invisible line. I promise."

I decided that I could do this. I was capable of sharing a bed with him. He handed me the remote with a smile, and I surfed through the channels until I found something I could fall asleep to. I covered myself with the shared blanket. The ocean scent that was so distinctively his was soaked in the soft sheets and pillowcase. I sunk in, surrounded by warmth.

"You know you can take a breath." He watched me carefully through his sleepy eyes.

I let out an obnoxiously long puff of air. "Better?"

The bed trembled from his laugh. "Yes." He rolled onto his side, his back facing me. "Night, Eve." He was fast to go back to sleep after that, leaving me to inspect the cracks in the ceiling, with the hum of the TV in the background.

An arm crossed over my stomach sometime in the morning. Malcolm murmured incoherent words, but he was sleeping peacefully. His long lashes stretched low on his cheeks. His skin was so smooth, not a blemish or visible pore in sight. The dark Mediterranean tan blended in flawlessly with the color of his hair. He was beautiful and powerful. Maybe he was what the ancient gods created, and the manuscript described, something so powerful it could tear a country apart. Malcolm could do that, at least he could to me, and I knew what that meant.

I scoured over the rest of him. A light scar ran from the top of his shoulder blade all the way down the back of his tricep, stopping right before his elbow. There was so much I still didn't know about him. How did he get that scar? Was it from an accident? Was it from his father? He clearly had contempt for the man. There had to be reasons behind it. Maybe the scar was one of the reasons. The thought that a father could do that to a child made me sick. From the sound of it, Malcolm's parents were not nurturing. He had told me several times that he raised his sisters.

I wanted to scoop him up and take him between my arms, but I was sure it might scare him right out of bed if he woke up to me, spooning him. I bundled up on my side, my back to his front. The movement caused him to stir. He sat up on his forearms and pored over me.

"I didn't mean to cross the invisible barrier between us." His deep groggy voice was going to send me way over that "invisible barrier."

"It's okay. You only crossed it a few minutes ago." I shifted onto my back again.

"How'd you sleep?" The sheets had slipped, exposing his chest. Deep lines curved around his shoulders and down his sides and stomach. I had never seen him work out, yet he was clearly in great shape.

"Do you work out?" I verbalized the question I was mentally pondering by accident. "I mean...." I twirled a piece of my hair. "I slept good. I don't remember falling asleep or waking up in the night. Thanks for letting me use your TV." I whipped the comforter off my legs but immediately tossed it back over me.

"Your room is freezing!"

He moved his legs next to mine, his body heat dissolving the chill. "To answer you, I work out a few days a week, mostly lift weights and run, and occasionally I swim. Do you want to get breakfast before we head over to the museum? If we bring Rose a chocolate croissant, she will be your mate forever."

"Chocolate will do that to any woman, especially chocolate covered in delicious flaky dough. Breakfast sounds good, as long as coffee is involved, but I am not ready right now, and it's too cold to get up."

"Stay here while I get ready."

He got up from the bed and the heat left with him. I bundled the blankets around my legs to gain some of it back. The sound of the shower lulled me back to sleep.

"Are you going to get out of bed or sleep all day?" I woke up to him, practically sitting on top of me.

"Option two, please." My voice cracked from sleeping.

"Option one is the only option."

"No," I mumbled into the pillow.

Before I knew it, I was in midair. He tossed me over his shoulder. My butt was directly in his face; my shorts had travelled to my ribs with the motion. He was getting a full view of my ass.

"Malcolm!" I shrieked, "Let go of me!"

"Mmm, no." He pocketed my keys and cell phone and carried me out the door.

"Put me down, you turkey!"

His hearty laugh sloshed my stomach around. "Did you call me a turkey?"

"Ugh, MAL!" I hoisted forward, but it was pointless. He constricted my movements. My shorts travelled up further with my curvy thighs pressed together. He was definitely getting an eyeful.

"You know that every time you struggle…." His free hand flared out right underneath my ass. "I like what I am seeing."

"Malcolm?" A soft voice came from behind him. I lifted my head, but all I saw was pointed red leather pumps

"Mom?" Malcolm let go of me, and I plummeted to the

floor as he turned around. My feet tumbled to the ground, and I crashed to my knees with a crunch.

"Ouch," I cried out

"Hell, I'm sorry, Eve." He raised me by the elbows and stood me up, checking me over to make sure I wasn't injured. I quickly adjusted my shorts while he was acting as a blockade.

I stepped around him when I was decent to come face to face with a short woman. Her dyed blonde hair was cut sharp at her chin. Stunning teal eyes glowed off her tanned skin, similar to Malcolm's, but hers held less life; they were more callous. Her nails were manicured, and her makeup was painted on to precision. She stood up straight and stiffly, not a hair out of place.

Next to her was a younger girl. She was taller than me and had many of the same features as Malcolm, and the woman I now knew was his mother. Her dark brown hair was to her midriff, her eyes a deep chocolate brown, almost black. Her nails weren't manicured or colored, and she was paler like she spent most of the time indoors. She was beautiful, but in a way that took a moment to see.

"Mom, what are you doing here?" He swayed between his mom and the girl, rattled and vexed.

"Nice to see you too, honey. It's only been a year." She was speaking to him but glaring at me. Her eyes were stone, not even a single blink.

Malcolm shifted closer to me, trying to track his mother's eyeline up onto him. "Sorry, you're right. It's nice to see you." He approached her, giving her a stiff hug like there were daggers between them.

"You too." She broke away first, commanding him to tell her who I was in Italian. Unfortunately for her, I knew how to speak her language.

I answered before he could, wanting her to know her games wouldn't work on me. "I'm Eve Monroe, the new archivist."

Her face moved a fraction, dismayed by my knowledge of her language. "Marie Archer, Malcolm's mother."

I thought it odd that she had kept her married name. It must have been for status. I stuck my hand out for her to shake. She took it limply and then tossed it away. I was going to reserve my judgments and name calling for when I was alone.

The girl standing next to Marie poked Malcolm in the side. "Oh, this is one of my sisters, Daphne." Daphne saluted sweetly to me, and I returned the gesture. "What are you guys doing here? I was going to pick you up this weekend and move you in myself."

"I tried to call you last night, but you didn't answer." Daphne measured me up and smiled. "Mother decided that since she hadn't seen us all year, she would help us with the move, and for some reason, she wanted to come today." Daphne's irritability was noticeable.

"I wanted the girls to settle in without any distractions." It was obvious that she considered me a distraction by the way she said the word and glared. "And I know you will be busy with everyone else moving in this weekend too. Layla is waiting by the car with their things while we came up to get the key to their room. We were thinking we could get some lunch together after that."

I didn't know why, but every word that came out of Marie's mouth felt dishonest.

"You should come with us, Eve. That way, we'll know you better," offered Daphne.

Marie stood coldly beside her. It was disturbing how little she moved, and it was also clear that I was an uninvited guest.

"That's very nice of you to offer, but I have a meeting I am afraid is going to take all day. In fact, I should be getting ready for it now." I couldn't be happier that I had an actual meeting—otherwise, I would have felt obligated to go, and the idea of having lunch with Marie shooting nasty looks throughout the whole meal was not appealing.

"Eve, wait!" Malcolm caught up to me, snaking out his fingers. He grasped my wrist, running his thumb in circles. I gazed beyond him to Daphne and Marie. Marie sneered at his action, but Daphne was smiling. "Sorry about this," he murmured.

"Nothing to apologize about. You didn't know," I whispered back. "Your mom is...is umm, severe." That was the nicest yet most honest word I could come up with.

He pressed into my pulse. "Sorry."

"Stop saying sorry, you turkey."

He smirked. His bland reaction to his mother was so opposite of how he interacted with me. "Tell Rose I couldn't make it and let me know what you find." He pulled out the leather tube, my keys, and my cell phone from his front pocket. "And later, we will talk about how you never told me you knew Italian."

I hurried into my room before any other scoffs were thrown my way. Since I was meeting Rose in a professional capacity, I dressed nicer than my normal jeans and shirts. I put on a long sleeved black dress that bunched on one side of my hips and matched it with dark purple ankle boots. I quickly did my makeup and tossed my sketchbook and jacket into my small backpack. I wasn't comfortable with not having the leather tube secured to me, so I placed the artifact into my bra. The leather was slightly itchy, but I felt it was better than risking having my bag stolen and worrying about losing a priceless artifact.

Malcolm was leaning against a dark green SUV, his legs crossed at the ankles. His mood had depreciated with the arrival of his mother until he saw me approach. "Wow, I don't think I've seen you in a dress yet, and I like what I am seeing." It wasn't only the compliment that made me blush. It was the way the edges of his eyes flared up, and the change of tempo in his voice. "You don't like compliments, do you?'

"Not really used to them." I gathered a piece of hair behind my ear.

"I can't believe that. You're too beautiful to—"

A girl surfaced from the other side of the car out of nowhere. "I don't think I've ever seen you flirt before. It's very entertaining," she lulled in amusement.

Malcolm's fists balled up. "Quiet, Layla. The adults are talking."

"I will not be silenced!" she screeched.

A grin spread over his face. Layla came to his side and wrapped her arm around his back. He looked at her in adoration. Layla was nearly identical to Daphne but was closer to my height, with well-toned limbs. She was built like an athlete. Her skin matched Malcolm's, presumably from spending a lot of time out in the sun. Layla had put some effort into her appearance. Blonde streaked her brown hair, and her face was lightly powdered with makeup.

"You must be Eve." She surveyed me, making her own observations. "Mal has told me about you. It's nice to put a face with your name." She stepped away and back to the trunk of the car, her attention not holding easily.

"She has a lot of energy and a short attention span," I told Malcolm.

"You have no idea how much energy she has, and I have no clue where she gets it. The rest of us are relatively subdued." He found an unruly strand of my hair. His finger twirled it around until it fell back into place.

I giggled at his ignorance. "She gets it from you. You are chock full of energy…well, around me, that is. I better go before it gets too busy, and I miss out on that chocolate croissant for Rose."

"Is the letter in a safe place? You won't lose it?" He tugged on the strand again. If he was trying to fix it, it would never happen.

"It is secured to me safely, I can assure you," I said, smirking at my secret hiding spot.

"What is that supposed to mean?" He let go of my hair, giving up. I stepped around him, leaving him to guess where the letter was.

I was determined to take the underground. I felt confident in my abilities to navigate the system by myself, even though it was the first time I had ridden the trains on my own without Malcolm. I was wrong in the assumption of my navigation skills. I hopped on the wrong train. Once I made it onto the right one, I got off at the wrong spot, almost a half mile away from the museum. Sweat was rolling down my spine, mostly from getting flustered from the tube, but also because the coffee shop where I waited was hotter than a sauna. I stood in line for ten minutes to order coffee, and then another ten to get my coffee and croissant. I made it to the museum late, but Rose still approached me with a welcoming hug despite my tardiness.

She was as pretty as I remembered. "Cute dress," she pointed to me.

"Thanks." I hugged her back when she enveloped me. "Malcolm couldn't make it. His mother came into town unexpectedly."

Her nose crinkled with a grimace. "She is such an awful woman. I always thought she was worse than Andrew, letting her child get abused and doing nothing about it because she loved money more than her son. I think she has spoken two words to me over the past fifteen years because I have made it very clear to her that I feel that way."

Rose had confirmed my earlier suspicions of Malcolm's abuse, but I was going to let him tell me his story, so I didn't try to coax out any further answers. "I am glad it's not just me who thinks she is heinous."

"Trust me, it's not. His parents are a nightmare."

I followed her to her office on the top floor of the building. She had a large window-facing cubicle. Calendars, whiteboards, and chalkboards filled the temporary walls.

"Wow, that's a lot of calendars." I should have told her how nice her office was, or something polite like that.

"I know. It's insane, but I have a lot of volunteers, and each of them has their own board and calendar. It's actually all very organized."

"Whatever works," I said, recognizing the obsessive need to be organized.

"That's what I tell myself on the days when I want to rip it all apart." Rose took a seat behind her desk, "The machine doesn't open up until ten-thirty. I wanted you two to come early so we could chat and get to know each other better."

"That's a good thing because," I reached for the pastry bag in my backpack, "I brought you a chocolate croissant."

She clapped her hands in excitement. "I was running late this morning and didn't get to eat anything. You're amazing." She yanked the pastry out of the bag, took a bite, and reclined back in her chair in complete bliss.

"I can't take all the credit for it. Malcolm did tell me to get it for you." I sipped on my coffee and picked pieces off my croissant as I let her talk about her life.

Rose had grown up with Malcolm, Logan, Wesley, and Owen. She and Owen had started dating when they were sixteen and had gotten married four years ago. Owen worked over by the university, and they lived on the other side of the river.

"It's really nice talking to a woman," I confessed. "I haven't had a conversation in person with one since I have moved here. My day revolves around conversations with men, and they talk a lot about football."

"Trust me, I know it. Logan has a girlfriend that I can't stand, but I think she is gone now. He doesn't date a woman longer than a few months. I can't keep track anymore. Wes married James, and Malcolm has never brought anyone around. I have been the lone woman since I was twelve. Sometimes I forget how to be a proper lady."

"In your defense, a proper lady is overrated." Not that I was ever one myself.

"I wouldn't know anymore," she disclosed, as red lipstick marked her coffee mug. She seemed like a lady to me. "I am nosy, so I'm going to ask you something because I'm dying to know. Also, I like you and would love for you to stick around. But what exactly is going on with you and Mal?"

"Nothing," I answered casually. It was the truth. "That doesn't mean I won't be around, though. We can get together whenever. I would love to have a night with just the two of us."

"I'm going to plan one." She flipped through her calendar. "I can't remember the last time I had a ladies' night. And are you telling me there really is nothing going on? We aren't blind. We can all see how much Mal likes you."

"I really don't think he is as interested as you all think."

"He is, trust me," she bolstered with encouragement. "It will take him time, though. He may be smart and fit, but he has no idea how to express his emotions. I think the bigger question, though, is do you have feelings for him?"

"I do." I didn't even hesitate answering. I had known how I

felt for a while. I honestly would have had to be dead to not have feelings, but I didn't think even death would prevent that. "It hasn't been easy to not have strong feelings for him."

"You should tell him!" Rose suddenly got excited, her hair bouncing with her energy.

"I can't. I don't want to complicate anything." I glanced around the space to see the time and found on the wall across the room that it was nearing ten-thirty. I couldn't have been more thrilled to be done with the conversation. His friends were great, but they were definitely nosey. "I don't want to miss my slot for the machine. I should get to work."

"Okay, but this conversation isn't over."

Taking her coffee with her, she brought me to a room filled with artifacts, excavating equipment, computers, scanners, and the oxidation machine. I wanted to play with everything, but I had to focus.

"I will leave you to it. Lock up when you're done and come back to my office."

She left me to my own devices. I removed the leather tube from my bra and carefully placed it in the chamber, along with a small razor blade and a set of tweezers. Sticking my hands in the gloves that were set up for me to reach into the box, I got to work. Carefully slicing around the seal of the leather tube, I wanted to make as little damage as possible. Once I cut the top, I was able to examine that there was a sheet of parchment paper rolled up in it. I used the tweezers to extract the paper and slowly unrolled it as not to tear it.

Beautiful cursive was written on the paper. It was in Latin, and the black ink hadn't faded, almost as if it were written yesterday. The airtight container it was held in for all these years had done its job and protected it.

C

Dearest friend. I hope this letter finds you. My soul is burdened, and I must confess, however, that I am afraid that I cannot even confide to our Lord. My trespasses run deeper than my veins. There are very few times in my life when I have admitted my wrong doings. At this time, I have made the most unfortunate mistake. My actions could have consequences for the entire country. I'm afraid my arrogance and quest to find the relic might be the undoing of England. The starvation I felt for it was greater than any emotion I had felt prior. There was no greater quest than to find the relic and have it in my possession. After I besieged Francis for it, causing great turmoil and war, it became known to me that the power was too great for me or anyone to possess. The idea of destroying it was as unbearable as the loss of my unborn children. However, I knew that I must for the sake of my country. To my dismay, the relic cannot be damaged. I have tried setting it to fire and melting it down, but it remains whole. I've taken an axe to it, yet it failed to split apart. The witchery placed on it is strong. My only resolve was to hide it, yet it always called to me, as if I could hear it bellow my name. The sins the Lord would bestow upon me for wielding it would be far worse than all my previous actions. I now know what poison is and that this power will be the death of us all. For the sake of our people, I pray its resting place is well hidden.

H.

A sudden swell of nausea fell over me. I had to take my hands out of the gloves to stabilize myself, and I took long whiffs of air in and out through my nose. The letter was signed with an H that was very similar to Henry VIII's signature. If it was from Henry VIII, then I had an overwhelming thought of betrayal. Could it be that everything I knew about that time period was a lie? I had spent all my work and time studying the Tudor time period. I thought I knew everything, and now there was a chance I knew nothing. I couldn't wrap my head around that. What was important right now was that H had had the relic in hand. He had written that it was still out there. It could even be in someone's attic, and they would have no idea.

I took several photos of the letter before I did the next most terrifying thing. I was running out of time to do an acid test to see if the parchment would be ruined with air contact. Sucking in the recycled air of the room, I turned the knob that slowly let air seep into the chamber. The paper rolled up at the corners. My heart stopped, and I prayed that I hadn't ruined this magnificent piece of history.

The door on the chamber flicked open, indicating that it was safe to take out the artifact. There was no visible damage to it from the exposure. I used the glove to roll up the paper in the leather carrying case and put it back in my bra for protection. I cleaned up the small mess I had made and raced back to Rose, although I wasn't sure why I felt rushed. Maybe it was the adrenaline from the new discovery.

Rose was sitting behind her desk with a pen in her hair and another one in her hand, jotting furiously on a packet of papers. Her attention went up when I softly tapped on her wall.

"Did you get what you wanted?"

"I sure did." I smiled widely.

"Are you or Malcolm going to tell me what you have discovered? He is a vault and refused to tell me anything."

"We can't." I was pleased that Malcolm had kept his word to me, even with such a good friend asking. "We want to have everything in order before making an announcement, but it could be big."

"That's very exciting. A new discovery is career-making."

"It is, but we have to make sure we have the facts in place. That's why we are so closed-lipped."

"Makes sense, but I'm still intrigued." She switched from her packet of paper to her keyboard, focused on whatever she was doing. It must've been interesting because her eyes never left the monitor. "I was planning on meeting Owen, James, and Wes after work for drinks. You were invited too, and James said he wouldn't take no for an answer."

"Sounds like fun. I'll be there. Let me know where you are meeting and when you get off work. I think I am going to go do some sightseeing for the rest of the day." As much as I wanted to go back to the office and research, I was forbidden by Shawn to do any work today. I had planned to do some sketching at the National Gallery. "I will leave you to your volunteers."

"Oh, let me walk you out." She didn't rise from her seat.

"That's not necessary." I knew that glaze on her face all too well—I had a similar one when I was busy with work. "I'll see you tonight."

Chapter 9

I was hypnotized within a Degas, trying to get the charcoal lines replicated perfectly with a pencil, but was getting frustrated in my work that it wasn't matching up. The flare of the ballerina skirt wasn't the same without that smoky smudge. My phone had buzzed for the fifth time in my backpack. I gave up on my drawing pursuit for another day and took my phone out. I had missed multiple calls from Rose. It was much later than I'd thought—the hours flew by when I was drawing. I quickly packed away my things and ran out of the building. The pub they had picked was by the university, and one that I had frequented before, so it didn't take much time getting there. I easily spotted the group outside in a circle, all of them being hard to miss because they were so attractive and stood out in the large crowd.

"Where have you been?" James called out, waving eagerly at me.

"I got caught up in my drawing," I said, as I went around giving everyone a hug. "Sorry," I panted from my short sprint. Wes held onto me a little longer. I was starting to notice a trend with him.

"You should draw a portrait of me." James gave me his profile, putting a fist under his chin.

"I don't know if I could capture your beauty."

He laced his hands together, sticking out his bottom lip. It was hard to say no to such a handsome, pathetic face. "Come on, give it a try," he whined.

I rolled my eyes. "Fine." For a split second, I thought about drawing a real portrait of him, but I had chosen to go with something else instead.

James stood still, not moving a muscle on his face, acting like one of the live models from art class, while I took my time pretending to draw him. I tried to act like I was concentrating, but I found it difficult. He really thought I was putting some effort into it.

Out of my peripheral vision, I saw Malcolm approach from my side, flanked by Daphne and Layla. I was about to say hi, but James stopped me.

"Don't get distracted by that delicious piece of man; continue to draw me." He went back to his pose.

"Yes, sir," I saluted him with my pencil.

"What's going on here?" Malcolm canvassed the group.

"James found out that Eve could draw, and he demanded a portrait from her," explained Wes, completely used to James's nonsense.

"Can I see?" Malcolm asked.

I tilted the sketch pad up so only he could look. He threw his head back and laughed harder than I had heard before. I smirked up at him. I'd drawn a stick figure of James drinking a bottle of wine and holding a flower.

"Let me see!" James yanked the pad out of my hand. He glared at the portrait and then at me. A small bubble of a giggle escaped him. He began inspecting all of my sketches once the laughing died. "Wow, Eve. These are actually really amazing—like, museum quality amazing."

Malcolm reached for the pad. James let it go without a complaint, and Malcolm thoroughly studied every drawing. "Eve, these are wonderful. You are...are perfect." He snapped his mouth shut like he'd accidentally let the thought slip from his mind. His cheeks flared with pink.

"You want a drink?" I asked, but it was more like a summons for him to follow me inside so I could talk about what I'd found, and maybe a little to pull him away from his embarrassment.

"Yes, I'll go with you." His hand etched a triangle on my lower back. "Girls, stay here. I will bring you back drinks."

With his hand still on me, we made our way inside the pub.

The picture of the letter was already up on my phone. I had read it a dozen times since I left the museum. Handing it over to him, he took it in his free hand, studying it for several minutes while I ordered our drinks.

"Eve. I don't even know what to say." He couldn't contain his excitement and picked me up, my feet dangling a few inches from the ground.

"I know," I choked out.

He put me back on my feet, but still held onto me, speaking into my ear so I could hear what he had to say over the loud noises. "Do you think that is a letter written by Henry VIII? The events that are described match up with his reign. What if the C is Cromwell or Charles Brandon?" I was thinking Brandon. He was the one person Henry VIII trusted the most, and while Cromwell was just another passing figure in Henry's life, Brandon had been around since boyhood. "We need to look into the places Henry lived or visited. That symbol has got to be there somewhere. This might take us a while, but I am willing to put the effort and time in. There is so much I want to talk about, and I have so many questions. I don't even know where to begin." Malcolm's enthusiasm was infectious, and I couldn't help but get even more giddy than I already was.

"Me too, but let's discuss this in a more private setting, later." We were back to back with a large crowd ordering after-work drinks, and I was afraid someone would overhear us. Even though I knew the majority of the people here wouldn't understand or care what we were talking about, I still wanted to be cautious in public.

He dropped the conversation after that. Grabbing the drinks, I threw my elbows out to escape the growing group at the bar. Malcolm was big enough to plow a path for us all the way back to our friends. He gave the two beers he was carrying to his sisters and then reached around my neck to take a beer from my hand, exchanging the beer to his other hand so he could keep his arm around my shoulder. Layla stared over in my direction, watching us.

"Eve, when do you want to go out? Does next week work?"

asked Rose, looking almost desperate to have some girl time. "I'm free anytime. I need to know the day before so I can go buy a new outfit."

"Why do you need a new outfit?" Malcolm questioned.

"We are going to get away from you men for once and go out, just the two of us, and I need something sexy to wear," Rose explained to him.

"Oh, me too!" I added, excited to go shopping and get dressed up. It had been way too long since I did shopping of any kind, and the impulse for buying new shoes was hitting me like it would an addict.

"Me three." James was quick to invite himself.

"You're kind of missing the point of the no men part, James," Rose sassed with her hand on her hip.

"What do you mean by sexy?" Owen asked. Malcolm echoed him, just now catching Rose's previous comment.

"You know, when a woman is attractive wearing a dress, fixes herself up and wears heels, and possibly gets a free drink or two out of it. I know I don't do it often, but it does happen," Rose answered, explaining it as if he needed step by step instructions.

"But you're married," Malcolm said with abhorrence and then swiveled to me. "And you're...."

I could've sworn he was about to say mine, but it fell short on his lips. That would have been ridiculous, though—my mind must've been playing tricks on me. I did a double take to make sure I wasn't crazy, and I couldn't quite place the somber look that flashed over him. My whole body got this weird pulsing sensation—I could feel it from the tips of my toes to the strands of my hair.

"Eve's what exactly, Mal?" Wes mocked, halting that weird pulsing sensation for me. "A friend, according to you. She is allowed to be sexy. I mean, so is Rose, but it's not like she will do anything." Wes poked her on the shoulder. "But Eve is free to do whatever she wants."

Malcolm stiffened beside me, "You're right; she is a friend, which is why I'm not comfortable with men gawking at her because of an outfit."

"And why do you suppose that is?" Wes nudged him, not stopping his taunting but only amplifying my need to know Malcolm's answers.

"I think I need another drink." Malcolm marched away. This time Layla and Daphne followed him.

"That was mean." James struck Wes on the back of the head. "And I am going shopping with you two. Let's go out on Friday and shop in the middle of the week after work."

Malcolm took much longer to get drinks the second time than the first. When he returned, he removed my finished beer and slipped a filled glass in my hand out of nowhere. But instead of coming back to my side, he made Daphne change spots with him and watched me as I made conversation with his friends.

~*~

The evening summer sky was fading away and careening into darkness. Layla had drank too much and was slumped up against Malcolm with her eyes closed. "I should get her back before I have to carry her," he told us.

We all nodded in agreement that she needed to get to bed. The rest of them didn't seem like they were going to go anywhere, but I wanted to get some rest before the hectic weekend.

"I will help," I offered, propping my shoulder under her and steering her away from everyone. Daphne said bye for us and stalked up to Malcolm's heels. We each took turns herding Layla's stumbling feet in the right direction. "I hope you don't mind that I have commandeered your friends," I said to Malcolm when Daphne was ahead of us, taking a break from the incoherent Layla.

"Not at all. It's fantastic that you get along with them so well." The apartments were in view. I almost sang out in joy because my shoulder was burning from the weight of his sister.

"For the record, I am not interested in doing whatever, with whoever, when I go out with Rose." I wasn't sure why I needed to tell him that when we weren't even talking about it. I chalked it up to my mouth having a mind of its own.

"That's your business, Eve. But if I can be honest, it would bother me if you decided to do...," he cleared his throat, "whatever or whoever."

Chapter 10

Students and parents were scattered everywhere, and boxes and bags were stacked in the hallways, making it almost impossible to move around. I had left the door to my room open, so I could easily hand out keys and answer any concerns, which was a mistake. About every five minutes, a parent would come around with a need, want, or complaint. Eventually, I had them write down the information and assured them I would take care of it. I was trying to get some work finished up for Colorado, but it was becoming increasingly frustrating.

Malcolm swung through my door in the late afternoon. "This is the worst day of the year," he forced out in complete misery. When he was tired, his R's rolled more. It was such a pleasurable sound.

He fell onto my bed and tried closing his eyes, but another panicked mom came in to tell me that her daughter's mattress was very uncomfortable. She all but stormed out when I told her I would get to her complaint by next week. It would have been a full out tantrum if she hadn't stopped and scanned Malcolm, who was still lying down, his arms stretched up with his hands crossed behind his head, looking so casual and comfortable, like he was a permanent staple there. I didn't hate the thought of that either. He winked at her, and she tripped on her feet as she left the room. I scoffed at his arrogance.

He was fully aware of his effect on women and me. "I don't know how you can be so nice to them, especially when they are pretentious like that. I really appreciate you doing the majority of the work today. I've done this three years in a row by myself, and

I've decided this day goes right up there with Satan's birthday as the worst possible day of the year."

I was pretty sure Satan's birthday wasn't an actual thing, but I wasn't about to correct him on what he thought the worst day was. "I have a little trick." I wheeled my chair over a few inches to my fridge and tossed him a clear plastic bottle. He unscrewed the cap and took a swig, nearly choking on the contents.

"Is that vodka?" He coughed into the back of his hand.

"Sure is. Now drink up and let me finish this work," I demanded, needing to get the last few pages of the cataloging I was working on done. Malcolm's presence was a big distraction. He obeyed me without another word.

The interruptions had stopped, and I was able to close my door and dive heavily into my work. After several hours I was ready for a nap and about to unwind under the blankets after a long, infuriating day. When I glanced behind my shoulder at Malcolm, who had been quiet for a while, I was hoping that meant he had calmed down. His torso was covered in my blankets, with muscular limbs on display poking out from the four corners. Under the sheets, I could see his stomach rise and fall at a steady pace. He was fast asleep. The bed looked even more tempting than it had a few seconds ago. There was not much convincing needed on my part that we were going to share a bed again. I quickly slipped on clothes to sleep in, but I saw that he was still wearing his shoes. Gently I untied each lace, slid them off his feet, and removed his socks with two fingers. Even his feet were exquisite.

I adjusted into the bed with only a small amount of room left for me. "Thanks for letting me stay over," he mumbled. His mouth was closer to me than I expected. "I am too tired to walk back."

"It's only fifty steps," I replied, yawning when I turned my head into the pillow.

"But I'm more comfortable here." He inched closer, limiting my space. "With you."

"That's great, but I am not. Can you slide over more?" I strained my back, attempting to move him over, but he didn't budge. His powerful muscles were unyielding.

He tossed his weight to the other side of the bed, leaving me with slightly more space but still not enough. His legs kicked in the air, and before I knew it, his pants were off.

"I really hope you're wearing underwear." I knew that was a half lie the second it came out of my mouth.

"I am still clothed. No nudity on this side of the bed." He moved the blanket closer to his chin and slid his hands behind his head, taking up both pillows. I was forced to place my head on his bicep. They flexed on the back of my head. "Did I ever tell you thank you?"

I racked my brain to figure out what I had done recently that warranted a thank you but was coming up short. "For what?"

"For helping with Layla and being polite to my mother."

"You don't need to thank me for that, Malcolm." There was a long moment of silence. I thought he had fallen asleep again.

His chest elevated like he was keeping something massive and weighty inside. "My father was abusive." He paused, then exhaled slowly. "Not all the time—or I should say every day. On good days he was my best mate. When I was a child, we'd play football or cards. He would tell me how proud he was of me when I received good marks. But then it was like a switch was thrown, and the physical abuse felt like it was unending. Once, he threw me into a stone fireplace. Not just shoved me, but picked me up and hurled me in the air. My arm caught most of the collision. That's how I got the scar. Believe it or not, that wasn't the worst of it. He would say the only way to experience real pain was to feel it physically. I grew up thinking the way I was raised was how everyone was raised, but when my friends didn't go to school with bruises, I knew it was just me. Andrew was—is, a manipulator. He would use everyone and everything to get what and where he wanted, including me and my achievements. It was lucky for him that I was intelligent and athletic, and lucky for me as well. If I was a weaker boy, it would have been a lot worse. I know it.

"The physical abuse stopped when I was a teenager. I suddenly was bigger and stronger than him. I had spent a lot of time training myself physically. At that point, he knew he could no longer take me, but he still had the mental manipulation over me. I kept my distance from him as much as I could, but I also grew up in a privileged household and was used to certain luxuries. I know that it was twisted, and there is possibly still something wrong with me, but it scared the hell out of me to live without certain things, so I stayed near him until my trust fund was handed over to me when I was eighteen. I left for a while for my own sanity, but never too long because of Layla and Daphne. I had raised them basically by myself from birth. My mother ignored all the abuse because she was rewarded with trips, jewelry, and a posh life. She left when the girls were six months old, and I was ten. My father, remarkably, didn't abuse them physically. But he was also never around them, and I would've never let that happen. He left me, and a caretaker when I was at school, to be responsible for them. My father had no real interest in the girls. They each have their strengths, but to this day, he tells them they don't compare to me. It's all mental with them. Luckily, the girls know who raised them, but I worry every day that the damage my parents did to them has had everlasting effects.

"It was not until they were teenagers and could take care of themselves that my mother wanted to be a part of their lives again. I know they both would do anything to get away from them, but like me, they have a certain way of living and are waiting for the day when they can get their money. Andrew and Marie changed it to where they must finish uni first and must follow their commands until then. Which leaves me here, still under my parents, because I love those girls and have to make sure that they can thrive. That is why I am so closed off and rarely let anyone in. How could I possibly throw someone into my disastrous life? That's basically tossing them into a pit full of poisonous snakes and telling them to survive."

I didn't know what to say. I wanted to say thank you for telling me and finally opening up. I wanted to ask what prompted the sudden change in heart. I wanted to cry. I wanted to protect him and seek out his mother and father. But right now, all I wanted to do was cling to him in a way that nobody had done before. I lifted myself up and adjusted on top of him, wrapping my body around him. He stiffened, his arms remaining behind his head, and then he softened and crossed them over my back. I held onto him, not letting go, wanting to give him the stability he needed and badly deserved. We didn't say another word to each other. I felt his heart beat irregularly against me. Soon it evened out, and we stayed like that until we both fell asleep together.

~*~

Thumping on my door woke me up from a peaceful sleep. I was glued to Malcolm's chest. He was still holding me as if I were some type of support for him. I forced myself up with much regret and shuffled sleepily to the door.

"What?" I squawked with disdain.

Daphne was standing in front of me. She cowed back with my unwelcoming response. "Have you seen my brother? I can't find him in his room or his office."

"Sorry," I uttered, a little nicer this time. "Yeah, ummm, he is in here." She peeked around the door and saw him sleeping on my bed. I stepped out into the hallway and closed the door, so we didn't wake him. "He needed to talk and fell asleep."

She wiped her small fingers down her soft jaw, having picked up that habit from him. "I worry about him. He carries a lot of responsibility. I'm happy he can talk to you about it. He doesn't typically talk to anyone, including us." At that moment, she looked older than eighteen. The hardships of her family weighed on her too.

I gave her a sympathetic smile, "I know we don't know each other well, but you can always talk to me too." She didn't say anything, but I didn't expect there to be an immediate response. "Why did you need Malcolm?"

"Oh yeah." She shook her head, remembering why she was there. "My sister is not well, and we need his help. I need him to get her some food, water, and aspirin. A few of us got together last night and went out."

The realization hit me at that moment that Malcolm and I had slept through most of the late afternoon and night, and it was now the next morning. I couldn't remember the last time I had slept that long and hard.

Dark chocolate hues ran across Daphane's patiently waiting eyes, pleading for some type of response from me. "If you can keep watch over her for thirty minutes or so, I will be back with what she needs."

"Thank you." She folded her hands together and bowed.

We both tiptoed back into our rooms. Malcolm was a brick. He didn't move an inch, even when my keys clanked to the ground, and I cursed because I was incapable of being quiet.

I went to the coffee shop across the street. The barista behind the counter knew me by order now. "Large mocha." She already had the cup off the top of the stack, writing it down with a black marker.

"Better make it two." I also ordered coffee for the Archers and enough food to feed all the residents of the apartment building.

I hoped I could juggle all of it back successfully without spilling anything. I had a coffee stacked on top of another one when a chill ran through me, making the hairs on my arm stand up. I spun around, the coffee balanced on its edge. I was able to wiggle it back to its base, but I had to let go of the bag of food. I squatted to pick it back up.

Over the lid of the cup, I saw a man watching me in the distance. I couldn't make out any distinguishing features, only that he was tall and wearing a hat, shielding his identity. His head turned when I walked across the courtyard, keeping him in my peripheral. All the warning sounds went off in my brain. That was not a good man. I picked up my pace and scurried inside to the safety of my building. Sneaking back into my room, I found Malcolm right where I had left him, eyes still taped shut. I got a bottle of aspirin from my bathroom and delivered the food, drinks, and medicine to Daphne's door directly across the hall. She let me in their room with a welcome smile.

The apartment was much larger than mine. It actually had a bedroom and a living room. The living room had a large pink fuzzy rug in the center of it, with silver pillows on a black couch. The design didn't strike me as Daphne's style.

"I am going to take a guess and say Layla decorated?"

"Was it the pink rug that gave it away?" She took the coffee and food from my hands and arranged it in the kitchenette that was exactly like mine. "I don't really care about the design of the room, and sometimes it is easier to let Layla do what she wants."

"Why didn't you get your own loft?" I knew there were several still available in the building.

"Never thought about it. We've always shared a room, even in our big house, where there were many rooms. I think we both feel safer together."

She portioned out the food and aspirin for Layla and went down the hall to the bedroom. I heard Layla wallow from under the door and took it as my queue to leave.

Back in my room, I let Malcolm sleep while I worked on the manuscript, continuing with the world's most impossible translation. I was stuck on one particular page where I was sure half of the words were made up. I wrote down a sentence on my note pad that almost resembled a sketchbook of doodles. When I got bored or was trying to really sink my mind into the manuscript, I found myself absent, mindlessly drawing the symbol all over the paper, almost like a preteen girl drawing hearts of the boy she had a crush on in school. There was something a little off about the penmanship with this particular author, and then I remembered that Da Vinci used to write backwards, and so maybe did this person. I wrote the sentence forward, but it was still in a language I couldn't decipher. Typing it into the search engine, the results came back as Ukrainian, translating into, *made from the bone of the woman*.

"What the hell?" I said out loud to the room, knowing there was no one to answer me.

"Morning." Malcolm yawned, causing me to flinch and force my palm down on my keyboard, freaking out my computer.

"More like afternoon." I gestured to the clock on the nightstand while I pressed down on the power button, hoping a restart would stop whatever was flickering across my screen.

"Whoa. I haven't slept this late in...ever, really."

He stood up from the bed and stretched. His shirt rode up,

showing off those amazing indents, but the best part was the tiny boxers he was wearing. They conformed to every muscle and cord of his athletic legs. My mouth gaped open as he bent over to get his pants and pull them on. He was molded to be absolutely immaculate.

"Are you checking me out?" He sizzled with smugness.

"No!" I closed my mouth, searching around my desk frantically for something, anything. "Just looking for a pen."

"Like the ones in your pen holder?" He pointed to the cup that was loaded with different colored pens and grinned. "Or the one on that piece of paper in front of you?"

"Thanks." Mumbling, I squinted blankly at the blue laptop screen until my eyes burned. "There is food and coffee in the fridge for you."

"Why?" he questioned, reaching into it and pulling out his cup of coffee I had ordered.

"Because I am a nice person and because Daphne came to the door this morning. Layla had too much to drink and needed sustenance."

"Hell!" He lunged for the door.

"It's all right, Malcolm. I took care of it. She is fine now. They both are." It had been hours since the morning too. My guess was that they weren't even in their room anymore.

"What? You took care of it?" He ran his hands through his hair, "Why? Are you sure she is all right?" The questions came off bitterly, and as if he was questioning my ability to take care of a drunk girl.

"Yes, Malcolm," I tried and failed to hold back my annoyance. "I took care of her. And why? Well, because she is your sister, and she needed the help. I am positive she is all right, but by all means, go check for yourself."

He left my room in agitation. I didn't know what that was about. I had thought he would've been happy he didn't have to take care of them for once. He had acted as if he were offended that I helped.

Malcolm never came back to the room after he left. I spent the rest of the day taking care of the list of problems that parents had written for me. I was going to put it off until later in the week but decided to get it over with. I had become very familiar with the maintenance man and apologized every time he had to come back to the complex after fixing a problem, and another one popped up. I was exhausted by the time evening rolled around—the enormous amount of sleep from earlier was already lost on me.

I was about to go to bed when Shawn came to my door in a nice button down as if he was going out for the night. "You up for some dinner?"

"I guess." I hadn't eaten anything besides the pastries I had bought for breakfast, and food was outweighing my option for bed.

He waited as I changed my clothes five times. I was in a mood, and nothing was fitting right. "We can do this some other night if you want," he called through the closet door.

"No. I am good. Give me a few more minutes." I settled for leggings and a sweater that was a size too big to cover my hips that felt like rolling hills today.

"You look great!" He practically yelled when I came back into the room with a scrunched up, unappealing look on my face. "Now can we go?" Shawn already had my bag in his hand, ready to leave. "I have to apologize to you, Eve," he started as we began walking. "It's not lost on me that this is the first time we have gone out together since you moved here, and that is not all right with me. I know it's entirely my fault too. I feel like I talked to you more over the phone thousands of miles away than I do now."

There was something very disjointed about what he was saying. I truly believed the words coming out of his mouth and the sadness behind them, but if there was full truth in the meaning, then he would've made the effort. I couldn't help but feel like there was something he was hiding or holding back from me, and that was the reason he avoided me.

Shawn leaned to my side as if he was going to say something else, but it never came. I wondered what else he was keeping from me until we made it down the street and stopped at an Italian restaurant shoved into a small space between two large office complexes.

It had been an adjustment for me to not wait for a hostess to seat me every time I entered a restaurant. I always stood there for several seconds until I remembered I had to seat myself. I did the same when Shawn opened the door for me, and I stood inside the entrance until he walked past me and sat down at an open table. A waitress zoomed right up to us and immediately began flirting with Shawn while I read over the menu, unfazed by the attention that was normal to him.

"I love your accent," she swooned as she stroked his arm.

I rolled my eyes and made a face at the menu. I selected pasta with some type of red sauce that I didn't care about, as the waitress was almost demanding my order. I knew she would stay longer if I let her, and I wanted to enjoy my limited time with Shawn, even if I couldn't help but feel there was something lacking between us. She got my queue and left the table, but not without touching his upper arm first.

"Be nice, love," he smirked. "She might do something to your food."

"Do you ever get tired of women flirting with you? Don't you ever want to settle down?"

He took my hand that was on top of the table and intertwined our fingers. "I will never get tired of it, and I have thought about it, but you weren't interested."

My eyes widened. "What?" I was completely taken aback by his words. "You…you never said anything to me." Malcolm's comments floated back to me. *He thinks you're the one that got away.* After all these years, how could I have missed this? Was I really that oblivious to other people's feelings, especially since people I hadn't yet met knew before I did? I was at a complete loss.

He waved his hand in the air, brushing it off like it wasn't a big deal, but maybe it was. Maybe this was the thing he was holding back from me."I figured it would be a moot point. You had laser focus, and I was barely a thought to you. Don't worry, I got over you quickly."

"Sorry." I swallowed the knot in my throat. "I thought we were really close friends. I'm glad I am that easily forgettable, though."

"I didn't say it was easy, and we were great friends," he agreed, "but there was always something more for me. Now I know those feelings were more like how I would feel about a sister and less about a girlfriend. It was an odd realization for me because I had never had a close woman friend that I hadn't fooled around with."

I smiled, exhaling so much air I thought I might pass out. I was relieved, knowing I couldn't handle having that kind of talk right now with him, especially when my affections were tied up with another man. "I consider you family too."

"Good. Now that we have that out of the way let's talk about Mal. I know that both of you are interested in each other. You spend every minute together."

I really hoped I wasn't about to get the lecture on dating coworkers. Any more serious talks today was going to make my head explode.

Just as Malcolm's name was brought up, he appeared out of nowhere, like a damn genie coming forward when he was summoned. His sisters flanked either side of him. "What's going on here?" Malcolm zeroed in on our intertwined hands, sneering at them.

"I was about to tell Eve that she should pursue you beyond being just friends." I was going to die of embarrassment. I couldn't believe he had said that out loud. I squashed his hand and twisted his fingers. "Christ, Eve!" He released his fingers.

Malcolm tossed his arms up in the air. "Why does everyone keep pressuring us to be together? It's not going to happen! I don't want to be with her!" He was talking so vehemently that a number of the restaurant patrons put their attention on us to see what the commotion was about. "If I did, I would be with you already," he exploded in the middle of the crowded restaurant. Sweat beaded all over my skin. The walls were caving in on me, and the heat in the building suddenly rose several degrees. "Eve." He snapped his finger at me. "Are you listening?" A group of girls sitting at a table at the other end of the restaurant were snickering and pointing at me. The waitress carrying our drinks stopped and turned right back around, not wanting to get in Malcolm's crossfire.

Tears welled in my eyes. I studied the grains of wood on the table; there was no oxygen coming or going from my body. I needed some space and fresh air. I was also about to cry, and I didn't want to do that in front of Malcolm.

"Sorry, Shawn," A few tears slipped away from me. "I need to go."

I stood up, my utensils clattering to the ground, and I practically sprinted out the door. I heard Shawn call after me, but there was no way I was going back. I would never go back to that restaurant again.

I ran the few blocks to the river, and once I hit the pedestrian walkway, the well of tears sprung out, and I cried over the bridge. My tears dripped into the Thames, mixing in with dirty water like they never existed. I stayed there for a long time. The longer I stayed, the angrier I got at Malcolm, which made me burst into tears even more. It wasn't his actions that were more embarrassing than anything. It was his words that wounded the most, mostly because I knew they were the truth, and I had been putting off that realization for a while. A few passersby would stop and stare, but I ignored them and kept on crying.

"Eve, what are you doing here?" called a voice that I immediately recognized as Owen's.

"Oh, hi, Owen." I sniffled, wiping away my tears. Malcolm and his friends had this uncanny ability to appear at the worst times. "I am out to stretch my legs." That was a bald-faced lie, but I didn't want to talk to Owen about what was going on. I barely knew him.

"Right." He stretched out the word, not buying my lie at all. "You want to come over and talk with Rose? James was planning on coming over too, and I'm tasked with cooking dinner. There will be plenty of food."

Talking to James and Rose sounded tempting, but I knew Owen was only inviting me because he felt sorry for me. "I think I am good, but thank you."

Owen cupped the back of his neck. "You see, the thing is,

Rose would suffocate me in my sleep with a pillow if she found out that I ran into you in this condition and didn't demand that you come over."

I blew out a snotty laugh. "Don't want to be the cause of your death and the reason why Rose would be sent to prison."

"Very good." He smiled genuinely. "Then you are coming with me." With that, it was settled, and I blindly followed him down the walkway. "We don't live too far away."

Once we crossed over the river, he was only two blocks away. The building was older, like most of the ones on this side of Thames, but it had a few more floors over the rest of the nineteenth century structures. We stepped inside to floral wallpaper that was much more modern than the architecture but still dated enough to remind me of my grandparents' house and climbed steep stairs to the fifth floor. The door from the steps opened up to a very large penthouse apartment overlooking the river.

"Whoa. Nice house." This place must have cost a fortune. It was all still Victorian with high arches, very detailed designs in the plaster, and dark running boards with wood floors.

"Thank you. We bought three apartments and renovated them into one. We moved in about six months ago."

The living room was filled with furniture that matched the time period of the house, but a large television was hung on the wall facing a couch that was out of place for the century-themed home. On the other side of the room was a dining table that could fit twenty people easily. Floor-to-ceiling windows lined the wall that led to an outlandishly large patio. I could see the tips of Westminster Abbey and Parliament. To wake up every morning and watch the sunrise over the London skyline would be extraordinary.

The backs of Rose and James's heads were protruding from the tall-backed couch. Owen cleared his throat to get their attention, and they simultaneously turned and popped up.

"Look who I found on my way home," explained Owen to my unexpected arrival.

He made me sound like I was a stray cat he'd found on

the streets. I really hoped my eyes had lost their puffiness and returned to a normal shade of white because I didn't want the interrogation.

"Eve!" both of them chanted. They were filled with so much happiness to see me that it instantly made me feel good about myself.

Before James came in for a hug, he yanked my jaw to the light. "You've been crying?"

I wanted to curse my betraying red and puffy eyes. "It's nothing," I replied, smiling big, trying to cover it up.

"Wine helps everything, including nothing." Rose went into the kitchen and poured me a large glass. Owen was on her heels, divulging something to her in hushed tones.

I sat on one of the many chairs in the room and took a large gulp of the sour liquid. The acid helped to wash away the salty taste from my tears. Rose was smart enough to bring me the whole bottle, and one for James and herself. James had his phone out, taking pictures like a mad man and sending them off to god only knew who. Conversation was so easy with them. We talked about nothing in particular, which was exactly what I needed: some time with friends.

After finishing half of my second bottle, Rose finally asked me the dreaded question I knew would come. "So Eve, are you going to tell us what happened tonight? Owen told me you were crying on the bridge."

I was going to give Owen the evil eye, but he wasn't facing me. He was focused on adding the toppings to our burgers. "No," I abruptly answered. "I don't want to talk about it."

"Come on. We are your friends. You can tell us anything." Rose egged me on with a purple tongue.

"Fine, but I need to be clear. I don't like being in large groups of people, and when I get embarrassed, my anxiety goes through the roof, and the tears sometimes happen."

"I like the disclaimer," Rose joked. "But it is okay to cry if you are upset. It doesn't have to be because of a reason. I mean, I cry all the time. Last night I cried over a commercial about a duckling going to Disneyland. Owen thought he was going to have to send me away to a psychiatric ward. But anyway, continue."

"I cried that my lilac bushes died," added James. "Poor Wesley is used to it now."

Their confessions made me feel better. "I went out to dinner with Shawn, and we ran into Malcolm. Shawn had mentioned to him that we should be together, and then Malcolm went off the rails. Yelling in the restaurant that he didn't want me, and if he did, he would be with me already. It was so out of the blue too, especially after last night when he opened up to me about his past." Rose and James gave each other knowing exchanges. "Am I missing something?" Are you guys going to fill me in on what you two know?"

"What did you do after he told you about his past?" Rose pried before answering me.

"Slept with him." I shrugged.

James spit the sip he was taking back into his glass. "WHAT!"

"No! Not like that! Geez, James. I mean…we held each other until we fell asleep."

"WHAT!" yelled James again. "You actually shared a bed with him?"

"Yeah, that is what falling asleep together means," I said with exaggeration. I pouted into my empty glass, but Rose promptly filled it back up, "It's not a big deal, and it's not like that was the first time."

"Wow." Rose opened her mouth widely, trying not to slur the one word. I thought it was amusing that they were both in wonderment that Malcolm was sharing a bed with me. It's not like I was the first woman to, but then again, they might not know that.

"Yeah, wow," mimicked James. "Is his body amazing?"

"James!" Rose smacked his chest with the back of her hand. "You are getting off track."

I smirked up at him. "Amazing," I mouthed to him. "It's like every muscle was chiseled out of marble, and his ass…." I cupped my hand. "I mean, it's…." I was at a loss for words. I squashed my lips together and breathed out, creating a low hum. All the wine was making me confess way too much.

"I knew it!" James excitedly hollered, making Owen fumble the plates he was carrying to the table.

"But enough about that." Thinking about Malcolm's body almost made him forgivable. "What am I am missing?"

"I don't know for sure," Rose began, "but he confided in you. Got close to you. And you didn't run away screaming like he expected. Instead, you embraced him, and that scared the shit out of him. Now he is driving you away because he thinks his life is too complicated for you. Perhaps he thinks you deserve better."

"If he really thinks that, then he isn't as smart as I thought." I pointed my finger at them, but my finger looked like it had a second one growing out of it. The wine was at full swing now. "I refuse to be okay with being embarrassed and yelled at because of his insecurities. That's what I don't deserve, and that's why I am upset."

"I think all of us," James made a large circle with his hand, "want you two to be together. We all love you and think you would be good for him, but I hate that he did that to you. It makes me want to give him a piece of my mind. But knowing Mal, I guarantee that he is already beating himself up for this. You mean more to him than you know, trust me on that."

I slung my head back against the chair and closed my eyes, expelling my frustration. "I am still mad at him until he gives me a reason not to be."

"We are upset with him too." Rose held up her glass for us to cheers. James and I obliged.

~*~

My mouth was as dry as a desert—I was literally dying of thirst. I rolled off a bed to get a bottle of water but was a little scattered at my unknown surroundings. I was trapped in a large white room with a giant bed in the middle of it. James's copper hair was splayed out on the pillow next to mine. Flashes of last night came back to me. James and I had agreed it would be best to stay the night and thought it would be fun to have a sleepover and share a bed. I was glad we hadn't tried to paint each other's nails like we wanted to. It would've been a colorful murder scene in here with all the white bedding.

I cracked open the bedroom door to slip out. The sun shining in from all the large windows was nearly blinding. Maybe that amazing view wasn't as spectacular as I was originally thinking. I felt around for the kitchen counter to gain my balance.

"Fun night?" I jumped halfway across the living space at the sound of Malcolm's voice.

My heart thudded in my ears from the scare, but I refused to let him get to me in any way. The anger only got worse after last night. Navigating to the kitchen, I took a bottle of water out of the fridge and chugged it in a matter of seconds. Going to the sink, I filled the bottle and repeated the action twice before I was satisfied. The pounding in my head had slowed a bit, but I was in no condition to even be out of bed. I took my phone off the charger and read through my messages. I had missed a message from Shawn, which reminded me—I would have to go to work today. That thought almost made me vomit, but apparently, I had prematurely called myself off work for the day. He told me to have fun and that he was sorry for dinner. I was thrilled that I didn't have to work. All I needed now was a hot shower, clean clothes, and coffee. I had several missed messages from Malcolm but chose wisely to not respond to him, much like now. I had also told Wesley that his husband was some seriously enticing eye candy. A long groan came out of me when I saw all the pictures that James had taken.

"Eve, can we talk?" Malcolm sighed, his eyes watching my every move.

I glowered at him, contemplating the idea, but nothing nice or productive would come out of my mouth.

"She doesn't want to talk to you. It should be obvious." Rose came from a door behind him. "And I am not talking to you either."

If her crazy hair was any indication of how she felt, it was most likely similar to me, tangled and out of control. She took a bottle of aspirin from a cabinet, dividing out enough of the little pills for the three of us. I snatched up a pile and inhaled it.

Malcolm stood up from his chair and came over to me in the

kitchen. His hands clamped down on my shoulder, forcing me to stay in place.

"What are you doing here anyway, Malcolm?" Rose demanded for me.

"Owen let me know she was over here."

"Betrayed by my own husband." Her hands flailed.

Malcolm's hand skated to my neck. His blue eyes were dulled, murky, and strained, anguish crippling the corners. "I am sorry."

"That's not good enough," I roared. "Do you even know what you're sorry for, or are you saying that so I won't be mad at you anymore?"

Malcolm took a step closer to me. My hands clenched the edge of the countertop. He lifted my head up with his hand, his thumb gliding over my bottom lip. His head tilted to the side. The dull in his eyes was gone; they had changed to lustrous jewels. He drifted them from my lips to my eyes and back to my lips again. He moved in closer, leaving a minute amount of space between us. I gasped. Rose gasped.

"What's going on?" Owen called from somewhere in the living room. Malcolm stepped back, letting go of me, causing my desires to be entrapped and torment me.

"Dammit, Owen!" Rose stomped her feet. "You have the worst timing!"

"What did I do?" he howled, his mistake lost on him. "I think I should go. I don't like to be here when Rose has that look on her face."

"Where are you going?" Rose demanded.

"To work. It is Monday after all, and Malcolm has some accounts he needs to close."

"Oh, so you didn't come over here to apologize to me?" The anger I was carrying was more palpable now.

He shifted from one foot to another. He must've known that whatever his answer was, it wasn't going to be right. "I was going to apologize to you, regardless."

"Wrong answer." I marched out of the room.

"Eve, please." He tailed me, right on my back.

"Save it. Whatever you have to say won't make me less angry.

I'm not some kind of toy you can play around with. I do have feelings. I think you need to leave." I didn't have the authority to kick him out of a house that wasn't my own and one that he was always welcome in, but I was hoping Rose would take my side.

"Still mad at you too," Rose called from the kitchen, backing me up like I was hoping.

"Me too!" James sung from the doorway of the guest room, still not fully awake or dressed.

Malcolm didn't budge. He was stubborn in his resolve to make amends. "I don't think you're a toy." His voice cracked as he reached out to me, but I jumped out of the way.

"Then stop treating me like I'm some kind of game." I was going to cry again in front of everyone. It was the last thing I wanted, besides not having this argument with our friends watching.

"Come on, Mal, I think we should leave," Owen spoke up, coming to my rescue again. He strapped his briefcase to his body and dragged Malcolm out the door.

Once the door shut, the tension eased out of the room. "Let's go shopping today since we all took off work," James suggested, lessening my sullen mood.

"I might need to clean up first and wash my face, but I am good with shopping and a lot of food."

~*~

I was squeezed into the tiniest dress I had ever tried on. The corset top was cutting off my air supply. "I don't think this is going to work." I tripped out of the dressing room. "Besides the fact that I can't breathe, my breasts are spilling over."

"Whoa." James's reaction was telling enough that this was not the right dress. "What about you, Rose?"

Rose stepped away from the mirror in a black halter dress that fit her thin curves beautifully. "I think I will get this one too." She already had a pile of dresses in the dressing room, not to mention the bags she had from the five stores we had previously visited. I had only found a pair of black heels. I knew they were uncomfortable, but James had insisted I had to get them.

I went back into the fitting room. One last dress was left for me to try on, and I had made the decision that if this dress didn't work, I was done for the day and would make something work from my closet.

The dark green fabric was snug on my full hips and chest, but I was able to breathe freely, and even though it was long sleeved, it plunged deeply in the center, giving me enough volume. I bent over to make sure it wasn't too short. It passed the test, and no underwear was showing. I had to get James's approval first, even though I was going to buy it no matter what.

James stood up from his seat and gave me and the dress a once over. "If I were straight, I'd be all over you."

"Thanks." My mouth twitched to the side as I squinted at him. "I think."

"If you don't get this dress, I am going to get it and dance around the house in it for Wes." The image of James dancing around in a dress was almost too good to pass up, but I knew I wouldn't find another one.

"I will save Wes the embarrassment and get it."

"I know he would appreciate it. Are we all in agreement that I am going to girls' night with you ladies? Because I need a new outfit too."

"I don't know. We really wanted to spend time with just the two of us," I taunted.

"Yeah, you might put a cramp in our night," Rose added, but Rose and I both knew James was coming with us, invited or not.

"You both know that isn't true. I make everything better." He was so confident in his personality. It was admirable, but he was right. James could turn a boring room around.

I touched my finger to my chin, pretending to think about it. "What do you think, Rose?"

"Well…." She held her words for a long pause. "I think it will be all right if you come."

"Yes!" He pounced up from his chair. "Now, let's go find something fantastic for me to wear."

Chapter 11

It was easy to avoid Malcolm for the rest of the week. I was still torn up, and he hadn't tried to apologize. What was worse was that I missed him. An ache in my chest increased every day I didn't see him at my door or in the office. At the base of our relationship, he was my closest friend. I was saddened. I couldn't even talk to him about my day, but that didn't stop me from keeping my space. I didn't linger in the hallway by the room, and I kept my door shut most of the time. I felt like I deserved an apology, and I wasn't going to be the first one to break.

By the time Friday night rolled around, I was ready to get away from the university. The walls in the archive and my apartment had become more of a trap than a retreat. Cranking on music, I danced around my room as I got ready, preparing myself for a fun night. I slipped on my dress, which felt as good as I remembered. My hair wasn't on its normal riot, so I kept it down and let the red spirals calmly tumble. I ended the look with red lips.

My phone chimed through the music. It was James letting me know they were outside waiting for me. I closed and locked my door right as Malcolm stalked out of the girls' room. I tried to dodge out of his way, but it was impossible. He took up so much space.

He froze at the sight of me. His tired eyes browsed across my face and scoured my body. They lingered a little longer at my chest. "Oh hell," he hissed through gritted teeth.

"Still not what I want to hear."

I stormed past him and headed to the stairs and out the front doors, but Malcolm was following. James and Rose were standing beside their significant others.

"I am confused. Did we change plans?" I was really hoping not; I needed this night.

"No," James answered. His pink button down shirt and dark gray pants that we had spent three hours shopping for were tighter than mine and Rose's dresses combined, but somehow the outfit worked in his favor.

"They are here because they are going out with Mal." Rose was always gorgeous, but tonight she was exquisite. Her red dress, if it could be called a dress, was painted to her body and made short by her long legs. From where I was, I could see that Owen was choking her hand like he was afraid to let her go out in that outfit.

Malcolm stopped by my side, seizing my wrist. "Can we please talk?" he pleaded.

"About what?" I challenged sarcastically.

"Eve, come on." My cold shoulder was even wearing on me. When I didn't interrupt him, he rushed on. "First, you are stunning. I don't know if I am comfortable with you going out dressed like that without me there. You might end up with a stalker by the end of the night."

"Malcolm, this isn't an apology. And honestly, I am at that point where an apology isn't enough."

"Eve, let's go," James yelled impatiently to us. "The people of London need to see how good I look."

Even in all the seriousness with Malcolm, I couldn't help but smile at James. "I should go." I pulled my wrist out of Malcolm's grasp and left him there with slumped, defeated shoulders.

~*~

James had hijacked our plans, and we ended up going to a nice, wallet-busting restaurant. It was a good thing I had recently gotten paid by the museum. The drinks were overpriced, but the company was worth every minute. We were there for more than half the night until James's hips swayed to the music in his chair.

"We need to go dance." He slurred his words.

Rose and I agreed. I would've never gone dancing if I didn't have a few drinks in me. We left the restaurant linked together. James led us to a club on a busy street. The bass was visibly vibrating the windows of the cars parked on the road—a long line curved around the edge of the warehouse. Rose and I headed towards the back.

"What do you think you're doing?" James put his hand to his mouth. "I don't wait in line. When you're this dazzling," he ran his hands along his side, "you go straight through the front door."

He took our hands, and like he said, we went right in without anyone saying a word. Neon lights flashed dimly at the ceiling. It was smoky and smelled like the kind of sweat that was made when bodies were pressed together. James drove us forward to the bar. In all the darkness and crowd, one body stood out. He was hard to miss because not one man in the club could ever compare to him.

"James, what is Malcolm doing here?" I yanked back on the collar of his shirt.

"I'm sorry, Eve. He was messaging me all night and was practically begging, and I couldn't help but tell him where we were going." I cursed at him, but the intense thumping music covered it up. Rose was frowning, not happy with the new development either. "Don't be mad, please. You two are miserable and need to talk. I am only being a good friend and helping you along."

"I don't want to talk." I crossed my arms. "I didn't want to think about him tonight. That's kind of the point of a girl's night."

"Avoid him, then." He tugged me toward the bar. "Come on, I will buy you a drink." I knew avoiding him wasn't going to be an option. Malcolm had come here for me, and he wouldn't let me slip away that easily.

"You will buy both of us multiple drinks for ruining our night," Rose told him as she ordered us a round.

Wes came up from behind James and clung to his waist. "Order me one too," he requested. James obeyed after giving up his cheek for a kiss. The bartender deposited four glasses on the bar. I drank mine in seconds because I knew the arrival of Wes meant Malcolm wasn't too far behind.

"I'm going to dance," I told them. Rose began to follow me but was cut off by Owen, who immediately shrouded her entire outfit. Paranoia read all over his thin, long face. A little saddened that I was now alone, I straightened my back and turned to the dance floor, bound to have a good time.

"Want to dance with me?" Malcolm yelled loudly over the music, emerging from behind me.

Spinning around, I bit the inside of my cheek. He was perfection. A gray long sleeved shirt clung to his body in a way that made me want to run my hands down it. I could practically feel the lust seeping off him—or maybe it was from me.

"No." I forced that one word out, thinking I was the only woman that could say no to him and mean it.

"Eve, how can I apologize when you keep avoiding me?" He dragged me onto the dance floor without waiting for my response.

I stood in front of him with firm fists and a stiff body. He lifted up my arms, folded them around his neck, and broke apart my balled fingers. His hands slowly travelled down my arms once I clutched the back of his neck and seared themselves to my waist. He brought his body to my hips, holding them firmly against me. They swayed to the beat of the music; it was mesmerizing. I didn't want to look like a fool and stand there while he danced. I relaxed and followed his lead, getting lost in how he felt. Every grind and sway thrilled me. My fingers drifted from his neck and ran through his thick hair. I lowered him to me, burying his head in my neck, and his hands covered the length of my spine. I closed my eyes, enjoying his warm breath dancing along my skin.

The song ended, but Malcolm didn't leave me. He kept up with the beat of the new music. After a while, I didn't know how many songs had passed, and I didn't care that I was dripping with sweat from our constant movements and how tightly our bodies were pressed together. I wanted to stay in this moment forever. Flashes of light came from the stage and almost immediately took me out of my trance, slinging thoughts back in my head. I shouldn't be here. His touch was now torturous, and every motion of his body and stroke of his fingers elevated my forbidden feelings.

"I need to go," I whispered, hoping he didn't hear me.

"Please don't go. I need you to stay." To prevent my escape, he kissed the edge of my jaw with a flicker of his tongue. "Damn, I missed you." He tucked me in more, even though I didn't think it was possible to get any closer. "There are some things I need to say to you."

Against my better judgment, I stayed. "I'm listening."

I felt his lips curve up at my ear. "Eve— "

"Sorry to interrupt whatever is happening here," Wes rushed in. I broke apart our bodies, a rush of cooler air hitting my dress. Malcolm set his glare on Wes, causing him to stumble on what he was about to say. "We have a problem with Logan. He got in a fight with some guy and is bleeding in the toilet. We should get him home."

"Shit." His glare transformed into that hard line that didn't give anyone a clue of what he was thinking. He gathered my hands in his, holding them to his chest. "I am sorry, Eve. I need to take care of this."

I couldn't really say no. His friend was in need. I had waited so long to hear what he had to say, I could wait a little longer. I released his hold and gave him the most accepting smile I could muster.

He didn't move, though. I could see by his jerky movements the struggle he was facing to leave or stay. I wanted him to stay, but I knew he wouldn't. Logan's well-being was just as important to him.

"Don't take this as me leaving you. I promise we will pick this back up tomorrow." He stepped around me and disappeared into the crowd with Wes to help Logan, leaving me on the dance floor by myself.

James and Rose came to my side. "We're back to the three of us again." Rose danced, getting into the rhythm of the music.

"Is everything all right with Logan?" I shouted over the music.

"He will be fine. The guys are going to take him home. What was happening with you and Mal?" James twirled me around, joining Rose in her pursuit of making the biggest hole on the dance floor.

"We were dancing," I said, jiggling my hips with them.

"That was more than dancing. I think the whole club got a show from you two." James bent low, shimmying on his way up.

We stayed at the club for another hour. Rose and I were getting tired of swatting men and women away from James. Eventually, the music and sweaty people became too much for all of us, forcing us to head back home in the early morning.

I yanked off my uncomfortable heels, relishing in the moment they hit the cold, flat floor of my room. I stood there in absolute paradise until someone started rapidly banging at my door.

"Eve, I am so sorry to bother you, but I can't find Malcolm," Daphne called through the thick wood.

I swung open the door. "Daphne, is everything all right?"

"No." She was on the verge of tears. "Layla is not well. She drank too much, again, and now she is sick. But she is also uncontrollable and keeps on shaking. I think she is having an anxiety attack too."

I darted out and into the girls' room. It reeked of vomit, and by the sight of it, it was covered in it too. Layla was convulsing in her bed. I went into the bathroom, running a washcloth under cold water. I sprinted back to put it on her forehead while painting small soothing rings with my thumb on the back of her neck and humming an off-pitch, unknown tune. I was well versed in the remedies of an anxiety attack. The rocking and shaking had decreased. I told her to focus on the poster across the room while I went to talk to Daphne, who was sitting on the floor at the bedroom doorway.

"Daphne, why don't you go get some sleep in my room tonight? I will stay up with Layla to make sure she is okay."

Daphne hesitated, then yawned. "Are you sure?"

"Yes. You are on the verge of sleepwalking anyway. You should get some good rest tonight. I promise that if I need you, I will come and get you."

"Thank you so much, Eve." She bounced up, her words following her as she exited quickly. "I really appreciate this."

With Daphne gone, I was left with Layla and her mess. She was still throwing up every few minutes. I forced her to drink some water, reassuring her with every sip that it would make her better. When I thought there was nothing left in her stomach, I searched through their cabinets for any kind of food and came up with some crackers. Breaking them into little pieces, I popped them into her mouth one at a time. She fell asleep, with one still dissolving on her tongue. With her sleeping, I rinsed out her trash can and cleaned up some of the mess. Layla stirred and called for me. I came over with the can, and she threw up the half chewed cracker.

"Water." She reached out for a bottle. I handed it over, and she began to weep again. "You must think I am pathetic."

"I don't think that at all."

"I hate my dad," she slurred, confessing into her pillow.

"I know you do, Layla, and you have every right to. But we all have our demons. Granted, yours is always in your face and is hard to ignore, but you have to learn how to deal with it."

"You don't know what I have been through," she spat back.

"I don't. But I know what your brother has been through, so I can imagine." I closed my eyes, thinking his abuse was far worse. "My father left me when I was six months old, too, like your mom did." I rarely talked about my biological father. The hatred was buried deep, and I never let it boil up.

She lifted her head up as far as she could. "Did he come back?"

"No, but I know he's still alive, and he actually started another family a year after he left my mom. I used to wonder why they were good enough to deserve his love, but that my sister and I weren't. I still get those feelings from time to time, and I have to tell myself that he is the one missing out. I have done all these great things and experienced so much. There wasn't one time that I missed out on my life. But he missed all those moments that made me who I am, and he will never ever get them back. And you know what else? My actions were never based around him. I was the one to decide what to do with my life, and there is something very powerful about that. Layla, you have to find what makes you powerful and thrive off it."

Her slender body quaked under my hand—she was crying again. Her tears poured out for a long time. My hand never stopped soothing her until she wore herself out with tears and slept. I watched her until the sun came up. Thinking that it would be unfair for Daphne to clean up her sister's vomit, I went to work on cleaning the room. The overwhelming smell of disinfectant was the only thing keeping me awake; sleep was wrestling with me hard. My dress was getting itchy, and my hair stuck to my shoulders from sweating all night long. All I wanted to do was strip down, take a shower, and go to bed.

I was putting the last of the vomit covered clothes in a plastic bag when the door flew open. Malcolm charged into the room, Daphne pulling him back by the forearm.

"Shhhh." I hushed him before he could say anything.

He surveyed the room, taking a step over to Layla. He placed his large hand on her forehead.

"She is okay, Malcolm. She had too much to drink and was having a panic attack on top of that. I calmed her down and took good care of her." Trying my best to convince him, I was afraid that he might act the same way he did last time and go another week without talking to me.

"And you cleaned," Daphne squealed silently. "I was having nightmares about all that vomit."

"I put her clothes and towels in the bag. They should go through the washer or be thrown away." Malcolm didn't say a word to me. He was brimming with remorse for Layla. "I need to shower and sleep. Can you do the rest, Daphne?"

"I can." She hugged me but gagged, confirming that I smelled as bad as I thought.

"Anytime, Daphne. I will do it a hundred times over for you two."

Malcolm scowled at me. "Why didn't you come get me?"

"I had it under control, Malcolm. We didn't need you." I tried to sass, but the effort was lost in my sleepiness.

An emotion that I couldn't place strained his face. It was a rarity to see him crack from his usual stoicism, but he could never really hide his devotion for his sisters.

"Eve?" Layla stirred with a quivering voice. "Thank you."

I bent over and kissed her on her damp forehead. "You're welcome."

I left the three of them together, going straight for my shower, jumping in without a care for the water temperature—I needed to wash and scrub away the vomit. My head fell to the side, and my eyes closed. The water was like a lullaby. I heard my name being called, but I thought it was from a dream and dozed back to sleep.

"Eve?" My name was called again.

I stuttered a silent curse in surprise. Positioning the handles to off, seizing the spray of water, I lazily dried myself with the towel, leaving water spots on my back and shoulders, and slipped on a shirt that went to my knees. I should've been more cautious about going into my room with some unknown voice yelling my name—maybe I should've grabbed a weapon of some sorts—but all I had was a hairbrush, and that would last for about two seconds as I attempted to hurl it at my intruder. I thought back to whether I had locked my door or not but couldn't recall. I kind of figured if someone wanted to attack me, they wouldn't question if I was in here or not. But it didn't take long to find out—Malcolm was in the middle of the room.

"Mal, what are you doing here? I almost attacked you with a hairbrush. You can't come into my room whenever you want, especially when I am in the shower."

A one sided grin crawled up his cheek. Without a word, he struck out his long arms and curled them around me, gluing me to him. I was pinned. The water from my hair dripped from my back and splashed on the floor. He flexed, lifting me up, giving me a chance to secure my weight around him. My feet dangled several inches off the ground. His face was even with mine, matching up our lips.

"Eve." The way he thirstily called my name let loose the hunger that had lain dormant in my bones, but a large yawn escaped from my mouth instead. I tried to force it back down, but it was too late. That grin turned to a full smile, "Come on, let's get you to bed."

Instead of going to my bed, he carried me to his room without my protest. I didn't really know what was happening or what he was doing, but he gently placed me on my back. The bed was still warm, the sheets twisted into a small pile against the wall. He unwound them and wafted the comforter in the air. It slowly parachuted over me, and he smoothly moved in. With one agile flip, he had me on my side and gathered into him. He glided his hand under my shirt, flattening it out on my stomach. His touch was sweltering on my wet, chilled skin.

His lips found their way to my ear. "Thank you." He kissed behind it. "And I'm sorry. I am sorry for speaking to you the way I did. I am sorry for making you cry and dragging out your anger longer than I should've. But most of all, I am sorry for lying to you. I want to be with you, Eve. I've wanted it from the moment I met you, and I never knew I could feel that way. You brought something new and entirely foreign out of me. I've never felt the need to change who I was or how I reacted, but with you, I want to be better. I have so many barriers, and all I want to do is break them down and give myself over to you completely. But I don't think I am capable of that right now. I am going to work on that for you. For me too, but I need time. I know it isn't fair to ask you to wait on me. But I'm doing it anyway because I need you. I need you by my side. I need your kindness, your humor, and I need these kinds of moments we have together. I know I can give you everything you deserve and desire, so please say yes and allow me the time I need."

His body constricted when I didn't immediately answer. I already knew I could give him the time. Never in my life would I ever be able to find what we had, and I had to see it all the way through, even if it wasn't fair and, at times, was heartbreaking. "I can give you time."

"Thank you," he exhaled, releasing his anxieties. "I promise it won't take me forever." He moved in even closer to me. The fabric of our clothes was the only space between us. "You can sleep now."

I laughed. "Thanks for the permission." I yawned

dramatically, but that was exactly what I did.

Chapter 12

Wet snow was beginning to build up on the window of the archive. December had crept up so quickly. There were only exams left, and then the students would be packing to go home for the holiday. I had missed Malcolm that morning. After one of the professors quit, he had taken all of his courses, including an early class that required him to be at work an hour before me. I had a rough time getting out of bed with the weather this morning and skipped out on our daily coffee run. He had also told me yesterday that he couldn't meet up tonight to go over the manuscript. I hated his new schedule. I barely saw him during the day, and he rarely went out with the group on our weekly meet-ups. If it weren't for James's hourly texts and calls, I would be lonely. I couldn't complain, though. We had become very close.

A notification sounded on my laptop, letting me know I had new email. I opened it up to find a message from Dante. He was back in town and wanted to meet up for drinks tonight. I replied with a yes and told him to send over an address to me. I was eager to quiz him about the symbol. We hadn't made much headway since the discovery of the letter at the Tower of London.

Malcolm had mentioned a while back that he wanted to join me when I met up with Dante. I thought I should check to see if he was available. I could text him, but I really wanted to see him. I wanted that surge of electricity I got whenever he touched me, even if it wasn't exactly the kind of touching I wanted. He had been very conscientious about not crossing that particular line, but he still got handsy.

The snow was still falling. Going to see him would require me to venture out in the cold, and my skirt was not winter weather attire. I knew Malcolm would warm me up quickly just by being near me.

"You're thinking about my brother, aren't you?" Daphne came in with her bag strapped to her shoulder and two cups of coffee in her hand. The archive was her new study spot after classes. She knew it was empty and that I was there if she got bored and wanted to socialize. Lately, that was a lot. It was like having my own little sister.

"How'd you know?" I hopped down from the window seat.

"You get this look on your face. It's like you are smiling at nothing but thinking really hard."

"Are you saying I don't think hard all the time?"

She giggled a cute sound. Daphne had never talked about being interested in anyone before. I chalked it up to her being studious like myself—or maybe she was like Malcolm and was scared to get anyone involved in her life. "Thinking comes easy to you. Navigating Malcolm is the hard part."

"That is true. But speaking of him, I should go try to catch him before I can't." I thought I might be able to find him between classes at his office.

I ran across the courtyard in my short boots and skirt. My sweater was the only protection I had from the elements. I had only been in the building where his office was twice but had not actually had a chance to see it. All I knew was that it was on the second floor. I slowly walked the hall, reading the nameplates on the frost-covered glass doors. I found Malcolm Archer in the middle of the hall. I knocked on the door, but no one answered. I jiggled the knob to see if it was unlocked, and it was, so I invited myself in.

His office was not as organized as his room. Books tracked the walls and overflowed to the chairs. His desk was mostly clean, except for a few stacks of tests and papers that needed to be graded.

I took the top book off one of the stacks, flipping it over to see what the cover was. I smiled that I had picked up *Emma*, one of my favorite books. I sat on the edge of the desk and began reading while I waited for him to return.

The door creaked open right when I finished Chapter One. Malcolm hadn't noticed me yet; his face was buried in a file. He was dressed in a nice pair of black slacks that curved around his beautifully shaped body. They were secured to his hips with a belt and suspenders. A white collared shirt was neatly tucked in at the waist. The sleeves were rolled up to his elbows. Letting my eyes travel slowly up to his chest, I felt blessed that I was able to gaze upon something so exquisite every day. He smiled brightly when he realized I was waiting for him.

"Hi." He gave me a once over with a gritty voice. "Have you been reading my journal? This is one of my fantasies—you sitting at my desk in a skirt, and your hair in those braids that I love."

"I don't know. You were pretty detailed in your journal about glasses, and I'm clearly not wearing any," I teased, wishing he did have a journal. I would love to know what thoughts ran through his head.

"Minor detail." He prowled forward. I remained still on the desk, waiting for him. He divided my closed legs with his knee, forcing them to open as far as the hem of my skirt would take them. He drifted forward, his hands on either side of my hips. I clutched my fingers around his suspenders.

"Does this mean that the time is off?" I breathed, pulling on his suspenders and moving him closer into me. I wanted him to say yes so bad that I could taste it.

He hung his head, knowing exactly what I meant. "No." He took a step back. "Sorry."

I crossed my legs, gathering myself. "Don't be sorry. I don't want to make things more complicated."

"I agree." He fastened his hand to my knee. I was right about him warming me up. My skin was hot even before he touched it. "Believe me, I will make it worth the wait."

I swallowed. "I know." My response was laced with more disappointment than I'd intended. It had been almost four months since he told me to wait. I knew he needed the time, but the wait felt unending.

Malcolm lifted up my jaw with his finger, his blue eyes peering deep into mine. "Hey, you know it won't take me forever."

"Yes." I smiled to assure myself and him that I believed that. "Anyway, the reason why I am here is that I am meeting Dante for drinks tonight and taking the train to Hampton Court tomorrow." I'd decided about Hampton Court right at that moment since I had the day off, and I needed to get back to work on finding out more about the manuscript. The months had gotten away from both of us. "I thought you might want to join us."

"Damn. I wish I could, but I have a faculty dinner tonight, and I am heading back home tomorrow. The girls want some things from the house. I was going to spend the rest of the weekend there before exams and do some grading in peace. All the student interruptions are distracting. But let's get together when I get back. I feel like the two of us haven't done anything together in weeks."

"That's because we haven't. It's only been work for you. I know the group misses you."

"I don't believe that. James is annoyed with me. He won't return any of my messages."

"That's because Wes is driving him crazy staying at home all day, and you aren't there to entertain him so that James and I can get some privacy. You should take them out for drinks, shirtless. James will forgive you then."

"I will consider it." Laughing, he uncrossed my legs and yanked me forward to my feet. "I have to get to my last class. Let me know how dinner goes with Dante. And are you sure you can make it to Hampton Court fine?"

"Malcolm, I made it to London by myself. I'm pretty sure I can figure out a thirty minute train ride."

"Here. Take this to be safe." He retrieved his small pocket knife from his front pocket.

I flashed him a dumbfounded sneer. "That's so sweet. It's almost like flowers, but more practical."

"That mouth of yours is cute."

He slipped the knife in the pocket of my skirt and then curved his fingers into the waistband. I instinctively enclosed my arms around his neck. This was becoming a familiar position for us.

He lifted me up so that our heights matched. "I will see you in a few days. Don't forget about me."

"Not likely, unless someone more attractive comes along."

"Pffff. That's not possible."

He kissed the end of my nose. I wanted to disagree with him, but it wouldn't be true.

Chapter 13

Dante wanted to meet at a piano bar all the way on the other side of the city. I hadn't had time to change so, with the snow, I took a cab. It was almost an hour before I got there. The place reeked of cigar smoke, and the only light was from blue strands along the brick walls. The soft rhythmic keys of a jazz tune I had never heard was shadowing in the background.

Dante was waiting for me at a single top, with what I knew was a gin and tonic in his hand. His long gray beard reached the top of the table, his hair was twisted back into a low bun, and the tan sports jacket was hanging over the back of his chair. A red bow tie held up the collar of his shirt, and I already knew his pants were too large because they had to fit around his belly.

Dante raised his glass when he saw me. He never stood up for anybody, partly because he didn't want to be vulnerable to the chance of human contact and partly because he didn't think anyone was deserving of standing for.

"Dante," I sang out as I took a seat across from him.

"Eve. I am so happy you are here." I knew he was genuinely happy, even though he always had an icy surface. "How are you taking to London?"

"Great! I can't picture myself anywhere else now." I signaled for the waitress to bring the same that Dante was having.

"So how is the college?" he asked curiously. "Have you had a chance to meet Andrew Archer yet? He is an outstanding person."

I coughed. I wanted to object, but I knew that was Malcolm's business, and not many people knew about his childhood. From what I knew, which wasn't much—all my information came from Daphne—Andrew Archer was considered a highly regarded member of society to the people in his crowd. "Not yet. It has been a busy school year so far."

"I will have to set up an introduction for you. How did you like the Vikings exhibit?" He changed the subject so quickly, it almost caught me off guard, but not surprisingly. Dante liked to be the center of every topic and even more so craved praise. "I have spent years cultivating it."

"It was great work, very detailed." If I had said anything less, he would've stormed out with a top shelf bottle of gin and left me to pay the bill, and destroyed my small reputation on top of that. He wasn't one for criticism of any kind. "How did you know that was Freydis's sword? There is very little documented on her." I had found that out after I scoured over every Viking book or article I could find.

"There is a small symbol on the sword. You'd really have to inspect closely. But after much research, I found that Erik the Red had that symbol etched into several items after his daughter Freydis was born. Most of the armor that was predominantly female had that symbol etched into it too. My team and I came to the conclusion that the sword belonged to Freydis because of that, along with the carbon dating."

I couldn't help but think that information would've been in the books somewhere if that was the case. "Very interesting. Have you seen that symbol anywhere else, or do you think it is exclusive to Erik the Red's ancestry?"

"No, I never saw it before." He shifted in his seat. He was trying not to act uneasy, but with the slight change in his demeanor, I knew he was lying. "Why do you ask?"

I did a mental check and voted on not telling him about any of my findings, especially since he was unwilling to let me in on his. I wasn't willing to expose anything either, and there was something about the callousness of his response that I didn't trust. "It was really great work, Dante. I can't wait to see what you come up with next."

"You should consider helping me with my next project. I

could use you on my team." He rattled the ice in his glass.

"I think Shawn would tie me to a chair and hide me away in a closet before he'd let me go to work for you." Shawn and Dante had had a huge falling out several years ago. I didn't know the details of their disagreement, but I knew they had pitted their people against each other. I was one of the few that stayed neutral.

"He is an ass." He yelled his disdain for Shawn for anyone to hear. "When you decide to leave that prick, you can work for me." He soured at the mention of Shawn.

"I will keep that in mind." I was ready to leave, knowing that Dante was only going to get grumpier. "I should go. I have some work to do before the term ends." I flopped twenty quid on the table, paying for his drink too. "Don't be a stranger. Let's plan another time to get together, and I promise I won't bring up that prick again."

He cheered his glass to me, then brought it to his lips, finishing it off. He flagged his finger at the waitress for another drink and pocketed my money. That was typical Dante, but his eccentricities were amusing to me, and one of the reasons why I liked him so much.

The moment my foot left the bar, a message came through on my phone. It was from Dante. *It was great seeing you, Eve. We will catch up again soon.*

I didn't respond. There was no need to. He would contact me when he was ready.

Since I hadn't had dinner, I picked up a sandwich on my way home, walking the rest of the way after the taxi dropped me off at the sub shop. My stomach turned from hunger, but I was able to make it home before my feeble body couldn't take the pains anymore. I was about to dig into it when a tap came at my door. I knew it was Daphne by how delicate it was.

"Come in, Daphne," I hollered through the door.

She came tumbling in with a bunch of books in hand. "Hey, Eve. Sorry to bother you, but can I study here? Layla has a study group over, and they aren't exactly studying."

"No problem. Sorry about the mess. Just find a place to set up shop." I had books sprawled all over my room. There had been a span of history on my floor and couch for the last week. I was scavenging through every resource for the symbol.

She picked the only clean space in the room, which was my bed. I cut my sandwich in half and gave her the rest.

"Thanks," she murmured

She didn't make a peep for the rest of the night. That was one thing I liked about her; she knew when to be quiet. I had my head in my research and didn't realize the time had ticked by and that it was after midnight. Daphne was curled into a ball, fast asleep on my bed. I went across the hall to check on Layla, but I could hear that there was still a lot of commotion going on in the room. I didn't want to make Daphne sleep in that chaos, and since my bed was now occupied for the night, I needed to find a place for myself. I thought about sleeping on my couch, but the effort it would take to clean up all my books seemed like a lot of work. Malcolm's bed was the most inviting out of all my options. I really hoped his door was unlocked—he tended to forget to lock it in his rush lately. Lucky for me, it was. I called out his name to see if he was in, but there was no answer—he must have still been out with the staff. I let myself in and took the liberty of getting comfortable in his bed.

Chapter 14

The motion of the bed dipping and blankets shifting woke me up. A warm body lay next to mine. “Sorry I am sleeping here,” I grumbled into the pillow, not wanting to open my eyes. “Daphne confiscated my bed.”

“I am not. Well, only sorry that I didn’t get here sooner. If I knew you were going to be here, I would have left that dinner hours ago.”

An incoherent noise came out of me. I was too tired to make real words. Malcolm made sure not to cross that invisible barrier again, but I wanted to be near him. I spun to my back, scooting next to him, and tangled our fingers together, my palm lying flat on his. I waited for a moment for him to resist, but he didn’t. He held onto my hand tightly.

When I woke up, my stomach was cemented to Malcolm’s exposed back, and I was launched over his torso. That invisible barrier went right out the door when I fell asleep. I slowly shifted away, but he resisted and held onto my arm and leg. There was no way to control how my unconscious state reacted to him.

“Where do you think you’re going?” He didn’t sound very tired.

“Back over the line. How long have you been up?”

“It’s too late. You already crossed it. Now you have to stay over here, and I have been up for a while.”

“Why didn’t you wake me up or roll me back over?”

“I like how you feel against me,” he said simply.

A fire exploded low in my belly. I smirked into his shoulder, placing a delicate kiss on it.

"Mmmm. Shouldn't do that in the morning." He rotated onto his other side, facing me but giving us some space. "So how did dinner go with Dante?"

"It was good to catch up, but it was quick. I aggravated him by bringing up Shawn." Malcolm nodded. He was aware of their feud too. I explained to him what Dante had told me about finding Freydis's sword. "But when I asked him if he had seen that symbol in other places, he lied."

"Interesting. I bet he knows more than he is letting on about it, but I wonder if he knows the significance of it."

"I don't know. I think he does. Besides being intelligent, he has been researching different cultures for twice our lifetimes. I didn't want to pump him for information, though, at least not without letting you know first or being there with me."

"I appreciate that. Try to meet up with him again, but do it over the break so that I can go with you."

"Okay. I will try to set something up again." I knew the next thing I was going to say wasn't going to go over well. "There was something else that Dante also mentioned. He thinks I should meet your father, and he can make arrangements for it."

Malcolm stiffened coldly. "I wasn't aware they knew each other. But then again, I try not to know much about Andrew's life. None of that matters, anyway. You will not be meeting him."

"Why not? I do work for him. And then there's you and whatever we are doing together." I gently pressed into his bare chest. "Not to mention how close Daphne and I are. It might be a good idea. Don't you think it will inevitably happen? This way, it will be on a professional level, not like how I met Marie, with me thrown over your shoulder and my shorts in my ass."

He pushed a stray hair behind my ear. His fingers lingered on my neck. "I liked your shorts in your ass. But I don't want you meeting him at all, personally or professionally. I will do everything in my power to keep you as far away from him as possible. There is no more discussion about this, and I know Daphne would agree with me."

"But I don't see how you can stop it." There was no way he could stop Andrew from going into the archive to introduce himself. In fact, I was curious as to why he hadn't done it already.

"I will stop it." His eyes flashed with determination. "I don't want you to be near that kind of cruel person."

I still didn't see how he could make that possible, but he was determined. He started to get up from the bed. "Not so fast. There is one more thing."

He waited for me to say something, but I took my phone from the bookshelf and snapped a picture of us, trying to get as much as I could of his defined abs. His hair was messy, but it added to his sexiness. My hair was a replica of Medusa's; little serpent tendrils sticking up in every direction. I sent the picture over to James with the caption "sleeping together."

Malcolm barked out a laugh. "You know he is going to crop you out of that picture and carry around the photo of my chest until Wes catches him."

"I can't really blame him. I might actually do that myself. It's almost too beautiful not to." I began cropping myself out of it, but he swiped the phone out of my hand.

"Don't you dare take yourself out of there. You're too beautiful." He positioned himself on top of me. His knee was between my legs, prodding into my thigh, as he held himself up by his hands. "I love your hair. I love how it's always crazy, even when it is pulled back. You're so composed, but your hair never is, and it somehow fits you exactly." His finger stroked, where my hair met my neck. He shifted his weight from his hands to his elbows, bowing to his side and bringing me with him. "You have no idea what you do to me, do you?"

"Show me then," I challenged, not wanting to wait for him any longer.

A pleasurable sound escaped him. "In time, doll."

He held me to him until the smell of someone's coffee maker drifted down the hall and under the door. My stomach roared from the scent.

"Coffee," I whispered to myself.

"Did you say coffee to yourself?" he mocked.

"Don't make fun of me. I should get going anyway. I want to spend as much time as I can at Hampton Court."

My phone buzzed from the other side of the bed. James had written back, "Fantastic. Now go lower." Malcolm took the phone from me and took a picture of his feet. "He is going to expect something every day now."

"At least he won't be mad at you anymore."

"I don't know if that is a good or bad thing. By the way, I called my mate, Will, who works at Hampton Court doing restorations. If you request him at the ticket counter, he will give you a pass that will allow you to go everywhere, including the off limit places."

I got very giddy. My legs kicked out, and I flew out of bed. "You have friends in high places. I should keep you around."

"You're already stuck with me, so it's too late for you to change your mind now. But I can drop you off too. Daphne and I are headed that way anyway. You would just have to take the train back home. Wait here while I get dressed," he demanded. "You'll need help waking Daphne up."

~*~

Daphne looked so angelic when she slept. It reminded me of one of those medieval paintings in which a mother cradled a sleeping infant. "This might get deadly. I would stand back." Malcolm gently patted her on the shoulder. "Daphne?" he sung softly. He was so loving to his sister. It was very sweet to watch.

When she didn't budge, he did it again. This time she took the pillow and slammed it in his face. "Go away, Malcolm!" He patiently stood there, waiting for her to settle back down, and repeated himself. "Get out of here!" She covered her head with the comforter.

"You're too nice." I elbowed him out of the way and stole the blanket, exposing her to the cool air of the room. Taking the pillow that had landed at Malcolm's feet, I pelted it back in her face. Springing up onto the bed, I began jumping. It only took a few seconds before Daphne was on her feet.

"I am up. Geez, Eve!" She stormed out of the room, slamming the door behind her.

"You're welcome." I was getting ready to leap off the bed, but Malcolm caught me around the waist midair and tackled me down.

He landed on top of me. "That was the quickest I have ever seen her get out of bed. You're brilliant, doll."

"I do have an older sister. I know how to agitate someone to get what I want." My hands casually went to his back. "Why do you call me 'doll'?" I had grown fond of the nickname that he made for me on the first day we met but never knew the reason behind it.

"Every doll I have seen has silver eyes like yours, not quite blue, green, or brown. That was the first thing that came to mind when I saw them."

"Are you saying they are lifeless like a doll's?" I closed them shut, suddenly self-conscious of them.

I felt his finger brush the end of my lashes. "Not at all, especially when I do this." The whole weight of his body dropped on top of me. He ground his hips down on mine and propelled forward. My eyelids flew open from the unexpected motions. Malcolm was unbearably close to me. "Definitely not lifeless." He thrusted again, forcing me to toss my head back, and a long, pleasurable sound came out of me. "That...," he stammered. "That was the best sound I have ever heard." He directed my head down with his thumb. Our heartbeats met in speed and heaviness. I knew what was going to happen next; he was about to kiss me. I held very still, not wanting to scare him away.

"Let's go!" Daphne came barging into the room. "Stop whatever you two are doing." She covered her eyes with her palm. "I need coffee."

"She sounds like you." He rolled off me, erasing our almost moment.

"I must be rubbing off on her." I got up from my bed, yet again disappointed. I needed the next best thing after Malcolm. Digging around in my wallet for some money, I handed some bills to him. "Can you go get coffee for us while I get ready?"

"Is that all I am to you two?" He let my money flutter to the floor. "The coffee runner?"

Daphne answered "yes" for both of us.

"Fine." He took Daphne with him, leaving the money where

it was.

Chapter 15

Daphne was loaded in the back of his Jaguar, and I was in the front, sitting in the city traffic.

"Thanks for letting me sleep in your bed last night, Eve. Sometimes it doesn't seem like Layla and I are even related. We have nothing in common except how we look. Even then, that's a stretch." She sipped her coffee, waking her and her mood up.

"I know that's not true," Malcolm interrupted. "You two are very close."

"We are in some ways. But if we weren't related, I don't think we would be friends."

"My sister and I are complete opposites too, but there are enough similarities to make us really close. I know you and Layla are like that. Like how you and your brother. You have the best parts of your brother. You're intelligent, caring, respectful, loyal, a hard worker, and loving. There is a lot that makes you completely different, but that doesn't matter. You are still friends."

"Right," Daphne squeaked. "I like being like Malcolm, though."

Malcolm chuckled. "I don't think that's a good thing."

"It is a great thing," I declared with absolute truth.

"Is that so?" He smacked a hand on my thigh.

"Yes," I replied, ignoring the placement of his hand. It crept slowly inward between my legs. I lifted his fingers up one at a time. His thumb was left kneading gently on the inseam of my jeans. I removed his thumb but kept it in my fingers, outlining the nail. He snarled his top lip at me. I tried to hide my smile, but couldn't.

"Stop flirting, you two, and pay attention to the road with both hands on the wheel," Daphne fussed from the back.

Malcolm let me keep his hand but revved the engine and hit the gas, causing Daphne to yelp. The car only made it about a hundred yards before it stopped again.

We made it to Hampton Court in the same amount of time the train would have taken, but the company was better. Malcolm parked his car and left Daphne in it. He escorted me to the ticket counter and asked for Will.

Will showed up a few minutes later, and I was almost positive he was the ghost of Hampton Court. He was my height, with translucent white skin, white hair, and white brows. The only color he had was the dark halos under his eyes. He was even wearing white coveralls. If I saw him wandering the hallways alone, I would be scared out of my mind.

"Mal, it's good to see you, mate." He grasped his shoulder firmly.

"You too, Will. Thanks for doing this for me. I know Eve will really enjoy seeing everything."

I made my introduction, and he gave me a lanyard with a badge that read All Access.

Will leaned into us. "If anyone asks, tell them you're helping me with the historical accuracy of the restoration."

"I am sure she could help you with that. This is her genre of history," Malcolm boasted proudly.

"That's good to know. I might use you at some point in time, but I have to go back to work now. Have fun, and don't break anything."

He left before we could say thanks. "Interesting guy."

"He is, but he is a good one. Let me know if you find anything." He dragged me in for a hug, "Thanks for saying those things to my sister. I am glad she has you as a friend."

"All true, but she needs to hear it more. I don't think anyone actually tells her that."

"I'll work on it." He kissed my cheek. "I will miss you, Eve." He kissed it again, lingering a little longer this time.

"You too, Mal."

I didn't want to leave him, so I held on longer. He didn't seem to mind us standing in the middle of the driveway, letting people watch us embrace to no end. Finally, I let go, and so did he. With a look of yearning from both of us, I trekked the long walkway that led to the main entrance.

Gargoyles stood on the sides of the red brick entrance. I examined every brick of the large main courtyard, taking my time and soaking in the fact that I was standing in the same place where so many people's footprints had stepped from my most beloved time period of history. I knew I was there to find anything that had the symbol on it, but I was so caught up in my own desire that I almost completely forgot my purpose.

I made my way to Cromwell's old apartment, which was converted into a toilet by Henry VIII. There were signs and videos relaying the stories of the Tudor time period, but I knew every fact and detail by heart. I moved onto William III's apartments. The large tapestries and detailed paintings, furniture, and fabrics could keep me there for days. From the windows, the gardens appeared to go for on for miles, making me eager to discover what was outside.

A large portion of the day I spent outside in the oddly sunny weather, after having snow the day before. Making my way toward Henry VIII's apartments, I stopped in the middle of the Great Hall, seeking out a very specific design in the woodwork. I spotted it from across the room. There it was: an A and an H, the only remaining marker that Anne Boleyn and Henry were together. Henry had commissioned all the lettering to be destroyed when their situation took a deadly turn. In their haste, one was overlooked. I had studied history every day since I began my career, but there was something about this moment I was in, and the relevance of what those letters meant, that made me emotional. I had the urge to wipe away the wetness in my eyes, but for some reason, I wanted to keep them there as a momentary reminder that I could have this kind of sentiment over a point in time.

Walking through the room and down the corridor, I came to a halt at the chapel. It was blocked off for renovation, but then I remembered I had all access. I showed my badge to the guard standing in front of the scaffolding and explained to her why I was there. She let me in without further questioning.

Some of the dark wood floor was lifted up from the ground, and a few pews had been dislodged for staining. I stepped over the missing floorboards, careful not to disturb any of the work. Every detail was beautiful, from the ceiling to the floor. I went over to the altar. A wood panel was missing from underneath. If I hadn't been canvassing every detail, I wouldn't have spotted that there was another wooden plank under the missing floorboard. I don't know what it was that drove me to stick my hand into the small opening that led under the altar—maybe instinct. I couldn't wedge my fingernails under the old board to lift it up.

I instantly thought of the knife that Malcolm had let me borrow to keep myself protected from I still didn't know what. I reached into my backpack and drew out the knife. Casting the small blade up, I plunged it into the board, causing it to splinter, and it broke free. I reached around for something but came up short. Lying on my stomach, I let the hole devour my entire arm. It was halfway under the altar when my fingers made contact with what felt like a box. I inched forward, palming the box, and carefully pulled it out.

I had to hold in a squeak because my hand and the box were covered in cobwebs. I shook them off like my hand was on fire and flicked the ones that were on the small wood box aside. I used the knife to pry the lid open. The lid tumbled to the ground and bounced off the floor, echoing in the empty room. I held my breath to see if anyone would enter because of the commotion, but nobody showed.

I gasped when I saw the contents of the small box. My finger fumbled over an amulet that was ivory colored, appearing to be carved out of some kind of bone. I was hoping it wasn't the bone of a woman like the manuscript had said. A gold chain, not as ancient as the amulet, was wrapped around it.

The amulet was in the shape of the symbol we had been searching for. The bone curved into soft curls and edged out where the symbol became sharper. My finger tested the firmness and structure, but when they touched it, a vibration shuddered my core. It wasn't uncomfortable, almost like a jolt of electricity, as if I had run my feet over carpet. I was drawn to it; there was a magnifying force. I reached out again—this time, I held onto it for a longer amount of time. The bone was solid, not brittle at all, considering its age. The vibration lessened under my fingers, but there was still a dull sensation. Was this it? Was this the relic? There was only one way to find out.

Without a second thought, I looped the gold chain around my neck and placed the amulet under my shirt so it would make contact with my bare skin. The vibration stopped once it was against my chest. I waited for something to happen, but there was nothing. There was no difference. I was the exact same. I closed my eyes and concentrated on being more powerful. Nothing. I reached out my hand to move an object with my mind—still nothing. I sighed. It was possible that the magic was depleted or made up, or that this wasn't the relic at all, just a replica. I pieced all the boards back together, burying the small wooden box in my bag, and kept the amulet around my neck. I was done for the day, partly because I didn't want to be caught stealing from historical property again. Also, I wanted to go home and read through the manuscript.

Chapter 16

Once I was on the train and seated, I took out my sketch pad to pass the time. I let my mind wander, and my pen sketched out the beginnings of the symbol, marked on the back shoulder of a woman. I graphed out a densely wooded area that was surrounded by an ancient building. The woman and two men were huddled, centered around fallen trees. My hand sketched bodies scattered on the ground. The corpses were mutilated; arrows and blades were burrowed into them. Bile rose in the back of my throat. I had to force my hand to stop sketching. I didn't know why I had been drawing that. The scene was out of something I had never seen before.

I pinched my eyes closed, erasing away my new morbid art, and turned to a blank page. I wanted to attempt something happier. I drew the tower bridge from the viewpoint of the Tower of London. Wes and James came to mind. I sketched them hand in hand, positioned on top of the gateway. I finished by the time my train made it to the station back in London.

It was dark and cold outside, but the train stop wasn't far from the lofts. I hustled back to my room as quickly as possible to get out of the elements. I catapulted myself into my room, switching on the lights at the same time. A body lay motionless on my bed, causing me to leap two feet in the air and giving my heart a cardiac workout.

A mop of wavy red hair was atop my pillow, a thick build sprawled out, covering the entire space. James was faced down on my bed.

"James," I called softly. No answer. I walked over to the bed.

"James?" I poked him. He was cold to the touch. Panic set in. "James?" I cried out, shaking him. He still didn't move. I checked his neck for a heartbeat but didn't find one. I ran to my bag to get my phone and call an ambulance, but then he whined out a noise. I ran back to him. "James, are you alive?"

He curled his side and formed up into a ball. "Barely?" He questioned the word.

How was that even a question? It was a yes or no answer. "What are you doing here?"

"Layla and I went over to Logan's tonight, and I walked her back after a few drinks. I was going to go home, but I didn't make it very far." He spooned into the pillow.

"I thought you were dead. I couldn't find your pulse, and you are freezing."

"Really? Because I am burning up and might need a trash can."

I rolled my eyes and got him my trash can and water. I tore my comforter away from him, not wanting him to get sick on it, and replaced it with a thin sheet. My bed apparently had an open invitation for everyone but me to sleep in. I swept all the books off my couch and stretched out, my feet hanging off the end. I dialed Wes to let him know that James was staying with me tonight.

He picked up before the ring even went through. "Eve, have you heard from James? I can't reach him at all. He was supposed to be home two hours ago." The alarm for his husband was apparent with each crack of his words.

I felt awful that he was so worried. "I found him in my room. He couldn't make it home and thought my bed was a good place to stop." It was a good thing I had given him a key a month back after I locked myself out twice and had to stay the night at their house.

"Do you want me to come over and help?" he offered.

"Not necessary. He is in good hands," I answered, putting his mind at rest. "Enjoy a night alone. I will return him tomorrow in one, maybe two, pieces.

"Thanks, Eve." The unease leaking out of his tone became

more stable. "I'm going to watch football all night." His laugh was almost evil.

I got off the phone with him and called Malcolm. It went to voicemail, instructing me to leave a message. I missed the sound of the beep because I got lost in the way he said his last name. There truly was not a sweeter sound than his thick deep voice. I stuttered on my introduction but got around to saying my name eventually. "I found something at Hampton Court. Show you when you get back. You have also been replaced as my bed buddy." I hung up and sent him a picture of James in my bed.

Chapter 17

I got a minimal amount of sleep. I was worried that James would stop breathing, so I got up every hour to make sure he was still alive. I had left the amulet around my neck. There was a small voice in the back of my mind that told me I should always wear it and keep it close to me, but I wasn't used to sleeping with jewelry. I would choke myself every time I tossed around from side to side.

Orange hair sticking up on all ends, with no rhyme or reason to their placement, approached my side. "Eve, are you up?"

"My eyes are open, aren't they?"

"Some people sleep with their eyes open. I didn't want to assume."

I scrubbed my open eyes with the palms of my hands. "What do you want, James?"

"Coffee, and breakfast." He stood up from his kneeling position at the couch. "I am going to take a shower, too. Hope that's okay."

"Do whatever you want. Just let me sleep for twenty more minutes." I covered the pillow over my ears to block out all the outside noises, but the repeated ringing of my phone was unavoidable. I gave into it and picked it up. "What?" I snarled sharply into the speaker, feeling sorry for whoever was on the other end, about to get my wrath.

"Whoa. Sorry," apologized the sultry voice of Malcolm.

"Sorry, Mal." I perked up a bit. "I didn't get much sleep last night. I thought James might die."

He chuckled. "Yeah. The first time I was with him when he

fell asleep while drunk, I thought he had died."

"That's what happened to me. It made me paranoid all night." I had thought about calling Wes so many times last night to pick him up, but I wanted to give him a break, which I was sure was much needed. I needed to get back on track before I went on a tangent of my sleeping pattern from last night. "But that's not why I called you. I found an amulet in the shape of the symbol underneath the altar in the chapel. I don't think it is the relic, though. I don't feel any different when I wear it."

"Eve!" he scolded, utter silence filling the other end. I thought maybe he had hung up on me, or there was a problem with the connection. "You stole an artifact from Hampton Court?" he said, finally breaking the unnerving quiet. "That could or could not be the relic, and now you are wearing it? What if someone saw you steal it? What if someone sees you wearing it? You promised you would be cautious, and then you put it on! What if it was the relic, and the text was right? It could have done everlasting damage to you."

I hadn't thought about any of those points, and now I felt silly that I hadn't. For some reason, I was drawn to it. It was as if I knew exactly where to find it, and it called to me, the dangers be damned. Now I didn't want to take it off like it belonged to me.

"I don't know, Malcolm, but I will make sure it is hidden when I wear it. And I think it's best if one of us keeps it on us. And might I remind you that you stole from the Tower too." I was stretching for a reason to make my crimes less credible than he was making them out to be.

He blew a shallow breath into the phone. "I can't argue with you, and somehow we are going to have to make these findings legal if we get published. Please be safe, Eve. I don't want to think about anything bad happening to you, especially when I am not there."

"I am very capable of taking care of myself, Malcolm." I stuck my finger in the air, waving it around like he was in front of me. When I realized he couldn't actually see me, I relaxed my finger.

"Trust me, I know you are, but I need you to promise me."

I appreciated his worry, but I knew I would be fine. It was

probably best to appease him anyway because this conversation would be argued into circles. I grumbled into the speaker, "I promise."

"Thank you." He didn't sound happy, though. "Can you also check in on Layla for me every now and then? She isn't used to being by herself."

"I will check in on her. She and James went to Logan's last night and made it back here. That's when I found James in my bed. Wes was about to have Scotland Yard send out a manhunt for him."

"Poor Wes—he has his hands full. James needs to be kept busy, and with winter here, there isn't much to do on the grounds."

"I told Wes I would keep him entertained for the day. The rest of the week is a different story."

"Speaking of work…," he said slowly.

"I didn't say the word work at all." Almost questioning myself, I wondered if I was losing my mind from lack of sleep.

"I need a favor, and I'm jumping right into it. Shawn was supposed to cover my evening class tomorrow, but he had to cancel. Can you take over? It is the last class, and I usually do a question and answer to help for the testing."

Silent. I was silent. I did not like speaking to groups of people, even in a teaching style. I had tried it once with Shawn's class back in Colorado but failed miserably and ended up showing a movie instead. After that, I vowed I would never do it again. Thinking about it made me nervous and flushed.

"Are you still there, Eve?" I could hang up on him and ignore his calls until he got back into the city. "I know you don't like public speaking, and I wouldn't ask, but you are my last and only option."

I don't know what unnatural force made my mouth open and utter my next words, but I couldn't say no to Malcolm when he needed a favor. He rarely solicited anyone for help. "I guess."

"Really? Are you sure?"

"No, I am not sure." Closing my eyes, I tried preparing myself for the future dread. "But yes, I will do it. Don't get mad at me when you get complaints that I didn't speak or got sick."

"You will do great." He sounded so reassuring and confident in me. "And I owe you."

"Okay." My thoughts were far off in the distance, thinking of all the ways I could embarrass myself. I heard Malcolm say what room number the class was in but tuned all other instructions out.

"Did you get all that?"

"Sure."

"Thank you, and let me know if you have any problems."

A sarcastic chortle slipped out. "Okay." I only had a two word vocabulary all of a sudden.

"One last thing Eve. You are my one and only bed buddy. I really hope I'm yours."

"Sure." I wasn't paying attention to what he was saying anymore. I said "bye" and abruptly hung up on him.

It took me until I was in the shower to realize what he had said to me about the bed buddy and that I also should have been paying attention to the information he was giving me about the class. I should call him back and tell him that my bed only belonged to him, and then casually bring up the class. But I was too ashamed to do that and somehow brainwashed myself into thinking I could figure it out on my own.

~*~

James and I went out for breakfast, and then I dragged him around to all the antique stores to find a picture frame for the drawing I had done for them on the train yesterday. I didn't tell him what the frame was for or that it was for him because I wanted it to be a surprise, but maybe I should have. He was throwing a fit that he was bored, and when I picked out a frame that matched their home, he would immediately veto it with a face of discontent. Finally, we found one we agreed on, and I purchased it quickly before he changed his mind. We made it back to their house before dark. I snuck off to the bathroom to place the sketch in the frame.

Wes entered the front door as I exited the bathroom. "Thank you for keeping him entertained all day." He gave me his usual long hug. "I really needed it."

"It was my pleasure, but you really should get a daily reward. He has as much energy as a puppy."

"I really should, but most days, I love that energy; it gets me through my days." The way he still cherished James after so many years of being together was admirable.

I refrained from making a swooning sound, even though it was really hard not to. "That is really sweet, Wes, but today you get a reward." I handed over the frame to him. I got nervous for a moment that he wouldn't like it. It was that inner criticism that every artist has.

"Eve, this is wonderful." He gathered me into him. "I can't believe you drew this. The detail is beyond anything I have seen—it's surreal."

I rested my chin on his shoulder. "It was nothing, and I did it on the train yesterday. I wanted to sketch something happy, and that came out. I thought you might like it."

When he stepped back, his eyes were watery. It was odd to see him cry—he was usually so sturdy—but this was the second time he had gotten emotional around me.

"What's going on here? Why is Wesley crying?" James roped his hand around Wes's back in consternation, consoling his love.

"Eve wanted to draw something that made her happy." Wes handed the frame over to him. "She made a picture of us."

James fastened onto my shoulder and held onto me too. Both very emotional men were glued to each side.

All the affection was making me jittery. I needed to get out before I was sucked into a crying triangle. "I'm glad you guys like it, but I should really get going. I have a busy day tomorrow." I was not entirely sure what I was busy with, but I left before they forced me to stay for dinner.

I didn't make it to the end of the Tower grounds before I got a text message from James. Malcolm and Wes were also a part of the message. *Mal, if you don't want Eve, we are going to keep her for ourselves.*

Malcolm immediately responded. *Who said I didn't want her*? I smiled into my phone.

Wes chimed in. *Too late, you lost your chance. We have already made a small bed for her in the closet.*

I wrote in, *I am not a house elf*! I roamed the dark streets, not paying attention to where I was going, too focused on the conversation.

Malcolm replied, *What is going on? Why are you keeping my girl in your closet*?

The words "my girl" had my heart thumping and distracted me. I clipped shoulders with a man walking toward me. The bump was swift, but forceful enough to take me back a few steps.

"Sorry," I called out, but it fell in the air. The man was already gone, moving briskly down the walkway.

In my collision, I missed a chunk of conversation. James had told Malcolm what I had said about the drawing and sent him a picture of it. Then there was a lengthy explanation on how they got teary eyed and were enjoying much needed quality time together.

Malcolm sent me a private text. *Bringing couples together one drawing at a time.*

I was about to respond when I felt a presence behind me. I glanced over my shoulder. A black shadow was several feet from me. I stopped, tripping over my toes, and the shadow stopped. When I moved forward, it moved forward. I caught a glimpse of the face of the shadow that was mimicking my movement from the street lamp—it was the same man I had run into a few moments ago. Was he that upset that I had bumped into him? A fleeting thought of turning around and talking to him came and went. I knew it wasn't safe to speak with him when he was clearly following me. I briefly thought I should veer off route, but the walkway was the busiest street at this time of night. I picked up my pace, but it didn't matter. I could still sense the presence of the person. The amulet around my neck hummed softly against my skin. I almost stopped dead in my tracks when it began to vibrate, but I figured that continuing to move was the best thing. The vibration of the amulet increased to almost a burn when the pathway ended, and I was forced to veer off the busy street.

None of the businesses were open for me to hide in the few

short blocks I had left to the college, and it was rare to see a taxi driving the road I was on. I figured that if I was going to get kidnapped, it would be best if someone knew about it. The discomfort of the amulet was nearly a distraction from me dialing Malcolm's number, but I fought through it.

He picked up on the first ring. "Miss me that much?" he joked.

"Mal, I think I am being followed," I hissed into the phone.

"What?!" His voice elevated with concern. "Are you sure?"

I turned my head to the side slightly to see out of my peripheral. The man was still there, keeping his distance. "Yes."

"Eve, can you get somewhere safe?"

"No, but I am a few blocks from home." I couldn't tell if my heart was throbbing or if the amulet was battering out of control.

"Okay, stay calm and hurry back home." The panic rising in his voice didn't calm me down at all.

"The amulet is vibrating," I hurriedly said as softly as I could. "I think it is warning me of danger." I didn't have any proof of that, but it was like it was talking to me.

"Shit. Please tell me you are almost there."

I nodded, which was ludicrous because he couldn't see me. "Yes."

The amulet burned my sternum. It was on fire, and the pain was almost unbearable. The man was much closer now. If he picked up his pace, he could be on me in a second.

"He's getting closer. I am going to run."

I didn't wait for a response. I pumped my arms with the phone clutched in my fist and sprinted the last block. My feet stomped up the cobblestone and skidded into the lobby.

A security guard was sitting on a couch. He came to attention when he saw me fly inside.

"I think I was being followed," I quickly told him, my lungs trying to obtain as much of the stale, artificial air as possible.

He went outside, and I didn't waste any time racing to my room. The hallway was flocked full of people, all buzzing around. Almost all the classes were over with, and the partying had begun before exams commenced next week.

Layla was talking to a boy, but she left her conversation when she saw me. "Eve, is everything all right?"

I was about to answer her, but flames ravaged through me. The center of the spark was at my chest. I crumbled to my knees. The amulet felt like it was shredding my skin. Every single cell was being sliced open. My phone had slipped to the ground and shattered into tiny pieces, but I didn't care. I curled up in the fetal position, unable to get a sound out, not even a cry.

"Eve!" I heard Layla scream through the fog. A cold hand lay on my shoulder, giving me some temporary relief from the extreme heat. "Should I call an ambulance?"

"No," I withered out. "Help me to my room." I started to crawl, but my limbs gave way. It felt like I was getting stabbed with large thick needles.

A hand scooped under me. I was able to haul myself to my feet, but my weight was shifted to Layla and a boy as they dragged me to my room and laid me on my bed. The softness of the mattress did nothing to comfort me.

Layla paced around my room while on the phone, agreeing with whatever the person on the other end was saying. Fatigue washed over me; my eyelids sank to my cheeks. The lights in my room switched off, and I heard the door click shut. I was left in silence and the scraping of glass shards that were flowing through my bloodstream. I wanted to sleep. I tried to sleep, but my skin was still on fire, and every time my eyes closed for too long, I'd get nauseous. The nausea had overtaken me.

I slithered out of bed, landing on all fours. I didn't have enough strength to stand. I crawled down the hallway to the bathroom and let out what felt like a week's worth of meals in the toilet. The coolness of the tile on my legs was too nice to leave. I planted my face down. It felt so good I needed all my skin on it. I slowly stripped off my clothes. Each sweep of my fingers hitting my skin made me want to scream out. The amulet was the last to go. I somehow managed to put it in the pocket of my jeans, thinking I needed to hide it away. I had hoped that when I took it off, the pain would stop, but it didn't. I fanned out on the tile, letting my skin cool, which helped me to relax.

My eyes opened, but my brain was foggy. I was aware enough to know that I was in between dreaming and awake. The lights were so bright, and every object was blazing with a halo, forcing me to believe I was dreaming. A dark figure materialized at the door, speaking in a language I didn't understand. Malcolm's voice bounced around in the back of my head, but it couldn't be Malcolm. This man was speaking another language, and Malcolm was at his childhood home four hours away. He must've been a figment of my dream.

He hauled me to his body. Without a doubt, I knew I was dreaming because Malcolm wasn't Malcolm anymore. His skin was glowing an amber color. It was so smooth and radiant. I peered into his eyes but had to turn away because the blue light that emanated from them was penetrating brightly into the heavens.

"Are you a god?"

He didn't say anything. Instead, he sat me on an even colder floor. Splashes of cold mist bounced off my skin, the droplets rhythmic and soothing. My teeth began to chatter with a chill. The water stopped, and a towel covered me. I folded into the skin of the man. A familiar scent caught my nose.

"You smell like Malcolm. He smells like the ocean. I want to know if he tastes as good as he smells," I confessed to the stranger.

"Jesus," the stranger spoke with a gritty voice.

He positioned me back in bed and bound his body to mine. I was still wet from the water, but that didn't bother me because as the god settled in closer, I was thrust deeper into my dream.

Chapter 18

There wasn't much sun shining in through my small window, but what did seep in was blinding. I vaguely recalled what happened last night. I was running away from the person that was following me and then fell to the floor from the extreme pain. I also remembered crawling to the bathroom and having a dream about a godlike Malcolm coming to my rescue. The fire had left me when I made it back to my bed, but my muscles still were weak and atrophied. I kicked the large comforter off and splayed out in the middle of the bed, still in my underwear. A creak from the floor cautioned me that someone was in my room. I really hoped it was Layla checking in on me. She had been very worried last night, and I had no strength in me to ward off an attacker if it wasn't her.

Malcolm's sultry energy filled the room.

"What are you doing here, Malcolm?" I asked him, surprised by how and why he was even here.

"I drove from home last night after Layla told me what happened."

"Thanks, but you didn't need to. I was fine." I covered the blankets over my exposed body.

"No, you weren't, Eve. I found you in the bathroom, burning up. I had to give you a cold shower and put you to bed." The skin around his eyes was dark and sleep-deprived. He must've arrived here in the early morning and stayed up watching me.

"That was you? I thought I was dreaming."

He let out a strangled laugh. "I know you wanted to know if I was a god, and you mentioned a few other things."

I knew he was talking about my confession of wanting to see if he tasted as good as he smelled. I was so embarrassed I wanted to go hide in my closet and rock myself in the corner.

He stepped out of the darkness and knelt by my bed. Uncertainty littered his handsome face. "How are you feeling now?"

"In less pain, but I'm fatigued and tender." He palmed my calf, squeezing the strained muscle. It felt too good to tell him to stop.

"What happened? The last I heard was that you were running home, and then I heard Layla scream your name, and that was it. The phone disconnected. I had to call Layla, and she told me that you fell to the floor."

"I don't know. When I made it back, it was like every part of me stopped working. I couldn't breathe or move, and then it felt like I had been set on fire from the inside out." As I talked about it, I could taste the burning on my tongue. I left out the part where I thought it was caused by the amulet. "I've never felt like that before."

He massaged my leg deeper, and a moan escaped me. His eyes expanded with the sound. I tried to contain it, but his hand was absolute magic. "It could've been your body reacting to being scared."

"Maybe." I'd let him believe that for now and sunk in under the covers.

His hand massaged up to the back of my thigh. "You should take it easy today; gather some strength. How about we go to my room? That way, I can take care of you and grade my papers. You can watch movies all day." He inserted his other hand under my side and scooped me up. The blanket slipped and exposed a copious amount of skin.

"Wait, Malcolm, I should put on some clothes." I tried covering up my stomach.

"Not necessary. I like what you are wearing."

I rolled out of his grasp and flopped on the bed. As quickly as I could shuffle, I went to the closet, changing into sweats.

Malcolm's bottom lip stuck out. "I prefer you with no clothes on."

"Thanks." I backhanded his hip. I only made it to the hallway before Malcolm swooped me up and carried me the rest of the way to his room.

His bed made me feel like I was encased by clouds. After he turned on a movie, he came back to the bed and began working his hands on my legs. My body wanted to tense, but it wasn't physically possible for it to; I was so weak under his hands. I rolled onto my stomach so he could get more of me. Those magical hands hit my back, and I almost died in ecstasy. Sounds I never knew I could make expelled from my lungs as he hit every knot and sore bone.

His hands halted. "I need to stop." He got up from the bed and went into the bathroom before I could tell him no.

I laid there in serenity, with not a thought in my mind until he came back out with damp hair and a tense jaw.

"I can leave." I sat up. My head spun, causing me to fall back.

"No, I want you to stay." He scattered out his papers on the floor. "I shouldn't do that anymore, though."

I didn't want to leave either, so I began watching the crime drama he put on for me while he went to work, occasionally laughing at what I assumed was an amusing answer.

I was halfway through the movie when something came to me. The manuscript had read that only a certain person could wield the relic. If the amulet was truly the artifact we had discovered, what if it didn't work because I wasn't one of those people? If that was the case, who was capable of wielding it, and where could I find them? Maybe that was also why I had gotten sick. The relic was trying to give me strength, but I couldn't handle its power. What if there was a bloodline that held the strength to carry the relic? I thought of Freydis and her sword. If she had attached the amulet in the hilt of her sword when it was constructed, it would have left a little etching mark like there was. I should try to trace that lineage as much as I could. There was a lot of genealogy resources here in London, and I knew of one person that could possibly have the answers that I needed. Dante.

I went for my phone to call him but remembered that I had

shattered it. I complained to myself, but it was loud enough for Malcolm to hear.

"Are you that bored already?" He swiveled up from his papers, wearing glasses I had never seen before.

"Why are those glasses so stunning on you?" My thoughts had slipped away from me yet again.

He grinned, his cheeks grazing the bottom of the frames. "You said it yourself. I am a god."

"I was delusional."

He got up from the floor, his body towering over me. "Delusional, really?"

Coasting onto the bed, he crawled closer to me, his eyes framed by thick rims. They brought out every feature in his face, sharpening the curves of his cheeks and nose. I tried to divert my eyes, but they wouldn't move. His hand looped around mine, and he brought my fingers up to his lips. He brushed each finger over his tongue, gently sucking on the tips. "I want to know what you taste like too." My mouth fell open—I was lost for words. He sat back and smiled with a wink. "What are your plans for Christmas?"

"I...I...." I stammered, caught off guard by the quick change in conversation and the surge of desire that stormed in my stomach. "I haven't really thought about it, except I know I won't be going back home." I was possibly going to order myself food and watch Christmas movies all day.

"Rose, Owen, and I co-own a flat in Paris, and we all go there with Wes and James for the holiday. We have been doing it for years now. I know everyone would really like it if you came."

"You own a home in Paris?" I stammered, confounded that I didn't know that detail about him.

"Yes. We were originally going to split it as a vacation house, but we all end up going to it at the same time. It's a loft by the Louvre, with five bedrooms. It's fairly large for that area of the city, but we got it for a good price and did most of the renovations ourselves. Well, mostly Rose and me. Owen isn't good with power tools, but that doesn't matter. What matters is that you say 'yes' to going with us."

"I don't know. I will think about it." It would be great to see Paris. I could check it off my list, but going on a trip with Malcolm felt too personal.

"What is there to think about? You're friends with everyone, and we want you there."

"I don't think licking someone's finger constitutes them as a friend, but I had it in my mind that I would get some alone time here, watch Christmas movies, and eat chocolate by the pound."

"You can do that in Paris, too. I can even provide the chocolate. Christmas is a few days away, and we are leaving after my exams. Take the time to think about it, but I really want you there, Eve."

"I will think about it," I told him, but already knew I wouldn't be joining them. Spending a week in the city known for romance with the man I was longing after, who didn't want a relationship, was difficult to say yes to.

Malcolm's phone went off beside us, reminding me that I needed to go buy a new one. "Shit, it's my father." He stood up and left the room with heavy steps to talk to him. He came back in almost immediately with a wry face. "I really hate to say this, especially since you aren't well, but do you think you could still cover my class tonight?"

Some of my strain from the day had been released because I figured that with Malcolm back in town, I wouldn't have to teach his class, but now the anxiety was back, ringing out of my ears.

"I am sorry, Eve, but my father found out I was back in town and wants to have dinner. He wants to talk about my teaching position for next semester. I think he wants my focus to solely be on that. No more work for Shawn." Sitting on the bed, his knees touched mine.

"What do you think about that? I know you like teaching, but I also know you don't want to be locked into a place where your father is going to live out the rest of his career."

"You're right on both accounts. I think I'm going to try to negotiate a four year contract until the girls are done." He straightened his back, confident in his new plan. "I want them to experience traveling like I did, but I want to be close to them for as long as I can."

"I don't know how much control you can have over that."

He flapped his hand in a flippant way, suggesting that he would be having a say in their decisions. "Anyway, are you still okay with covering?"

NO, my brain was screaming, but that's not what passed through my lips. "Yes, but you might have to go over things again with me. I wasn't paying attention last time."

"I thought you might not have been." He went over what I needed to know, which basically wasn't much. It was a general overview of the Renaissance period, which I could recite in my sleep.

"You're going to have to leave my room in order to teach my class."

He yanked at the hem of my sweatshirt. He wasn't dressed in his normal casual clothes, but more suitably for work and to meet with Andrew, I guessed. The day had sped by quicker than I wanted. I was going to stay in Malcolm's bed until the last possible second.

"Give me a minute or ten longer."

"Any other day, I would be thrilled for you to stay in my bed all day, but I am leaving now. You don't get a minute." He dragged me out of the bed and his room, locking the door behind him so I couldn't run back in. "You'll be fine." He combed a piece of hair off my face, but it coiled right back up.

Time went in slow motion the moment I stepped into the large classroom. The room expanded out into miles worth of desks, and the brown speckled carpet was like a tar trap, solidifying me to one spot and capturing all my fear and anxiety. Sweat pooled down my back as I faced the crowd. They were all at attention, waiting for my introduction. My vision tunneled, but I got myself to get one word out at a time.

"Mr. Archer couldn't make it today. I am Eve Monroe. I'll be doing the review tonight. First off, I don't know what is on the exam. Mr. Archer explained that it would be a general overview of everything you had discussed this term." There, I did it, and without stuttering. My feet loosened from the carpet.

A hand shot up in the air, plummeting my earlier confidence. Blood stammered in my ears. I needed to calm myself. I knew this history, and I could answer any questions that came my way. I called on the girl, waving her hand eagerly.

"Who was considered to be a major creator of architecture?"

"Donate Bramante," I recited, not even thinking about it. "He served as principal planner for Pope Julius II. His works include St. Peter's Basilica, Tempietto at San Pietro, and the Belvedere Court." The whole class was listening attentively. "Also, Filipino Brunelleschi, who was considered one of the first architects. He constructed the dome of Florence Cathedral. Leon Batista Alberti and Andrea Palladio were others."

The class and I went back and forth, and before I knew it, an hour had passed, and the class was over. "That's it for the class. If you have any questions for Mr. Archer, you can find him at his normal office hours." I sounded so professional; I impressed myself.

"Where can we find you?" Someone shouted from the back. A rumble of agreement ran up the aisles.

"You can find me in the archives for most of the day. If I am not in or you need some help outside of my working hours, you can email me."

For the first time all year, I had a reason to use my university email. I wrote it neatly on the whiteboard and dismissed the class. Several students stayed behind to pick my brain further. After another hour passed, I had to call it a night.

~*~

Malcolm was buzzing around the hallways in the morning. The dinner had gone well. There were other members of the faculty there, and since he didn't have to solely deal with his father, it went better than expected. He had solidified the four-year contract with the university, which included a pay increase, even though he didn't need it. After the next spring classes ended, he didn't have to be in the lofts anymore and could live wherever he liked. He kept on telling me about this place he had an eye on that was between the school and Wes's place. I was happy for him but a little glum that I would lose my coworker in six months. It wouldn't be the same without him, especially in the apartments.

"I should take you out to celebrate," I called to him as he zoomed around the hall.

He stopped, picked me up, and spun me around. "I have to take you out for covering my class. I got several emails from the students. They raved about you."

I couldn't help but laugh. "It appears we have a date planned," I replied, stumbling on my feet when he put me back down, "but it has to be tomorrow night. I told Shawn I would meet him for a drink tonight before he left for Georgia for the break."

"What about this afternoon?"

"I have to get a new phone, and I told the girls I would take them shopping for Christmas gifts," I explained

"Tomorrow is better than not seeing you at all. I will meet the guys tonight since it has been a few weeks. Have you thought any more about Paris?"

"It was only yesterday that you invited me. I haven't had much time to think about it." That was true. I didn't think about it because I knew I wasn't going.

"I don't understand what the big deal is. It's not like it is different from any day here."

I let my lungs fill with air; I figured the truth was best. "Malcolm, it's no secret that I want more with you, but you aren't ready to reciprocate those feelings, which is fine. But taking a trip with you, especially to a city like Paris, wouldn't be good for either of us."

He hadn't shaved this morning. The small growth worked well for him, but what didn't? "I haven't made it easy for you, have I? It won't be the same without you there."

It hadn't been easy, and some days, when he innocently held me, were harder than others. But I couldn't put the blame entirely on him. I perpetuated contact, too, even though I knew the outcome would not change. "You have done the holidays without me for your whole life. I know you will still have a good time."

"I don't care that I've done every holiday without you before.

I now know that I've missed out because you weren't in my life." He took my hands in his, smoothing out the tops of them with his thumb. "It won't ever be the same again. I need you—"

The girls came whizzing out of their room, purses in hand and ready to spend money, forcing whatever Malcolm had to say to fall away. Layla yanked me by the forearm. "Sorry, brother. We have gifts to buy and money to spend."

I gave him a wry smile in response.

Chapter 19

Layla was holding a black garment up to her body, swaying her hips in the middle of her room. She wanted to show us what she had bought when Daphne and I left her in a store to buy Daphne a Christmas gift.

"Is that a shirt or lingerie?" I asked, choking on the water I was drinking.

"I actually don't know. I think a dress. That's how I am going to wear it anyway."

"That's pretty risqué for a shirt or a dress. Who's it for?" The black lace was see-through in the center. Thin straps held up the low cut top, and it scalloped at the short end.

Layla blushed. "No one." She put the cloth back in the bag.

I didn't believe that for a second. There was no reason to buy something like that unless it was for someone to see her wear it.

"Don't worry, Eve. She won't even tell me who it is," Daphne complained.

I eyed Layla.

"I will tell everyone when I think it is serious enough to mention. Let's not talk about me anymore." I almost choked again. Layla was hiding something because, in the five months I'd known her, she always wanted to talk about herself. "Why aren't you going to Paris with us for Christmas?"

"Yeah. Why?" Daphne added.

"I think it would be best if I spend my time here." It was the quickest and easiest response I could think of without going into detail. They were my friends, but I saw them more as little sisters, and there were some things I chose not to confide in them about.

That was reserved for James and Rose.

"That's not actually a reason," Daphne argued.

"I have to get ready for drinks with Shawn." I quickly went to my room before they could ask more questions about my relationship with their brother.

~*~

It was unseasonably warm for the middle of winter, with no rain or snow or overcast for the next few days. I left my coat behind and opted for a thick sweater with a high neck. I took my time going to the pub. London was really beautiful during the holidays. Decorations were everywhere. It added a little extra magic to the city that already held so much magic for me.

The pub was packed, as expected, inside and out, but Shawn was nowhere in sight. I texted him a message on my new phone that I was waiting for him outside. After thirty minutes of waiting and no response, I tried calling, but it went straight to voicemail. I left him a more than slightly annoyed message and told myself that I would give him fifteen more minutes, then would leave. I watched a group of people socialize and ramble on about how they hated their boss for another twenty minutes. I didn't know why I felt the need to let Shawn know I was leaving, but I did it anyway. *Leaving the pub. Tired of waiting for you. Not happy.* Hitting the send button, I pocketed my phone and retreated back to home.

It was quiet when I rounded the corner to leave the pub. The streets weren't flooded with the usual crowd of people. There must have been something about the holidays that made everyone go home early. I crossed over a dark alley only a few blocks away from the uni when I suddenly lost control of my forward momentum and slammed against a brick wall. The shock of being completely taken off guard left me utterly useless as a man in a ski mask crouched towards me.

"Where is the relic?" A sinister voice boiled up from under the mask. He grasped his fingers into my shoulder and dug in with his nails like a titan.

I screamed out, but there was nobody around to hear me. He jammed his hand over my mouth, causing my front teeth to slice open my bottom lip with the force, halting anymore screams.

"Tell me where the relic is." His demand slithered malintent through my ears and down my spine. I held my tongue, tasting the metallic flavor of my own blood. I refused to let someone like him have possession of such a powerful piece of history. He palmed my forehead, slamming the back of my head against the wall.

A crackle sounded in my brain, and everything became hazy. "I don't know," I mumbled through his hand.

Switching his hand from my mouth, he clasped it around my neck, joining both his hands together. He crushed my throat. "I know you have the amulet."

"No."

Wheezing, a tear slipped away from me. The fear that was building was almost as blinding as the blow to the back of the head, but it didn't block the vision of a large fist closing in on the right side of my face. Pain ruptured behind my eye, and blood dripped from my nose, stinging the fresh cut on my lip. I had never been hit before. The action imploded my temper. I thrashed out, my limbs flailing, but he choked my neck harder, constricting air from passing through to my lungs.

He lifted one hand from my neck, giving me a small rush of air that I desperately needed. He ripped the high neck of my sweater all the way down to my chest, exposing my bra. I hadn't worn the necklace since it had made me sick. It was still sitting in the pocket of my jeans on my bathroom floor, and I couldn't have been more grateful for that. His dark, nothing, black eyes explored my skin, not seeing what he wanted, and his other hand slipped off my neck. He reached for something behind his back, and I knew this was the only moment I would have to get away.

Although I had never hit anyone before and my body felt like it was going to give up, I balled up my hand and swung out my arm as forcefully as I could. My fist collided with his teeth, shredding the skin on my knuckles. I lifted my leg and kicked him in the groin with all my anger. He tumbled to the ground, and I ran as fast as I could, ignoring the throbbing of my head and back. Small specks of water sprayed my face, and then the sky tore open, pounding larger raindrops, almost as if the weather increased with my rising fear. The rain had distorted my view further, making it difficult to see my surroundings.

I glimpsed behind me. The man was encroaching on me fast. I picked up as much speed as I could, making it to the courtyard of the university. My shoes hit the grass, causing my feet to slip out from under me, and I stumbled to the ground. Hoisting myself up, I gained my footing again. Checking to see if I was still being followed, my attention directed behind me, I bounced off something solid and once again fell. A large hand landed on my back. I screamed as loud as I could to scare away whoever was on me.

"Eve!" Malcolm roared clearly at me. Instantly I knew I was safe, and like the rainstorm, my tears broke free and fast.

"What's the matter?" He knelt down, worry piercing his question.

"I...I was attacked." I whimpered each word through sobs.

"What?!" He tried to assess my injuries, but my hair was plastered to my face, and any light was being blocked by the dark, cloudy skies. "Are you injured?"

"Y...y…y…ye...." I attempted to spit out the word, but I couldn't control my shaking. I wrapped my arms around his neck, needing the security that only he could bring me.

"Breathe, Eve." He sounded off, not his normal composed self. His unease made it difficult for me to gather myself. "I've got you now. Trust me." He cradled me in his sturdy arms and carried me through the doors. I buried my face in his chest. I couldn't stop my tears and the tremors of fear.

Malcolm maneuvered me to the edge of his bed. When he shut the door and locked it, I was able to even out each breath. A stream of blood was coming from my nose and lip, and the water from my hair was mixing in with the blood, causing a thin pale pink liquid to drip at a steady pace to the floor. He sat beside me with a washcloth in hand. He slanted my jaw up with delicate fingers, gently brushing away the mop of hair that was covering my battered face.

"Shit," he cursed as he wiped away the dirt and blood. His

hand was controlled and sturdy, unlike mine, but that mouth of his was set in a cold line, with eyes devoid of color and emotion. He became aware of my exposed chest, with my bra on display. "Goddamn it!" Breaking his composure, he handed me the washcloth, stood up from the bed, and left the room. I heard him curse in a different language on the other side of the door.

The pool of blood and water on the floor was like a parasite eating at me. I had to get rid of it—it was a reminder of what had happened. Maybe if I cleaned it up, it would wipe away the memory. I knew it was illogical, but I had to try. I painfully got on my knees, and with the washcloth used for my face, I started cleaning up the pool. The only problem was that the towel was already wet, and it was spreading the blood around instead of soaking it up.

"What are you doing?" Malcolm questioned, with ice packs in his hand.

"I am cleaning up my mess." Biting down on my tongue, I pressed the towel into the floor with more vigor.

"Eve." He knelt next to me. "You don't need to do that, doll."

The more I tried, the more mess I made. A tear splashed in the puddle from frustration, adding to my impossible task. More tears fell, and my head sunk low in defeat. Malcolm drew me back into his lap. I cried again while he rocked me.

"Thank you," I sniffled into the sleeve of his shirt.

"Don't say thank you. I didn't do anything." He held an ice pack up to my face, holding it into place, not letting it slip down from the tears. "I need to know what happened."

I gathered control over myself as much as I could. "I was supposed to meet Shawn for drinks tonight. I waited for him for an hour, but he never showed. I was walking down an alley, and out of nowhere, I was thrown against a building by a masked man. He slammed my head against the wall." I reached around to the back of my head. There was a big knot already forming. "He wanted to know where the relic was. When I wouldn't tell him anything, he punched me. He knew I had the amulet. He began to choke me, and then he ripped away at my sweater to see if I was wearing it. When he realized it wasn't on me, he reached for something behind his back. That's when I punched him. I never hit anyone before. I don't think I did it right because I hit him in the mouth, and now my hand really hurts." I raised my bleeding knuckles to him. There was a long gash across them from where his teeth had scraped my skin. They had already puckered red. I wondered how bad my face was. "After I hit him, I kicked him in the crotch. He fell to the ground, and that's when I ran, and then…you know the rest."

Malcolm let out a rocky stream of breath. How could he have endured years and years of this pain? I bet the fear I felt was a fraction of what he had gone through. Suddenly I was really sad for him, which caused the tears to come out again, even though I thought I was empty of liquids.

"You're safe with me, doll." He took my uninjured hand in his. "I wish I could take this pain away for you. I would do anything for you not to feel this way."

"I am sorry." I watched the tears stream down his muscles.

He went to place his hands around my neck but then hesitated. I was sure there were marks from when I was being choked. "Why are you sorry?"

"How could you deal with this fear, anxiety, and pain for half of your life? I had never been hit before, and it was so paralyzing it rendered me helpless. I can't believe this happened to you all the time. It makes me so furious."

Malcolm yielded his rocking motion, the curves of his cheeks and the sudden roundness of his eyes, making him appear as if he were was struck with bewilderment. "Eve, you are sitting here bloody and bruised, and all you can think about is me. I honestly don't know what to say." He placed his forehead on mine. "There will never be another woman as good as you." He grazed his lips on my shoulders.

I winced from the tenderness. "Sorry."

"Stop apologizing." His hands went to my hips, and he dipped into me. "Why don't you go take a shower? It will help you loosen up. After you're all cleaned up, I will bandage your hand." He held onto me as he stood to his feet. His strength was immeasurable. Carrying me to his bathroom, he turned on the hot water. "I'm right out here if you need me."

Malcolm left me by myself. I stripped off the rain-soaked clothes and stepped into the shower on auto-pilot, not having anything left in me to expel emotion or energy. I let the water wash away the blood and dirt. Droplets stung the skin that was freshly cut. I washed myself clean with his soap. The bathroom filled with the scent of Malcolm and immediately calmed me. I stayed in the shower until the water got cold, which I didn't think was possible in such a large building.

Wiping away the steam on the mirror, I examined the damage on my face. Under my right eye, red skin had puckered and swelled at the point of impact. The cut on my bottom lip had stopped bleeding, but there was still a split that was going to leave a small scar. The worst was my neck and shoulders. Long fingerprints enveloped my neck and encased my shoulders, with little indents from where his nails had buried into my skin. They already held a purplish tint. I didn't want to think about what would have happened to me if I didn't get a chance to take out my attacker. I was angry, but most of all, I was frightened and exhausted. Never in my life had I experienced so much horror.

I didn't want to look at myself anymore. It was going to make me sick. I tied a large towel around my chest and stepped out into the short hallway.

"Hell, Shawn!" Malcolm yelled into his phone. "No, she isn't all right!" I'd never seen him so heated, but I knew he had it in him, and I wouldn't want to be Shawn right now. Malcolm was fuming enough for both of us, and there was something about that that I enjoyed. I didn't know if that made me a terrible person or not. "I think it would be best if you stayed away from me and her for a while." I was eavesdropping from around the corner but had caught Malcolm's attention. He hung up the phone without saying another word and paced around the small space.

"Maybe I should go back to my room." I made for the door, my condition obviously too much for him.

He stood in the way of my exit. "Eve, I am not letting you out of my sight. You are staying with me tonight, and for a few nights after that, honestly."

The thought of being alone didn't sound appealing. All I wanted was to feel safe, and Malcolm could provide that for me. "Fine," I said, not putting up much of an argument. "But, I need a shirt to sleep in." I clutched onto my towel in fear that it would fall.

He hustled over to his closet and found a T-shirt. Before he handed it to me, he carefully examined the bruises on my neck and shoulders. His face was stamped cold again, not letting what he was feeling out. "Let me ice these, all right? Then we can go to bed."

I nodded, twisting my hair around to let him have full access to my neck. The ice burned with the first contact of skin, but soon it helped to numb the throbbing. After a few seconds in one spot, he'd change the position, taking the coolness across my bare shoulders. His expression never changed, but the pulsating rhythm of his chest told me that he was affected by all of this. "Your hand doesn't seem bad, and the skin didn't break too deeply. If it's still tender in a few days, we should go to the hospital. In fact, we can go now to make sure your hand isn't broken, and the back of your head is fine."

"I don't want to go anywhere." I was sure of that. I wanted to hide away and not think about what had happened to me. "I'm a little banged up, that's all."

"You don't have to act brave around me. You're more than a little banged up, Eve." He reached for four small white pills on his dresser and a bottle of water, "At least take some aspirin. It will help if a headache starts and with the muscle aches. If you get to it early enough, you can avoid a lot of discomfort."

"Are you speaking from experience?"

He dropped the medicine in my hand, urging me to swallow. "I know what works best."

I didn't doubt that, and I followed his directions because of it, drinking the whole bottle of water in the process. My stomach rumbled with the contact of water. I hadn't eaten anything since lunch, and even then, I only had a small salad.

"Are you hungry?" One of Malcolm's eyebrows glided up. "I can hear your stomach."

"I could eat. I know it is late, but I don't think I will be getting much sleep anyway."

"I will give you privacy to change, and I'll order us some food." He backed out of the room, keeping his eyes on me until he couldn't.

Releasing the towel, I maneuvered the shirt on over my head. It fell short of my thighs. I dug around his drawers for boxers and came up with a pair that had fire breathing dragons on them. In the seriousness of the night, the cartoon dragons made me burst out in laughter. How in the world did he end up with these? Nevertheless, I slipped them on. For a moment, I stressed that I wasn't wearing a bra, but that thought left quickly because it wasn't going to be the kind of night where he noticed my lack of undergarments.

He came into the room and closed the door behind him. "I ordered Chinese. I hope that is okay."

"Sounds great." Chinese actually sounded delicious. I needed to drown myself in greasy food.

"I thought you might like that." His neon gaze traveled up my legs to my shirt. Maybe I would have to think about underwear. "You here, wearing my clothes, makes me ecstatic." He rubbed his jaw. "I only wish it were for different reasons."

"Sorry." My cheeks flared. Why was I apologizing so much? "For now, can we discuss why you own these boxers? The dragons are really doing it for me."

"Those were actually a Christmas present from James last year." His whole face turned bright red. "I used to have a thing for dragons as a kid, and when James found out, he thought it would be hilarious to reprise my obsession. So for years now, on my birthday and Christmas, he gives me dragon related items. I have a box of it all at my father's house."

A giggle escaped me. I had to see that box one day.

A crack of a smile crested on his sharp cheeks. "What else can I get you? Do you need another ice pack? More water? Anything or everything, I am here for you."

"I want you to hold to me." For the first time, I wasn't embarrassed by my own honesty. He was the only remedy I needed at that moment.

"I want that too." He held my hand in his, bringing it to his mouth. He added a small amount of pressure to the wound from his lips. "I want to take a quick shower first." I hadn't noticed that his clothes were still wet from the rain, and spots of my blood were on his shirt from where I had cried into him. He tossed me his phone. "Let me know if the food gets here before I get out." I watched him walk down the hallway and take off his shirt, getting a sneak peek of his rigid back.

His phone reminded me that I didn't know where mine was. I tried calling the number on his, but it went straight to voicemail. Shit, that was a brand new phone, and there was a chance I had dropped it somewhere between the alley and here, and by now, it was destroyed by the rain.

Malcolm's phone rang in my hand. I blamed the fact that I jerked it in the air and threw it half across the bed on tonight's events. The caller ID flashed James when I reached for it. "Malcolm, James is calling you," I yelled at him through the door to the bathroom.

"Pick it up." He was barely audible over the running water, but I was able to make out the words.

"Hello?" The greeting came out more like a question.

"Eve? Oh, thank god you are safe! I have been trying to call and text you. You've ignored me for hours, and that isn't like you. I thought something happened to you."

"I lost my phone. Is everything okay?"

"I'm having a minor crisis, that's all." I could picture him falling back on the couch, his hand flying to his forehead in a very dramatic, James-like way. "I have no idea what to get Wesley for Christmas. He is so difficult to buy for. He likes boring, plain things, like books and stationaries."

Malcolm emerged from a quick shower. His face was smooth from a clean shaving, and his hair was slicked back, showing off all the angles of his face. The plaid pants he wore hung dangerously low on his hips. "What's James up to?"

I had to tell myself to close my mouth so I wouldn't drool. "He is having a crisis. He doesn't know what to get Wes for

Christmas," I told him with my hand over the receiver.

"Give me the phone." Malcolm reached for it, and I handed it off. "James. James. James." He was such a patient man. "You called my phone. Who else would it be? Listen, James. Eve isn't well and can't talk. I need to go take care of her. Can we talk about this later?" Malcolm grunted a few more sounds and hung up. "Still need me?" he asked at the edge of the bed.

"I need you," I practically begged.

"Good, because I need you too." He glided into the bed. Propping up against the wall, he placed a pillow at his lower back. He spread his legs and tapped the space between them. I moved to him but was still stiff. My back barely touched him.

"Relax," he crooned to the top of my head.

I forced my muscles to let go of the tension, my back loosening into him. I slouched, resting my head on his firm chest. He intertwined our fingers and crossed our arms over my stomach. Closing my eyes, I let the motion of his steady breathing soothe me. I forcibly shoved down everything that had happened to me tonight. All I cared about was that the relic was safe.

"Do you want to talk about tonight at all?"

I shook my head, no. "I only want to keep doing this." I pushed his arms tighter into my stomach.

Chapter 20

I was sitting in the position I had been for the last four hours. After dinner came, I felt tired again, but every time I closed my eyes, the dark sunk-in eyes of the man in the mask haunted me. Malcolm was sleeping next to me, but I knew it would only last for about another half hour. He was on a routine. He would wake up, tell me to try and get some sleep, and then fall back asleep until the next time. I turned the TV on and the volume low to not wake him any earlier. I think he was worried I was going to have some sort of mental breakdown, but it wasn't going to happen. The relic was the root cause of my attack, so it was obvious that someone else knew about it and its power. They knew I had it, which led me to think I was being followed, possibly from the very beginning. I couldn't risk it getting into the hands of someone dangerous. So even though I didn't want to, I had decided that I would wear it again, keeping it close to me at all times. I was tempted to sneak back to my room and get it, but I didn't want Malcolm to be upset that I left him.

He stirred again, this time pulling at me so that my back laid flat on the mattress. "Sleep, Eve. If you don't, you are going to hurt worse in the morning."

"Every time I close my eyes, I see his face," I confessed.

Malcolm rolled onto his stomach, covering most of my body with his. Throwing his leg across me and holding me in under him, he buried his face into my neck. "You are safe with me. Remember that." He stroked my injured cheek with his finger. "What can I do to help you sleep?"

"You being here is enough. I don't know what I would do

without you tonight." His lulling finger on my inflamed cheek began to hypnotize me.

I woke up early in the morning. Malcolm was still on top of me. Normally I would love the contact, but I couldn't lay down any longer. I slithered out of his hold, tired and sore. My feet hit the floor. Every muscle burned with each step back to my room. I immediately went to my bath and took another long shower. I was about to put the amulet around my neck when I heard someone in my room. Placing it back in the dirty jean pocket, I tossed it in my laundry basket, thinking it would be safe in there temporarily.

"What are you doing up?" Malcolm's hair was out of place. He had covered his chest with a shirt but was still wearing those plaid pants.

"I am getting ready for work." No matter how bad I was damaged, I had no intention of sitting around all day.

"You need to take the day off. I changed my day to watch you." Scrutinizing my decision, he must have thought I was a lunatic by the way he studied me.

I put my hands on my hips. "Why would you do that? Were you serious about not leaving me alone?"

"Dead serious." He crossed the room, closing the rift between us. He twirled my hair around his finger. "I am determined not to let anything else happen to you, and if that means staying by your side until I am one hundred percent sure you're safe, then that is what I will do."

"Mal, I really don't want you to do that. I have to continue with my routine. Otherwise, I will get too dependent on you and never want to go anywhere without you."

"What's so wrong with that?" he appealed, ignorant to my logic.

"Mal," I squinted at him, "that's unreasonable."

"I don't see how." His tone went up an octave. "Let me take care of you."

"I am not saying you can't." I threw my hands in the air. "I want your help every now and then, and I want to do the same for you. But you don't need to be glued to my side twenty four hours a day because you feel the need to be responsible for me. I am not one of your sisters."

He was wordless; the sister part might have been a cheap shot. The ticking of my clock was the only sound in the room. He reached out, hitching on to my slacks at the belt loops. "I will always try to keep you safe and protected, but I will work on the other part."

"Good." I was still heated from our short disagreement.

"So, what do you want me to do today? Stay here or leave?" I had to give him credit for trying to change so quickly.

"Why don't I work half the day?" I was proud of myself that I was compromising. "Let's go get some coffee, and meet up for dinner. I will stay with you tonight also." As much as I didn't want to admit it, I wasn't ready to be alone at night.

"I can deal with that." His lips latched to my forehead.

"Eve, where are you?" Layla's voice called through the thick door just as it hurled open.

Before she could invade my privacy, I stepped out into the hallway with Malcolm. "What's going on, Layla?"

She grimaced at the sight of me. "Malcolm told me you were injured last night, and I wanted to check up on you. He didn't say it was this bad, though."

I gave him the evil eye, as much as I could. I wanted to keep my injuries as private as possible.

"It wasn't his fault. He was running around the halls last night, not acting his normal self. I pretty much forced him to tell me what was going on." She patted my shoulder softly. "How are you doing? You look terrible. What happened?"

"I'm fine. Thank you for checking up on me." I avoided the "what happened" part and ignored the looking terrible comment. Daphne came out from her room, running at full speed. She pitched herself into me. "Ouch, Daphne. Not so tight, a little sore this morning."

"I was worried last night. Malcolm said he would let us know how you were doing, but he never came by." She pinched him in the side. He didn't even flinch. It was probably more aggravating than anything.

"I'm just sore. I was headed out to work, so it isn't that bad."

I saw Shawn's silhouette in the distance, anchored by an older man. The man was tall, with a lean, strong build. He had a full head of gray hair and dark brown eyes that held a menacing quality to them. His sharp jawline, high cheeks, and sloping nose were so similar to Malcolm's that I knew within an instant that the man was Andrew Archer.

Malcolm stiffened beside me when he saw him coming. Taking a protective step in front of me, half his body was covering me. Malcolm puffed his chest out. As he stood up straight, I could tell he was grinding on his molars by the way his jaw was set. Layla and Daphne observed the shift in his attitude. They both immediately changed direction and headed for their room.

"Daphne. Layla." Andrew's stern voice boomed in the hall. "Are you not even going to say hello to me?"

They simultaneously rotated stiffly on their heels. Straight elbows were met with clenching fists. It was the most twin-like I had seen them yet.

"We have to go study for exams," Daphne announced in an unexpectedly commanding manner. It must have been unusual because Andrew stopped in his stride and glowered directly into her chocolate eyes. She didn't move, blink, or balk. She had a determined sneer set on her tiny face. Layla kept her head and eyes glued to the floor.

Andrew bared teeth in the most sinister smile. "Glad to hear it. Your mother and I have very high expectations for you, Daphne."

Apparently, there were no expectations set for Layla. Daphne took her sister by the forearm, and they went into their room without another word.

"What are you doing here?" recited Malcolm in the same tone Daphne had.

"When one of my staff members gets attacked, it is my duty as the dean to make sure they are well."

Malcolm eyed Shawn. Shawn mouthed back his apologies. "I can assure you that Eve is fine and doesn't need your concerns."

Andrew smirked. Malcolm's discontent was amusing to

him. It was as if Andrew thrived on the game of hatred and manipulation they played back and forth. I had no intention of stepping out from under Malcolm and introducing myself.

"Eve, can you leave me and my father alone for a moment?" He didn't adjust his head or body to me. He was like a lion protecting his lioness from an unwanted intruder. I turned my back to them.

"I like a woman who takes orders from a man," retorted Andrew.

I stopped. My nails dug into the palms of my hand. I considered for a moment if it was worth it to give Andrew a piece of my mind. And fist. Now that I knew I could hit someone and handle a hit back, I was ready to fight. Sure, I would most likely lose my job, but I wouldn't care about that. It would be worth it. The only thing that made me put one foot in front of the other was Malcolm.

I shut the door behind me but heard Malcolm tell Shawn to leave as well. Shawn only halfway listened to him because he lunged into my room.

"That," he pointed to the door, "is a situation I never want to be put in again."

"Agreed, but you know what other situation I don't want to be put in again?"

For the first time, Shawn was able to get a full view of my face. "Eve, I am so sorry." His fingers reached out to my cheek, but I backed away.

"This isn't the worst of it, Shawn." That anger I had for him not showing up was there and amplified with last night's events.

"God, Eve. I can't believe this happened to you. I don't know what to say but to apologize profusely."

"Why don't you start by saying why you stood me up last night?'

"It's really stupid, but I fell asleep and didn't even hear any of your calls or texts. It was only when Mal called that I woke up. I know this wouldn't have happened if I would've shown up. Can you please forgive me?"

It was true that I possibly wouldn't have gotten attacked

if he was there, but this was about the amulet, which Shawn knew nothing about. If it didn't happen last night, it would have inevitably happened. I also couldn't fault him for falling asleep. He had been as busy as the rest of us. "Yes, I can forgive you, but don't do it again."

"Thank you, Eve. You don't have to go in today. I am leaving for the airport in an hour. You know you do get the same time off I do. Right?"

I rolled my eyes. "Yes, I know that, Shawn. But I like working and have nothing better to do. Besides, I am leading a study session today, so I was planning on going in no matter what. I will take the week of Christmas off, maybe...."

"Are you sure you will be fine here by yourself over Christmas? It's not too late to go home, or come to Georgia with me, or go to Paris."

"I am sure." I was ready to have some quiet time alone. "I have a little bit of work left to do for Colorado, and I will even have time to get some drawing in."

"As long as you forgive me, I will be able to leave London a happy man."

Malcolm returned, anger steaming off him. He didn't interact with Shawn, still upset with him. Shawn left, not wanting to stick around for Malcolm's wrath, and I couldn't blame him.

"Did Shawn apologize?" I was afraid if the answer was no, Malcolm would chase him down the hall and drag him back by his collar.

"Yes. I forgave him. It wasn't completely his fault. He doesn't know the circumstances that revolve around the attack."

Malcolm was still stiff and uptight. Impulse drove me to do my next move. My fingers found the edge of his shirt. I inched them up to the sides of his waist. I had to repeat to myself not to run my hands over his stomach. Malcolm's marine eyes transformed into sapphires. I squeezed, but his stomach didn't squish like mine did. My fingers sprang back like a rubber band.

"It's me and you now."

His forehead was flush against mine. I regretfully removed my hands out from under his shirt. "I try not to let him get under my skin, but sometimes it feels like an impossible task, especially when you're the topic of conversation. Thank you for staying away from him. I'm sure it was difficult for you not to respond to what he said. You know I don't think that way, right?"

"Mal, you're a thousand times a better man than your father. I wanted to react to him. I think sickly that was what he wanted, but he wasn't worth the response. You...you on the other hand…." I longed for him in a way that I never had before. I wanted him to know how I felt. I wanted to demolish all the walls.

"And you…." His lips brushed the side of my cheek. "I feel the same way about you, too." It was like he was reading my thoughts. "Come to Paris with me. We leave tomorrow after my exams. I can't leave without you, especially after last night."

I was throttled back by that. Was that the only reason why he wanted me in Paris after I already told him the reasons why I wasn't going to go? Did he want me to go so he could keep an eye on me? "I am not going to go with you."

He jerked up like I had slapped him in the face. "Then, I am not going. I need to know you are safe."

I crossed my arms, clearly not happy with him. "You will not stay here. The girls are so excited to go and spend the holiday with you and your friends! You will not disappoint them because of me. We have also been over this. I can take care of myself. I don't need you around me all the time. I don't need your pity or obligation. I am not going to go on this holiday with you because you have some kind of instinct to protect me. That's not enough for me!"

"Eve, it's not—"

"No, Malcolm! I can't do this anymore! I can't handle the disillusion, and honestly, the heartache. Can you leave? I don't want to see you right now."

I knew I was having a tantrum, but at this point, it was agonizing waiting for him to be ready and feel more than some type of burden to be responsible for me. The anguish that seized his face was unbearable. It was as if I had broken him. He didn't say a word as he stepped out the door and slammed it behind him.

I hated myself for saying that, but I was also in no mood to be my usual self. Feeling my defeat inside and out, I couldn't help the few tears that had slipped away from me. Needing to keep busy and not think about my broken heart, I decided to go out and get a new phone yet again and buy Christmas gifts for everyone. With the study group at the end of the evening, there was no time left in the day to steep in my thoughts. With my day laid out, I was determined to see it all through.

Before I left, I dug the amulet out of my laundry basket and hung it around my neck. There was a small vibration, but it stopped when it made direct contact with my skin. It was like I was wearing a normal, unenchanted, gift-from-the-gods necklace. I had so much to figure out about the necklace, mostly how it worked. I thought my earlier hunch that it had something to do with a bloodline was right on. Once I got my phone, I would call and demand if Dante knew anything.

When I went into the phone store, the man at the counter, the same one that had helped me yesterday, took pity on me and got me a phone almost for free. I think he took one look at my face and figured I had had a tough night. Before I left, he slipped me a piece of receipt tape. Scrawled on it was his phone number. I snorted to myself. There were other options out there for me, even though I only wanted the most impossible options. I thought James would get a kick out of it. I sent him a picture of the number, and my phone rang within seconds of the notification that the picture was sent.

"I still have a little something left in me," I greeted him, doing a toe tap in the middle of busy London.

"Girl, you have a lot in you," he laughed. "Malcolm would be cross that someone else was encroaching on his territory."

"First off, I am not territory, and second, Malcolm wouldn't care at this point. I think I ruined everything, and I'm sure he doesn't want to speak with me for a while."

"That man couldn't stay mad at you for more than ten seconds. He has it bad."

"I don't believe that, but for some reason, I'm still out here wandering around trying to figure out what to get him for

Christmas."

"Why didn't you tell me you were shopping today? I still have nothing for Wesley. I need your help. I'm putting on pants now and meeting you." There was a commotion on the other end, and then the sound of a zipper. He was serious about the pants.

"I will head towards you. And put on more than pants, please."

I hung up and made my way towards the Tower. On the walk, it hit me how comfortable it was that I was strolling around London by myself and going to places like the Tower on a regular basis. It was only six months ago that I fantasized about this place, and now I would go by all these historical markers and be completely unfazed by them.

~*~

"Eve!" screamed out James from five hundred yards ahead of me. He began sprinting with arms wide open. He stopped halfway through to catch his breath, which I knew was an act because he had an intense workout routine every morning. He was absolutely my favorite person. He slowed when he saw my bruised face. "Eve, what happened to your pretty face?" he roared in horror.

"I was supposed to meet Shawn for drinks last night, but he never showed. I was attacked on my way home." I tried my hardest to not make it sound like a big deal. I didn't want him to ask many questions because I didn't know how capable I was of lying to him.

"Oh my god!" His arm landed on my shoulder, and I flinched with the weight. He frowned at me. I stretched the collar of my sweater to show off my bruises. "I can't believe this happened to you. It hurts my heart. What happened to your attacker?"

"I don't know. After incapacitating him," I flashed my bruised knuckles, "I ran like hell out of there."

"Remind me not to ever mess with you." He punched the air.

"Yeah. I am pretty tough." I exhaled with exaggeration.

"Why didn't Mal tell me last night? All he said was that you weren't well."

"Might have something to do with you being overly dramatic

about not finding Wes a gift."

"Speaking of…." He made my attack old news, which I was okay with. "What should I get him?"

"I actually have an idea for him, and I know exactly where to get it."

"I don't know how I survived my life without you." He latched us together. "So tell me all about what is going on with you and that handsome friend of ours."

I recalled our argument and how hurt he had looked, even the part about the slammed door. "I think I need to take a break from Malcolm. Things have gotten way too complicated, and I don't have much patience left in me. I need some time alone to clear my head."

"Eve, you have the clearest head of anyone I know, but you have given him more than enough time. It's no longer fair to you." I appreciated how he supported me. I knew that no matter what happened, James would always be with me. "I can talk to him to see what he is thinking."

"No, James," I held out my hand in a stopping motion. "I don't want you to get stuck in the middle. Malcolm and Wes are so close, and so are you and me. I don't want you to think you need to pick a side. If Malcolm and I don't progress, then I want to make sure we all remain friends. And even though I'm not spending the holiday with you, it doesn't mean you aren't getting a gift from me."

"Oh, good. I was so worried about that," he smirked at me. "And I can't guarantee you that I will stay out of the middle. This is what I do best. So what am I getting Wesley?"

I would bet my life that James would be meddling in my business as soon as my back was turned, but maybe a little help was necessary at this point.

"According to you, he likes boring things, like books, which is not the best thing to say to someone who is surrounded by books every day. But I remember him talking about his love for the classics. I stumbled on a store awhile back. It has quite a large collection of first edition classics."

~*~

For someone who didn't have an obsession with books, James spent a long time combing over every novel. I hadn't found anything, not even something for myself. After hours, James came away with a rare signed copy of *The Secret Garden*. He ended up paying way too much for the book, and that was even after he had negotiated on the price.

"Thank you so much for the idea, Eve. I know he loved this book when he was a child. Could be why he married a gardener." He did a little dance all the way to the end of the street.

"That makes the gift more meaningful. Now I have to leave you for the day. I still need to get you a gift. I will see you when you guys get back." I gave him a large hug. "Have a great trip and happy holiday."

"You too." He returned the hug. "I will see you soon."

We parted ways, and I made my way to another store down the road. Much of the store was filled with old Coke bottles and beat up frames that were labeled as antiques. All the aisles were hoarded with junk the owner thought he could make some profit off of.

A small display case held pocket knives of various sizes. One of them caught my eye. The handle was about three inches long, overlaid with opal, and had a tiny black border around the edge of what looked like onyx. Opening the blade, the transition felt good. There was no rust on the joint, and the blade was newly polished and in great condition. I rotated it to inspect the other side and almost dropped it on the glass case with what I saw. At the top end of the blade were the initials M.A. They were beautifully engraved in an old fashioned script, next to the date of 1822. What were the coincidences that this knife had Malcolm's initials on it? I had to get it for him.

"Five hundred pounds," the cashier stated when he realized I was interested in it, but he sounded unsure of his estimate, and I took advantage of that.

"One hundred pounds," I offered. I knew this knife was worth some money, but not five hundred pounds—three hundred at the most.

"Four hundred," he countered.

"One hundred." I didn't blanch. I set my narrow puffy eyes on him. Maybe it was because my face was bruised, but he agreed on one hundred. I was proud of myself. I had spent less money than I thought I would today, between the phone and the gifts.

I was planning on drawing something for Malcolm too, but I could do that later. I had to get back to the study group. Rushing back to the archive, a large group of people were huddled around the old door. I unlocked it, and they all flooded into the room; I was sure that over half the class showed up. I had cleaned up the archive almost to perfection. There were no more books and documents thrown everywhere. After it was all picked up, the room was rather big. Daphne and I had searched for chairs and small tables about a month ago to make it another space for students to study, even though she was the only one to ever use it.

"I am amazed by the turnout," I told the group. "There are more of you than I expected."

"Mr. Archer's exams are notorious for being impossible. I think only about ten percent of us have received higher than a C," shouted a girl with light blonde hair sitting on the floor.

"I have been in three of his classes. They are all like that. He likes very detailed and cited work," claimed a boy behind her.

"At least he is easy on the eye," someone from the back of the room declared. I thought it was the waitress I had met at the pizza place a few months back. The entire female population followed with agreement.

Deciding it was best to move on from that subject, I couldn't help but be possessive of him. "I would really like for all of you to pass with high marks."

We got to work quickly. The two-hour study session transformed into four. I really could have been there all night. History flowed out of me, giving me a buzz that was indescribable. This was my passion, and I was so lucky I got to work with and enjoy it every day. By the end, the students were getting restless, and the conversations lagged. I also saw Daphne's petite frame waiting for me in the hallway.

"I think we have covered a lot. Good luck tomorrow, and if

you need study help for next semester, you know where to find me. Have a great holiday."

Daphne came in once everyone had left. She was carrying a small bag with her. "Was this your study group for Mal's class? Did the whole class come?"

"I think only ten people didn't show. Malcolm is going to be thrown when he grades those exams, and most of them pass."

"I don't know if that will make him happy or upset. He really likes the fact that his exams are impossible. I hope he is happy, though, because he has been in a bad mood all day, and I can't handle him being like this. It's exhausting."

"Sorry about that." I touched the back of my head, where the large knot was. "That's my fault."

"I figured. He has been cursing your name all day in conversations he's been having with himself. But that's not why I am here. I wanted to give you your Christmas gift early." She handed over the bag to me.

"Thanks, Daphne. Yours is in my room. Can we go back and get it?"

"You will have to give it to me when I get back. Mal and Layla are waiting outside for me. We are going out to dinner, just the three of us."

I was happy that they were able to spend some family time together. I stuck my hand in the bag and pulled out a small jewelry box. I opened the lid. A platinum ring was in the center of the box. A small squat circular opal, similar to the handle of the knife I'd gotten Malcolm, was set into the band. "Oh, Daphne, it is beautiful." I picked it up. There was an inscription on the outside of the band. It read "*sanguis in corde, sed sororibus*" in Latin, which I knew translated to "sisters not in blood, but in heart." Tears sprung to my eyes. "I love this!" I sniffled, slipping the ring on the pointer finger of my right hand.

"I wanted to let you know that you have changed my life. You have given me so much confidence in being comfortable with myself, and I know no matter what happens, we will always be sisters." I agreed vigorously, too emotional to say anything. "Anyway, I better get going. Layla and Mal were already complaining about being hungry before I came in here."

"Thanks, Daphne." I wiped away tears.

I was overwhelmed by the strong relationships I had formed in such a short time here. I never knew that I could have this much love for people who were complete strangers to me a year ago.

Chapter 21

I had expected Malcolm to come to my door and say goodbye, but he never did. I was upset with him, but mostly with myself. I couldn't get him out of my mind, especially since I had spent all day drawing the picture for him. I was very intentional of making each curve of his jaw exactly right, and the way his hair swooped to the side right above his eyes. To the left of him were his sisters. He held that pose of admiration that he always carried around for them. Daphne was next to him. Malcolm's hand fell on her shoulder, while Layla's head was rested on Daphne's, with her hair behind her ears. I impressed myself with the drawing. I typically didn't put that much time and detail into my work, but the end product almost resembled a black and white photograph. I placed it in a frame I had picked up earlier and carefully wrapped it, along with all the other gifts. My hand was cramped from all the drawing and more swollen than it had been since the day I used it for punching my attacker. If it didn't get better, I was going to have to get it checked out.

Christmas Eve was the next day, and I was planning on doing some research on the ancestry of Freydis and ordering in food. I had changed into my traditional Christmas garb of green flannel pants with snowmen patterned all over and a red sweatshirt with a reindeer in the center. It was laughable, but I had worn it for the holidays for the last five years, and since I was by myself, I was going to wear it for the next two days to really get into the spirit.

My phone woke me up at five in the morning. I hit the ignore button, but it went off again. The caller ID flashed Wesley. I picked it up, thinking something was wrong, "Hey, Wes, why are you calling so early? Is everything all right?"

"I am sorry." He didn't sound that sorry, I thought.

"For what?" All of a sudden, my door sounded like it was getting trampled on by a herd of elephants. "What the…?"

I opened it, and Wes's face greeted me. "I already apologized, so you can't be mad."

James came barging in behind him. He planted his hands on both sides of my upper arms and pinned me on the bed.

"What are you doing?" I bucked my legs out, but James was stronger than me.

Wesley fled into my closet. He came back out a minute later with my weekend bag, stuffing pants and shirts in it. "When James told me that you weren't coming with us, I refused to accept that. So we bought you a train ticket to go with us."

"Wes, I don't want to go! Let me up, James." I struggled, but it got me nowhere. I heard Wes clattering in my bathroom. Somehow he found my makeup and toiletry bag. "Cute boots." He packed my favorite knee high boots into my bag. "All ready!" He zipped the very full bag closed.

"You can't make me go. I am not changing, and I am staying right here!" I went slack, giving James my dead weight. There was no way he could get me up.

"You don't need to change." Wes smiled sweetly. Without any struggling, James schlepped my dead weight up and tossed me over his shoulder like I was a sack of potatoes.

"How can one person be this strong?" I pouted as I realized my plan to break free was futile. I was hoping they would forget my passport, and I wouldn't be able to get on the train.

Wes took my phone, charger, and keys off the side table. "I know it comes in handy."

"Oh, don't forget these, babe." James pointed to my pile of Christmas gifts. "And get her passport and wallet. She keeps them in her backpack."

There went that idea.

"You're so helpful." Wes stood up on his toes and nuzzled his cheek.

We were out of the room before I could protest again. Wes

locked up, and James kept me over his shoulder as they walked casually out of the building and down the street. The only people that were out so early in the morning were the ones that slept on the streets. If it were busier, I would've yelled for help. Someone would've thought I was being kidnapped and saved me, but as it were, nobody even cared. James and I went unnoticed to the train station, where he finally let me go and plunked me on my feet.

Wes held me around my midsection, herding me up to the passport window. The attendant didn't even grill me. She stamped the page and motioned for me to move along. Wes pushed me forward, the train already at the platform. James lifted me up the steps and directed me to our seats. He held onto my knee until the train jolted forward into motion. I stuck out my lip. It was official—I was going to Paris.

"Don't pout, Eve. You had to know we couldn't do this trip without you. Besides, you are getting a free trip to Paris," Wes said from across the aisle. They had me trapped from both sides.

I would have never thought they would kidnap me, but Wes was right—not too many people would have dragged me out of bed and forced me onto a train to a beautiful city. I inched down, lounging in my seat. "You're right. Thank you for the trip. I should enjoy myself." I didn't want to be ungrateful, and I could make a plan to try to avoid Malcolm. It shouldn't be hard; he didn't want anything to do with me anyway. "Can you let me change clothes, though?"

"Oh, no way," James laughed. "This is your consequence for being such a nuisance, and your outfit is amazing. Why would you want to change?"

My bag was sitting on the seat next to Wes. I was tempted to pretend to go to the bathroom, grab my bag, and make a run for it so I could change into something less humiliating, but I knew the attempt would be stopped before I even started.

Wes had fallen asleep by the time the train picked up full speed. I had to listen to James talk about the different kinds of flowers indigenous to France for three hours. In the six months I had known him, I had not once heard him talk about plants and flowers. I wondered if it was some weird travel tick. Whatever it was, I was ready to plunge myself out the window of the speeding train. The train's brakes screeched to a halt, and I flew off the seat to get away from that conversation.

We took a taxi from the train station to a commercial building. There was a coffee shop, a patisserie, and two boutiques. From what I could see, it was two or three blocks from the Louvre. I could see the tips of the building and the Eiffel Tower from the ground. "Where are we?" We stood in front of a large white building from the French Renaissance, with *fleur-de-lis* plastered to the outside trim. "Is this the house?" I was in awe of the large complex.

"They own the whole building, but only the top floor is the living space."

I followed James to an industrial door around the back. We climbed the emergency stairwell to the top floor. A short hallway led to a mustard yellow door. That must have been Rose's choice. It was her favorite color. James knocked once and then let himself in. My heart was drumming rapidly. I was not ready to face Malcolm yet. I didn't know what to say to him.

"We're here," James sang out, making a grand entrance.

Owen, Rose, Malcolm, and Logan were sitting at bar stools at a large island that went directly into a kitchen. Light cement floors ran throughout the whole space, and exposed ductwork and piping opened up to high vaulted ceilings.

"We kidnapped Eve too." Wes pointed out the obvious from behind me. "In her snowman pants and all." I smacked him. He rubbed the center of his sternum. "Ouch."

Everyone except for Malcolm got up from their seats and greeted us. He observed my every move from the kitchen with a callous scowl, like I had trespassed in his territory. All the commotion brought Daphne and Layla out from a room. They nearly tackled me to the ground. I yelped from the roughness, still not at one hundred percent.

"I almost forgot you were injured," Layla said. "I don't know why, with how bruised your face is." I didn't think she meant it to sound as offensive as it came out.

"You know, Malcolm." James dumped his bag and sauntered over to him. "When I enter into the room like the damn Prince of England, you should really get up to greet me."

Malcolm stood, clasped James's hand, and shook it, "Good to see you, mate," he welcomed halfheartedly.

"Not what I was expecting. Did you see that your friend Eve is here too, Mal?"

He shoved me forward, causing me to be toe to toe with Malcolm and forcing me to make a decision to talk to him or not.

"Hi," he mumbled.

"Hi," I sheepishly returned.

"Wow, that was very heartwarming." James rolled his eyes. "Are you still mad at her? Because if you are, it can't be from that silly argument. Eve was scared. She had every right to be. And let's face it, Malcolm, you need to put the poor woman out of her misery. Now, be adults and make up."

"I am sorry," I offered, making the first gesture. "James is right for the first time ever, and it's none of his business, but I am sorry." I swallowed the bile that was coming up, just thinking about what I was going to say next. "It's obvious at this point that if you were interested, you would be with me. I can accept being your friend, but I think we need to draw up some boundaries."

Malcolm didn't say anything. Taking a sip of his coffee, he walked right past us and went into a room at the end of the large living space.

James blinked at me in astonishment. "That was rude. Forget about him. Let's enjoy our time together."

Malcolm's actions bothered me, and I couldn't help but feel out of place and not welcome. I wanted to go home and spend the holiday by myself in my room.

"I know that look on your face," James spoke softly to me so nobody else could hear it. "Stop what you're thinking before you even say it. You are welcome here, and wherever I go, you go, and that's it." He rubbed the center of my back.

I gave him a weak smile. I loved that he was always on my side, but still sad about it all. I think James felt bad because he handed over my bag. "You can change into normal clothes now."

"I appreciate all your effort in getting me here, but I think I need to go back home. I can't be around him right now, and I don't want it to be uncomfortable for anyone." I searched on my phone to find the next time for the train to head back to London.

"I get it, I do, but I wish you would stay." He was so disappointed, it almost made me change my mind.

"There is a train that leaves in two hours." I clicked on the checkout button and purchased my ticket back home. "I'm going to change and then head out. I'll leave the gifts here for everyone." I hoisted my bag to my shoulder. James pointed me to the bathroom. I changed into the first outfit I saw, which was a sweater and jeans. I wasn't in there for a long time, enough to put on a brave face to tell everyone goodbye.

The living room was empty when I came back out. Only James and Rose were in the kitchen, working on cooking food. "Where is everyone?" I asked them.

"They went out." Malcolm took a large step out from behind a support pillar. "I told them all to leave, but James and Rose insisted on staying. I think they are afraid of what you might do to me."

I turned around. His muscles were tight. There was nothing about his stance that read he was in a good mood. "But I wanted to say goodbye to everyone before I left."

"You're not leaving, Eve." He slowly rocked his head from left to right.

"Why the hell not? You don't want me here."

"Because I have waited for this moment for weeks, and I will not let you ruin it." He directed his attention to the couch. "This was not how I wanted this to go, but I am doing it anyway because you are stubborn, and I keep finding myself apologizing to you."

"What are you talking about?" I questioned because he wasn't making any sense.

"Sit, and I will explain." He went to the couch first.

I knew he wasn't going to let me leave without talking to him first. I stomped to the couch and heaved myself on the opposite end, not in the mood to do this with him now. My attitude didn't go unnoticed either. He got up and took a seat closer to me.

"Let me start by saying I didn't want you here because I wanted to keep an eye on you and make sure you were safe. I mean, there is and will always be a part of me that needs you near me because I know I can protect you properly. But I really wanted you here to give you your Christmas gift. I am going to give it to you early now because we can't wait any longer." He bent over, retrieving a rectangular box from under the couch. "Sorry, it's not wrapped."

He handed it over to me. I wasn't sure what this had to do with what was going on between us, but I lifted the cardboard top anyway and uncovered a beautifully leather-bound, handmade sketchbook. The right hand corner of the front cover had my name branded into the rawhide. "Thank you, Malcolm. It is very pretty." I smiled at him but was baffled on why he couldn't wait to give it to me.

"Go to the last page," he urged.

I turned the book to the last page. In the middle of a blank sheet were two words.

Time off.

"Time off," I read out loud. "I don't understand. What does that mean?"

Before I could have another thought, his lips were on mine. They were satin and smooth, how I'd always imagined. Every motion of his was like a charted out map over my lips, but I was thirsty for him. I had wanted this for so long that the sensation of his mouth pressed against mine was overwhelming. All the emotions I had stored away came exploding out of me. I wanted to cry and laugh at the same time. I balled the collar of his shirt into my fist, dragging him closer to me. He groaned with the pressure, shifting his body onto me. My back hit the arm of the couch, and I sunk down, forcing him on top of me. The movement made my breath catch, causing my mouth to part slightly. He took advantage of that and slid his tongue in. It collided with mine, moving in unison. I was greedy. I wanted to taste him, touch him. I wanted every inch of him on me. My hands went up the side of his shirt. My fingers were met with soft skin, which was firm over his back muscles. His response was immediate. He thrust his hips into me, and even though I didn't think it was possible, he kissed me more fiercely and with more urgency than before. His motions were savage and were driving me to the edge.

"Wow," a voice echoed in the background.

Malcolm suddenly stopped. He slowly lifted up, forcing me to whimper from the separation. The sound stopped him from leaving me, and he sweetly kissed my lips. Water sprang to my eyes. My feelings were all over the place. I had never in my life experienced such an extraordinary passion before.

"That was...there are no words," Rose squeaked from across the room.

"Words fail me too," James added.

I was officially creeped out that our friends were watching our first kiss. Malcolm cleared his throat, but the water at my lids flooded over and trickled on my cheeks. I tried to wipe them away on the sleeve of his shirt without him noticing. I was completely embarrassed that crying was my first reaction to him kissing me.

His face warped from lust to fear when he saw the moisture on his sleeve. "Did I hurt you?" his accent cracked.

"No." I hurried my answer. I didn't want him to think he was causing me any harm. "I don't know why I am crying."

"It's because you're so happy," James squealed. He was clapping while skipping around.

Malcolm soaked up my tears with his lips. They tenderly ran from the bottom of my eyes to the corners of my mouth, tasting the salty water. "I'm happy, too," he softly professed to me.

"We need to celebrate!" James ran into the kitchen.

Malcolm's hand clenched on my hip, and he adjusted me, so I was sitting in his lap. I shifted, settling myself in between his legs. "Easy doll, we don't want to give them a show." I cocked my head to give him a devilish smile. He caught that smile and swept his lips over mine once more. I could kiss him all day long, and my life would be perfectly content.

James returned with four glasses filled with red wine. He lifted his glass. "To you two coming to your senses."

Malcolm's lips caught my shoulder, then neck, and then my

ear. He raised his glass also, but I hesitated. Was this something he really wanted or was it pressure from all of us? I had wanted this, but did he? "Wait. Wait." I paused, everyone mimicking me. "Are you sure this is what you want, or are you succumbing to your friends? You don't have to do this because of me either. I meant what I said earlier. We can be friends."

Malcolm took my glass out of my hand and placed it on the coffee table. He gave James and Rose the sign to leave the room, but they didn't go anywhere. They were way too eager to be involved in our relationship. He raised me up off his lap, and I sat cross legged by his side. His hands cupped around my jaw. "I can't take a step without thinking about you anymore. It's impossible to breathe when you're away from me, and there is nothing I want more than you. I want you to know and be involved in every part of my life, the good and the bad. This has nothing to do with other people. I want so much more than to be your friend. I have never been more sure of anything. So, can time be up now? Can we be together?"

"Eve, if you don't say yes, I will." James held his hand over his heart.

I lifted myself up with my legs still crossed, meeting his lips. I touched my mouth to his and smiled into him. "Time off."

He kissed me briefly, which was a good thing because anything more and I would be making Rose and James very uncomfortable. I got the wine glasses off the table, and we clanked them together. The bittersweet flavor washed away the new taste of Malcolm, and I wanted to savor that for as long as I could. Rose and James went back into the kitchen to finish the meal prep for the following day.

I took advantage of their absence and launched myself on top of him, straddling my legs over him. "I want you for a little longer before everyone gets back."

"I like the sound of that. We should take this somewhere more private, though."

He grabbed my butt and stood up. It was amazing that he could carry me like a weighed nothing because I definitely weighed something. He found the way to a room and positioned me on my back on the bed. His body hovered over me, heat filling the small space between us. He kissed the crook of my neck, moving up until his lips nearly reached mine. I closed my eyes, anticipating the weight of them, but they never came.

"Everything all right?" I lifted the lid of one eye, peeking up at him.

"I can't believe I'm about to say this." His thumb swept over the bruise around my eye. "I want to make sure we do this right. We shouldn't miss any steps. I think we need to take it slow. I want to take you out first, or a few times, really."

It was sweet that he wanted us to go on dates and do all the right steps, but I felt like we had moved slowly enough over the past months, and I was ready to give myself over to him. It wasn't easy for me to say yes, but I couldn't say no to him either. "Does that mean you don't want to do anything?"

"Oh, God, no." His tongue grazed the bottom of my mouth. I nipped at him, and he returned the action with a long deep hold to my lips. "How are you doing? Your eye and lip are still really bruised."

"They're fine." There was a sting with each touch to the lip, but I wanted him more than the discomfort of my injuries. "I can endure it. Can I ask you something?"

"Anything."

"Earlier, you mentioned that you had been waiting for weeks, and this was not how you planned to tell me, but that I was too stubborn. Were you planning on telling me you were ready over Christmas?"

"I had been wanting to tell you for a few weeks now. The restraint was almost unbearable, but I wanted to make it memorable for you. And what better time to do it than over Christmas in Paris? There were so many times I could've, probably should've, told you. But I had an elaborate day planned out for you after Christmas morning. Then you told me that you didn't want to come. I was trying to sway you otherwise, and after you were attacked, I thought for sure you would come. But you're so damn stubborn. On my way down here, I made the decision that I was going to leave after the Christmas gifts were opened and come back to you. When you showed up, every single plan I had went out the window, and if I didn't tell you now, you would have left."

I felt bad that I had ruined all his planning, but I liked the way he told me. It was a moment I would never forget. "You didn't have to come up with something elaborate. All I wanted was you, and that would have been more than enough for me."

"That response right there is why you deserved this to be memorable. Not lying in bed or in my office, or because we were both scared after your attack. I wanted it to be more for you than on the couch, and I know it was a feeble attempt with the journal, but it was the only thing I could think of to do quickly. I will make it up to you a hundred times over, though." His eyes danced around my face and down my neck. "Are you wearing the amulet?"

The question caught me off guard and was completely opposite from what we were talking about. Pushing him off me, I sat up, fingering the chain. "I am."

"I need you to be careful when you wear it. It makes you a target." He held up my hand that had refused to shrink back to normal size.

"It's safer with me than anyone else. Plus, it doesn't work. I have tried everything short of a magic spell." I explained to him my theory about it only working with a specific family.

"If that were the case, then why would Henry go to war for it, unless he didn't know it could only be used by a specific family. Can I see it?"

I removed the bone carved symbol from under my shirt. "It's very old, but it's durable."

Malcolm reached for it, but when his skin made contact, it sizzled on his flesh, "Shit! I think it burned me."

"It does pulse for me from time to time."

He wrapped his hand around the whole piece, and smoke fluttered up. A small pink mark began to pucker in the shape of the symbol. "I can't touch it. How come you can?"

"Do you think it is only you, or that other people can't touch it, also?"

I got up from the bed to answer my own question and went into the kitchen. Twisting into James for a side hug, I intentionally let the necklace hit his skin at the end of his shirt sleeve.

"Ouch. What was that?" He bobbed out of my hold.

"What?" I tried to act as clueless as possible.

"Something burned my skin." He massaged the side of his arm.

Malcolm and James couldn't touch the amulet, but I could. What did that mean? It couldn't have meant anything serious because it still hadn't worked. I wasn't stronger. I couldn't use the force. I could still get injured. So what was it?

"Are you going to stand there and stare off into space, or help us?" Rose waved her fingers at me.

"Yes, of course. I will make the pies." I went to wash my hands, hiding the amulet back under my sweater. "You want to help me, Malcolm?"

Rose and James both laughed so hysterically it almost scared me. "Malcolm can't cook to save his life. He can't even mix sugar into coffee correctly."

"It's not that bad!" He crossed his arms, forcing the muscles up. "I only did that twice, and are you ever going to let that go?"

"Never." James tossed a dishrag at him. He caught it before it hit his face. "But if you want to stand in the middle of the kitchen in the way, make yourself useful and take off your shirt."

"That's not going to happen. I have exams to grade, anyway." He kissed the back of my neck before he left to get the exams and settle in at the island.

I worked on rolling out dough, when several curses came from his direction.

"What's the matter?" Rose asked. "Did they receive bad marks this year?"

"No. The opposite, actually. I'm eight exams in, and all of them have high marks. It's unusual." He scraped his red pen at his temple. I tried to hide my grin, but I was failing. "You had something to do with this, didn't you?"

"Maybe…after I taught your class, I was requested to host a study group. Most of the students showed up."

He removed his glasses, pinching the bridge of his nose. "How could I spend months going over all this, and they fail almost every exam and paper, but in two sessions with you, they know it all?"

"Well, I do know things. A lot of things." I came to his side to read over his marks on the papers. There really weren't that many. "They did tell me your tests were next to impossible."

He transferred me to the countertop of the island, hurling the papers to the side, his knees touching the outside of mine. "You are ruining my reputation. I should have known you could outsmart me with the whole class."

He leaned in to kiss me, and his tongue met mine. Every motion brought out a new desire in me. I wrapped my legs around his thighs and forgot all about the pies. I wanted to go back in the bedroom, and the way he purred over each pass of our tongues suggested he wanted to also.

"Is this what we should expect from you two from now on?" James snuck in between our faces and bonked a wooden spoon off my head.

Malcolm yanked the spoon out of his hand and snapped it in half with ease. "Yes," he answered, handing the two halves back to him. "Is that a problem?"

"No, I like seeing this side of you. But you might want to explain to everyone what you are doing."

James took the ends of the broken spoon and tapped them on both of our noses like some type of fairy godmother. Malcolm turned his head, and I peeked over his shoulder. The others had come back, and we were the center of attention.

"I think it is pretty obvious what they are doing," Owen answered. "I don't think we need an explanation."

"Great, because I wasn't planning on giving one."

They all took Malcolm's response and dispersed to their own business, but Daphne was right on his back, clinging to him from behind. He held up his hands like he was going to surrender when he pivoted around.

"I am so happy for you," she sobbed into his shirt.

He stroked her hair. "Why are you crying?"

"I never thought you would get here. I thought you were going to be single and lonely forever."

I held back a chortle. Malcolm sought me for guidance, but I was at a loss of what to do. "Sorry, I'm emotionally spent after this week." I hopped off the counter and continued my work with the pies.

Rose came over to save him and took Daphne into a room for her to cry inconsolably. Malcolm went back to grading, huffing every few minutes. He was never going to let me near one of his classes again.

Chapter 22

James had been taking a nap on the couch after he was done with his dinner prep, and Wes was tangled in him. Rose, Owen, and Daphne were off walking around somewhere, and Logan and Layla were chatting quietly at the dining table. I had finished the last of the five pies I had made. I might have gone overboard with them, but I couldn't help myself.

Malcolm came around the island to get a cup of water. He leaned in behind me, filling his cup from the faucet while I was at the sink, not even bothering to push me out of the way. He kissed me on the cheek. He had always been touchy with me, but now that we were together, he had no problem putting his lips on me. I wasn't about to complain about it, but it was still foreign.

"We should go for a walk. This is your first time in Paris, and you have spent the first five hours in the kitchen."

"That sounds great, actually." I stood up on my toes, kissing him swiftly on the mouth as I tried to get used to our new physical relationship.

Logan and Layla trapped us in the kitchen before we could leave. "We have something to tell you," Layla announced. Then she braided her hand in Logan's. He didn't refuse her; in fact, he took a side step closer.

Oh, no. I knew where this was headed, and it wasn't going to go over well. I gripped Malcolm's upper arm as a reminder that I was right beside him and on his side. Malcolm fixed in on their connected hands. He stood up straight, and all the happiness we had cultivated over the last several hours seeped out of him.

"Hell no," he spat sharply. "No way is this going to happen!"

"It's already happened," Layla spoke up, defiant and ready for a fight. She was so much like her brother.

James and Wesley were now up from their nap and had joined us in the kitchen, in disbelief at the new couple.

"Logan, are you joking with me right now? Please tell me this is a goddamn joke?" Malcolm braced his back against the counter, his hands balled into fists. If one wrong thing was said, he was going to break.

"It's not, Mal. We weren't going to say anything unless it got serious, but now it has," Logan said, speaking up for the first time.

"He wanted to tell you after the first time," Layla stepped in, a little sweeter, "but I was the one that wanted to keep it casual."

Malcolm gripped the top of my uninjured hand tightly. "I can't hear this. I don't want to know the details. All you need to know is that this is over with as of this point."

"That's not going to happen." Logan's stance shifted to a more challenging one, and I braced myself for the worst. "This isn't your choice; it doesn't affect you."

"Doesn't affect me? Doesn't affect me!" Malcolm questioned harshly with disbelief, "Logan, you have a new girlfriend every three months, and Layla is way too young to know what she wants. When one of you decides it isn't going to work out, which will happen, then you are going to have to make not only me but all of us, pick between my friend, who I consider a brother or my actual sister."

"Layla is different, Malcolm, and I wouldn't risk our relationship unless I thought it would work out." I had to give Logan credit for trying to stand up to such a fierce, terrifying force.

"How is this different from any other girl, Logan? Sorry Layla, but Logan has a type—young and pretty, typically blonde, and likes to party. But then he gets bored and moves on to the next one. I refuse to let my sister be another number for you."

"It's different," Logan implored. "She isn't another number to me. I love her."

Malcolm's head snapped to him, eyes sharp but oddly lifeless.

His chest didn't beat from breathing. He didn't even a blink or tick a muscle from his clenched jaw.

"Oh shit," Wes cursed what we were all thinking.

I thought for sure Malcolm was going to go for Logan's neck, but instead, he silently went out of the kitchen, walked into his room, and shut the door without making a single sound.

"That can't be good," James puffed out.

"Can you go talk to him, Eve? Talk some sense into him," Layla begged. She was on the verge of tears. Her brother's approval meant more to her than she let on.

All eyes were on me. This wasn't my responsibility. As the girlfriend, my responsibility was to comfort him. "I will talk to him, but I don't think he needs any sense talked into him. I am on his side with this." I made a path to his room, hearing Wes tell Logan that what they were doing was not right.

I entered through the doorway, shutting the door behind me. The room was dark, the only light from the window that faced a building. If I peered down, I could watch the passersby on the street. He had designed the room similar to the one at home. It was minimal, with a large dresser that held a television. The bed was bigger here. It could easily sleep six people, but it had the same black satin sheets. Matching nightstands were on either side. There was no bookshelf, but that didn't stop there being a pile of books on one of the end tables, along with a reading lamp.

Malcolm's attention was out the window.

"How you doing?" I softly sung, stepping in front of him and blocking his view.

"I need a distraction. I can't think about this right now." He shook his head like he was trying to let his thoughts escape.

"A distraction I can do." I pushed my hands hard against his chest and backed him into the bed. He stopped before he fell over.

"What are you doing?" he grinned. Everything that had happened was now washed away, according to the glow in his eyes.

With enough force, I drove him to fall over and land on the mattress on his back. "As much as I respect the fact that you want to take things slowly—and I will take your lead on that—there are a few things you should know about me."

I straddled his body, slowly migrating to within centimeters of those magnificent lips, my tongue barely touching.

"What should I know?" His voice was raw and filled with excitement.

"I may be nice, but I am also pretty naughty." His eyes flared with desire. "And I waited for a long time to put my lips all over your body. I can't let you take that away from me."

My hands worked under his shirt, slowly rolling it up to his shoulders. I shuddered with the display of his firm muscles. My lips inched their way over to the cords of his abs, kissing each one as I travelled south.

"How did I get so lucky with you?" he growled.

My mouth found its way to the indents right below his hips. My tongue lingered, enjoying its newly found playground. With every tantalizing moan that came from him, I followed the thread lower and lower until his waistband acted as a barrier where he had forbidden me to go. He rasped my name, and the anticipation was too much for me to stop. I wanted to test exactly how forbidden it was. As I unbuttoned his jeans, he didn't stop me. I slowly worked on the zipper—still nothing. I was getting further than I expected.

There was hammering at the door, halting my pursuit. "Don't speak, and they will think we are sleeping." My breath danced along the surface of the elastic of his boxers. The knocking stopped, and I began my pursuit once more.

"Malcolm, we need to talk," Logan broadcasted from the other side.

"I am busy, Logan. Go away." Malcolm's voice was gruff.

"No. I am not leaving until we talk," he demanded.

"I think you'd better speak with him. Sounds like he is serious." I lifted myself off him.

"Fine. Give me a second," he huffed at the door. "I am going to kill him for so many reasons." He pivoted me around, now on top of me. "We will pick this up later." He lifted his weight from me and worked up his pants. I watched him button them, fixating on the button like it was ice cream, and I had been on a diet for months. "Goddamn, don't look at me like that, doll." He kissed me hard, pulling on the hair on the back of my head and causing friction on my lips.

I gasped for air when he released me. He opened the door when I motioned that I was ready. Logan fell forward, and I stepped past him, scowling. "Sorry, Eve." He apologized in passing, knowing exactly what he had interrupted.

James was on the couch. I plopped next to him, resting my head on his shoulder. He palmed the side of my face, making sure not to touch the bruise. "How's he doing? What did he say?"

"Not much." My cheeks flared pink. Good thing James couldn't see my face.

"Did you even talk to him about it?"

I cleared my throat. "He wanted a distraction. That's what I gave him."

James panted, "I am jealous."

"Don't be too much. He wants to take things slow, do it right. So I am not getting very far." Closing my eyes, I got tired all a sudden. It had to have been from all the excitement of the day. After all, I had been sleeping in my bed in London that morning, with no boyfriend, and hours later, my life was different.

"He is like a different man with you. It's fun to watch."

"More like torturous. Where is Layla?"

"Wesley took her for a walk. That girl is trouble. Don't get me wrong, I love her, but she has always been difficult. I can't blame her entirely, though, and Logan should know better than to get involved with her."

"It's like a living daytime drama. Never a dull moment in this series." I was including myself in that drama.

"You couldn't be more right, but this time we can sit back and enjoy the show, now that you and Mal are together. There had to be something new, didn't there? Before you know it, Wes and I are going to want a kid."

"Do you want one?" I placed my hand over my heart. I would spoil that kid rotten.

"Calm down. No, we don't."

I sat back with a pout.

Malcolm and Logan surfaced from the room. Logan was smiling, apparently pleased with the conversation. Malcolm was not as pleased. His face was pinched with a scowl. He picked me up from my spot, stealing my seat, and forced me onto his lap. He fastened his arms around me tightly.

"I don't think I will ever get used to you being so handsy with someone," James said. "I have known you for ten years and not once experienced this."

"Get used to it; it is only going to get worse. Well, for you. For me, it will only get better."

A response was on the way out of my mouth, but the amulet vibrated furiously. At first, I thought I was having a heart attack. My heart fluttered so quickly I couldn't breathe. A high pitched ring broke all sounds in my ear. I brought my hands to my face. They were twitching uncontrollably. A milky fog laced over the room. I couldn't see what was in front of or beside me, and then it stopped suddenly—no more vibrations from anywhere. The fog cleared away, and I was face to face with Caribbean blue eyes.

Wetness dripped from my nose. I wiped it away with my palm to see that it was blood. I didn't know if the amulet was guiding my thoughts, but I knew what this feeling was. Someone dangerous was close by, and I was tired of playing cat and mouse.

"Someone is watching us," I muttered, untwisting from Malcolm, and ran out the front door before anyone could stop me.

Swinging my head from left to right down the hall, I saw that no one was there. Sprinting to the stairwell, taking two steps at a time, I burst out into the cold, wet Parisian air. I heard Malcolm and James call my name behind me, but I didn't care. I was determined to find out who had been harassing me. My bare feet pounded on the cobblestones. I let the amulet guide me. The harder it vibrated, the closer I knew I was. It took focus to forget the electricity in my veins, but I had tunnel vision. Nothing else mattered—it was like a switch had flipped, and I had only one goal.

I rounded a corner, coming to a crowded intersection. The

amulet stopped vibrating, which also made me stop. Since I didn't know who I was running towards, I didn't know which direction to choose. I leaped to a small alley to the right of me but was yanked back.

I whipped around, about to strike whoever had me, but the flawless face in front of me made my fist unfurl at my side. "Eve, what are you doing?" James clasped his hands on my cheeks, his eyes frantically trying to focus in on mine.

I was lost in the crowd of people, searching for whoever was watching us. I caught sight of Malcolm jogging up. His chest was beating briskly from the unexpected exertion.

"I don't know what's wrong with her, Mal. She won't listen to me." James moved aside to let Malcolm in.

He flung me to his chest. My ear could hear his sporadic heartbeat, jolting me into the present.

"He was here," I whispered, not loud enough for James to hear. "The amulet was trying to warn me."

"And you thought running after him would be a brilliant idea?" He was on the verge of breaking the calm in his voice. "He is dangerous, Eve. What do you think he would do to you if you caught him? He has no problem beating you to get what he wants." Malcolm was right. It was a stupid impulse, but one that I couldn't contain.

"I am sorry." I shivered, realizing how cold it was and that I wasn't wearing shoes.

"We aren't done talking about this, but we should get you inside."

James put an arm around me. "What the hell happened, Eve? It almost looked like you were having a seizure, and then your skin went white as a ghost, and then you got up and ran. You ran really fast, faster than I've seen most people run. I thought you weren't athletic?"

"Speaking of…how come you got to me before Malcolm? I thought he was in good shape too?" I was hoping that the mention of competition was enough distraction for James not to think about my erratic behavior, or apparently my new ability of superhuman speed.

"I am clearly in better physical condition," James boasted. "You should work out with me, Mal. It might make you faster."

"I don't think that's a good idea." Malcolm curled his arm around my back as we walked side by side. I loved the comfortable closeness we had now, but I had a feeling it was more to keep me by him for fear of me running off again. "I would be afraid you would try to touch me the whole time and not get anything done."

"That's a good point." James rubbed his fingers on his temples, almost like he was trying to wipe away a thought. "I would do that. And I don't think boxing is my kind of workout anyway. I'm a gentle soul." He fluttered his lashes.

"When did you start boxing?" I asked Malcolm. That was news to me—last I heard, it was running and swimming.

"About four months ago." He shrugged, "It helps with control." I knew that control meant anger, and the rest of his emotions, he kept bottled up inside.

When we came into view of the loft, Daphne was standing outside, with Owen behind her grasping her shoulders. He was standing tall; his muscles expanded, making him appear bigger than he was. They were talking to a couple. The closer we got, the more recognizable they became. The cropped blonde hair of a petite woman and the gray hair of a tall man; the Archers were here.

"Shit!" Malcolm sprinted to them. We followed behind him.

Daphne saw us coming and waved for the three of us to stay away, but Malcolm bolted forward, ignoring his sister. "Stay here and watch Eve," he told James.

James put his hand on my stomach as I stepped forward to follow. "Stay, love. You don't want to get involved. Trust me."

"But Daphne—"

"Owen and Malcolm have her."

James was right, and Malcolm didn't want me near them. I had to respect that, but it didn't mean I had to like it.

Andrew saw James and me and called us over. Malcolm stopped mid-sprint. He mouthed "no" to us, but Andrew called us over once more, this time with more authority. Malcolm was torn, but he waved for us to come. We slowly made our way to them, taking our time. Malcolm captured my hand and led me the rest of the way. His elevated pulse on my wrist was the only indicator that he was angry about this meeting.

"James, it is good to see you again," Marie spat with apparent disdain, not even acknowledging my presence.

"You too, Ms. Archer." He emphasized the Ms. part, maybe as a little jab to remind her that she wasn't actually married to Andrew anymore. "Your hair is adorable," he responded with the same disdain as her. I had to hide my smirk, but James didn't.

"I don't think we have officially met Ms. Monroe. I am Andrew Archer."

Andrew bowed to me with such a polite smile, but all it reminded me of was a serial killer. A happy, perfect façade, but below the surface, a darkness larger than anyone could ever fathom. Malcolm made sure I was far enough away to avoid skin-to-skin contact with him, and for some reason, I appreciated that.

I smiled curtly and said, "Hello," keeping my introduction short.

"What are you two doing here?" Malcolm seethed from their unexpected appearance.

"We wanted to see our children over the holidays." Marie pretended to be appalled that he couldn't understand their sudden appearance, but even I could tell it was an act. "We wanted to take you and the girls out to dinner tonight. And then we will leave you all alone for Christmas."

"No," Daphne spat at them. "I will not be going to dinner with you, and neither will Layla and Malcolm. We can arrange something when we get back to England." Daphne spun around and stormed into the building, leaving the Archers to three feral men and me.

Andrew snarled at Daphne's disrespect. "You need to have better control over her Malcolm, much like Monroe here."

I frowned, counting to ten in my head so I wouldn't say anything, but ten came and went. I tried twenty next. The longer I counted, the more enraged I got, but I managed to keep my mouth shut, bruising Malcolm's hand in the process.

"I think you'd better go," Malcolm commanded.

Marie and Andrew delivered their goodbyes without a fight to James, Owen, and Malcolm, but when Andrew got to me, he put a hand on my shoulder and drug me forward. All three of them took a step closer to me. Malcolm tugged on my hand. I hated that his father shared so many physical characteristics with Malcolm.

Andrew placed a hand under my jaw delicately, but I cringed with the touch of his skin. Malcolm was about to rip my shoulder out of the socket. "I hope you are treating my son well. He means a lot to me."

His words were like a parasite invading my whole body. I clenched my jaw, wanting nothing more than to take a bath and scrub away his touch on my skin. I leaned forward into his ear instead. "I will protect him at all costs, even from you." I hoped he took it as the threat I intended it to be.

Dark, dangerous eyes were glued to me, searching for a hint of fear. He wouldn't find any. He would find anger and protection and a slew of unpleasant words. "I believe you and understand."

He let go of me, and they departed, leaving us standing in the middle of the sidewalk. Malcolm released his lock on my arm. I waved it around, trying to get out the numbness. He did the same to his hand. "What did you say to him?"

I stretched out on my toes, barely reaching his lips, and kissed them tenderly. "That's between me and Andrew."

"Where are your shoes, Eve?" Owen pointed to my bare toes.

I tried to hide them behind one another. "Long story, but I'm freezing and hungry. Let's go inside."

Malcolm held me back at the stairwell while everyone else went upstairs. He gathered me into his chest and held me until his pulse settled down. "When it comes to you, nothing turns out as I planned, and I am sorry for that."

"I know you didn't want me to meet your father," I said into his shirt. "And you didn't plan on my injuries or this entire trip, or maybe even me in general. But you can't stop certain situations. Now, it's about how we get through it all, and I really hope we can do that together."

He bent down, placing a delicate kiss to my lips. But I elevated it, gripping him tightly. I consumed him, wanting him to believe me when I said we could get through anything together.

Chapter 23

All of us were crammed in at a small table with a red and white checkered tablecloth. I was sandwiched in between Malcolm and James. Logan had forced Layla to sit on the other side of Malcolm. I was consuming large chunks of bread because my stomach was trying to eat my insides. Malcolm was so rigid from today's events that his shoulders bulged from under his sweater.

I supplied him with a glass of wine that I had filled to the rim to take the edge off. "Mal, we are all here having fun, and you look like you want to run away."

He cuddled up even closer to me. I took a sip of his wine to urge him again. He took it out of my hand, and in three large gulps, it was gone. He refilled it from the bottle between us. "I think Layla is trying to curse me," he commented in my ear, his tongue stroking around the edge. My fingers fumbled on my bread, which flew halfway across the table. In my fumble, I tipped over my almost-empty water glass. It spilled off the edge and onto my pants.

"Damn it," I hollered. Thankfully it was only water. Using my napkin, I dried myself as much as I could.

"You are so clumsy. I love it," he laughed loudly. I smacked him in the stomach, but his muscles were so dense they were like a brick wall, causing my injured knuckles to throb. "Ouch," I blurted, skimming over the red skin with my other hand.

Malcolm caught the hand and kissed at the red welts. "When we get back, you are getting this examined." He kissed it again and placed it in his lap, keeping it protected from any further damage.

The thrill of him being mine made me tingle. I had no idea that I could be this happy with one person.

The smile that spread over my face was permanent, but Layla was not sharing in my same happiness with her brother. I waved my finger at Logan, who was at the end of the table. He caught my small gesture, pointing at Layla and her scowl; he got what I was suggesting. Logan took her hand and held it on top of the table, mouthing, "I love you." She did the same in return, instantly brightening her mood but ruining Malcolm's in the process. He took down another glass of wine. It was like trying to referee a game of ping pong played by toddlers. With my hand in his lap, I pinched the inside of his thigh. My thumb pursued the spot between his legs. There was no mistaking what I was touching.

He flung his head to me, brows raised high. "What are you doing?" he moaned in my ear.

One side of my mouth tipped up. "Naughty side, remember?" I rasped back, skating my hand up a few inches more.

"You're sinful." His hand that was around my shoulder forced me to him. The way he kissed me wasn't appropriate for the public. I could taste the sweet wine on his tongue. My hand fell from between his legs. My whole body was lax and dizzy from the intensity of it all.

"You two are going to get kicked out if you don't stop soon," Layla vented, turning her bad mood on me. "But then again, it would be best if you left."

Logan shook his head with defeat. We all knew this wasn't going to go well if they kept going back and forth.

Wes hammered his napkin angrily on the table. "Can we please have a nice friendly dinner with everyone? It's rare that we are all together, and since this is Eve's first Christmas with us, we don't want to scare her off to not come back next year," Wes scolded both of them. "And Layla, if Malcolm wants to kiss his girlfriend, for God's sake, let him. You should be happy he found someone. I know the rest of us are." Wes took a mouthful of his wine after his rant. We all followed his lead, not knowing what else to do.

I leaned into Malcolm and said, "He is a great best friend."

"Sure is," he praised with appreciation. "He has always had my back."

After Wes commanded that they stop bickering, we all settled in with our wine and food. Layla was still sulking, throwing mental daggers at Malcolm, but every now and then, she would put on a fake smile. Eventually, they drank so much that they forgot they were mad at each other. And unbeknownst to me, when they had too much to drink, they would slip into speaking Italian. Daphne was telling him a joke, and he could barely keep it together. He was so carefree and full of happiness, his whole body lit up. I could look at him like this for a lifetime.

"You're awfully silent over there. What's going through that smart brain of yours?" James fastened me back into his shoulder, coiling his arm around the front of my neck.

"I like seeing him like this."

"It's because of you," Wes spoke from over James's shoulder. "Don't get me wrong. He normally is great to be around. But he is lighter, freer with you if that makes any sense at all."

"It does."

I sipped on my wine, cuddled into James, with Wes watching over us. The night was late, and I was flushed from all the drinks. James was like a mattress, and my eyes couldn't help but sag.

"We should get going before I have to carry you home." I had somehow ended up on Malcolm's lap in my brief nap.

"No," I yawned. "You're having fun. We can stay."

"Rose is sleeping on Owen, too, and Layla is back to being mad at me. I think it is safe to say we can call it a night." He hauled me to my feet. I clung to his waist as we exited the restaurant. I was too sleepy to stand on my own.

"Wait." I stopped both of us. "I didn't pay."

"*Bambola,* I paid for us," he chuckled.

He had called me doll in Italian, and I loved the way it sounded on his full lips. I repeated the way he said it over in my head. It was almost like a melody, but then it stopped because I realized what he'd said about paying. "Don't distract me with your Italian words. You know I don't like it when you pay for me."

"I do know that." He propelled me forward to keep us moving. He wasn't walking in much of a straight line; the alcohol had been working through his system. "But I made you so uncomfortable earlier that you felt the need to buy a train ticket, which I know wasn't cheap. I owe you that money back. Also, now that we are together, our previous arrangement no longer stands. And before you argue with me, let's talk about this later. I have drunk too much to make any valid points right now."

"Fine." We would be talking about it later, but for now, he was in such a good mood I didn't want to hamper that in any way. I was also tired and had had too many drinks to make any sense either.

He raised an eyebrow. "That was too easy. What are you plotting?"

"We will talk about it later." I winked at him.

The outside had dampened, and my long sleeved shirt was no longer providing me with much protection. Malcolm rubbed up and down on my arms, trying to create some type of heat, but it wasn't working.

The moment we got in the door of the loft, I ran into the room and dove into the bed, trying to get rid of the chill under the covers. Malcolm joined me after getting us water from the kitchen.

He tucked me in under him, our bare legs intertwined. This was my favorite way to fall asleep now. Nobody else could make me feel as safe as he did. "Your legs are freezing!"

"I'm cold-blooded." He was hot on top of me, helping my skin to absorb the heat. "Did everyone go to bed, or are they going to stay up?"

"Everyone went to bed, and Layla made it a point to make sure I saw her go into Logan's room. I don't like that at all because I know what they were doing."

"I know." I kneaded his back in condolence.

It didn't take long for him to lightly breathe in my ear at a steady pace, already asleep. I pouted to myself. I was planning on seeing how far I could test this whole taking it slow thing, but that would have to wait for another night.

Chapter 24

The Christmas morning sun broke through the window of Malcolm's room. Heat pooled in, causing sweat to break around my hairline. Malcolm was on the other side of the bed; it was too hot to sleep next to each other. I got out of bed to get some fresh air out on the patio. When I reached for a cup of coffee, I noticed that my hand had become disfigured overnight. It was twice the size it was yesterday. That wasn't a good sign. It was stiff and sore and difficult to fully grasp the cup with. But I would have to deal with that later; for now, I wanted to enjoy the cool Christmas breeze outside.

Logan was sitting at a bistro table, having the same idea I did. "Mind if I join you?" I muttered. The coffee hadn't worked its way to my brain yet.

"Not at all." He cleared away some newspapers he was reading. "Are you okay? I mean, after yesterday."

"Yes. How is your situation?" I didn't envy Logan right then. I knew Layla and Malcolm were putting him in a tough spot.

He took a sip of his coffee. "I tried to smooth things over with Mal, but you saw both of them last night. I don't think he will ever be completely all right with it, and Layla is Layla and will have the attitude always. It was really bothering me that he didn't know, though. I was the one that had to force Layla into telling him. We could have gotten married, and she would still want to keep it a secret."

"I think as long as both of you are happy, he will come around. It can't be easy for him to have another man step up in her life. He is used to doing it himself. But no more big announcements for a while."

"Thanks for the advice. Happy to have you around. I don't think I have told you that yet." He tipped his mug to me. "Happy Christmas, Eve."

"Merry Christmas, Logan." We sat there in silence, drinking our coffee and enjoying the air. It wasn't an awkward silence. It was the kind that was welcoming and appreciated in the early morning.

We finished our coffee right before everyone stirred.

"Here comes the stampede," I said.

"The silence was nice while it lasted," he agreed.

Layla came skipping up and bounced on Logan's lap. He grunted an "umpfh" sound. "Morning, babe." She had more excitement than one should in the morning without coffee first.

"Morning, love." They began kissing in a way that made me uncomfortable, forcing me to go inside.

My target was the kitchen, but Malcolm caught me by the torso before I could make a step in there. "Where you going?"

"Give you one guess." I looked longingly at the coffee pot.

"Coffee?" He forced my head to him. "You might have a problem."

"There is no such thing." I kissed him softly on the lips.

"I'm sad that I didn't get to see that naughty side of yours last night."

"It's a little hard to see my naughty side when you are passed out."

"I wouldn't have minded." He teased his lips on my neck. His hands found their way under the back of my shirt, crawling up my spine. Arching into him, there was no need for coffee when I had him in the morning.

"Let me get coffee for you since that's why you keep me around anyway." He reached for the mug in my hand but didn't take it. He frowned at my inflamed knuckles. "Your hand is worse. Does it hurt?"

"Yes, but it can wait until we get back." I didn't think it was a big deal, but the way he was reacting made me think he did.

"No. Tomorrow, we are going to the doctor." He picked me

up and lifted me onto the island in the kitchen. Finding an ice packet from the freezer, he skimmed it over my hand. "Don't move, and keep ice on it."

"Why can't I move?" I swayed my shoulders. Saying the words made me want to get up.

"Because I want to keep doing this." He leaned in and kissed me again. I loved the way his lips felt on mine.

"As much as I like watching you two, can we please open gifts?" James called from the couch. "I am going to have a heart attack if we don't get to it soon," He already had a pile of gifts in front of him. All I could picture was a ten-year-old James in red pajamas running around his house early morning on Christmas Day, waking up his parents so he could open gifts, much like now.

Layla and Logan appeared from the balcony with red faces and lips. Malcolm muttered his discontent, but it was clear enough for Layla to hear. She whipped around and kissed Logan in front of us all. Her hands drifted down his shirt and rested on the button of his pants. The kiss was heated and seducing, and poor Logan was taken so off guard by it that he didn't stand a chance.

"God, I can't watch this anymore." Malcolm covered his eyes and spun right back around to his room.

"Layla!" James screeched. "Can you stop the drama for one day? I would like to open gifts and be merry, damn it."

Layla retreated to her room with a slam of the door.

"Could you two try to be nicer to Layla? This isn't exactly easy for her either," Logan scolded Wes and James. "I am already struggling with Mal. It would be helpful if I could get a break from you two. We are family, after all."

"That's exactly the point, Logan." Wes got up and made his way to the center of the room. "There are two families involved here, and it's not like we can go separate ways when you break up. We aren't going to pick sides. Both of you will have to deal with the fallout without us. I also can't even imagine what goes through Mal's mind when he sees you two together. It's his sister, Logan. You do understand that, right?"

"And we all know how difficult Layla is. She has been that way for as long as I have known her, and you have known her for longer," James explained from underneath his pile of gifts. "You are with her now, so you have assumed the responsibility of her actions."

Logan's ears were turning red, and his body was swinging from side to side. He was outnumbered, and I felt bad for him, even though I didn't agree with him either. I knew there would always be a rift unless some resolution was put into place.

"Why don't we all agree on this," I began. "Logan worries about Layla and tries to keep the affection to a minimum in front of Malcolm, at least until he gets more comfortable with it all. I will worry about Malcolm. Let's not talk about what could possibly happen if they break up. How about we all focus on what is happening now."

"I can agree," Logan eagerly said, ready to have some type of remedy. We both looked toward Wes for a response.

"Fine by me. It's on you two now." Wes sat down by James, patiently waiting while James piled his gifts on top of him too.

After thirty minutes, Logan had managed to get Layla out of her room. Malcolm had come out after he changed clothes, and James was happy as he sat amongst his horde of unopened gifts. He gave us all permission to let the opening commence.

When I opened Rose's gift, a giggle escaped. She eyeballed me. "Is there something humorous about my gift?"

"Open yours from me, and you'll figure it out."

She tore into the small box, wrapped in purple paper, and pinched a small gold chain bracelet with gold charms on it between her fingers. Each charm reminded me of a moment in our friendship. She started to laugh too.

"What's so funny?" asked Owen.

I held up my gift—it was the exact same thing I had given Rose. Even most of the charms were the same.

"Great minds," she clucked, tilting her coffee to me. I did the same.

Malcolm hadn't unwrapped anything from his pile yet. He was watching Layla carefully. "Are you going to open anything?"

I urged.

"Sure." He didn't, though.

"You know you begged me to spend Christmas with you, and now it's like you don't even see me here."

"Okay." He kissed the side of my head, oblivious to the words I was saying.

I watched Wes open his gift from James, ignoring Malcolm's attitude. Wes rattled the box. "I don't think it is the usual shirt or tie. What could it be?"

James winked at me. Wes saw the sly gesture. He tantalized James by tearing one corner at a time. James nearly yanked it out of his hands and ripped it open. Finally, the box was open, and Wes gasped at the sight of the book. It was the best reaction. "Is this a first edition?" He carefully opened the pages. "Oh my god, it's signed too! Where did you find this?"

"In a small little bookstore that Eve took me to. I can't take all the credit."

"Yes, he can," I told Wes. "We spent hours in there. He had to pick the right book and knew exactly what it was when he found it."

Wes gleamed. "It was my favorite book, made more special because I married a gardener." He nudged James in the neck and kissed him sweetly.

I placed the small box that held the knife for Malcolm in his lap, nudging it to him eagerly. He opened it halfheartedly, keeping his eyes on Layla as he removed the paper and lid to the box. After a minute of the lid being open, he finally looked down, and his face fell completely flat as he stared at the opal encrusted pocket knife.

"If you don't like it, that's okay." I was not sure what to say to his reaction. Maybe I didn't know him as well as I thought.

"It can't be," he mumbled, flipping up the blade and reading the inscription. He sucked in air between his teeth.

"Can't be what?" I questioned his skepticism.

"Where did you get this?" He balled it up, sealing it in his fingers.

"At a small little store on the north side. It had a bunch of junk in it, but when I saw this, it spoke to me that it should belong to you."

He laid a shaky hand on my cheek and kissed me. He was feverish, though, putting everything into it. His hand tangled in my hair, and somehow I ended up sitting in his lap. His mouth was glued to mine as if I was giving him life, and he wanted to take every ounce of it. He slowed after what felt like a glorious lifetime. His inflamed lips matched mine.

He unfurled his fist, showing me the small knife in his palm. "This knife belonged to my great grandfather, who I was named after. My grandfather, Harvey, gave it to me before he died when I was five. It had been passed down from his father. Harvey never gave it to my dad, perhaps because he knew what a monster he was and that he wouldn't appreciate it as much as I did. I carried this knife around with me everywhere. It was the only thing I had of Harvey's, and that made me feel safe. I don't know if it was out of resentment or cruelty, but Andrew took it away from me when I was seven, along with several of my other treasured items. He told me he had thrown everything away, but like always, he obviously lied about that. I can't believe you brought it back home to me. You have no idea what that means."

I couldn't believe that either. My intention wasn't to bring back a lost heirloom. I only thought it matched him so well.

"And trust me when I say that I very much know you are here." He kissed me again, but I had to move away.

"We won't finish opening gifts if you keep on kissing me like that." I ran my fingers on his jaw. My stomach dipped, and a new hunger surrounded my heart. I knew what it was, but I refused to acknowledge it yet. I handed him the drawing. I didn't know how this one would go over, especially after I had given him what he thought was the best gift in the world. "This one isn't going to be good as a precious family heirloom. Sorry."

"I am sure I will love it."

Suddenly I hated my own work. "I should take it back." I reached for it, but he held it over his head, out of my grasp.

"Doll, it will be great."

He quickly removed the paper so he could see it before I had a chance to run off with the drawing. This time I closed my eyes. I didn't want to see the disappointment on his face.

"You did this?" His voice sang deep with the question.

I opened one eye. "Yes. I know it's not very good. I shouldn't have given it to you."

"Are you joking? This is really good. I don't know what to say."

"No, it's terrible. You don't need to be nice."

He put the frame on the couch. "Eve, stop," he said, smushing my cheeks together. "I love it. I'm keeping it, and it is really good. I couldn't want for anything more, not even the knife, because you made it for me. And I can tell you put a lot of effort into it. This has been the best Christmas. I'm the one who feels bad. You gave me these thoughtful gifts, and all I gave you was a sketchbook and…well, me."

"You are the best gift." My lips found his again. Nobody wanted or cared to bother us in our moment. "So, I should take the knife back, then?" I teased.

"You will have to pry it out of my dead hands." He hid the knife in the front pocket of his jeans. "Let's go for a walk before we eat. Paris has some pretty interesting things. I don't know if you have heard of the Eiffel Tower."

"The Eiffel Tower construction began in 1887 and ended in 1889. It's three hundred and twenty four meters high," I listed off.

"You're like an encyclopedia; it's very sexy." He stood up, taking me with him. "Eve and I are going out alone," he added, in case someone had the urge to go with us.

We went back into his room so I could change. I dug around in my bag for underwear but came up short. "No, no, no! I am going to kill Wes."

"Why?" Malcolm came out of the bathroom, untucking a corner of his shirt that got stuck in his pants. "What did Wes do?"

"He managed to pack everything, including a pair of stilettos," I held them up by the thin crisscross straps, "but he failed to pack any underwear for me."

"Oh, we are definitely not leaving the room."

"You know, for someone who wants to take it slow, you sure don't talk or act like it."

"I am only human. A good looking one, but you're irresistible with underwear. But without and with those shoes…." His hand went up to his jaw, running it over the smooth surface of his skin.

I rolled my eyes at him, yanking a pair of jeans and my boots out of the bag. "Are we counting this as a first date?" I was hoping he would say yes, so we could push some things along.

His chest shook. "No, this walk is just a walk."

"Fine, but remember that I will be wearing nothing under these." I waved the jeans in his face. He raised an eye. I fondled his lower back on my way into the bathroom. He growled back at me.

Chapter 25

The rain from yesterday had dried up, and the sun had made a special showing for Christmas. There weren't too many people out. They were still enjoying the Christmas morning or at mass. Walking hand in hand, we made casual conversation as we headed towards the Eiffel Tower. The large structure came into view; lattice metal worked all the way up to the peak. It was very much what I had expected from seeing pictures and replicas throughout my life, but the actual act of standing in front of it was a different experience.

"I have seen so many amazing things in my life, but for some reason, every time I see this structure, this sense of calm surges through me," Malcolm confessed, "It's probably because I have such fond memories of Paris. Rose's family is originally from France, and they would come here for the holiday. Since all of us were inseparable, we would come here with them. That was among the few times I was away from my parents and where it was all so easy, without troubles." His story gave me a whole new appreciation for the monument. "Remind me to thank Wes for dragging you along, no underwear and all."

I playfully jabbed him on the back of the leg. "I need to use a restroom before we walk around more. Stay," I ordered.

"Yes, ma'am." He saluted me.

I stepped around to one of the giant legs that held up the Eiffel Tower and found a small public toilet. For the middle of the morning, I was amazed that there was nobody on the streets or in the park across the road.

A dark shadow crept up behind me as I was walking into the

bathroom. "I thought I told you to stay."

I turned around, but the face I saw wasn't Malcolm's. Long gray hair was put up into a ratty ponytail; small pieces stuck out from his head. The white beard was filled with crumbs from bread, and a large stomach was bursting out of a red Christmas sweater.

"Dante?"

"Eve. I have been looking for you." He slithered forward as if he were going to attack me, but that was an absurd thought.

"What do you mean? You have my number. You could have called me."

"That's not what I mean, and you know that." I backed away, on the defense. His eyes were deranged. "Where is the relic, Eve? I know you have it."

I stopped moving. My suspicions were right. He did know about it, and he was hungry for its power and strength—I could see it in his face. It had to be what was driving him to act this way.

"I know everything about it, Eve. I've been searching for it my whole career, and you've only been here a short time and have already found it. I should have had you on my team from the beginning, but you would never leave Shawn. But that doesn't matter now. I saw that security video of you and the Archer boy at my exhibit, examining Freydis's sword. I knew you had seen that symbol before, and I have been tracking you for months. I don't know how you obtained it, but I know it's in your possession."

Dante had been my friend and mentor for years. I refused to believe that he had any part in being the one to cause me so much agony; it couldn't be possible. I had trusted him with so much in my past. This version of Dante broke my heart. Regardless, I needed to accept it, and then maybe he would go away, or Malcolm would show up and scare him off.

"It's a myth, Dante. I have searched everywhere for it. I don't have it. Your sources are wrong," I implored, trying to talk him off the ledge.

"No!" he yelled, hopefully, audible enough for Malcolm to check to see what the commotion was about. "Wars have been started over this relic. There are texts that talk about the power of the amulet. It gives you strength, protection, and absolute control. I wasted my life on it. Hand it over, Eve."

He howled and hurled me across the grass with all of his strength. My feet caught on their heels, and I fell backwards. I tried to brace my fall with my hands, but the injured one was already so weak that my head bounced off the cement. The contact was blinding. My head swirled, trying to find a place to focus. I rolled onto my side but cried out. It was too much strain on my arm.

"Tell me where it is!" he shouted, and this time I knew Malcolm could hear.

"Go to hell," I cursed at him.

Dante kicked me in my side with the point of his large shoe. "Not until I get the relic."

He kicked again. This time there was a crack, and blood pooled in my mouth. I couldn't do much, not even talk. He could beat me all he wanted, but he wouldn't dare to do anything more because I held the information he needed. I was waiting for another blow when Dante fell to the side, his eyes shut. He was out cold next to me. Malcolm stood over him with tight fists. I whimpered with relief and pain.

"God, Eve." He crouched. His hands were flying, not knowing where to place them. "Where did he hurt you?"

"Everywhere." The blood dripped out of the side of my mouth. I spat it in the grass, holding back tears. It was easy when I was this bitter and filled with adrenaline.

"I need to call the police." He dialed a number and spoke in French too fast for me to understand. For a brief moment, I saw him shake. I didn't know if it was from anger or fear. After this week, both of those emotions had to be in the forefront. He hung up on them and put his full attention on me. "I should have gotten here sooner. This wouldn't have happened if I had."

"I am fine. Just make sure he doesn't wake up."

I watched Dante closely, not that I would be doing anything if he became conscious. I tried to set myself up but fell back. My head was dizzy, and the motion made me nauseous. Two large blows to the back of my head in a matter of days couldn't have been a good thing. Sirens blared in the distance. I hoped they were for me because all I wanted to was sleep and not wake up for a very long time. I closed my eyes.

"No, doll. You need to stay awake until the ambulance gets here." He kissed the top of my brow, keeping his hand on my forehead. But his eyes were trained on Dante, checking for signs of consciousness.

The police arrived, along with the ambulance. I was completely lost in the conversations and interrogations. For some reason, it never crossed my mind that my knowledge in reading the French language didn't translate to speaking it. I was only able to pick up a few phrases and words here and there.

The police officer spoke to me in English, making it easier for me to keep up. "Do you know this man?" he asked, as the emergency techs loaded Dante into a van, cuffed to a stretcher.

I choked on the taste of my blood before answering, "I do. His name is Dante Rich."

Malcolm came to attention. "That was Dante? Oh, Eve…," he began, sympathetically.

"Don't. Not right now." A bubble rose in my throat. The rage I had been carrying since Dante attacked me was evolving into heartbreak. I couldn't handle his empathy right now. It was going to gut me open.

"Of course." He stroked my lower back, not pressuring me any further.

I was loaded into the back of the ambulance once I was done with the police.

"I can't ride to the hospital with you, but I will take a taxi and meet you there," Malcolm told me when he didn't get in the back.

"I could be awhile at the hospital. You should go home and enjoy the rest of Christmas." I didn't want him to waste the day away in the waiting room for no reason.

"That was the most absurd thing I've ever heard you say." He stepped away from the back doors so the police could close me in the vehicle.

The pounding in my head and questioning of the paramedics,

along with the blaring sound of sirens, prevented me from thinking in detail that my attacker was Dante, the man I had revered for so many years. All I kept on repeating in my head was, how could he do this to me? Was the amulet worth destroying friendships and livelihoods over? Not for me, it wasn't.

Chapter 26

I was wheeled inside and into a large communal room that only had two other people in it. Since it was Christmas morning, the hospital wasn't busy, and it made the process quick. The doctor came in shortly after X-rays with my prognosis. Malcolm was able to join me at that point.

"You have a fracture at your wrist," the doctor spoke in English, "and we will have to reset a few of your fingers. Your accident from earlier in the week has damage, too. There are two hairline fractures on your middle and pointer fingers at the knuckle. We need to put you in a cast for eight weeks. I can do that here, and when you get back to London, you can make arrangements to remove it. You also have two cracked ribs, which will cause bruising and discomfort, but there isn't much I can do about that. The headache you have is normal after taking a hit like that. Getting some rest and pain medication will help."

"When you say reset my fingers, do you mean breaking them back into place?" The sound of that was terrifying to me. I had never broken a bone before or had a doctor readjust anything. The idea of a chiropractor alone scared me.

"Shall we?" He indicated that he was indeed taking my hand to put everything back in place.

I turned my head and closed my eyes. Malcolm bent his arm around my head and forced my face to his chest. He had been reserved the whole time. He was skilled in masking whatever mental state he was in. I blamed it on his childhood. The jolt of pain was substantial, but it was the sound of the bones cracking back that put a shiver on my spine.

I was fitted for a cast. It felt bulky on my weak bones, almost like there was an anchor tied to it. I got instructions on how to take care of it—or I thought they were instructions. The nurse barely spoke English, but Malcolm understood her well enough. She also handed me a bottle of pain medication.

They released me to the real world, which was more threatening than when I had entered the hospital. I had doubts about everything. Who exactly could I trust now? I had thought Dante was one of those people, but I was wrong, and that had made me feel humiliated and defiled.

Tears burned my eyes as I kept my vision out the window of the taxi Malcolm had waiting for me at the hospital entrance. I didn't want him to see the bubbling water. He reached for me, but I dodged out of the way. All I wanted was to be left alone.

The trip from the hospital to the apartment was too short. I needed more time to gather myself before I faced everyone and the million questions that would inevitably be asked. Malcolm paid and sped around to my side to open my door. My tired bones slowly made my way to the alley door. If I felt this terrible now, I didn't want to know how it would be tomorrow.

"Mal, can I go straight into the room and let you tell everyone what happened? I can't handle explaining it all, and you should also enjoy your Christmas. I know Rose and James put in a lot of work for the dinner. Don't let me ruin that."

"You haven't ruined anything," he mewed, "and we can still have a Christmas. I can bring food to the room and stay with you. I think everyone would understand."

"I want to be by myself, Malcolm." The side of his mouth slightly curved down with a frown.

When we entered the apartment, I avoided the conversations from the kitchen, thanks to Malcolm, and beelined it to the bedroom. I ran the water in the bathroom sink and washed down the pain medication. My headache was increasing as the adrenaline from the day had drained away. I tried not to think about all of it, but I couldn't shut off my brain. Was this relic really worth all the destruction and all the hassle on my end? I knew the answer to that before I even finished my thought. Yes, it was worth it. But I should have known more about it before I decided to wear it. It was too late for that now. I couldn't change the past. I had to be prepared for what was to come. There were more people out there that knew about the relic. I knew Dante wasn't the only one. The thought of Dante undid me. I let go of the tears I was holding back all morning.

A small knock, then a crack of light, came from the door. I covered my head with the sheets so Malcolm couldn't see me. "Hey, doll. I know you wanted your space and time alone, but I wanted to check in on you and make sure you don't need anything. Also, everyone is very concerned. I think they wanted to make sure you were alive."

"You can tell them I am alive," I sniffled under the cover. "I need to sleep for a day or two."

Malcolm took hold of the sheet and brought it to my neck. His fingers collected the tears. I felt like lately all I did was cry in front of him. He sunk in the bed and laced in next to me. I gathered myself, not wanting to give in to any more tears.

"You're allowed to be sad, Eve. You can show me that side." He watched me with intensity, sweeping his eyes over every inch of my face.

"That is all I have been doing." I wiped away the remainder of my damp face on the edge of the sheet.

"I don't think that at all. You have endured so much. Your resilience is impressive. I actually admire it. I hate that this has been the worst trip for you. I wanted it to be memorable, but not in this way. I will make arrangements to go back home tomorrow."

"What?! No way. This is my first time in Paris, and I want to enjoy it." I refused to let Dante ruin Paris for me. "I don't want this memory to be associated with this holiday. I need to stay. But first, I might need to sleep. And three more things."

"Anything," he urged, so eager to help me in any way.

"One. I need you to enjoy the rest of your day. I expect to hear laughter out there. Two. Save me a pie. And three. A kiss."

"The first one will take some effort, and the second one is already done. But the third...."

He was on my lips before he could finish the sentence. They

flew over me, but I wanted more, like always. The pain pills were working their way through me, and I was able to swing my leg around his hips and pull him on top of me. I would never grow tired of the feeling of his muscles. His mouth found a spot below my ear that drove me to the edge. He slipped off the strap of my tank top, making a pathway down my collar bone. My hand found the button of his pants and unbuttoned them before he could stop me. He didn't, though. He let me slink them off his legs. I thrust up once they were off and led him in closer. His hands and lips fluttered all around my stomach. Holding onto my sides, he danced his tongue along my hips. His head dipped lower, and with his hands climbing up, they grasped both sides of my ribs. I tried to suppress my whimper from where I was kicked, but the sound caught his ears. His hands and lips stilled on my skin.

"I'm fine," I said, holding in a spasm of pain. "Keep going."

"Not a chance. I already feel guilty for not preventing this, and I don't want to be responsible for any more of your pain." He rolled off the bed, taking his pants with him. "Also, as much as I want to continue, you are high on drugs, and that's not how I want all this to go." He drifted into my ear. "I want you to feel everything."

I made another whimpering sound, but for a different reason.

"What can I say. I am a little naughty too." He smirked at me, fastening his pants and leaving the room with a cocky stride.

I fidgeted in bed for a few hours. Malcolm had my blood boiling in all the right ways. He could take my mind off everything that was going on. A burst of laughter came from the other side of the door. I was glad their Christmas wasn't ruined by my misfortunes. I took another pill, without water, and attempted to sleep, but it wasn't working.

I was hit with a large craving for pie, and I knew myself well enough to know that if I didn't feed that craving, I would be up all night thinking about it.

I limped out of bed, straightening my hair, but I knew the waves were out of control and untamable. I went straight to the kitchen and found a whole pie in the fridge and a fork. I was definitely high, thinking I could eat it all by myself. I found Malcolm sitting on one of the big reading chairs and made myself comfortable in his lap. I didn't even bother to see who was around me or care to listen to their conversation. He kissed my shoulder without a word while I dug into my dessert.

"You look crazy." James pointed to me.

"I am two pain pills in and hungry. Leave me alone." I poked the air at him with my fork and scowled. He held up his hands, taking my threat seriously. Their conversation carried on like I wasn't even there, and that was fine by me.

I only made it four bites in before I got sleepy. I put the pie on an end table closest to me and nuzzled into Malcolm, too tired to go to bed. He didn't mind that I was using him for one purpose. He nestled me to him, which made it easy to fall asleep.

Chapter 27

I rolled from my back over to my side but immediately had to change directions. The medication had stopped working sometime in my sleep, and now every muscle was aching. The last I remembered, I was sleeping in Malcolm's lap, and now I was in his bed, his warm body next to me. I reached out, my fingers caressing the side of his hip.

"Don't do that." That was not the voice of Malcolm.

I opened my eyes and let out a sharp scream. "What the hell are you doing here, James?"

"I wanted to make sure you weren't scratched by a zombie because last night you were a pie-eating zombie."

"When there is pie, I can't help what crazed beast comes out of me," I joked, hoping that my lighter demeanor would ease him.

"What's going on in here?"

Malcolm came out of the bathroom, water dripping off his body. It was almost like slow motion, the way each drop of water descended down his golden tan skin. I was jealous of how those drops caressed the hard planes of his body. They suddenly made me thirsty. I wanted to drink the water right off him. Every muscle twisted with every curve of his body. The small towel he wore was only hiding what I could assume was his best feature. His hair fell across his forehead in a glorious mess. The water darkened his eyelashes, highlighting his aquamarine eyes.

"Oh my god, heaven, and stars." James pinched my thigh. "I know I should look away, but I literally can't."

"Neither can I." We feasted on him.

"James, what are you doing in bed with Eve?" A small twinge of disapproval flashed in his eyes but went away suddenly.

"I wanted to make sure she was okay. What are you doing, wet and sexy?" He bit his lower lip.

"I heard Eve scream and rushed out of the shower, but now you two are acting like I am on display." He turned around to go back into the bathroom.

"Good lord, the back is better than the front!" James hollered.

I agreed, both of us rumbling like we were spectators at a sporting event and applauding the skill of athleticism.

Malcolm faced us and walked backwards to the bathroom.

"I really thought he was lucky to be with you, but now I am thinking you are the lucky one. That boy is glorious," he confessed once Malcolm was behind closed doors.

"Yeah, I am very lucky."

"On a serious note," he sat up cross legged, "are you okay? You have been through a lot this week. How's your sanity?"

"It's ruffled but still sturdy. I think my body has taken the biggest toll." I held up my newly casted hand. "But honestly, there might be some type of breakdown headed my way, and that will involve crying, drinking, and lots of food."

"When that happens, I will be right there doing it with you. You are my best friend. I'm always here for you."

"You only like me because I send you pictures of Malcolm."

"That is an added perk." He high-fived my broken hand. "I'm being truthful, though. Whenever you're ready to talk, I am here and don't bury it for too long. That will do worse damage."

"I love you." I had never spoken more truth in my life. He had been my rock since I moved to England and had gotten me through the ups and downs of my new dramatic life.

"You too, Eve. Now get up and brush your teeth and hair. We all want to see non-zombie Eve and spend the day with her."

"Fine, but I do need to take it easy today. Doctor's orders."

"We can do that. Skip the meds, and let's drink Bloody Marys and have leftovers."

That sounded better than what I had planned, sleeping all day and trying not to think about Dante and this cursed relic. "I'll see you out there."

Malcolm stepped into the room right when James left. He was fully dressed, and his hair was now damp.

"Where'd the towel go?" He scoffed at me for a response. I was serious. I wanted the towel back. "James has convinced me to be sociable and drink Bloody Marys. I am going to take a shower and to try to be halfway presentable."

"You need help in the shower?" He gave me his hand to get out of bed. I had to take it, knowing I wasn't able to get out of it on my own. Once I got to my feet, I was more stiff than I thought.

"I would love some help in the shower, but that might be going too fast for you."

He stepped forward, hooking his fingers into the elastic of my pants. Since Wes had forgotten to pack me underwear, there was nothing blocking me from being exposed once he took them off. He was hesitant but then dragged them down my legs until they fell to the floor on their own. He kept his eyes on mine. His chest rose when he tugged on my shirt, and he carefully took it off me. He left my eyes, going over every inch of my curves.

"Shit." His hand ran between my breasts and around my back. He stepped forward and splayed his hand on my bottom. My bare chest tickled on his shirt at his stomach. "You are so damn beautiful. All I want to do is worship you. I thought I could do this, but I honestly don't think I can. Do you really need my help?" His restraint was impressive.

"No. I can do it. I might need help getting dressed, but I'll let you know."

I sauntered away from him, swinging my hips. When I shut the door to the bathroom, he was standing in the same spot with glossed-over eyes.

Taking a shower with a cast was more complicated than I expected. I got more water on the floor than in the shower. I had to soak up the mess with towels, saturating three of them. It was also difficult getting dressed with one hand and bruised ribs. I was hoping that someone could tackle my hair. If it wasn't untangled while wet, it would never untangle once it dried.

I crept out into the living room with my brush in hand. Only

Malcolm, Rose, Wes, and James were out in the large space. "Where are the others?"

"Layla, Logan, and Daphne left early, and Owen is recovering from last night," explained Rose.

"Whoa. You let the girls leave with Logan? I know I was out, but it wasn't for that long."

Malcolm got up from his chair and took the brush from me. He began combing my strands before I could ask for help. "Layla didn't really give me a choice, and Daphne promised to chaperone. Logan said he would help the girls with moving more stuff out of our father's house."

"You aren't worried about them running into them?" I was surprised by the uncharacteristic change in his feelings.

"No." He yanked off a hair tie from the handle of the brush. "They let me know that they went to Spain for Christmas and would be there for the week." His fingers flew nimbly across my hair.

"So, it's the adults for the next four days." Wes pushed his feet under James.

I was thrilled about that. Not that there was anything wrong with the girls or Logan, but Malcolm couldn't fully relax when the girls were around. He was always keeping one eye on them, making sure they had everything they needed. Malcolm twisted the tie around the ends of my hair and rested a perfect braid over my shoulder. I didn't question his knowledge on how to braid. He did have to raise two girls.

I sat next to Wes on the large couch. He put his hand on my head, and I snuggled into him as comfortably as I could. Malcolm handed me a Bloody Mary with a straw. I drank it quickly, needing something to take the edge off my discomfort.

"Eve, I have to talk about this," Rose said, taking a sip of the thick red juice. "How could Dante do this to you? I thought he really respected you."

Malcolm was back in the kitchen, making me another drink before I could ask for another. I was hoping he would hurry because I needed his guidance on what to say to them. We couldn't tell them the real reason. "I...I don't know."

"In honesty," Malcolm spoke up, "this has to do with the project Eve and I are working on. We have come across a new discovery that could be much bigger than new books or a step up in our careers. We have evidence of wars beginning and ending. The current events of history that we all know could be changed by this if we can gather all the research and do the detailed work. Money and power would come along to whoever breaks the news. Dante had been doing work on it for his entire career, keeping it in the dark, knowing the greatness of the discovery. He found out that Eve and I have been doing our own work, and he got greedy and power hungry. We have made great strides, and Dante has not. We can only speculate that he wanted to steal our work and wouldn't take no for an answer."

Malcolm was right—Dante became power hungry, and it was probably in both aspects of the meaning, mystically and concretely. If he ended up figuring out how he could draw the power from the relic, it would bring a source of control that I didn't even know or understand. It was hard to imagine the possibilities when I couldn't even get the damn thing to work. However, even without the so called power, Dante would rise quickly to the top with the perspicuous knowledge of the vast impact it had over numerous cultures and religions.

"I never knew that being a historian and an archivist was so competitive and dangerous." Wes's mocking was clearly laced with sarcasm. We should've had the safest jobs out there, sitting behind books and research papers.

"That goes to show you the significance of our discovery," Malcolm shot right back. "And before you ask, we are not going to say anything to anyone until we have all the facts. We definitely can't tell you now for your own safety."

"But Dante is in jail. The threat should be gone." James challenged Malcolm's reasoning.

"I don't think he is working alone," Malcolm confessed. "Who does he associate with at work, Rose?"

"He has a whole team of people, not to mention the director and other historians and museum professionals. The list is endless, really."

"That's not much of a lead. By the time we went through the list, I am afraid the other person would come forward." Malcolm came back to his chair with drinks in hand.

"So what am I supposed to do? Wait around until someone else finds me and beats me for information?"

Wes flinched with my bluntness, but that was the truth. I was the one with the relic, and no one in their right mind would go after a man as strong as Malcolm.

"I won't let anything else happen to you." Malcolm commanded it with so much conviction that I wanted to believe him, but I knew that wasn't the truth. I didn't point that out to him, though—my attacks had taken a toll on his ego, especially when he was so protective.

"Regardless," said Rose, fiddling with the toothpick of her olive, "shouldn't you report this? Let the authorities know what is going on?"

"The French authorities know a part of it now. I don't want to relinquish what we have collected and start an investigation. It could literally create a war if it got out, especially when we don't have all the research." I was hoping that Dante was sane enough to not reveal anything to the police, but I had clearly misjudged him before.

"I don't like this at all." Rose crossed her legs. "Is this worth risking your life over?"

"Yes." I didn't hesitate. I had thought about that all last night and the answer was easy, no matter how many outcomes I played out in my head.

"Malcolm, do you agree with her?" she asked condescendingly.

"I am sure Eve has thought about this more than I have, but I have been thinking about this non-stop for months, and I do agree with her. Eve and I need to protect this finding at all costs. Don't get me wrong, I hate seeing her like this. It eats away at me constantly. All I want to do is take away the pain and take out every single person involved, but this is bigger than all of us."

It was the first time he'd openly talked about it. We'd put off that conversation for some time, and I was truly afraid that he would disagree with me and make me choose between him and the relic.

"I don't like this, but I trust both of you, and if you say all this is worth it, then I will support you." James and Wes agreed with Rose, and that ended the conversation.

James and Malcolm had gone to the patisserie and cafe that were in the building to get us something to eat. Wes turned to me once they left. "I know you are done talking about this, but I want to make sure you know what you are doing."

"I do, Wes. I believe what I am doing is the right thing." If I didn't, I would be ripping the amulet off and trying to figure out ways to destroy it.

"All right. Then we need to arrange self-defense classes for you when we get back. I don't think you should be unprotected either, so I don't plan on giving you much space."

"I think self-defense classes are a great idea, but—"

"No. Don't argue with me about sticking to your side when Malcolm or James aren't around. I don't think you understand. If anything serious happened to you, Malcolm would not make it out on the other side. He would never be able to bounce back, and if I am being honest, neither would James. James has had my group of friends, and they have welcomed him openly, but it's not easy to come into a group that has been friends since childhood. He never had a close friend until you came along." Wes put his hand on top of mine. "You can't devastate them, Eve. I won't let you."

His plea was heartbreaking, but he was right. I couldn't do that to that either of them. "Fine. But you have to do the classes with me."

He smirked. "Okay. I need to get back into shape anyway. This might motivate me. Also, so we have everything out in the open, I would be devastated too.

~*~

I was making myself another drink, trying to numb the pain, but I was going to need some meds soon.

James and Malcolm came barreling inside. They had four bags of food between them. "You do realize there are only six of us now?" I questioned with a lifted eyebrow.

"We weren't given a choice. It's one of the perks of being their landlord." Malcolm took a gulp of my drink before putting down the bags.

"Could also have something to do with the baristas flirting with Malcolm," James added.

I narrowed my eyes in on him. I knew it happened a lot—he was godly, after all. But now that we were together, there was a layer of possessiveness that laid on the surface of my brain.

"Don't be upset, Eve. You couldn't help yourself either." He gave me a charming smile that almost blew my pants right off.

"Ugh." I threw a piece of cheese at his face. It missed and hit his shoulder. He picked up the piece and tossed it in the trash across the room, making the shot.

He shoved his hands in the back pockets of my pants. "You have nothing to worry about, you know that?"

I stuck out my bottom lip. He caught it with his teeth, gently working on it to get me closer. It worked. I met his teeth with my tongue. He opened his mouth and let me explore but retreated before I wouldn't let him stop.

"You really shouldn't get jealous. I could never find another woman who kisses the way you do."

I flushed with embarrassment. "Sorry."

"Trust me, it's nothing to be sorry about. Now, what can I get you to eat?" He served out several breaded treats.

"I'm not hungry." I moved slowly and carefully away from him. I was uncomfortable, but I didn't want to complain about it.

"Wait, wait." He stepped out in front of me. "The only thing you have eaten the last day and a half is four bites of pie, and olives and cheese from the Bloody Mary. You'd tell me if something was wrong, right?"

"Of course, I would. All I need is to rest up so we can go out tomorrow. Don't worry too much."

I made my way to the large chaise lounge, thinking it would be more comfortable on my ribs than the couch. Wes turned on a show about a psychic detective and put a blanket over me. Owen stumbled out of his room for the first time all day. His skin was an awful shade of green, and his hair was racked with sweat. He flopped onto the chair next to me. He grunted twice at me and then once at Rose. She seemed to know what that meant because she brought him a plate of food, coffee, and a Bloody Mary.

Malcolm was the last one to join us. He held out a coffee mug for me with a large smile, like he'd made some great achievement. I took a sip. Richly sweet sugar hit my tongue, forcing me to immediately spit it back out. "What did you do to it?"

"I thought you liked sugar and cream in your coffee?" He was dumbly stumped by my reaction.

"I do, but I don't like the whole eight pound bag in it. I do actually want to live after I drink it." Sugar coated my mouth. I drank half my Bloody Mary so that the acidity would help get rid of the taste.

"I told you," James snorted through belly rolling laughs.

"I love that you tried, but you might want to leave the coffee making to the professionals, and you have solidified yourself in never cooking for me."

Kissing his palm and wrist, I carefully shifted forward so he could sit behind me. When he got comfortable, I covered most of myself and him with the blanket. His hand went under my shirt; his pinkie slid under my pants. I stiffened. The pinkie creased into the band. The rest of his hand smoothed out on my stomach. His thumb thoughtlessly moved in spirals around my belly button. I fell back into him, enjoying the peace for the rest of the day.

Chapter 28

I was having a showdown with a pair of scissors. I really didn't want to cut the sleeves off my shirts so I could wear them, but I had to be able to wear something over the next three days, and it was far too cold to wear a tank top. I picked up the scissors. I could reuse the same shirt for the remainder of the time. Sorting through my pile, I tried to eliminate all but one, but Wes had packed all my favorite tops. A large sweater floated over the pile from above me.

"We can share for the rest of the week. Plus, I am sure your jacket won't fit over your cast."

I held Malcolm's sweater to me. It was going to be gigantic, but I thought if I paired it with leggings and boots, it would work fine.

Malcolm helped me to slip the sweater over my head, releasing my hair from the collar. "Do you want your hair up or down?"

"Down is fine. It will help keep me warm."

"I can think of other ways to keep you warm." His eyebrows moved up and down, causing his dark hair to bounce across his forehead.

I chuckled at his ridiculous gesture and drug him out the doors of the building to the bitter cold air. I had been waiting a lifetime to see the treasures of the Louvre, and today was finally the day. Walking briskly to the museum, we were lucky enough to not have to wait in line outside. Europe had known how to do museums properly. They were big and vast, every room filled with pieces of history and artwork that were unsurmountable to me.

We were discussing a time to meet up in the massive lobby when a heavy tap landed on my shoulder. I turned to face a thick arm covered in tattoos. The dark ink ran right under the black sleeve of a shirt and up to the collar.

"Tucker?" I gasped with surprise.

"Eve! I knew it was you. I saw the hair in the cameras, and it's unmistakable." Tucker's light brown hair was cut short at the sides and longer on top. He'd grown since the last I saw him. He was almost the size of Malcolm, but his muscles were bigger and more bulging. He was more attractive now, but I knew I wasn't his type. He would be more interested in James or Wes. Tucker met my height to give me a quick embrace. He wasn't much of a toucher, but after six years of not seeing each other, contact was required.

"You saw me in the cameras? What are you even doing here? Last I saw you was at the end of sophomore year. You were moving to Canada."

Malcolm took a step into me, his hip pressing up on my side. I secured my hand on his lower back.

"I finished school in Canada and moved to France. I'm the assistant director of security here." It was only then I noticed that there was a small earpiece in his ear with a corked wire dangling behind it. "What about you?"

"I live in London. We are here on holiday. This is my boyfriend, Malcolm." That was the first time I had told anyone that wasn't in our inner clan that Malcolm was my boyfriend, and it easily fired off my tongue. "Malcolm, Tucker and I used to be neighbors in college."

"Nice to meet you, mate." Malcolm grasped his hand firmly and gave a hearty handshake. Tucker returned it. Being in security suited Tucker—he had the build and the appearance for it. I wouldn't want to come face to face with him if I was trying to steal from the museum. I smirked inwardly at the fact I had stolen two artifacts and gotten away with it without encountering someone like Tucker.

"These are my friends, Wes and James." Apparently, Rose

and Owen had left in the midst of our conversation, not wanting to wait any longer. Tucker held onto Wes's hand for a very long time. He smiled widely when Wes made his introductions.

James took a sheltering step in front of Wes. "I'm his husband, James." He broke their connection. Tucker took his hand flimsily for a brief moment but never took his eyes off Wes. James was on the verge of a battle, willing to fight for what was his.

"I won't keep you, Eve. I have to get back. But call me to catch up." He picked a card from his back pocket and handed it to me. "You should also check out the paintings in the Italy room. There is one in there that has always reminded me of you." He fingered another card and passed it over to Wes. "Call me if you get bored."

He winked at him and disappeared through a door to a secure room. That was Tucker, bold and completely out there on getting the things he wanted.

James's mouth flew open in disbelief. "Can you believe him? He was hitting on Wesley right in front of me!"

"That's what I have to deal with every day. Now you know what it's like." Wes crinkled up the card in his hand, but the smirk on his lips led me to believe he didn't mind the attention at all.

They bickered back and forth, getting Malcolm involved in their argument. I waited patiently for them to finish. My hand on Malcolm's back followed his muscles. I loved how they created a ridge from his spine. Even over his thick sweater, I could fondle the edges. My thumb hooked in his back pocket, and I cupped his meticulously formed ass. He cocked an eyebrow at me, and I squeezed a little tighter. The cold line that he typically wore on his mouth spread all the way up his temples, showing teeth. That was a smile worth paying millions for.

He removed my hand and integrated it into his. "Let's get out of here before they make a scene, and you grab me in more inappropriate places." He leaned down, with his lips hot on my hair. "Not that I mind. Want to go to the Italian paintings? I want to see what reminds Tucker of you."

I nodded, sucking on my bottom lip—it was hard to stop the habit after it got cut. I had wanted to see the painting also, curious as to what it could be, and if I would even know it if I saw it.

The paintings in the large rooms were spectacular. I wished I had the skill and technique of these artists, especially when canvases were as large as the walls, depicting detailed scenes. The way the fabric was layered on the clothing was so realistic. I could admire how they made the material look so shiny and flowing for hours. I roamed the long hallway, eyeing all the pieces. Malcolm had crossed to the other side. He was studying another mural with his hands behind his back, lost in whatever thoughts he was having.

A painting a few frames over caught my eye. A woman wielding a small dagger was standing naked in a field. Red hair that was like cooled embers was tangled wildly around her face and shoulders. The face of the woman was nearly identical to mine. I took a step closer. Her nose was slightly longer, and her jaw was more oval, but it was me if I were a Renaissance painting. At the woman's feet, in the yellow and white flowered fields, was a man with his chest cut open. Dark grey clouds stormed over the scene. Warriors surrounded the woman, and more bodies were sprawled on the ground. It reminded me of the drawing I had done on the way back from Hampton Court when I first found the amulet, but the woman in my portrait was different. She was smaller and more savage. I could still picture her fierce face.

"That woman could be your twin." Malcolm stepped up beside me. "That's bizarre. I mean, she has a different jaw and body shape, but…." Malcolm was completely entranced in the woman.

"Do you think I'm related?" I asked numbly as cold air skipped along the back of my neck. There was a small plaque next to the painting. "Unknown artist. Painted in 1600s, depicting a story of a Grecian woman in 600 AD, who was known to be the guardian of her village," I read out loud.

"Eve." He reached out to touch the painting, but I hit his hand away. "Look what's around her neck."

I examined her neck but didn't see what he was seeing. "There is nothing there." Malcolm pushed me forward till my nose was almost touching it. There was a slight darkening of skin right between her breasts. The shadow formed into the edges of an amulet. The paint was faded, but a thin chain wrapped around her neck, securing it into place. My heart stopped—not even one single beat. I knew what this painting meant, but I didn't want to believe it.

"I...I...." My legs moved before my brain did. They lunged back and down the hall, running away from the painting, away from it all. Unfortunately, my injuries didn't allow me to go very fast or far. I only made it to the end of the room before Malcolm pivoted in front of me.

"I can't, Mal," I exploded, getting the attention of several people.

He cradled my head to quiet me down. "You don't have to now. But you had to have known that you were a part of this, that the amulet belonged to you. You're the only one that can wear it, let alone touch it. The painting is further proof that you are her descendant. There is no mistaking that you're related to that woman."

He was right, and I wondered how long ago he had put those pieces together and not told me. I, on the other hand, hadn't always known it because the relic hadn't worked for me. The only thing it had done was cause me trouble. "Tell me we will figure this out, and I'll be okay," I pleaded. I needed to hear that it would all be all right from him because I couldn't believe it myself.

"I will be with you every step of the way, and I will do everything possible to keep you safe. I promise. I've never been so sure of anything in my life." He pressed his mouth on mine to seal his promise. "Since you aren't ready to accept all of this, let's go knock the crowd of people out of the way so we can see the Mona Lisa. And when you are ready, I'll be right here to talk about everything."

I didn't think I would ever be ready to accept any of this, but I knew I had to. The longer I put it off, the more dangerous the unknown would become.

Chapter 29

We were sitting on the train back to London. Malcolm's head was resting on my shoulder, and his lashes fluttered with some type of dream he was having. I was trying to finish the sentence of my book, but the thought of the relic was preventing me from going any further. I hadn't once spoken about it over the last three days. I still wasn't ready to fully grasp what it all meant for me. I wished the train would change directions and send me back to Paris, where Malcolm had left a rose on my pillow every morning, and we had strolled by the Seine, enjoying my complete avoidance of real life.

"Don't be irrational, Rose," Owen demanded. They'd been having a disagreement about where to spend the New Year the whole train ride back. Owen wanted to go see his parents and brother in Finland, and Rose wanted to stay in the city. James would glance up from his book every few minutes to listen to them, and then would roll his eyes at me. Wes was peacefully clueless, listening to music.

"Eve, no!" Malcolm mumbled in his sleep, wrenching open his eyes, fully awake. He was lost and panicked, but then found me next to him, and he exhaled with relief.

"Having a nightmare?"

He kissed me before answering. I would never grow tired of how his lips felt on mine. "Yes." His hand fell to my inner thigh. "But I don't want to talk about it. Let's talk about what we are doing for New Year's Eve. I was thinking about going to Edinburgh."

"Don't tell me you own a house there too?" I wouldn't have

been surprised if he did.

"Not in Scotland. I was going to get a hotel room."

"Well, have fun and a happy New Year." I played with his hand on my thigh, making his fingers dance.

"You are coming with me, so I know I will have fun. We are going to spend a few days alone and get to know each other better. I have a few ideas in mind of what I want to do." His hand dipped lower between my legs. I threw my head back against the seat, biting back a blissful melody. "What do you say? Come with me to Scotland, and I will show you what spending alone time with me means."

"Are you trying to bribe me into going with you?" My knees shuffled slowly together with gratification.

"Absolutely." He smiled wickedly, his eye trained on the way my breasts moved from the motion of his hand.

"It's working." He didn't have to bribe me. If Scotland was going to be half as good as this trip, I would've gone. But if Malcolm was ready to show me another side of him, the side I had been waiting for, that was a bonus.

"Fantastic." He peeled his hand away from my thigh.

The train jerked to a stop right as Malcolm's phone went off. He pulled the device out of his backpack and answered it, and transitioned into speaking French. All I caught was that he was speaking to a police officer. James and Wes helped me with our suitcases as we stepped out onto the platform with the group. Malcolm spoke fast, visibly troubled even after he stopped talking, and clutched the back of his neck. Before he spoke, his face went blank. The news he had wasn't good. I knew that bland expression well.

"Dante killed himself this morning in his jail cell. I don't want to go into detail, but they are calling it a suicide."

I couldn't move; my legs felt like they were weighted with sandbags. How could Dante do that? Was he that far gone that he felt like his life had to end if he didn't have the amulet? I couldn't, or didn't want to believe that. It wasn't the Dante I knew—but then again, none of it was. Despite what he had done to me, Dante had been a major influence in my career and a friend. I wanted to see him pay for what he did, but I didn't want him dead—I wanted justice. There was a harsh sting of remorse, underlined with regret and bitterness for his loss.

Everyone was talking at once, but it was all white noise to me. Dante was alive a few days ago, and now he was gone. Somehow, as dense as my legs felt, I had managed to walk out of the train station and was out on the street in the wet snow. I waved goodbye haphazardly to my friends, or what I thought was them, and stumbled to the road, not really paying attention to where I was going.

"Eve, wait up." Malcolm jogged over to me.

Without any warning or sign, I cried. He held me to his chest. I couldn't tell if it was my tears or the snow that had soaked his shirt. But regardless, he stood there with his hands on my head and let me take out all my feelings on him. "I don't even know why I am crying. He did betray me, after all."

His chin settled on top of my head. "Because even with the betrayal, he was still your friend at one point in time, and you cared for him."

"I hate it all," I sniffled. Maybe I needed to accept the fact that Dante was deranged and let him go. It would do me nothing to continue to grieve over a man who didn't care about me. "Let's get you inside before you catch a cold. I got you all wet with my tears. I also forgot to say thank you for the week. It was really special to me, despite the injuries and casualties."

"You don't need to thank me. I want every day to be special for you." He shivered with a chill.

"Seriously, did you buy a copy of 'How to be the World's Perfect Boyfriend'?"

"I wrote the book, doll."

He kissed my hair, and I lightly smacked him in the side. He took that hand and wrapped his around it as we hurried back to the university. Even though being back meant I had to face the challenges of the relic, it felt good to be home.

I turned on my light switch and smiled at my small purple bed. "By the way you are salivating at your bed; I'm assuming you want to sleep in your room tonight." He swept away snowflakes off my hair.

"I do." I never thought I would miss that stupid bed so much. "Is that okay?"

"As long as I can sleep in that tiny bed with you, then I am okay with it."

"I think that could be arranged. But first, we should get these wet clothes off." I tugged on the hem of his shirt and pulled it up until it was over his head and in a pile on the floor. I bent down to kiss his belly button. His skin was ice-cold on my lips, which made me worry. He typically ran hot. "Are you cold?"

"Yes, but if you keep doing that, I will warm up quickly."

I yanked off his pants, exposing his flawless bottom half. I ran the tips of my nails up the back of his legs until I got to his boxers. They were ice-cold, too. "A shower will help warm you up too."

He arched a brow. "Let's get going, then." He had my clothes off and on the floor quickly. My mouth was on his. He picked me up with one arm and carried me into the bathroom. I made sure the water was hot before I shoved him in, leaving me on the other side. "What are you doing? Are you not joining me?"

I waved at him with my cast. "You forgot."

"Damn it, I did forget. I had some really exciting things planned."

He stepped under the showerhead. The water loved his body. I'd never seen anything quite like it. I left him to finish undressing and to shower in privacy. I put on dry clothes and dove into my bed, spooning the comforter. My shoulders shimmied with the excitement of sleeping in it.

~*~

Noises from the bathroom woke me up. I peered over at my clock. It was four in the morning. Malcolm's absence was easily noticeable in the small bed. I waited for him for twenty minutes, but he didn't return. Tiptoeing to the bathroom, I rapped lightly on the door. "Mal. Are you all right in there?"

He didn't answer, but the door slowly opened. He was standing in front of me but was off kilter. "I think I got a cold or the flu." He sounded stuffy, and his throat was hoarse. My hand caught fire when I checked the temperature of his forehead.

"Let's get you to your bed." I helped him to his room and tucked him in, placing a bottle of water next to him and a cold cloth to his head. "Try to get some rest, and I will pick up some cold medication in the morning. I will be on the couch if you need me."

"Stay with me, please."

The way he pleaded tugged at me. I rested by his side, and for a brief moment, he held me, but then he tossed around for the rest of the night. Unease kept me up with him.

I was groggy when I got up to go to the drugstore to get medication. I tripped over my feet a dozen times, and squinted at the cashier when she told me that hairbrushes were on sale. Like that would help me be more presentable. I also stopped to pick up soup and a gallon of coffee for myself.

Malcolm was in the same place where I had left him when I came back, lying on his back covered in a pile of sheets with a mobster movie on in the background.

"How are you feeling?"

He let out a long miserable moan as a response.

"If you rest up and do what I tell you, you will be back on your feet in a few days."

I poured a small cup of cold medicine. Handing him a water bottle, I told him to drink it and then take the medications. I heated some broth in the microwave and brought it back to him, watching him intently to make sure he listened to me.

"I've never had anyone take care of me before, not when I was sick when I was little or when I had to bandage my wounds."

The confession took me aback. "Your mother or housekeeper never brought you soup or medication?"

"Not once. My mother didn't care or wasn't around, and the housekeepers were only there to do a job. It was only when I was older and went off to university that my sisters got a nanny." Every time he told me about his past, it broke my heart a little piece at a time. It was hard to believe he was so well adjusted after coming from such abuse. "If I had the energy, I would be getting you naked and doing what I planned to do to you in

Scotland, as a thank you."

"You can thank me when you're better." My tongue ran over my bottom lip with the thought.

"You're perfect." His eyes hung low. He let out a long wheeze and then fell asleep. I made myself comfortable on the couch with my laptop.

I launched into my extensive study into my ancestry. It was time to face my reality, and the only way to figure things out was to do what I did best—research. I didn't know much about my father's side—all I knew was his name and birthdate. I typed that information into the computer and attempted to rummage through all the people with his name.

Malcolm slept for most of the day. I had ordered more soup when he rung out a yawn, letting me know he was awake. "Did you stay here all day?"

"Of course, I did."

"God, I wish I could kiss you." His stomach thundered from across the room.

"Food should be here shortly, but for now, drink some more water." I pointed to a glass I'd placed on his bookshelf.

"What are you working on?"

"Exploring my family tree."

He perked up, pushing himself into a sitting position. "You're ready to see how you're involved?"

"I think I need to." I swallowed deeply with the thought of what I might find.

"You said that sometimes the amulet would act as a warning for danger. How come it didn't react to Dante when he attacked you?"

"I thought about that, and I couldn't remember if it did or not. I was kind of in another world, spending the day with you. I really wish I could see Dante's research, though. I'm sure he has notes on it somewhere." Why was this relic even created if it was only meant for certain people to control? I had considered that so many times, and it was not like I was in any powerful position to make a difference. I was only an archivist. "What's the point of its creation?"

"What was the point of the Ark of the Covenant, the Holy Grail, Pandora's box, or the Book of Thoth?"

"Power, immortality, destruction. But nothing that was useful for civilization. All I know is that I can't keep on constantly watching over my shoulder."

"Come here." He moved over slightly, leaving space for me in the middle of the bed. I did what he wanted and rested my head on his shoulder. He swept away the nest of my hair and kissed the side of my head. "You know as well as I do that some research can take years. We have committed ourselves to this relic, so what choice do we have? Maybe now that Dante is gone, we won't have to be so cautious."

"I really hope so, for both our sakes." I knew that was wishful thinking, and so did he.

Chapter 30

Malcolm was still sick the next morning, but he was able to move around outside of the bed, even if it was slow. He was well enough that I could leave him alone for a few hours and do some more work in the archive. I retrieved all our books and documents from four hundred to eight hundred AD Greece and rested on the floor, making a vortex with my books and trapping myself in until I found something.

I came across one book with the painting from the Louvre. The explanation was the same as the other one. I studied the woman. There was no mistaking it—I was absolutely related. The hair alone was a giveaway.

"Eve!" I heard Wes call for me down the hall from the room.

"In here!" I yelled back. He came into the room with flushed cheeks.

"Thanks. I have never been here before. Thought I would be lost forever." Those were my sentiments the first few weeks I was there too. "James and Mal wanted to cook us dinner for New Year's Eve. Well, mostly, James does the cooking, and Mal pays for the food. Anyway, they went to the store and told me to pick you up and take you back to our place."

I wanted to say no because I still had so much work to do here, but spending a few hours with friends wouldn't kill me either. The work would be there in the morning. "Can we stop by my room first, so I can wash up?"

"Lead the way." Wes gestured me out the door.

The hallway to my apartment felt off somehow. A slight vibration from my chest arose, but it wasn't something that was too alarming.

The door to my room was ajar. I held my arm out so Wes would stop. "I locked my room before I left."

"Was Malcolm in there?"

I had to think over my steps this afternoon, but I knew I'd locked it. I was sure of it. "No, he doesn't have a key."

"Wait here. Let me go in first." Wes crept forward, surveying the room through the open door. It took all my willpower to stay put. Luckily, he came back out after two minutes. "Good news is that nobody is in there. Bad news. Someone was, and they did a number on your belongings."

I bumped past him into the room. Wes was right. Every item I owned was scattered on the floor. My papers and books were ripped apart. My laptop was smashed to pieces, lying mangled on my desk. All my clothes were in small piles that led from my closet. Not one article of clothing was salvageable. Even the soles of my shoes had large holes in them. My bathroom was demolished too. Lotions, shampoo, and conditioners were all emptied on the tile and shower floor. The makeup bag was empty, too. I didn't see the necessity of removing the powder from the compact, but there it was in a pile of mush in the sink.

I went back out into the main living space. My comforter, pillow, and mattress were slashed—white stuffing layered the floor as if it had snowed cotton and fibers. Beneath the snow mass was my suitcase that used to live under my bed. The lid was open. I dug through all the stuffing. The manuscript was gone.

"Oh, no, no, no, no." I stood up with my hands on my head. "All our research is gone!"

"Eve, we should get out of here before the intruder comes back. We can call the police at my house." He tugged on my belt.

"I don't have anything left, Wes! It's all destroyed." I was in disarray. All my possessions had been taken away from me.

He cupped the back of my neck, forcing me out the door. "I know, but we need to leave. Whoever did this was undoubtedly angry, and we don't want to be here if they come back."

He called James, and we made a plan to meet at their house. I had thought it was the safest place to be because it was a historic site, with security all around. I had nothing; no clothes, no shoes except the ones on my feet, and all our work we had done over the last six months was gone. All that was left was the amulet, and I vowed that I would cling to it no matter what. I clutched it under my shirt. My hand began to shudder, but it wasn't from the necklace. It was from my fear. I was thankful that Wes was there. He was literally guiding me every step of the way. He got me out of the taxi and onto his couch, handing me a cup of tea. The tea sloshed to the sides from my shaking hands, so I placed the cup on the table for safekeeping. I sat there with my head in my hands. No emotion, no breakdown, nothing.

Malcolm came crashing through the door, making me move from my position. He collided into me, clasping his arms around my back. His heart pulsated against my ear.

"Everything I own is destroyed. I only have the clothes on my back, and the artifacts were stolen. I am so sorry, Malcolm. I know we promised to protect that research."

"I don't give a shit about the work. All I care is that you are safe."

"But—"

"No." He gripped me at arm's length. "I don't care. We will get you new stuff. We have the amulet, and you are with me. That's all that matters. You are all that matters."

"What amulet?" James and Wes both queried from the kitchen.

I knew it was time to let them in on our secret. What I was about to tell them wasn't going to be easy, and I hoped they believed me.

"About six months ago, I found an old manuscript in the archive. There was an odd symbol on the cover that we had never come across before. After doing extensive translations, we discovered that the symbol was a representation of a relic that was supposed to be forged by some sort of god. Whoever had control over the relic had absolute power. At first, we didn't believe it. We considered it another myth, but we had run across clues that suggested otherwise."

"What kind of clues?" Wes asked, on the edge of his seat,

looking skeptical.

"A letter written from Henry VIII to who we think was Charles Brandon. We had also found the symbol on several other historical artifacts. I tracked one of the clues to Hampton Court, and although what I did was highly illegal, I actually found the relic." I removed the long gold chain from my neck and placed it in my palm, showing it off for the first time since I found it.

"How do you know that is the relic?" James glared at it as if it had eyes. "And no offense, Eve, but it doesn't seem like you have absolute power." There was no trace of disbelief in his voice, only curiosity, and I let out a sigh of relief in that. If he thought I was crazy, there was no way in telling what lengths he'd go through to get me lucid again.

"We know it's the relic because I have been hunted down multiple times for it. I wasn't as discreet as I thought I was being. Also...." I held out my hand for them to touch it. They both reached for it at the same time. Their fingers smoothed over the ancient bone, but like Malcolm, it burned their skin.

"What the hell?" James yelped.

I hated this part, but I pressed on anyway. "It belongs to me." That truth was still something I wanted to deny. I didn't want to have the burden of the relic, but it wasn't my choice anymore. "From what we can speculate, only a specific bloodline can carry and control it. We found a painting in the Louvre of a woman that eerily resembles me. She was wearing it. We haven't found enough information to back up that theory, though. Also, Freydis, daughter of Erik the Red, had the mark on her sword at the British Museum." Was it possible I was related to her? She was depicted to have hair like mine, but I didn't know how accurate that was. "There was an imprint on the sword. She must have figured out how it worked. Unfortunately, I haven't discovered that yet."

"Did you think that maybe she had it cradled into her sword because she couldn't physically possess it, and that was the only way to use the power?" James tried to touch it again, but there was a pop from the sizzling of his skin.

I looked to James, then Malcolm, then back to James. "Not really. If she wasn't able to carry it like me, but still used it, then that changes everything." If that was the case, that meant that anyone could use it if they knew how.

"But what does it do?" Wes's eyes were larger than a dinner plate. They were both taking this surprisingly well. I thought for sure they would have called an institution for Malcolm and I both, after talking about magic and ancient, powerful relics.

"We still don't know. All I know is that it does warn me when danger is nearby."

The amulet visibly pulsated in my hand, almost as if it heard me talking about it. I laced my fingers around it just as the front door flew open. Daphne stood before us, tears streaming from her pale face. A hand covered her mouth, and another grasped a gun that was pointed to her temple. Behind her was Andrew Archer.

"I'm tired of playing this game with you, Eve. Give me the relic, and I won't shoot Daphne."

"You wouldn't dare." Malcolm moved forward. Andrew released the safety on the gun, forcing Malcolm to pause.

"You know I would." The malicious grin that twisted on his face was so disturbing, it would give me nightmares. "Although I would hate to lose her. She is my favorite out of the girls. Don't underestimate how much I want that relic, son. Now, Eve, I am tired of stalking you. Scaring and threatening you didn't work. You're one brave woman, I give you that, with a hard right hook, but that relic belongs to me."

Shock plunged into me, sinking me deeper into the complicated web. Had Andrew known all along that I had a connection to the relic, and that was the reason he allowed me to work at the university? Or was it all coincidence and luck on his part? Dante was my only link back to Andrew and the relic—he must've played a part in Andrew's quest too. "Was Dante working with you?"

"We had a partnership, but he was impulsive and impatient. He wasn't willing to wait for you to make a mistake and show us where it was. Dante also couldn't keep his mouth shut about the relic. Half of his team knew about it. Unluckily for him, though, there are other people who have been searching for the relic for years, and his running mouth is what got him killed. But it got him away from me—no skin off my back, there. Only a few of us knew you had it. I thought for sure you wouldn't be stupid enough to wear it. It had to be somewhere in your room. To my surprise, it wasn't, but I did find that manuscript. You did great work with translation in such a short time. Shawn was right. You do have a gift. When you left for Paris, I searched everywhere in your room for it. I made sure to cover my tracks carefully. But tonight…tonight, I needed you to know that because Dante was gone, it didn't mean you were safe. Bad luck for Daphne that she saw me coming out of your room. I knew you two had grown close, and I needed some incentive for you to hand it over."

"Why not use me?" Malcolm offered and questioned, stepping up to take his sister's place so easily.

"You know I could never do that. You're very special to me."

Malcolm flinched; I knew those words were nails to his head. He didn't want Andrew to have any allegiance towards him, even if it was only made out of manipulation. "Also, Eve had made it very clear that you were her number one priority. I knew if I threatened you in any way, she would take me out, and I believe she is capable of that, especially with the relic. Isn't that right, Eve?"

I bit the inside of my mouth until I tasted blood. "Yes."

"Now, enough talking, and give me the relic!" He cocked up his elbow and jammed the barrel of the gun closer to Daphne. Her eyes widened with fear.

I stepped forward, ready to trade off a potentially life-threatening artifact, but Malcolm caught me. "Fine." He yanked out a gold chain from his pocket. Dangling from the end was a charm, an exact replica of the bone that was still clenched in my fist. The ivory appeared to be as old and aged as the one I was carrying. If I hadn't known any better, I would have thought that he was holding the real relic. When did he find the time to make that? It must've been in Paris since that was the first time he had seen it. "Give me Daphne first."

"No, give me the relic." Malcolm stepped to him, but I cut him off at the pass. Quickly snagging the fake relic with my casted hand, I crossed over to Andrew, thrusting Malcolm to the side. I meant what I said. I would do anything and everything to keep him safe, even if that meant having a standoff with a gun.

"Eve! What are you doing?" he hissed at me.

"Step back, Malcolm." I created a barricade with my arm. "Let go of Daphne." I advanced closer, with the replica held between my fingers.

Andrew dislodged the gun from Daphne's temple. I seized her by the elbow and whipped her to Malcolm. She scurried behind his back.

"Eve, we had a deal."

I tossed the necklace to him. "You can have it. It doesn't even work."

He caught it in midair, gun still in his right hand, "You evidently haven't done all your research. It has to be activated."

"Activated? How?" I clutched the real relic in my other hand to assure myself that it was still safe.

"You have to kill someone."

He pointed the gun at my heart. Three shots rang out, and I simultaneously heard screaming. I didn't know if the screams came from me or the other people in the room, but in an instant, I was on the ground. Wetness pooled at my back. It was warm, but then the feeling dissipated quickly. All of it did. I was aware that I had gotten shot somewhere, but all I could focus on was Malcolm hovering over me.

His hands were covered in blood. My blood. Tears streaked his beautiful face. "Eve, stay with me. God, please stay with me."

I couldn't respond or move. All I had was my thoughts, and they were fading fast. I knew I was dying.

"No, Eve. Don't leave me." He held my limp hand in his. "No." He sounded distant and faint, like the light in the room.

To be continued….

Coming soon, Book 2 The Chrysalis.

About the Author

PJ Bailey lives in Birmingham, AL, where she enjoys spending time being on the water and exploring the city and country. Her love of stories and books was cultivated at a young age, with a house filled from floor to ceiling with thousands of novels. From classics to old and new mysteries to sci-fi, and beyond, she has delved into many dimensions, which she contributes to spurring her imagination and crafting her stories. PJ can't wait to bring her readers along on each new journey as she unfolds her own worlds.

Inspired by her travels to far off places and her eclectic community of family and friends, PJ molds so much of her own experiences into her work by building worlds and characters that feel real, exciting, and disarmingly familiar. Her hope for her readers is to find the perfect nook to enthrall themselves in her words and lose themselves in the storytelling.

Made in the USA
Monee, IL
12 January 2021

57385257R10155